# BEST
# DESTINY

# STAR TREK®

# BEST DESTINY

## Diane Carey

POCKET BOOKS

New York    London    Toronto    Sydney    Tokyo    Singapore

POCKET BOOKS, a division of Simon & Schuster Inc.
1230 Avenue of the Americas, New York, NY 10020

ISBN: 0-671-79587-2

Dedicated to the young men and women
in the Vision Quest program, and to the crews of
the Schooners *New Way* and *Bill of Rights*,
who prove that troubled youth can not only be saved . . .
they can save themselves

What you from your fathers have inherited,
Earn it, in order to possess it.

—Goethe


Commanding a starship is your first best destiny.

—Captain Spock to Admiral James Kirk in
*Star Trek II: The Wrath of Khan*

# HISTORIAN'S NOTE

This story takes place shortly after the events chronicled in
*Star Trek VI: The Undiscovered Country.*

# FOREWORD

☆

Ahhhh! We're back and it sure feels good!

Diane and I have been on sabbatical for four years from the Star Trek universe, but we haven't been idle. We traveled back in time to write a three-book series set during the American Civil War. Though we are once more flying around in the future for humanity's best destiny, we're still working in the past—this time James Kirk's past.

At first we thought we would just swing back into Star Trek, concerned only about changes in Trek. We didn't realize we were bringing so many changes in ourselves.

Nor did we expect any connection between the genres . . . but the past and the future were way ahead of us. They had something else in mind.

After a few thousand pages of raking our Civil-War-era characters over the coals, the two of us found ourselves burgeoning with unexpected insight into what might have shaped the life of Captain James Kirk. Tiny events, not big ones, can ultimately make a hero, or fail to make one. Suddenly the tiny things were important, all because we had become so sensitive to the small events that shaped our own history. In writing our Civil War series, *Distant Drums, Rise Defiant,* and *Hail Nation* (Bantam Books, 1991, '92, '93), Diane and I have been hammered by the very lesson *Star Trek* has been trying to teach us all along.

Just as "the needs of the one outweigh the needs of the many," the actions of the one can overwhelm the actions of the many. Let me show you how.

In 1861 the European aristocracy saw the New World cracking in two, and smiled. The Confederate States of American, they felt, were the inevitable winners of the conflict. History gurgled with examples of weaker powers emerging victorious when defending their home soil. More significant, however, it seemed impossible to drag the rebellious states back into a "voluntary" union. To the European elite the United States of America—the big experiment in mob rule—was at an end. Now the Europeans would be justified in crushing any rising democratic sentiment on their own continent. They'd simply point over here and say, "See? Won't work."

Dismemberment of the United States was too tempting for the European powers to ignore. By 1862 Britain and France were poised to recognize the Confederacy and offer monetary and military aid to the new country—fan those flames! Watch that nation crumble!

They hedged their bets, however. They waited for one big Confederate military victory to prove the Confederacy's ability to not only survive Northern aggression, but end it. In a daring move that took advantage of infuriatingly timid Union General McClellan's turtlelike military pace, General Lee split his smaller army of grays into three parts and invaded the North. As the gods looked down upon the impending battle, the odds against the survival of western democracy were very long.

The gods and the aristocracy lost their collective shirts that day!

The North was dealt a wild card. One of General Lee's men lost a few pieces of paper that contained a complete set of orders for the impending battle. Now, if a cow had happened upon the orders and eaten them, this would have come to nothing but a historically insignificant belch. But instead, the lost orders ended up in General McClellan's hands, and the future history of the world was changed.

With Lee's battle plans in hand, a blind man on a three-legged horse could have led the Union Army to a flashing victory and ended the war then and there. Since it was McClellan who had the paper, the Union managed only a stalemate.

Because that accident with the piece of paper and McClellan's personality got together on the same day, North and South had to endure three more years of wartime carnage. The Confederate Army was turned back and the European powers never considered intervention so seriously again.

A minor incident in a day's work . . . a careless Confederate courier can't keep his paws on a few pieces of paper, so the United States of America survives its greatest trial.

If not for this one clumsy moment, there might not be a single unified nation here today, but a handful of squabbling nation-states each jealously guarding its borders. We'd spend our time suspicious of every bit of trade, every law, every traveler, arguing over who got to take advantage of whom, who got to set which rule, who should patrol which road, who got to toll which river. We would never have been able to pull together to build a society or nurse a flourishing economy.

There would be no "we."

How different would the world look today if the United States had not existed to play its role in the economic and military developments of the last century?

And what makes a hero? Single people can turn events, even if they're not dropping battle plans out of their map cases.

Later in the war President Lincoln finally found a hero for his war-weary country. A non-McClellan emerged, willing to fight with the firmness needed to end the civil conflict and reunite the nation. It was General U. S. (Unconditional Surrender) Grant. While Grant lacked General Lee's military acuteness, he made up for it with a pit bull's tenacity and the dispassion of a surgeon.

If we were inventing Grant's past from scratch, as we had the chance to do with Jim Kirk, would we create a polished youth, a successful collegiate, a square-shouldered officer?

Probably. But history taught us something else, just in time.

General Grant, later to become President Grant, had no success early in life; in fact, before the Civil War his life was marked by failure after failure. He was completely out of place in civilian life, and could barely feed his family during those days without a uniform. The war was Grant's last chance to avoid stunning mediocrity.

How might events have been different if Grant had been successful and wealthy at the advent of the war? Would he have been as driven toward success, having already had it?

Why was President Lincoln willing to take any personal or political risk to reunite the country? What is it that forges heroes like U. S. Grant, Abraham Lincoln, or, as we have tried to extrapolate, James T. Kirk?

*Best Destiny* is a Star Trek historical novel. Like the heroes of the real-life past, we know much about the deeds of Captain James Kirk. Through the television series, movies, books, and comics, Kirk and crew have been dragged through and survived a multitude of adventures.

But why them? What in our characters' pasts gives them that extra pinch of determination and guile it takes to survive the trials of space travel? What minor events and twists of fate, like those in the American Civil War, piled one upon another, resulted in Captain Kirk rather than Chief Surveyor Kirk, or Sixth Level Accountant Kirk, or Mr. J. T. Kirk, 101 No Particular Avenue?

*Best Destiny* is not a complete picture by any means. However, Diane and I do hope we've developed an insightful and entertaining peek into the steel personality of James Kirk while he was still raw iron and coal.

So join us in the future, and explore the *Star Trek* past. If you enjoy *Best Destiny,* perhaps we'll do more of the past . . . in the future.

And don't throw away any marching orders that fall into your hands. They might affect the path to your own best destiny.

Gregory Brodeur

# PROLOGUE

☆

USS *Enterprise* 1701-A
United Federation of Planets Starship,
Constitution-Class
Naval Construction Contract 1701-A
Captain James T. Kirk, Commanding

*"You'll retire with extraordinary honors and the boundless gratitude of an unfolding Federation. We have a real chance for prosperity in the galaxy . . . a large portion of that chance is due to your vitality of will, your fundamentality of purpose, and your belief in us, Captain Kirk."*

"Thank you, Mr. President. I don't know what to say."

On the starship's forward viewscreen, the president of the Federation took an uncustomary pause. His white eyes never flickered within his whey complexion and the frame of long, chalk-white hair, but today hope did luminate in them.

*"I could suggest something,"* he said, *"if you were willing."*

An "aw-shucks" grin creased James Kirk's face, and he fingered the armrests of his command chair for one of the last times.

"Thank you again, sir," he said. "We've had our time in the light. It's time for others now."

The president offered his idea of a nod, barely a movement at all.

1

His Deltan albinism made almost any expression something only the perceptive would notice.

*"We shall speak again,"* he said, *"and privately raise a glass to your career, sir, and to your officers. Starfleet Command has authorized Starbase One's interior occulting light to flash in alternate white and gold, as salute to the* Enterprise. *I shall consider it my privilege to sign your Bell Book personally in note of arrival, as this will be her last time coming in."*

"When we return to Starbase One," Captain Kirk pointed out.

*"At your discretion. No authority will supersede your own as to the final cruise of the* Enterprise. *Enjoy it."*

The president nodded his elegant shaggy head, those alien eyes seeming not to really see.

The screen suddenly went black. Only the audio system operated for a last few seconds, in the voice of an official communications person.

*"United Federation of Planets, Office of the President, Starbase One, out."*

Captain James Kirk wagged a finger toward the bridge communications station, noted the acknowledgment, and settled a little too calmly back into his command chair.

"I want to speak to Mr. Scott," he said.

No one acknowledged him. No one wanted to. Somehow protocol didn't fit just then. A moment later the communication tie-in on the command chair's armrest spoke for itself.

*"Scott here, sir."*

"Condition of the ship, Scotty."

*"Aye, sir. We've got all damaged decks evacuated and sealed off and isolated priority repairs. Warp engines are fine. Cosmetic repairs can wait, but I'll have the ship's engineering up to full integrity within twenty hours."*

The captain leaned an elbow on that armrest and lowered his voice. "Mr. Scott . . . you understand the ship is being decommissioned upon our return to Starbase One."

*"I do, sir. But if Starfleet Command is going to retire a spaceworthy* Enterprise *without my corpse rotting in her hull, I guarandamntee yeh they'll have pain doing it. I intend to make them*

*go down on record as having decommissioned a service-ready starship."*

Silence pooled on the bridge. There was no echo, but there might as well have been.

The captain was gazing at nothing, as though preparing to follow his vessel into that nothing. He and the chief engineer. Their ship.

"I understand," he said. "You carry on, Mr. Scott."

*"Thank you, sir, I will and a half. Scott out."*

The captain crossed his legs and leaned back as though to digest what he had heard, and what he had uttered back.

"Steady as she goes," he said to the helm before him.

On the quarterdeck behind him, a very thin man with eyes the color of water and hair that had gone merrily gray felt his own square features harden up. Dr. Leonard McCoy had waited all his life to become a country codger, and he was enjoying it. He could scowl openly at such exchanges. He could snarl at anybody, and not get hit in the mouth.

With an aggravated frown he stepped sideways to the science station, as he had a hundred times before in years past, and muttered again to the same person who had heard his mutters those hundred times.

"What can we say to him, Spock?" McCoy began, easily loud enough for the captain to hear.

A figure straightened inside the science station cowl. The entire bridge seemed to inhale as the alien presence turned to the ship's fore. Small, alert eyes brushed the bridge, set in the triangular features of his face that McCoy had once regarded as hard, cold, built deliberately on angles. Sober and thrifty—that underpinned the study of being Vulcan.

How old was the Vulcan now? McCoy skimmed the medical records he kept handy in his mind and tried to equate Vulcan years with human years. Failed, as usual. They just didn't equate. Spock's straight hair, once stove-black, was now a dignified sealskin gray. His quill-straight brows were still dark, still angled up and away, but were shaggier than in his youth, though they still made the Vulcan look to McCoy as did all Vulcans—like tall, skinny bats with clothes on.

3

Add them to the one feature that had made Vulcans so hard to take seriously . . . the elongated ears that came to points. McCoy had decided those ears were the reason Vulcans had given up emotion. They couldn't stand being teased.

Suddenly McCoy felt lucky to be standing beside this man. Despite the years of mutual antagonism, he and Spock had been through every form of effort, every kind of death, every kind of life together; each offered himself in sacrifice for the other time after time, and somehow they were both lucky enough to still be standing there.

McCoy knew he was also lucky to be standing next to the first Vulcan in Starfleet, the first of what had turned out to be many. The Vulcans had always tried to be unimpressible and self-contained, but because of this one, they had changed their minds.

Because of the young Spock, the impertinent radical who had shunned his race's Olympian seclusion, Vulcans no longer prided themselves on inaccessibility. They'd discovered that Starfleet, though founded by those silly humans and still primarily run by them, wasn't quite the lawless fluster the Vulcans had assigned humanity in the past, and that it didn't cause concussion to the art of being Vulcan. In fact, they'd found out that Starfleet emblemized law in settled space, was counted upon by dozens of defenseless worlds in a touch-and-go galaxy. The Federation was the great castle that protected them, and Starfleet was its knighthood.

Even enemies knew it. That was why there had been affluent peace for so long. Starfleet insisted upon it, had the muscle to back it up.

The Vulcans were now proud, yes, proud to be part of Starfleet, to actively defend the Federation, to participate in the strength that prosperity insisted upon, and they too bristled when that path was blocked. Those who had once turned their very straight backs on Spock in his Starfleet uniform now nudged their own sons and daughters into Starfleet Academy, eager to see them answer a bugle call they themselves had once rejected, and to see them participate in the spaceborne operations a thriving interstellar community simply had to have gone on.

Yes, things had changed.

Though he was standing right beside McCoy, Spock also didn't

4

bother to mutter, or even to lower his voice, on the bridge. This critical deck was built for acoustic perfection, so no order went unheard, no whisper unconsidered, no buzz unanswered.

On top of that, there was the captain's damned alertness. Like a leopard at rest.

"What can we say," McCoy sighed, "to make it easy to watch all the *Enterprise* fade into history?"

Spock shifted his weight. "The Constitution-class starship is no longer considered state-of-the-art in patrol/exploration craft, Doctor. That accolade now goes to the Excelsior-class."

"Excelsior-class," McCoy grumbled. "Looks like a swollen-up party balloon at a Starfleet shoving-off party."

The captain glanced at them, stood up, and casually circled his command chair, running his hands along the soft back.

"All things change, gentlemen," he said. "All things grow. It's our duty to be gracious."

He hesitated, gazing at the viewscreen and the enormity of space.

"How would it look to the young," he added, "if we botched our final duty?"

## USS *Bill of Rights*
## United Federation of Planets Starship, Excelsior-Class
## Naval Exploration Extension 2010
## Captain Alma Anne Roth, Commanding

"Contact Starfleet! Level One distress, immediately!"

"Trying, Captain! No power on normal channels! No power at all!"

"Then use abnormal channels! Get a message out before it's too late!"

"Aye, aye—switching to telemetry!"

James Kirk's hair had gone darker with age instead of lighter, as had his temperament, yet he still bore the tan of a sailor and the browns of a fox—acorn, walnut, toast, bone, berry—in his cheeks and hair. He had always been on the foliage side of the color wheel.

It was dark in the forest today.

"Jim," McCoy attempted, "just because you're retiring from command doesn't mean you have nothing to give. The Federation doesn't want you to retire from Starfleet—nobody does."

"Nobody?" James Kirk responded. "I've lived not only a good life, but a great one. I've cheated death a hundred times in the field, beaten the perils of space, and now the people who were kids when I was in my prime are in *their* prime. It's their turn. I can't take mine and theirs too. I've spent my time behind a desk and in front of a classroom, and neither of those are for me, Bones. They're decommissioning this entire class of starship in favor of the Excelsior-class heavier design, and without a ship . . . the best part of my life is over."

His two closest friends regarded him somberly. They were seeing all the changes in each other, and not so much how things had stayed the same. They were still together after twenty-five years, yes. Their legacy was approaching what appeared to be a close. They had all learned to look forward to retirement.

Still . . .

"I'm going to be an officer and a gentleman about it," Kirk said. He didn't look up at them. "It's time to lower the pennant, spend time on the family farm, rediscover old friends . . . go out on the oceans of my home planet and do some serious adventure of another kind."

Not even his two closest friends could decipher how deeply he meant those words.

"Captain, excuse me," Uhura said. Long familiarity with her deep, clear voice told them she was disturbed. Her chocolate features and those fashion-runway eyes gave the bridge a flavor of the exotic. "I'm picking up an echo of communication from *Bill of Rights.*"

Kirk angled away from Spock and McCoy as though he was glad to be changing course.

"Are we authorized to intercept that?" he asked.

"No, sir, not technically."

"Then why are you doing it?"

"Sir, it's coming in on the coded emergency channel, over telemetry," she enunciated carefully. "I'd say their audio was down, except that it's coming over the lowest grade signal capacity. In the Academy, communications students sometimes refer to that as the 'panic channel' because it reads like a last resort. Permission to accept and decipher?"

"Quickly." His brows came together and he spoke fast. Suddenly everyone who knew him was tense. They'd seen his instincts at work before. "Well? Haven't you got—"

"Sir—receiving an SOS from them!"

She worked more swiftly as stillness came over the bridge, leaving only the hums, chirrs, and buzzes of her systems at work and the sounds of a starship's bridge on automatic, running the ship as best it could while the people were busy—waiting—worried.

Then suddenly she wailed, "I've lost them!"

"Sir?" a young ensign interrupted from the starboard upper deck as she peered into her viewer. She frowned into her screen and didn't say anything else. But there was something in that one syllable.

And an instant later—

"Captain! Antiproton flushback!"

The head of every experienced person on the bridge suddenly shot around at her, as though she had cursed at a kitten—then killed it.

"Shields up!" Kirk barked at the helm, then spun around. "Spock, confirm that!"

The Vulcan was already laying his large hands upon the long-range sensor panel on the quarterdeck, while the other bridge officers were scrambling to go into pre-alert, as always when the commander ordered shields.

Kirk wasn't waiting. He dropped into the command chair on one thigh and snapped, "Chekov, lay in a course for the source of the flushback and engage!" Then he regained control over his tone and added, "Prepare for emergency warp speed."

The compactly built Russian at the helm pursed his lips but kept his voice in control. "Emergency warp, aye."

"Flushback confirmed, Captain," Spock reported. There was dark trouble in his tone now.

Kirk slammed his chair's comm link with a fist. "Engineer Scott, prepare our shields for forward-intense against antiproton flushback." Then he cast back at Uhura, "All hands on deck. Code one emergency."

She didn't nod, but went straight to her controls. Her voice thrummed through the huge vessel with an evenness that somehow intensified the urgency.

*"This is the bridge . . . all hands on deck . . . all hands on deck . . . code one emergency, repeat, code one emergency!"*

The emergency alert panels began to flash a steely electric-blue light. As it flashed, a familiar voice plunged up like a Celtic drumroll through the system.

*"Scott to bridge! Repeat and verify that forward-intense order. Did you say flushback?"*

"Kirk here, Scotty. Verified."

*"Aye, sir!"*

"Uhura, close all outgoing communications. Log the Perils of Space Rescue Response Clause, the time, stardate, circumstances, and decision to act without headquarters contact."

"Aye, sir, logging."

"Sensors on long-range, wide dispersal, Mr. Chekov."

"Long-range wide, aye."

McCoy frowned. He knew those tones too well from people with whom he'd spent a half century on the not particularly welcoming doormats of space.

"What's going on?" he asked.

No one paid any attention to him.

He was used to that too.

Careful not to trip or bump anyone as the bridge erupted into a flurry, the doctor moved cautiously back up to the quarterdeck and went sideways to the science station and its poised alien officer. There, he leaned on an elbow to make sure he was out of the way, and lowered his voice.

"Spock, what does it mean?" he asked. "I've never heard of antiproton flashback before—"

"Flushback," Spock corrected him. His mind was on more than just the word, yet he frowned as he said it. Even through Spock's poise, McCoy could tell it was a hated word.

"You haven't heard it, Doctor," he said heavily, "because antiproton flushback cannot occur in nature."

"When *can* it occur?"

Spock straightened then, posture tight, and looked at the forward screen as the ship shot into warp speed, and the galaxy blew by. He gazed at the long streaks of distortion as though all were new and very frightening. His angular brows drew tightly inward, and for some reason too personal to be voiced, he gazed at the back of James Kirk's head, the back of a captain intensely occupied with whatever lay before them.

The answer, even in its Vulcan reserve, was bitter.

"To our science . . . only in the explosion of warp engines."

Silence clacked between them. A sentence like that demanded silence, murdered for it, thrived upon it.

But this was a starship's bridge, and something was on their wind. Silence couldn't reign here.

Voices, voices, all over, from the depths. Sounds. Technology leaping to the call of men and women. Men and women leaping to the call of trouble.

Reports. Different voices. Each its own purpose.

"Science decks checking in, Captain. All hands ready."

"Engineering reports all hands on deck, sir."

"At warp two, Captain. Chief engineer signals ready for emergency acceleration on your signal."

The captain's voice.

"Emergency warp speed."

"Emergency warp, aye . . ."

The ship began a low whine, from her bowels.

"Warp three . . . warp four . . ."

"Emergency jump," the captain said. "Go to warp nine."

A pause. A nervous confirmation.

The surge of speed, eruptions of successive warping, without pause, without rest—*crack, crack, crack, crack.*

"Warp nine, Captain. Stressed, but holding."

"Go to yellow alert."

"Yellow alert, aye!"

*"Yellow alert, yellow alert . . . all hands to emergency stations . . . yellow alert, yellow alert . . ."*

# Part One

☆

# DEAD RECKONING

# ONE

Tension on the bridge could have been lifted and carried.

It would have cast the people into chaos, except for the anchor of the captain's voice. The captain on any ship was the only reason the crews could ever sleep or eat, for no one can sleep or eat where there isn't the anchor.

With that anchor on board, no storm was too bad, no fog too thick, no silence too damning.

Knowing the ship around them was screaming through space at warp nine, piercing through increasing waves of antiproton flush and heading not away from that horrifying fact of death but right into it, the crew clung to the captain's voice.

"Mr. Chekov, project our course and report what's there in a funnel of fifty light-years in diameter. Specify any outposts, Federation or otherwise, areas of contention, reported storms, and call up manifests of any shipping that has passed through that area in the past ten days."

"Aye, sir, projecting the course. I'll have that for you in a few moments."

"Short moments, Mr. Chekov."

"Aye, sir."

On the quarterdeck, the ensign who had first noticed the

flushback swallowed obvious guilt at having been the bearer of awful news. Wasn't her name Dimitrios? Demarris? De-something.

McCoy knew that look, had carried it plenty of times himself.

With nothing to do—yet—in this emergency, he stepped away from the science station and over to the other side of the bridge to the young woman.

She was trying to get some moisture back into her mouth while she tracked the surging waves of flushback and tried to pinpoint their source. Not an exact science at all, if her expression was any clue. Her hands were shaking.

"Don't drink coffee," McCoy suggested.

The ensign blinked, glared at him, confused. Then she turned back to her screen and squinted into it.

"I don't know what you mean, sir."

"Don't drink any coffee until whatever's happening isn't happening anymore."

She bit her lip, then only said, "Thank you, sir."

McCoy shifted his feet, watching the bridge personnel move tightly at their stations and the lights and panels of the bridge crackle with activity. A ship at warp nine was plenty active.

"It'll make you nervous," he added, "and you'll have to—"

"Yes, sir," the ensign snapped. "I understand. Thank you."

She wanted him to go away, and Leonard McCoy wasn't the go-away type.

"What's bothering you, Ensign . . . ."

"Devereaux, sir."

She swallowed a couple more times, resisted the urge to glance at him and damn him for his doctor's intuition, but then she lowered her voice and let it out.

"If there's something out there that made an Excelsior-class ship blow up," the ensign said, "what chance do we have?"

McCoy offered the girl an annoyed glare, then swaggered a step closer to her, took her elbow, and turned her away from her console.

She gawked at him as if he were crazy.

The doctor didn't care that he was interrupting her work. Didn't care that she had been the one to tell everybody that a sister starship might have just been blown to bits. He was concerned about something else.

14

He nodded down toward the main deck, to the command chair, and to the man in it.

"Kid," he said, *"that* is our chance."

Ensign Devereaux looked down there too. Through his grip on her elbow, McCoy could feel some of her trembling go away as she watched James Kirk in his command chair.

There was just something about Captain Kirk.

The ensign cleared her throat, licked her lips, and turned back toward her station. Halfway there she paused, and gazed at Dr. McCoy. She was still afraid, but not in quite the same way.

"Thank you, sir," she said. "I won't forget."

At the navigation station on the upper deck, Commander Chekov straightened from his backbreaking hover and turned to look at the heart of the bridge also.

"Captain," the Russian said, speaking around his own accent as much as possible. "I have put up the merchant marine manifests on this screen for you to review. There are very few, sir. And there are no storms, no contested areas, no border disputes, no reported hazards in the specified funnel of space, no Starfleet outposts, no unfriendly settlements, and only two star systems within a hundred light-years. One is uninhabited, and on the other there is only a Federation archaeological excavation on a small outside planet."

Captain Kirk came up out of his chair. He had always had trouble sitting when there was action going on.

"Name the project," he ordered.

"I have never heard of it before, sir," came the clipped answer. "It is logged as . . . Faramond."

If McCoy was any judge of people he knew and people he didn't know, no one else on board had heard of that place either. One glance around the bridge told him that.

But then he looked down again at the captain.

On the face of the man he knew so well, McCoy saw a glitter of dangerous recognition.

The captain turned like a policeman about to make an arrest. He paced behind his command chair, caressing it. He glared forward into the rage of warp nine as stars and space debris blistered past the main viewscreen. His brows drew together and his eyes narrowed. A fire came into them which his friends thought talk of retirement might already have killed.

Though he watched the screen before him, he was gazing into the past. His lips parted and he spoke, but not to anyone there.

"Faramond . . ."

# TWO

☆

*Forty-five years earlier . . .*
A rope footbridge over the swollen North Skunk River,
Mahaska County, Iowa

"Stick with me and you'll get the ride of your lives."

A surly clutch of teenagers clung to those words as tightly as they clung to the tatters of the ages-old jute footbridge. Beneath them, the swollen Skunk River lazily whispered *dare you, dare you, dare you* and suggested they fall on in.

"Don't look down! Nobody look down."

Immediately the grunts and complaints went silent. Nobody wanted to get chewed out by the stocky boy with the sawdust-colored curls and the stingers in his eyes.

"Keep moving," he added. "No looking down."

"It'll be our luck a tourist tram floats by and sees us," Zack Malkin said. He wanted to scratch his neck, but he didn't dare let go. "We're on the Tramway's historical trail, you know."

"They won't."

"What if they do?" Lucy Pogue spat. Her soggy, bloodshot eyes were wide and her hands twitched on the prickly ropes. "You didn't think of that did you, genius?"

"We'll wave at 'em, all right?" their leader snapped, scowling

17

from under the brim of his grandfather's touring cap. With a shift of his shoulders he rearranged his high school jacket to free his arms a little. "Shut up and keep moving. One step at a time. And don't look down."

"I don't like this, Jimmy," said a brittle, fragile boy who had trouble breathing. He didn't look down, but he did glance back over the third of the walkway they'd already crossed. "Nobody told us we'd have to cross something like this."

"There's going to be a lot out there that nobody tells us about. We've got to find out for ourselves," their leader said, "before it's too late."

Tom Beauvais squinted into the sun and cracked, "You mean before we get caught."

"We could just sit at home," Jimmy shot back. "Be real safe that way."

The only person ahead of him was a girl whose powdery complexion barely picked up the light of the western sun. Her small eyes were like clear gelatin—hardly any color but lots of shine—and they were tightened with fear. Her cheeks were large, the shape and color of eggshells, and on a less swanlike creature might have been ghastly.

Shivering, she murmured, "Jimmy . . ."

"Keep moving," he told her softly. "Don't try to hurry. We're not going to move any faster than you can go. That's why I had you go first. I'm right here next to you, Emily. Nothing can possibly happen."

Their muscular leader curled his fingers around the jute and packtwine ropes and willed the sixty-foot-long footbridge to hold up.

It stretched from one cliff to another, east to west over the river. It had two sides for handholds and a walkway on the bottom that once had been tight and safe—a *long* time ago. Now it was rotting. An adventure, or a death wish.

Jimmy gritted his teeth at it. It'd been there for two decades, so it could just stay there another ten minutes. He'd argued them down about how this was the best way to cross the Skunk without getting caught, and how the authorities would be after them by now, and anything else he could tell them to keep them in line. He tried to make this look easy, to pretend the old ropes weren't scratching his palms and to act light on his feet.

Giving the others his voice to concentrate on, he kept talking. "Always think four or five moves ahead. That's the trick."

"If it's such a good trick," Tom countered, "why didn't you think of one of us going across this wreck first to see if it would hold up?"

His brow in a permanent furrow, Jimmy tightened his eyes and tried to slip around the truth. "Better this way. Even distribution of weight."

He held his breath, hoping nobody would notice how little sense that made. He squinted into the west and ignored the sun's glow off his own peach-fuzzed cheeks.

Peach fuzz. That was his father's phrase. Peach fuzz, baby face, greenhorn. Damn his cheeks for fitting that description. Deliberately he looked away from the sunlight.

"We're pioneers," he said. "We're going straight up the Oregon Trail, just like the people who settled this country and put in the railroads and the towns like Riverside across this part of Iowa. Only instead of horses or steel, we're hopping the Stampede."

Though he had played for team spirit, his only reward was a nasty grunt from Tom. "Sure. We're going to hop onto the fastest train in North America while it's doing nine hundred kpm five centimeters above the ground, *in* a tube. That'll be a whole new definition of 'friction.'"

"Glad you're paying attention, Beauvais."

"Glad you can fly, Kirk."

Jimmy shot a glare at him. Warning.

"Even the Stampede stops once in a while," he said. "All we have to do is make Omaha at loading time and we're aboard. Next stop, Oregon, and next after that . . . South America."

"What're we gonna do when we get to South America?" Quentin Monroe asked.

"Anything we damned well please." Jimmy glanced past Lucy and Zack again to see how Quentin was doing, and hoped Beauvais would look after the little guy.

Quentin's brown face was ink-spotted with big black freckles, enhanced by his spongy black hair and perpetually worried eyes, which in this light looked like two more inkspots. Jimmy hadn't wanted to bring him along. Quentin was only fourteen and every-body else in the gang was sixteen, he'd never held his own in a fight, and he hadn't even been to the city, but there was something about the frail black boy that said I'm okay, I'll grow, I'll learn.

So here he was, on the great adventure with the big kids, and Jimmy had to live with the decision. There was no turning back now.

"Maybe we'll become archaeologists," he said. He tightened his brow and nodded in agreement with himself. Inch by inch he urged them toward the middle of the rope walk. "Hack through rain forests looking for the ancient Mayan city-states. Find out why they went extinct after a thousand years of—"

"They found those."

Jimmy stopped. So did everybody else. The bridge shuddered.

"What?" he snapped. "What'd you say?"

Quentin clung to the ropes and blinked. "They found them. The Mayan palaces. A long time ago. You know . . . how the twentieth-century archaeologists found lance heads in the walls, and later they proved that the city was under siege, and how the siege forced them to do all their farming behind the walls, and how the crop yields fell off, and how—"

"Where'd you hear all this?"

"It was . . . in our history of science book."

"Books!" Jimmy spat out. "You're going to believe what you read in some book? Why waste your time with a book when you can get out and live!"

Quentin fell silent, ashamed that he had wasted his time.

Jimmy shook his head and barked, "Keep moving."

Suddenly an arm of wind swept downriver, pushing the bridge with its enormous hand. The ropes started whining and the whole footbridge began to sway.

"Damn, I almost dropped my pack!" Zack complained, and tried to rearrange his load.

"Don't do that," Jimmy said. "You've got the fake IDs."

"How'd you get those, Zack?" Quentin asked.

"Tapped into the voting records for people who hadn't voted in five years. Figured they were long gone, so we took the IDs of any children they had who were the right age five years ago to be eighteen now. Took their numbers, and *bing*—we're legal."

"Damn. Good idea."

"It was Jimmy's idea. I just did the hardware."

"Told you," Jimmy said. "You don't have to worry about anything. I've got it all stitched up."

Lucy grimaced. "These ropes stink! What if they're rotten? What if they break? We'll die here like some goddamned trout in that rolling throw-up down there."

"We're only thirty feet over the water."

"Water can break your neck if you hit it at the wrong angle," Zack provided.

Lucy let her lips peel back and broke the looking-down rule. "My astrologer *told* me not to do anything dangerous this week. I *knew* I should've paid attention to the signs—now look where I am."

With a stern scowl Jimmy said, "Don't believe in it."

Zack nudged Lucy another sidestep west and called to Jimmy over the wind as it howled between them. "You don't believe in destiny?"

"Didn't say that," Jimmy called. "Said I don't believe in *pre*destiny."

"Why not?"

"Because somebody else has to tell me what mine is. That means somebody else is in charge. Means somebody else knows more about me than I do. Malkin, see this main line?" He put his hand on the only braided line on the side of the rope bridge. "That's the one you hang on to. No, the other one. Look at me. *This* one."

Lucy's voice sounded a little steadier when she spoke again. "I know there's something about the stars and when you're born and all. I've *seen* enough. I've had crazy things happen that can't be coincidence. Like when they advised me to start packing a knife, and the next week I had to use it."

Glad he had managed to distract her, Jimmy said, "The stars care whether Lucy Pogue carries a knife? We know what stars are. We know that's one." He spared a hand and poked a forefinger at the bright golden sky. "Am I supposed to believe some arrangement of things in the sky makes life just a package deal? A frame-up all set

21

before we're born? What if your mother trips on a pig like mine did and you're born a month early? Which date sets destiny—my birthday, or a month later? Which stars should I look at? A batch of hot atoms a billion light-years away has some influence on my future?" He snorted.

Some of the gang nodded. Others didn't. So he continued talking as long as they were moving.

"Destiny and predestiny are two different things. Predestiny is pointless. If it's true, we might as well turn around right now, go back to Riverside, and sit on our bulkheads, because whatever's going to happen's gonna happen anyway."

"How's destiny any different?" Tom Beauvais challenged.

A crooked grin danced on Jimmy's face as he leered back at them. "That's the one *I'm* in charge of."

From the west, the sun buttered his apricot curls and sweat glittered on his brow. To the others, he looked like a demon with a license to smile. If anyone in the group wondered how he had talked them into running away, a moment like this snuffed the thought. Something in the ballistics of Jimmy Kirk was tough enough and vivid enough to keep them going across the shabby old rope bridge, stepping one by one over their better judgments.

Zack coughed as the wind filled his lungs, and he forced himself to move along the ropes, to stay distracted, and not to look down. "Sounds like plain luck to me."

"It sounds like that, but it's not," Jimmy said. He held out one hand, fingers spread, as though gripping the imaginary brick with which he would lay his foundation. "Luck is blind chance. Destiny . . . *that* you *build*."

He eyed them, one by one, even Beauvais, until the belief returned to each face.

Then he said, "Move along. Twenty more feet and we're there."

The river whispered below. They moved slowly toward the west bank, a few inches at a time, each burdened with a backpack of survival supplies and foodstuffs.

Lucy's voice showed she was trying to keep control as she asked, "How are we going to find our way to Omaha?"

Jimmy helped Emily find a handhold. "Dead reckoning."

"Dead what?"

"Basic sail training."

"Who's gonna sail?" Tom cracked. "We're going on a cargo carrier!"

"It's basic seamanship, Beauvais. Get used to it. The captain's going to expect us to know this stuff. The STD formula. Speed, time, distance. If you know your constant speed and distance, like how far you'll go and how fast, you can figure how long it'll take. If you know your time and speed, you can figure how far—"

"Maybe we should go to space instead," Zack suggested.

"Space? Cold and empty. We got it all right here."

He dismissed the subject with his tone and twisted forward, watching Emily's tiny feet custodially. He moved his own feet carefully after hers, along the miserable knots and fraying lines that once had been sturdy enough to carry teams of Girl Scouts and Boy Scouts across the Skunk River. Long abandoned, the sixty-foot ropewalk had been left up for sentimental value as part of the Tramview of the Oregon Trail. He and Zack had worked for almost an hour breaking through the protective grating that kept hikers off the old footbridge. Zack could break into anything. That's how they'd gotten the food in the backpacks—it was how they'd gotten the backpacks. That's how they'd finagled tickets for the Stampede Tubetrain.

All they had to do was get to Omaha without being spotted for runaways, and they'd never be seen again.

Jimmy shook his head and forced himself to stop thinking about what they'd stolen. What choice did they have? They hadn't been given anything, so they just had to take somebody else's. That was fair.

*Snap*

"Ah—ah—Jimmyyyyyy!"

The shriek cracked across the ravine at the same moment as the rope bridge waggled hideously to the snap of parting jute—and Quentin went over backward. His hand clawed uselessly at a broken line, then at open air.

Lucy screamed, driving the needle of terror under all their skin.

Jimmy cranked around in time to see Quentin bounce against the ropes on the other side of the bridge and bend them almost all the way down to the level of the walkway. Part of the braided walkway caught the small of Quentin's back and bounced him stiffly, but finally held. And there he was, hanging.

The boy was arched backward over the outermost strands, his upper body in midair, hanging halfway out over the greedy water. His loaded pack yanked at his shoulders and held his arms straight out sideways. The whole bridge wobbled back and forth, back and forth, in a sickening bounce.

None of them did any more than freeze in place, clinging to their own ropes.

"Nobody move!" Jimmy bellowed. "I'll do it!"

"Goddammit!" Beauvais shouted. His face twisted. "This was your stupid idea! We could've just taken the long way, over ground, but no! We had to do it Kirk's way! Why does anybody listen to a blowfish like you!"

"Cram it, bulkhead. I'm busy." Jimmy unkinked his fingers from the scratchy ropes and forced himself to move back toward Lucy.

"Please, Jimmy," Emily murmured, "don't let him fall . . ."

Jimmy pressed her hand just before she was out of reach. "I'm not going to let him fall. Nobody else move. Quentin, hold still."

They were only a couple of stories up, but Jimmy knew it was enough to kill. Below, the muddy water chewed and gurgled.

Jimmy maneuvered around Lucy, then around Zack, careful not to dislodge either of them from their hold. The ropes shivered, but no more parted or frayed.

"It'll be all right," he said steadily. "Everybody stay calm. He just put his foot on the wrong braid. Nothing else is breaking."

"Tell the ropes," Beauvais snarled.

Jimmy's face flamed, and he stopped moving toward Quentin. "I'm telling the damn ropes!" he bellowed. "Leave me alone and let me do this."

Beauvais rearranged his grip and muttered, "Okay, okay . . . just get him."

Below them Quentin dangled backward, his hips tangled in the old ropes, and gasped as though he couldn't remember how to breathe. "J-J-Jimmy—"

"I'm almost there. Don't whine."

Jimmy reached Quentin and lowered himself to the braided

24

cordage, his own breath coming in rags. Old tendons wobbled and grated against the cross-braids, threatening to open beneath him. By the time he got above the dangling boy, his palms were bleeding.

Quentin's left foot was caught between two braids that had twisted as he went backward. If he turned his foot now, it would slip through and he would be tossed out like a circus performer on a springboard. No one wanted to point that out; they all saw it.

A finger, a limb, a joint at a time, Jimmy lowered himself to his hands and knees onto the walkway of the bridge. The old jute cut into the flesh of his kneecaps right through his clothing. He bit his lip, ignored the pain, and searched for a secure position over Quentin's entangled legs.

There wasn't one.

The ropes quivered defiantly under him, refusing to cooperate. Ultimately he arranged himself on his stomach across the braids, right beside Quentin's leg. He shoved an arm through the side ropes of the bridge.

"Monroe, give me your hand."

Nothing happened. Spread halfway out in open air, the younger boy was muttering unintelligible sounds.

"Monroe, what are you doing?"

"P-p-praying."

"Well, do that later, will you? Give me your hand."

"I can't—move—"

Jimmy lowered his voice, literally made it darker, grittier, meaner. "This is one of those times when you've got two possible destinies, right?"

"Mmmm . . ."

"Pick the best one."

No one else breathed, no matter how the rising wind pushed air between their clenched teeth.

"Now!" Jimmy ordered.

A brown hand arched upward toward the sky. Jimmy caught it, and hauled.

"My arm! My arm!" Quentin bellowed as his body cranked sideways, upward.

Jimmy twisted his fingers into the boy's shirt collar. "Beauvais, take his backpack. The rest of you, keep moving. Zack, you're in charge."

"What? I don't want to be in charge."

"You don't have any choice, do you?"

"This was your idea."

"Fine. Lucy can be in charge."

The bridge waggled.

"I don't want it either!" Lucy protested.

"We're more than halfway across!" Jimmy shouted. "All you have to do is go twenty more feet! How many decisions do you have to make?"

"I'll be in charge," Tom said as he slung the extra backpack over his shoulder.

Jimmy cranked upward the other way. "I didn't pick you!"

"We didn't 'pick' you either."

"Yes, you did. This was all *my* plan."

"Some plan! We're not even out of Iowa and we're already in trouble. You're all gas, Kirk."

"Look, any time you're ready to turn back—"

"Jimmy . . ."

The soft beck from above drifted down and silenced the disharmony.

Jimmy twisted back toward the others. "What is it, Emily?"

The girl stood with each narrow white hand on a side of the bridge, unable to push back her hair as the wind blew it forward over her cheeks and into her eyes. "Quentin," she murmured.

"I know, I've got him," he grumbled, and returned his attention to where it should have been.

Quentin's brown face had gone to clay by the time Jimmy hauled him up and pulled his legs out of the ropes he'd gotten tangled in. He had both eyes knotted shut and refused to open them until Jimmy threatened to leave him in the middle of the bridge.

Then Jimmy took him by the shoulders and almost broke his shoulder blades. "Quentin, this is how it is," he said. "We're going on. It's just rope. We're not going to be beaten by rope. Are you with me?"

He didn't wait for an answer. He straightened, placed Quentin's hands on the side support lines, nodded toward the bank, and started picking his way westward again. He didn't look back. Quentin would follow, or be left out there.

But through his boots he felt the pressure on the braided rope behind him, and knew he would win that bet.

On the bank Tom Beauvais was the last to jump onto solid ground. They turned to watch Jimmy bring Quentin all the way in.

Jimmy jumped onto the hard, rocky ground, pulled Quentin up behind him, then stepped aside as Zack and Lucy came forward to help Quentin stumble onto the grass.

When he turned and looked up at Tom Beauvais, there was mercury in his eyes. He took two steps forward, and *boom*—

A roundhouse right pitched Tom's head backward, and he staggered but didn't go down. He gathered himself and let fly a rabbit punch to Jimmy's midriff, but Jimmy saw the punch coming in time to tighten up. He had the advantage of *not* being too lean.

His buff curls flickered, his brow drew in, his eyes turned to arrowheads, and the heels of his hands struck Tom in the shoulder hollows. Another flash spun Tom around, and Jimmy had his challenger's wrist forced halfway up his spine.

Tom ground out a senseless protest and arched his back, then bellowed in pain.

Forcing the arm upward another inch, Jimmy asked, "Your way or my way?"

"Okay, okay, your way! Don't break it!"

Jimmy shoved him off and dropped back a pace, satisfied. Holding his arm and swearing, Tom stumbled away.

"I'll break it next time," Jimmy said.

The others looked away from both boys, embarrassed and unsure about their adventure.

He pushed through the others to Quentin, and his entire demeanor changed as he took Quentin by the shoulder and said, "Take a deep breath. Now take another one . . . you did it. You beat it."

Quentin managed a nod.

Jimmy turned him to look at the shaggy rope bridge as it waved in the wind as though to say good-bye. "There it is . . . everything you were afraid of. You went one step at a time and you trusted somebody. Now it's all behind you. Understand?"

As Quentin looked at the rope bridge, at how far it was back to the other cliff, and at how far he had come, his trembling slowly faded away.

It *was* behind him. He never had to cross it again. He'd done it.

He cleared his throat and said, "You're stronger than you look."

Jimmy smiled. "All right, everybody, mount up. Get your packs on and let's get moving. We've got a schedule to keep."

He strode cockily away from Quentin, leaving most of the group to stare at the back of his head, closed almost his whole hand around Emily's upper arm, and started walking her west.

"I," he said, "will take care of you. You don't need anybody. You don't need your teachers, you don't need your parents, you don't need your sisters . . . you need only me. By morning we'll be in Omaha. Then, four hours on the Stampede, and *zam*—we're in Bremerton, Oregon, signing on as deckhands of dynacarrier *Sir Christopher Cockerell.*"

"How old you are?"

"Old enough to get here on our own."

"From where you come?"

"From over two thousand miles. You guess the direction. We want to sign on. Work our passage."

As the six young people stood on the windy dock, looking very small, oafish, and overwhelmed beside the 58,000-ton dynacarrier, the German first mate gazed down on them from far above. The ship's rail was two stories up, and he wasn't going to waste time going down to the dock to talk to these children, no matter how they had demanded audience with an "officer." Suddenly he wished he could be wearing a uniform instead of denim and deck shoes. That would be funny. He could scare them even more.

He paused to light a cigar, shoved back his shaggy yellow hair, and tried not to laugh. Only two of the teenagers looked fit for duty at sea.

The others were . . . uncertain. He could see it in their eyes.

"You got your mama's okay to come here?"

Without a pause the boy shot back, "You got yours?"

The mate paced a few steps.

28

"This is no toy boat," he said. "What will you do on big merchant ship?"

"Whatever it takes," said the boy with the chamois curls who appeared to speak for all. He stood with one foot on a piling, leaning forward on that knee, boiling with the know-it-all cockiness of youth.

The first mate sucked on his cigar and strode a few feet along the ship's rail, turned casually away to get that smile out of his cheeks, then faced them again and paused. "Deckhands?"

"That's right," the boy said.

"What do you know about a dynacarrier? What I tell the captain I am bring on his ship?"

"You can tell him it's got a hull design that can be adjusted in sections by the navigation computer, and that she carries harvested crab, shrimp, and fish from the continental hatcheries to the statis outposts so they can be preserved and sent to our colonies in space. Tell him she's got telescoping masts with duckwing stabilizers that fold back in harbors and expand on the open sea. Robotics do most of the work and that she goes out of the harbor on antigravs and you turn off the antigravs and settle into the open water, because somebody figured out that cargo carriers don't have to be fast, just efficient. And tell him he's got six apprentices who want to learn to run the robotics."

The first mate wasn't particularly impressed, but he *was* amused. The boy had a belittling tone in his voice and an uncharming bitterness in his eye, but he'd obviously done his homework, prepared for this moment. Cheap labor. Hmmm . . .

"What you want for pay?"

"I told you," the boy said. "Passage, berths, food . . . and no questions."

Real cheap.

The first mate shrugged with his expression.

"I see what I can do."

Down on the dock Jimmy repressed any sign of victory and kept a stiff scowl on his face. He was sure the others were amazed. Deliberately he didn't look at them.

"How can you know all that stuff, Jimmy?" Quentin asked. "How did you know how to get us here on the train? It was a great trip! I want to go on that train again someday, don't you, everybody? I can't believe all the stuff you know, Jimmy!"

Jimmy narrowed his eyes and gazed up at the looming panorama that was their future—a red and gray sea monster stretching across their entire field of vision, loaded to the gunwales with ocean harvest, and rumbling.

"It's my business to know," he crowed.

Quentin appeared in his periphery. "What I mean is . . . how can you know if you don't read any books?"

Color flared in Jimmy's cheeks.

He buried his embarrassment in a cough and brought his foot down off the piling. He felt the heat in his face and turned away quickly to hide it. Above, three sea gulls circled, whistling with laughter.

"Well," he pushed out, "you . . . gotta read the right books."

He buried his blushing complexion by fussing with supplies and packs they'd dumped a few feet back on the dock.

"Jimmy?"

"Yeah?" He straightened suddenly, and found himself looking into Lucy's overused, overmade-up, over-everythinged face. It took some hard looking to see past the cake and lipstick and see she was still young. He lowered his voice. "What's the matter, Lucy?"

"You didn't tell certain people that this son of a bitch would be so *big*," she said. "There was nothing like this in Riverside."

"That's the point," Jimmy said firmly. "We're not in Iowa anymore, Toto."

"Why do we have to go on the ocean? I don't want to barf all the way to South America. Why can't they just fly cargo around?"

He felt the eyes of the others on him. Answers. They always wanted answers. Reasons to keep doing what they had decided to do.

Then he would give them reasons.

"You want to know why we don't fly?" he began. "If you're at the bottom of a well and you want to get to the other side of the well, do you climb all the way to the top, then walk around, then climb all the way down again?"

Lucy snarled. "Oh, sure."

30

"Why wouldn't you?"

She shrugged one shoulder. "Because it'd be brain-dead."

"Because it'd be a brain-dead waste of energy, right?"

"What's that got to do with this?"

"Earth's at the bottom of a well of gravity. If you want to move a half-million tons of harvested seafood, you don't use up energy lifting it thirty thousand feet in the air just to bring it down to the same level later, do you?"

"I guess not."

"That's why we don't fly cargo around."

"Hey! You, down there!"

He and Lucy turned, as did the others, looked up, and saw the first mate grinning down at them with a weird, devious glint in his eye.

"Hey! Captain say he won't notice if you come on board. Then we get a look at you."

*"Attention,* Cockerell! *This is Port Authority. You are being detained on suspicion of illegally transporting minors into international waters. Put your engines in neutral, fall off your course, and prepare to be boarded."*

Garish fog-cutting spotlights jabbed from the Port Authority hovercraft as it hissed toward the dynacarrier. Its aircatcher quivered like a sea slug's skirt.

The big hovercraft was dwarfed by the dynacarrier, but there was no doubt as to who was in charge.

At the *Cockerell's* bridge rail, the captain frowned at his first mate and said, "Damn you, Klein. These deckhands you brought on board—have they brought false identifications we can point at?"

"They all claim to be eighteen years old. I saw the cards, with pictures," the German responded. Then he grinned. "Just like last time."

"Stick to the story. Where are these children?"

The mate grinned wider, crookedly. "In the galley . . . scrubbing mouse shit from the corners."

The captain grunted. "Hmm. Thought they would be on sail computers, and they end up scrubbing—who is *that!*" He pressed forward against the upper deckhouse rail and peered down onto the

31

deck of the hovercraft as it came alongside their boarding ladder. "What is Starfleet doing here!"

Before the mate could answer, the captain was on the stairs to the lower deck.

"Contact the galley! Lock up those children!" he shouted as he dropped to the deck. He didn't wait for the mate's confirmation, but just hoped the ship's comm was buzzing.

The captain met the hovercraft, having worked down only part of the dread on his stubbly face—if only he'd shaved today! He barely managed to choke out a civil greeting to the Starfleet Security Division team as they stepped aboard.

Three men and two women, neat as a picket fence, none particularly amused or affording his ship the usual visitors' appreciation.

They weren't there to visit.

The highest-ranking officer was a muscular man with iron-red hair and no fun in his face, who obviously took this situation personally.

"Captain," the officer said, "you picked up six teenagers in Bremerton, just outside of the naval base. Where are they?"

"In custody, Lieutenant!" the captain said quickly. He pointed at a little coffee station near the middle of the ship. "We put them in the midships deckhouse as soon as we saw that their identifications were fake. We didn't know when we hired them—"

"Save it, Captain," was the growling response. "And I'm a commander."

He tapped his rank insignia with a forefinger.

"You can take it up with the Coast Guard," he said. "They'll be here in ten minutes to lodge charges against you and your parent company for antagonizing the laws of your host government and for illegal international transport of minors. This practice is going to stop. You're going to have to pay the competitive price for consenting adult labor, and that's it. Now," he added, "where are those kids?"

Sweating and turning purple, the captain snapped his fingers at the mate and shouted, "Get them!"

"Bringing them now!" the mate called instantly.

Coming toward them were several crewmen of the dynaship,

flanking the teenagers, all of whom were particularly grim. There'd been a fight. Two of the *Cockerell*'s crewmen were dabbing at bruises on their faces. Another was holding his arm and trying not to wince.

The Starfleet commander squinted, then glowered. "There are only five. Where's the other one?"

Viciously the captain shouted, "That bulldog! Where is he?"

One of the crewmen gestured back at the shabby white deckhouse. "He's fighting. Kicking and spitting. Crazy. Like a barbarian or something. Won't come out. No respect for nothing."

Everyone paused, and sure enough the deckhouse was physically rattling. From inside, the muffled noises of contention boomed. Bodies hit the old plank walls. Coffee spilled under the door and spread onto the deck. The door clapped and squawked against its hinges.

"Don't worry," the captain said, pulling at his mustache. "We have control, don't worry . . . we'll get him out."

But the commander gestured to the captain, the sailors, and his own people to stay behind, and he stepped forward himself.

*"I'll* get him out."

The teenagers averted their gazes and didn't meet his eyes as he stalked past them.

The captain and his sailors gathered closely and watched the Starfleet man get smaller on the huge deck. The man's fists were knotted, his thighs grinding like pistons, his head forward and his shoulders set, the wind picking up his blood-colored hair and flopping it down with every step.

"I wouldn't want to be that bulldog boy," the captain muttered.

One of the sailors rubbed a sore jaw and said, "I wouldn't want to be the Starfleet man."

The commander caught the deckhouse door handle at that instant and raked the door open so sharply that the others heard it shriek all the way across the deck. He disappeared inside.

Everyone winced in anticipation and waited, making bets inside their heads and wondering if they had time to make them out loud.

Almost at once the deckhouse stopped lurching.

Another ten seconds trickled by.

The deckhouse door scratched open, and three battered sailors slogged out with obvious relief, happy to leave that under-aged terror to somebody who was armed.

But suddenly there was no more thunder from inside.

Instead, the door opened one last time, and the Starfleet officer stepped into the spilled coffee, dragging Jimmy Kirk by the collar of his jacket so hard that the jacket was nearly being pulled off.

The boy allowed himself to be hauled, but like a convict in the hands of an abusive guard. He refused to look at his captor, only blinked into the sea wind as he was made to pass by his bitter comrades and stand before the captain and the Starfleet Security team.

"You see the problem we had!" the captain insisted to the commander. "We saw the mistake, but too late! Tell me—how did you get him to come out? We had to fight! It was terrible. You see my men's faces—all scratched and hit. How did you do it?"

The Starfleet man swallowed several times and stood braced against the ocean wind, holding the boy's arm with each of them standing as far from the other as possible.

"I didn't have a choice," he said. He looked at the boy then, and spoke with a digging shame. "He's my son."

# THREE

☆

"Petty theft . . . fraud . . . shoplifting . . . leaving school without permission . . . falsifying identification . . . breach of public security . . . unauthorized use of private credit lines . . . invasion of official records and illegal use of accessed information."

George Kirk's forefinger drummed on the galley's scratched tabletop, his face bayed by anger. With a flop of oxblood hair hanging in his face, brown eyes scowling, and his scarlet and white Security Division jacket collar bunched up under his chin, he looked like a mad rooster.

Under his boot soles, the rumble of the hovercraft provided a constant ugly drone. He was glad the two of them were alone.

"You strike off to see the world and this is the gang you follow? Lucy Pogue? Her juvenile record didn't give you a hint that maybe she was somebody you should avoid? Zack Malkin? He's got a computer crime file as long as his leg. Quentin Monroe? A skinny, sick kid. Brilliant choice. Tom Beauvais? The only thing lower than that backslider's goals are his grades. And Emily! *You* talked her into going, didn't you? A girl like that, on a dynaship! You not only follow these junior-league swindlers, but you entice somebody like Emily to go along? What were you thinking?"

He hesitated, but got no answer.

After a few seconds he lowered his voice. "You don't have a clue how to pick the right people to be close to, do you?"

At the corner of the table, against the bulkhead, as far down the bench as he could get, Jimmy Kirk sat with his knees flopped apart and his touring cap pulled low over his eyes, doomfully silent.

His father paused, ticked off five seconds, then shifted his feet. "Nothing to say?"

Like a prisoner of war, Jimmy remained resolute, stony, and refused to meet his interrogator's eyes. His wait-it-out posture was damningly effective.

"Okay, let's have it." Pacing across the tiny cabin, George demanded, "Who's the ringleader?"

Jimmy turned his head so his father wouldn't see the smirk that erupted on one side of his mouth. He tapped his thumbs on the seat of the chair, rattled his imaginary handcuffs, and remained uncooperative.

"Who was it that invaded the voting records? Zack, right? Was it Beauvais's plan? Are you going to waste your life following Tom Beauvais around?"

Jimmy folded his arms, belittling his father with his disinterest, and slumped further.

"How were you expecting to survive once that ship docked in South America and those people were done with you?" George demanded. "Do you have any clue how tough it is to make a living down there?"

"I'd have been fine."

George stopped, gaped down at the unenchanting representative of youth, and wondered what button he'd pushed to get an answer that time.

"Fine?" he echoed. "Okay, let's say you'd have been fine. Then tell me what's down there for you. Why would you want to go there?"

"Didn't want to live at home anymore."

"Why not? What's so bad about home? It's a decent little town, isn't it? Lots of fresh air, polite Amish neighbors still farming with horses, close to enough cities that there's plenty for you to do—*legally* . . . how do you think this is affecting your mother?"

The touring cap's brim came up just enough for George to see his son's broiling eyes masked by a band of shadow. The voice was a grim dare.

"Leave her out of this."

Another light snapped on in George's head. He widened his eyes and nodded.

"Leave your mother out. Sure. Easy. Like she's not home worrying about you. Like she got up yesterday morning and said, 'Oh, Jimmy's run away from home. Guess I'll fry a couple less eggs for breakfast today.'" He paused and changed to a tone that put this issue on the top of the list of crimes. "You should've heard her voice when she contacted me," he said. "If you had, you wouldn't say, 'Leave her out of this.'"

Stern as a circus firebreather, Jimmy folded his arms tighter and changed the subject.

"How'd you find us?"

George parted his lips to tell him, maybe get a good gloat out of all this, but then he changed his mind.

"Why? So we won't find you the next time? Forget it."

He continued pacing.

"Now you'll be looking for ways to avoid being found again, right? Why don't you tag along behind some light-fingered punk with a bright idea to *beam* out of Iowa? Does that sound fancy and intriguing enough for you? Violate beaming regulations, scramble the patterns? Adventure enough for you? It's real fast, y'know. I sure couldn't trace you, not that it would make much difference." He slapped his own thigh and added, "Your leg'll end up on some old lady's neck and I won't be able to do a thing for you anyway. Sooner or later you're just going to be too big for the safety net, Jimmy, and you're going to fall through."

He leaned forward on the galley table and glared at his son.

"Jimmy," he asked, "when is it going to dawn on you that rules exist for a reason?"

The words settled poorly against the hovercraft's hum.

He straightened. His head came into the direct line of the cooking light near the galley stove, turning part of his hair carrot-red as though in punctuation.

"What is it you want?" he asked. "What're you doing all this for? What do you *want?*"

Jimmy's eyes were cold. "Respect."

"I can't give that to you. You've got to earn it."

"Whooo," Jimmy mocked. "A zinger from the book of parental clichés. I'm burned."

His father straightened and swallowed hard. "I'm real disgusted with you, I want you to know that. Nothing like this is ever going to happen again. And when we get back to Riverside, we're going to figure out what to do about this."

Jimmy shifted his feet and, if possible, turned farther away. "You can try," he said doomfully. "But it's all just a broken mirror to me, 'sir.'"

"I don't know what to do."

George fingered the kitchen curtains and looked out across the tenant farmland he owned and the two Amish farms between there and Riverside. Off to his left he could see the English River almost flowing out of its banks.

A fleeting memory of crossing that river on a rented road-and-float vehicle flicked back at him. There he was, barely an adult himself, with his wife, a toddling son, and a brand-new baby boy, antigravving across a swollen creek that laughed at him for moving in the spring instead of waiting two months until the water dried up. George and Winona Kirk, and their boys, George Samuel, Junior, and James Tiberius.

George winced. Poor kid, named after a constellation . . .

*"James T. Kirk . . . say it, pal! Jimmy, look at me, buddy. Can you say 'James'? Say James Teee . . ."*

Images of their young family and the anticipation of the future shriveled as he realized what his younger son was becoming.

"What can I do?" he asked quietly. "He's too big to spank . . . I can't lock him in his room, can't give him extra chores . . . you can do things to a six-year-old that you just can't do to a sixteen-year-old . . . I can make him come home but I can't make him stay. I can't help feeling that he's salvageable, but he's fallen in with the wrong crowd and now he's tight-lipped as a convict. He's going to turn into one if he stays on this track, and I don't know what to do to head it off. The beardless twirp won't even talk to me. What can I *do?*"

Deep in the nearby farmlands, their Amish tenant and his four sons tilled the cornfields with horses and plows, mirroring a more distant past than George could imagine anymore. His mind was used to another kind of field, a field of stars, tilled by cranky, hard-working space vehicles held together with spit and spare parts, by people who rarely set foot on a real planet anymore. Only on leave . . . only in emergencies . . .

"I'm scared, Winn," he murmured. "My boy's turning into a gangster, and I can't stop it."

Behind him, Winona Kirk stood with her arms folded and her one shoulder poetically against the wall. She was a leaner, always had been, always had her shoulder or her elbow or a hand propped against something, and did her best thinking while holding up a building.

"Sam was never like this," she said. "Jimmy's strong and he's rebellious, always a smoke-chaser, looking for trouble and calling it fun . . . he's so much more skeptical than Sam ever was, so much less fulfilled . . ."

George turned and started to say something, but his wife's appearance there in the natural light struck him silent.

Her hair, a mass of tight buff curls, was too much like Jimmy's. She even had her arms folded the same way the boy did—both hands tucked under, fists knotted—not in relaxation, but in tension and thought. Neither she nor Jimmy ever folded their arms just to get them out of the way like most people did.

She still had her lab coat on and she didn't look so different from the girl he'd eloped with—how long ago? Almost twenty years?

And after twenty years, the only things they had in common were the two boys. No animosity . . . just not much in common.

It hadn't been a problem when they were eighteen years old. Being married had been impressive all by itself at that age. They'd wanted to be completely grown-up, big man and big woman. They hadn't seen reality lurking behind the wedding pictures. Prestige was the only trophy at that age.

Then one year, two, three, a couple of children . . . and they'd discovered that being together at eighteen and being together at twenty-five . . .

Between themselves, they'd made it work. For the children—

He sighed and walked toward her. "My emergency leave won't last forever, you know."

"I know," she said. "Forty-eight hours, eighteen of them gone already."

Her voice was utterly passive. She'd gotten used to his not being around. They both had.

But this . . . this was too much for her to handle alone. They both felt that.

He paced right past her and halfway into the dining room. "Maybe I should leave Starfleet."

"Oh, cripe, there's an echo in here," Winn said. "How many times have I heard that?"

She turned to lean against the other shoulder so she could still be facing him.

"How is it going to help Jimmy to see his father wandering around the farm, bothering the Amish workers, knowing you gave up your career because of him? And it'll straighten him right out to see Mom and Dad carping at each other." She smiled ruefully, but her eyes were forgiving. "You know how we get when we're too close together for too long."

"Well, I'm not helping him from out there, am I?" George desperately bellowed.

She shrugged. "You're having some kind of effect on him. First chance he got, he headed for open water, didn't he? All that sailing stuff when he was little—not wasted, apparently."

"And not enough, apparently," he grunted. "Well, you know Jimmy best. I'll help if I can, Winn. If he'll accept it—but I won't make any bets. Got any suggestions?"

She pushed off the wall without unfolding her arms. She moseyed around the room, staring at the carpet and biting her lip.

When she turned, she looked squarely into her husband's eyes.

"Take him into deep space with you."

George almost choked. "What?"

"It's an idea."

"Deep space? I can't do that! I'm in the Diplomatic Corps's

Security Division! Our missions are touchy! We deal with unstable cultures, unknown sectors, border disputes, angry representatives, assassination attempts—nothing you take a civilian on, much less a *kid* civilian! You get court-martialed for that! I go dangerous places!"

Her left shoulder went down and her eyebrows went up.

"Then go someplace not so dangerous this once," she said. She paused, strode to the window at his side, and leaned there for a change. "We'd better show him there's something better out there than what happened to him the first time he went in space, don't you think? There must be something that's routine to you, but that a sixteen-year-old will think is kind of enchanting. Isn't there? You've been promising him for years."

"I promised . . . but you know what happened . . . whole sections of space started to open up . . . I got called away—besides, he didn't seem all that disappointed. He didn't seem like he really wanted to go."

"George, look back. You know what it's like to be a boy. It's taboo to show emotions like those. He saw that Sam wasn't particularly bothered by not going, and he didn't want to throw a tantrum while his big brother stayed cool—you know how that is."

"Yeah, I know how that is."

"And he didn't want to make you feel guilty when you couldn't work it out. Eventually, I guess he realized it probably wouldn't happen." She paused, tightened her arms around herself, blinked out the window, and frowned. "Come to think of it . . . that may have been when he started to close up."

Turning a troubled gaze on his wife, George let the revelation hit him full in the face.

"Oh, God, is it my fault?" he murmured. "Is it all my fault?"

She seemed troubled as he said that, and faced him. "That's not what I was after," she said quietly. "He's responsible too. He's sixteen, after all. I know it's an age when you blame other people, but still . . ."

"I've got to do something," George said, pacing tightly. "I've got to fix this."

"I always knew he would go away someday . . . there's something

41

in his eyes. He can't stay home." Winona pulled at one of her own curls and twisted it while she helped him feel guilty. "Use some of those connections of yours. Why don't you do it, George? Your son needs more than just me these days. He needs to see a *man* work, not a woman. He needs to see his father at work. And you need to spend time with him too. Go ahead . . . take Jimmy into space on some safe little cakewalk. It'll be good for both of you."

*Ten hours later* . . .
A Federation utility ground-to-space stratotractor, in space over the U.S.-Mexican border

Jimmy Kirk sat smoldering where he'd been left in the miserable excuse for a galley, going over how his father could have caught him.

The porthole was thick and scratched and had evidently served duty as a dart board, because it had little round dirty spots all over it. Through those dirty spots, Jimmy looked down at Earth.

Around him the stratotractor growled and burped. The chunky, squared-off utility crawler had looked more like a sleeping rhino than a space vehicle when he'd first seen it only an hour earlier. But yes, it launched into space, and yes, it made orbit. When had vessels gotten so ugly? Didn't anybody care what ships looked like anymore?

Below, the planet was particularly sleepy. The sun was just setting over America, and there was a chalk-dusting of clouds in the north. Otherwise, not a storm to be seen.

Except here, in his own head.

He felt his mouth set hard and his teeth grind. It awakened something.

Here he was, in space. Big deal.

The walls were cold, the engines were a dull grumble, the view of space was empty and black, Earth looked like a lonely old woman with white hair, and every ship he'd seen so far was a battered old barge with too many space hours in its log.

"Damned depressing," he proclaimed to the porthole and the planet, and the walls. Obeying the twist of determination inside, he got up, and his eyes went into a stiff squint. "I'm not going. I'm getting off this junkheap."

He pulled his cap low over his eyes, raised his jacket collar like a cat burglar trying to hide his face, and started going through the crew's lockers.

# FOUR

☆

"George! You crimson dragon! How are you?"

"Don't ask."

"Contentious as ever, eh?"

"Robert, please. Couldn't you be a little less jolly once in a while?"

A lanky forty-some-year-old fellow in a sweater tilted sideways to see past his cross-grained old friend and peer from under an awning of fluffy brown hair at the stratotractor's foredeck lift. The opening was small, as was usual in these planetary station grunt vehicles, so it couldn't hide much.

"Where's Jimmy?"

"Below."

"Of course—good for you! Taking no chances. Don't want him to see you bashing dignitaries with a pole-ax like you did the last time, eh?"

"Quit rubbing that in! The greenhorn punk just wouldn't come up, that's all."

"Cat-and-doggish as ever, the two of you. What would I do if George were not George and Jimmy were not Jimmy? Ah, the Kirks!"

Robert April shoved his hands into his cardigan pockets, bunching the shawl collar up around his jawline, shoved the sweater forward until it nearly hid his gold command tunic, and regarded George with open affection.

He rocked on his heels and grinned sentimentally. Lean and casual, his expression always neighborly, Captain April still carried a forbearance that betrayed him as a Coventry uppercruster. He was a happy, broad-gauged English string-puller whose steady hand had kept Starfleet on good footing since the beginnings of the long-range exploration program. Easily imagined as Sir Robert or Lord Robert, he had come to be regarded by his crews as something closer to Uncle Robert. He was a man to whom life was a jubilee, who could even take the jading tedium of space travel without a hint of wear, and he was as comfortable here on a maintenance tractor's foredeck as he was on the command bridge of a ship of the line. He'd ushered hundreds of young inductees into space exploration as the Federation of Planets expanded, simply by treating them as though they really could do this remarkable thing and do it plenty well.

To that dauntlessness George now pinned his last chance.

"Have you got a mission for me?" he asked.

Robert tilted a little forward as though sharing a secret. "I've got . . . Faramond."

It sounded mysterious, especially the way he said it. George tried to get it in context, but there wasn't any.

"You got what?" he asked.

"Faramond," Robert repeated, smiling. "Faramond. It's a planet. And on it there's a newly discovered archaeological mecca. A massive project. George, wait until you see it!" He spread his hands illustratively. "They're dealing with an ancient *advanced* race. Think of it! With an ordinary dig we'd have to be careful, but we'd never stumble upon anything we didn't understand. But this—this is remarkable! The information at Faramond could boost Federation science and medicine forward immeasurably. It's comparable to scientists of Columbus's time stumbling upon a sunken nuclear carrier, complete with computers."

George tucked his chin and blinked. "Wow."

"Yes, very wow. And listen to this part—Faramond is a cold planet. No volcanic activity whatsoever for ten million years, and it's far from its star, so it had no heat to speak of at all. We've had to build huge atmospheric domes to work under. We're just now ready to start the actual archaeology."

"Why would some advanced culture bother with colonizing a planet they had to heat up? That's a hell of a lot of wasted energy, isn't it?"

"That's what we want to know," Robert corroborated. "If they were interested in it, perhaps we'd better be also. It wasn't used for farming or mining, yet it was a massive complex, obviously far beyond us. Then all at once the entire culture packed up and left. And here's the clinch . . . we haven't the frailest idea how they left."

"'How'? You mean 'why'?"

"No, George," the captain insisted. *"How."*

George squinted at him. "Are you telling me there's no vessel residue?"

"No vessel residue, no technological droppings, no fossilized dock casualties, in fact no remnants of docks at all, no fuel film, no space markers, nothing to take care of a ship," Robert said, and paused. He spread his elbows in a shrug without taking his hands out of the pockets. "So how did they leave? It's a sociological mystery. And, George, we are finally ready to start solving it. The Federation has asked me to break ground with the 'golden shovel,' so to speak. Very easy on our parts, nothing to it."

He hesitated, sighed.

"I'm so wrapped up in the starship program, I was thinking of turning them down until you contacted me about Jimmy, and I thought how much he might grow at seeing such a place, so far away. It's a minor diplomatic mission . . . well, I suppose it's not minor to the fellows involved, is it? Glad I thought of that," he added. "I wouldn't want to disappoint anyone."

George, even in this choleric mood, couldn't resist an appreciative chuckle and wondered how a gate-crasher like him had ended up with a friend like Robert. The thought eased him somewhat. Robert April was well known to shun the lionizing offered by a grateful Federation of Planets as it bloomed outward like a rosebush, wanted little to do with the celebrity he deserved, but he did understand people's natural need to fuss and cheer. George knew

Robert believed that's what kept the blooms on the roses—the spirit of exploration, as much as the purpose.

Drawing a breath that betrayed the tight hopes chewing at him, George heard himself say, "I'll go get the little gangster."

"Go easy on him, now," Robert admonished. "He's probably sitting alone, making a lip hang."

"Yeah, he thinks he's been bushwhacked. I'll be right back."

"George—"

He spun on a heel. "Yes, sir?"

Robert's mouth quirked and he raised both eyebrows. "I have a surprise for you."

As though he couldn't take a surprise, George held still and asked with his silence.

The captain grinned slyly. "We're going to take *her* out again."

For a moment George didn't understand. Then he felt his nerves twist and realized what was being waved before him.

"Are you kidding me?" he asked, staring.

Robert grinned wider.

Stepping feebly toward him, George gasped, "Are you telling me . . . that my boy . . . is going to get to ride on *her?*"

The silence between them tingled.

"I've gotten you out of your hitch with the Diplomatic Corps," Robert said, "temporarily at least, and you're going to be one of my officers again. Won't that be like old times? Here we are, thick as thieves, all set for adventure and chivalry. Be quite something for Jimmy to see, eh?"

He hadn't been told anything. Just asked a favor. Hadn't been given the details. Yet, Robert knew. Had sensed, pieced it all together, the needs of old friends. Even though he had too many other friends to count, Robert April had known what two particular friends needed.

How many strings had he pulled? How many favors had he cashed in?

*She* was going to fly again, for the Kirk boys.

Overwhelmed and unable to hide it, George simply murmured, "I don't know what to say . . ."

The captain gazed warmly at him. "She's spacedocked. We're almost there."

George's mouth dropped open. "You mean now? Right now?"

"Right now."

"Oh, this is—this is . . . I'll get Jimmy! He's gotta see her from the outside! How close are we? Where's she docked? No—forget that—it doesn't matter! This is great! Slow us down, will you? No, never mind! I'll move fast!"

He took the captain's nod as permission to leave the deck, and hopped the lift doublequick, and just before the panel slid shut he stuck his head back out.

"Robert, you really know how to ice a cake!"

On a station stratotractor, from anywhere to anywhere was a very short jog. A matter of seconds put George on the utility deck, stepping between mooring harnesses and powerloaders to the little crew galley where he'd left Jimmy sitting alone.

"All right, champ, on your feet. Wait'll you see—"

He stepped in, and another second told him the rest. There was nothing in here but the gurgling snack dispenser.

"Ohhhhh—no!"

He left the galley on the run, stumbled over two triaxial coils and a spooled umbilical, and this time didn't wait for the lift. This time he climbed the companionway ladders, squeezing past pitch adjusters, going directly from the trunk deck to the anchoring deck to the tonnage deck, right into and then past the crew saloons. He peeked into every portal, every cargo gate, platform, hatch, and hole, and got strange glances from the crew. They weren't used to anyone hurrying, much less a Starfleet Security guy, because nothing *ever* happened on a stratotractor.

Of course, they probably weren't used to Starfleet officers hitching rides on maintenance craft either.

He didn't stop, except for a brief few seconds in one of the six dispatch silos, where he spied a compact fellow in a Security uniform being pressed against a stored antigrav pontoon by two Neanderthal mechanics.

"Hey!" George shouted, stumbling off the ladder. "What's this about?"

Cocoa eyes and a burnished face turned to him and called in clipped Trinidad English, adding a West Indies spice to the dull deck. "Commander! Lieutenant Francis Drake Reed reporting for assault and battery! Kiss the stars at your timely arrival! Tell these walking rocks that my father was a priest and I never cheat!"

George waved at the mechanics and barked, "Back off, you animals. He's under my command."

The mechanics were bigger than any four of George, but obviously weren't used to being ordered around by a Starfleet officer.

George snapped at his subordinate and said, "Trouble. Fall in."

"But I've—"

"I said trouble! Jimmy's gone!"

"Cow poo. Where can he go on a flying garage?"

"That's what scares me!"

Drake Reed dropped a bow at the two mechanics he'd just fleeced and started to make an exit statement.

"Pardon, all the thunderclap and shivaree, but duty caaaa—"

And choked when George grabbed him by the collar and hauled him down that ladder.

In seconds they were clattering between decks.

"I told you it'd take two of us to watch that kid!" George blustered. "Why didn't you meet us at the embarkation port?"

"I didn't even know you were on board yet," Drake protested. "A witch doctor, am I? Brain juju? I can see through walls?"

"And I told you not to run any games while you've got your uniform on. All I need is a complaint from the dock superintendent against my own lieutenant for gambling on duty. What's the matter with you? They could yank this tractor's dock warrants for that! Do you know what a mess it is to try to get your license out from under a complaint? Every person on board can be waylaid indefinitely! Climb faster, will you?"

"I am a gentleman, not a lizard. Where could the unripe lambkin be?"

"I've got a hunch he's trying to get off the stratotractor while we're still in the spacedock area."

"Hunch away. I shall follow."

They dropped onto the messy shipment deck, and George gave his assistant a push through crated parts and structural segments.

"Check the removable airlocks! I'll check the workbees!"

49

"Right." Drake started away, then spun around. "What on a spice rack could he do in a removable airlock? They're only used for transfer of pressure-sensitive cargo, yes?"

"Don't underestimate that snot. If it leaves the ship, he could be in it."

"But they have no thrusters!"

"Go!"

George waved him off with a frantic thrash and ran in the other direction, toward the row of four one-man work pods that commonly peppered space around docked vessels. Ugly with claws, magnets, antigravs, and hooks, the acorn-shaped bees could attach to almost any section of any kind of ship or dock section while the man inside did mechanical or electrical repairs. Otherwise, the bees were pretty low-tech. So small they were nicknamed potatoes and their bays were called pantries, they couldn't get far on their own.

Barely far enough for a boy to blow away from a stratotractor. After that—a very hard landing.

Crossing with some difficulty into each pantry and checking the old-style hatches that took a workman's badge code to get open, George satisfied himself that two of the bees' hatches hadn't been tampered with.

The third one, though, was locked from inside.

He yanked his markline spike from its sheath on his holster and hammered the blunt end on the hatch.

"Jimmy! Open up! Open up, goddammit!"

There was no response from inside, but the on-line lights were blinking on the external skin of the workbee. It was preparing to jump.

"Drake! Drake, over here!" he shouted, and poked hopelessly at the outer control panels. Nothing worked.

He started to shout again, then heard Drake's boots thudding on the deck behind him, and kept his attention on the hatch.

Risking detachment of the workbee with a ruptured seal, George turned his markline spike to the pointy end and started prying at the flexible seals around the airlock hatch. All the fancy, flashy weapons in the galaxy couldn't match a simple eight-inch pointed steel spike at moments like this. If he could just rupture the seal enough—before the workbee jumped free of its cowls—the safety system would take over and the big metal things holding the workbee wouldn't detach it.

Just enough—

*Hshshshshshs*

"Got it!"

When the airlock seal suddenly hissed, both Security men felt the rush of jackpot and alarm that comes only at moments of truth. As the hatch gave against his shoulder, George's instincts and training took over and his Fleet-issue laser pistol swept out of its holster and into his hands as though it had a life of its own.

He plunged in, locked both legs, fell into aim-and-fire posture, and shouted, "Hold it!"

"George!" Drake blared.

Instantly George yanked up the barrel, stumbled, and gasped, "Jesus, what am I *doing!*"

He and Drake gawked at each other. Could have been funny. Should have been.

Then they both looked again into the workbee's pilot cubby.

There, not quite filling the man-size shell, cooking with resentments, plots, and plans, Jimmy Kirk was ready to make his escape. He seemed more disgusted than embarrassed at having been caught, and he didn't move or attempt to cover up what he'd been doing. Maybe he was even proud of it.

Amber eyes that had once gazed at George in adoration and respect now burned with thankless acrimony—and it took some of the red out of George's hair to see it.

The boy was dry ice.

"You're pulling a weapon," he said, "on your own son."

Jimmy's bulky, muscular body never flinched as he glared at his father. Still half-hidden between the touring cap and the raised collar of his high school jacket, his eyes showed belief in his own sentiments. He had moved forward on his decisions with all the force of a teenager, and apparently he had no concern that his judgment might be bad or his course off.

He remained silent, pillorying his father with a full load of mean-mindedness.

Knowing when to keep his clapper tongue quiet, Drake Reed

cautiously reached out and removed the laser pistol from his superior officer's hand.

His chest withering, George stared at his son and held out his bare palm.

"Jimmy, I . . . I'm sorry . . ."

Brooding, letting his victory burn, Jimmy refused to show his father the slightest sympathy.

Seconds ticked by without relief, until he finally said, "Didn't know the word was in your rule book."

George jabbed a finger at the boy's face.

"Look, you retract your bristles, bud! What were you thinking anyway? These potatoes aren't toys! There are a lot of ways to die in space, but the worst one is to die of stupidity. You can't get around the security on this thing. The jump codes are—"

*ENABLED ENABLED ENABLED*

"How'd you do that? I'm *in* Security and I couldn't break this security!"

The boy got up slowly.

"Too bad," he said.

He stepped past, barely brushing his father with a very cold shoulder, and got out of the workbee.

George sagged against the curved interior shell, touched a hand to his head, and groaned, "He's gonna be a criminal . . ."

Drake clapped him on the back. "Buck up, George. He can take my place as a Starfleet legend."

He left George near the hatch and moved into the cubby to shut the potato down and buzz for a repair crew before anything went wrong.

At least, that was his cover. George knew Drake was really giving him time to go out there and handle his son alone.

Not just time, but a push.

He swallowed a couple of hard lumps, then stepped out onto the deck, feeling as though he had a butt full of duckshot.

As far down the cluttered deck as could be, Jimmy had retreated to a coffin-size niche between two big cargo-antigravs. There, he was waiting.

George approached without theatrics, and stood just out of the niche.

In the mirror of Jimmy's expression, George's hopes saw themselves and shivered. The resistance was palpable.

"Life's just one giant setback to you, isn't it?" he asked.

The boy looked away from him, shoulders down, a foot braced casually on one antigrav's trunk.

"You knew which bricks to pull out," George began again. "You'd have breached the couplings and gone off in the potato without anybody knowing you were out there, without following any pattern, without announcing your presence in the maintenance channels—if you even got out of the pantry alive. You could've killed yourself detaching that piece of junk the wrong way. Or you could've killed somebody else if the pressurizing went wrong in here. You could've killed Drake or me."

He paused, searching for reaction. There was absolutely none.

"Do you even care about that?" George added.

Jimmy folded his arms morbidly. He seemed proud that he had used neither hindsight nor foresight, and remained deaf to reason.

"You know what my dad always says," he answered. " 'In space, you take your chances.' "

He stalked farther into the niche, like walking rocket fuel.

"Maybe you can help me a little here," George said. "What'll work with you?"

Jimmy's cheek was barely visible as he tossed a response over his shoulder.

"How about raising the side of my crib?"

"Y'know, there's a lot to see in space if you'd just unclench your tight ass and open your eyes!" George struggled.

"Thanks for the advice."

"How old do you figure sixteen is? Wait till you hit twenty. In the Academy they give you tests you can't even win!"

The boy turned, scowled at him, and refused to be impressed. "Any game can be won."

"Oh, is that right? How'll you ever know if you can't even get past the entrance exam?"

"I could get into Starfleet's monkey farm *if* I wanted to. Who says I couldn't?"

"Your grades, that's who." George pointed back at the workbee. "Why don't you put some of those smarts into your schoolwork?

You mother enrolled you in the pre-Academy program so you'd have a little direction, not so you'd have a reason to go become some half-cocked vagabond on Earth. You mother and I have always tried not to compare you to Sam, but—"

"What do you know about how things are on Earth?" the boy challenged. "What do you know about Mom and Sam? We've gotten along just fine without you. Our names aren't in your Fleet manual."

George flopped his arms at his sides. "So you're just going to sneak back to Riverside and follow that pack of delinquents around until you hatchet your life. Good plan."

"Guess I better spend my life dodging black holes and pretending aliens don't smell. Thanks for the advice."

The tone was completely composed, even dry. There wasn't even the satisfaction of scorn for George to cling to.

He stepped back, giving Jimmy room to not get close. "All right, come out of there. Captain April's waiting to see you. That's how it is, you know, when you come on board a ship, you report to your commanding officer."

"So now he's captain of a station tractor?" the boy commented as he moved with damning slowness toward his father. "Thought he'd be doing better by now."

"These things don't have captains, and you know it," George said. "Now, move. We're going to show you what he *is* captain of."

# FIVE

"Jimmy, hello! Why, you look as if you've lost your dog."

Captain April spread his arms in welcome as George pushed his son out of the lift.

Jimmy Kirk wagged a hand but refused to speak. Before him, framed by struts and strings of lights outside—were those part of the spacedock?—Robert April gazed at him with complete understanding and tolerance, and the last thing Jimmy wanted right now was to be understood or tolerated.

A shove between his shoulder blades told him he wasn't moving fast enough.

He stepped down to the foredeck, putting space between himself and his father.

Captain April was already gesturing him forward. "Take a look at the moored vessels, Jimmy. And the service docks. It's all quite stirring in its labyrinthan way."

Bitter refusals popped into Jimmy's head while he was trying to envision whatever *labyrinthan* meant, but he couldn't push out any cracks as Captain April gathered him toward the wide, curved viewportal.

Jimmy was stiff, but he couldn't help seeing. If he turned around, all he'd see was his father.

Out there, in geo-somethingerother orbit over Africa, was a

tangle of spacedockage whose organization wasn't immediately clear.

"Looks like a girder factory puked," he said.

"Yes, doesn't it?" the captain said with a grin. "All around here are merchant ships in for repairs or refits. They'll go a few at a time into the structural docks . . . and that bunch of angular things is the LBR complex for spacefaring vehicles not carrying passengers. Loading, building, repair. Isn't it pretty in its industrial way?"

The strings of docklights were garish, but the dock girders themselves didn't catch any light, not even the sunlight, and had probably been painted with low-reflective paint to keep unexpected flashes from being mistaken for docking lights or buoys.

*At least, that's what I would do,* Jimmy thought, and mentally retreated for a moment to imagine building a thing like this if he had to.

Rather than going around the skeleton of red and blue girders, the stratotractor plodded right through the center, apparently having all its passage warrants in order. Jimmy had tried not to pay attention, but he'd picked up enough casual conversation to know that warrants and patterns were the only way to keep robotic vessels, or any kind of vessels, from knocking into one another and into the dock brackets.

He cleared his throat and pressed his lips tight, annoyed with himself for having paid attention without meaning to.

"These funny-looking beams have names," the captain explained, pointing as he spoke. "They seem snarled up, but they're not really. Those extra-long ones are longitudinal antigravity pontoons. They're always in line with the longitudes on the planet's surface—don't ask me why. But the entire dockage can be dropped out of orbit and landed on the planet, or taken apart and pieces of it landed, with vessels inside. Doesn't happen very often, but now and again it's handy. Oh, look there. No, no, directly above us . . . crane your neck a bit—that curved area above us—see it?"

"I see it."

"That's called a head wall. The curved bows of most Federation-standard vessels fit right in there. See the slings and clews that hold a large ship in place on the cutting stage? And those over there are built-beams we call backbones. All these ships are being worked on in some capacity. You can see that each one is flashing a blue light directly between two red lights, vertical to the ship's lines? Those are their not-under-command lights."

Still aware of his father standing silent behind them, Jimmy only grunted, determined to remain undazzled.

As they passed through the metallic mess, stringed lights sprinkled their colors on Captain April's face and made the smile lines crease around his eyes. He pointed at several vessels, all different shapes and sizes, which weren't in the dock complex, but were floating free in space, tethered by umbilicals to orbiting tanks.

"Those barges and clippers are in for resupply," Captain April said. "That's why they're at external moorings. There's no reason to take up dockspace with them. Most of these are merchantmen under contracts of affreightment with the Federation. The large ones are the clippers. They'll go from here to the DLO ports, which means 'dispatch and loading only.' The big ones carry bale cargo. That's raw material that comes wrapped in bunches. Their holds are called bale capacity or bale cubic. Makes sense, doesn't it?"

"Yeah, great," Jimmy chewed out of the corner of his mouth.

"The smaller ones, the barges, usually carry bulk cargo," April went on, "which is anything stored loose, not boxed, baled, crated, or casked. Flowing stuff, like liquid fuel, for instance, or even water for outposts. They can get their Bill of Entry directly from the dockmaster, along with certificates of registry, bond notes, warehousing tickets, and Bills of Lading, without having to set foot planetside. All the customs inspections, trade appraisals, and damage surveys can be done right here on the spot. It's really all very smart and allows for what we call 'customary dispatch.' That's the quick, lawful, and diligent loading and discharge of vessels." He drew a long breath as though inhaling in a garden, then let it out slowly. "Ah, it still gives me a chill to see how well we carry on such things!"

Jimmy bit the inside of his cheek to keep from reacting. Trying not to show on his face that half of that information had just flushed in one ear and out the other without stopping to check in, he suddenly felt very small. The trick of getting himself and five friends from Iowa to Oregon had seemed tough enough. Now it withered against the problems of moving a spaceship and cargo from here to there. Space had seemed drawing-board simple while he was sitting on Earth . . . bills of what? What kind of tickets? Surveys? Notes?

Luckily, Captain April didn't look at him, but instead was waving a hand appreciatively across their view.

"All these are involved in what we call the coasting trade," he added. "That's moving cargo within the Federation of Planets, or to colonies settled by our member planets."

Jimmy tried to spit a "Who cares?" but couldn't. If it had been anybody else talking to him—

April's hand curled over Jimmy's shoulder.

"And there," the captain added proudly, "is Starbase One."

As the stratotractor left the tangle of dockage and came out into open space again, they saw before them the majesty of what mankind had built on its own doorstep.

A hard lump of air made Jimmy tuck his chin when he had to swallow.

Starbase One . . .

A man-made heaven, beside Earth.

A giant silver spool with thread of lights, rotating slowly on its own axis, whispering into a boy's ears, *First of my kind, first of my kind, welcome, welcome.*

Jimmy swallowed a smile. He offered Starbase One only a constricted eagle eye.

He tried not to listen, just as he had ignored the whispering of the Skunk River, but these things spoke to him somehow and he could never forget. That's how it had always been. The distance had always whispered to him. The sunset, the howling wind, the hum of aircraft, the shiver of sails. Anything a hundred miles beyond wherever he was standing. Testimonials to the great outside had always whispered to Jimmy Kirk.

He gazed down through the popcorn clouds at the planet below, at the detail offered to him by the special windows and the cameras that brought pictures up to the monitors above himself and Captain April, and, trying to keep a handle on his narrowmindedness, he muttered, "Guess you can't bathe nude in your backyard any-more."

"Mmm, guess not," April responded. "In fact, Starfleet has expressly requested that officers not do that."

A smile pulled, but Jimmy chewed it down.

"Before many more years," April went on, "I hope to have officers who won't have to worry about that sort of thing . . . you know, the kind who don't have clothes to take off."

Jimmy leered at him. "Huh?"

"Aliens. I hope to attract more aliens into Starfleet."

"Why? Who needs 'em?"

"Don't you think that would make service more interesting? More noninsular, so to speak?"

"Not for me. I wouldn't want to spend my time working next to some slimy lieutenant with a tentacle."

"Well, why not? You, the adventurous type who doesn't care what's around the next tree? Why, I'd have thought you'd be the type clawing to get out to space, Jimmy."

The boy turned suddenly and purposely dark. "I've been to space," he said sourly. "Once."

New silence broke out as the forward area opened up and showed spines.

April shifted uneasily, realizing his error.

"Oh," he uttered. "Yes . . . of course you have. Sorry."

Jimmy bathed in the syrup of satisfaction while keeping his face bitter, then coldly added, "Don't apologize to me. I'm one of the ones that lived."

Great. Played right into his hands. He knew his father was back there, holding his breath, hoping for a reaction.

There would be none. There would be only a prisoner's glower, only disdain for that which had taken him away from where he wanted to be, when they all knew he had a fair reason for never wanting to go into space again. They were taking him away from Earth, away from Emily, away from those who did what he told them to do.

Though he was seeing the glittering spacedocks and the magnificence of Starbase One, Jimmy peered only through his own savage tunnel vision. He worked so hard to keep his face barren that his cheeks got stiff and his eye muscles actually hurt. Squinting them a little in the docklights helped, and he hoped it looked like a frown. No matter how the struts glowed in the sun's aurora or how the strings of docklights shimmered on the transport ships, he refused to be impressed. He kept his body stiff and aweless.

It took every ounce of his willpower to deny his father even the smallest satisfaction. Keeping his face a practice in nonwonder, he stood before Niagara Falls and felt no spray.

After a few more seconds of calculated nothing, Jimmy got his reward.

"I'll go make sure Drake's all right," his father said from behind them. "Don't want him accidentally locked inside a damaged potato. I'll . . . be right back."

A twinge of victory ran up Jimmy's spine. His father sounded defeated.

Captain April turned. "George, didn't you want to see . . . you know."

As the lift panel slid open, George Kirk appeared surly and crestfallen.

"I don't know if I want to see her or not right now, Robert," he muttered, and simply left.

The panel sighed shut. Now Jimmy was alone with Captain April and that field of astonishments out there. They looked at each other.

No matter how he tried, Jimmy couldn't muster the same rude disregard for Robert April that he gave his father. So he kept his father in mind in order to keep the chill on his face.

"Who's 'her'?" he asked, bristling.

Captain April blinked.

"Beg pardon? Oh!" Then he chuckled. "Oh, you'll see soon enough. An old friend of your father's and mine, you might say. He'll perk up when he sees her, don't you worry."

"I don't care."

"You don't care? That's no way to talk, my boy."

"Isn't it? He held a gun on me."

"Oh, now, Jimmy!" the captain admonished. "Is this the same family I spend Christmases with?"

Jimmy shrugged. "Shows how he thinks of me, that's all I know."

"Certain it wasn't just instinct at work?" His grin twisted warmly. "A Security commander has to go on instinct more than most of us. Don't you realize that?"

Eyes still hard, Jimmy charged, "Is that a reason?"

"No, no, of course not . . . let's try to forget it, shall we? We're all starting out on a wonderful adventure. We won't let a bit of domestic sandpaper spoil it, will we? Of course not. Oh, look! See those little one- and two-man worker vehicles? We have funny names for those, like potatoes and hedgehogs and sandbaggers—"

"Sandbaggers," Jimmy repeated. "That comes from wooden racing boats."

The captain looked at him. "Does it? How so?"

Suddenly on the spot, Jimmy sifted for a nearly faded memory. "The East Coast . . . sandbaggers were racing sloops in the 1860s, I think. They had big sails with extra-long booms, and they used sandbags for movable ballast. Every time the boat tacked, they'd toss the sandbags to windward."

"Really! What a spartan way to run a race! Must've taken a great deal of skill and timing. Where'd you learn about such a thing?"

Sensing he was being cornered, Jimmy shoved his enthusiasm into retreat. He wasn't about to say where he'd learned that. It would mean mentioning his father.

"Just happened to hear about it," he muttered.

"It's champion that you know these things," Captain April said genuinely. "Spacefaring is just an extension of basic seamanship. Good fellow. Proud of you!"

He clapped a congratulations on Jimmy's shoulder and kept his hand there as he gazed at Starbase One.

Jimmy felt heat rising in his cheeks. He stewed in silence as the stratotractor moved across the starbase's main doors.

And *didn't* go in.

When he realized that, Jimmy straightened and frowned. "What's going on? Where are we going?"

A cagey grin appeared on Captain April's lips. "We're going around to the other side of the base, to the Starfleet box dock."

"Why? I thought we were going someplace on this—"

*Bucket of bolts.*

"—ship."

"Oh, no. We're going on another ship, my boy. Another ship altogether. Look . . ."

The stratotractor was just coming around the starbase, breaking out into open space with the planet glowing at their left, half in daylight and half in night. In the coal-black distance shimmered the thing April had called the box dock.

It was an elongated red hexagon hovering there in the blackness, peaceful and separate, glowing with rectangular lighting bars much softer than the strings of lights on the merchant spacedocks.

There was something inside it.

Something white.

Jimmy pressed his shoulder against the rim of the viewport and determined to remain composed. He would offer a nodding acceptance to whatever Robert April showed him, and an open derisiveness to whatever his father showed him. He made promises to himself. He folded his arms and let his hands go limp at his sides to show how bored he was.

"This is Captain April aboard Strato 838, requesting permission to approach."

*"Acknowledged, Captain. You're free to approach. Please use the port side arrival patterns and fall into magnetic tractor beam port-four for docking. We'll do the rest."*

"I will, thank you. April out."

A few more clips and taps, and the robotic piloting took over.

They drew closer and closer to the box dock, moving higher into orbit, up, up, up toward the box dock—until the angle of the dock's ribs could no longer hide what hovered inside.

Robert leaned forward in nothing but love.

Bathed in beaconage, there *she* was. The gazingstock of Starfleet. With the diamondlike poise of a resting Lippizaner stallion, a huge milk-white ship beguiled the blackness. Two pencil-shaped warp nacelles pierced back from her lower hull, implying speed. The lower hull, where mankind's genius of engineering found expression, provided the ship's sense of ballast. Robert knew those impressions had been designed into her in defiance of commonplace understanding that a ship in space could be shaped like almost anything. There was no wind resistance to consider here. Here, such a ship was designed for only two things: purpose . . . and raw inspiration.

He knew. He had been there at the beginning. Seen the design plans. Seen the flash in the eyes of the designers. Heard their gasps of hope. He had touched Starfleet in its embryonic years, known and worked with the intrepid designers who dared have ideas, and this was the brilliant white mystery that came from those ideas.

As they came around to the fore of the ship, Robert gazed up and smiled at the primary hull, spreading above their approach like the bell of a great bass horn waiting for a tuning note. For the first time they were given a view of the entire ship, without interruption by dock struts.

There was a sound at his side, barely audible. One of those little human sounds there's no name for but that all humans recognize.

Robert glanced—and noticed the change.

Beside him, Jimmy Kirk was canted forward over the panel, committing the deadly sin of enthusiasm. He forgot his sworn duty to melancholy, and stared.

Robert April placed a warm hand on the boy's hunched shoulder, and spoke with quiet adoration.

"We call her . . . *Enterprise.*"

"She's a starship, Jimmy . . . isn't that a masterful word? Starship . . . her express purpose is to roam free to untouched stars. And she has the power to do it too. She and her kind will hammer through the frontiers of space, approach and contact faraway civilizations, bridge cultures, learn, share, grow . . . she's a flintbox for the firewalkers among us. The starship *Enterprise.*"

He hesitated, drew another breath, then sighed heavily.

"Isn't she a royal flush," he murmured.

Before them was the calm, elegant antithesis of Iowa. Jimmy knew his lips were hanging open, knew his shoulders were chinked forward and that he was leaning on both hands as though he wanted to break right through this viewport and touch her—he knew all that.

And could no more stop it than get out and fly.

He was going to go aboard *that* . . .

"She's a testimony to just how much good mankind can do," Captain April went on. "The first of her kind. Our flagship. Her engines are the first full time-warp commodities. She's built for constant thrust, none of the usual getting up to a speed, then going on momentum. She just keeps going faster and faster until the captain tells her not to. We're not even sure how fast she'll be able to go eventually. Until now she's been on a few stressing-out missions, but soon she'll be embarking on a series of five-year missions in deep space. We're going to go out, take our technology with us, our medicine, our dreams, our tenacity, our willingness to help and the wisdom we've gotten from our own mistakes . . . we're going to climb aboard that mastercraft, and we're going to head out. In time there'll be a dozen like her, going in a dozen directions for years at a time. They'll be like the first pioneers who went out in a reed boat . . . no contact with anyone, no help nearby, relying on their own spit and thatch to survive. That's adventure, Jimmy . . . real adventure. Isn't she something to write home about?"

Behind them, George Kirk stood in silence with Drake Reed.

Robert and the boy hadn't heard them come back in—or were too captivated to notice. George's own attention was swallowed up too by the giant white angel, shellacked and mounted on ebony before them. He and Drake barely breathed at the sight of her.

George hadn't seen the starship in almost five years. Not since all the decals, pennants, and insignia had been added. He had known her only as a white-on-white masterpiece with lights. Now, though, she was decorated with red nail polish and black eyebrow pencil in fine, unblended lines, and she said who she was and who had made her, and she said it with all the simplicity and pride of naval tradition.

*NCC 1701 . . . USS Enterprise . . . Starfleet, United Federation of Planets.*

But even this wasn't the shock of the day for George Kirk.

Now he gazed no longer at the ship, not at Robert, who was softly talking, but at his own son—

—who was *listening.*

Jimmy the unbeguiled, Jimmy the hard, Jimmy the cold . . . was leaning so far forward he was almost climbing on the control panels. He was poised on all ten fingertips, his face a sheen of reflections from the starship.

For the first time in years, George saw his son's brick wall of disillusionment begin to crack.

"I don't understand the doomsayers among us," Robert was saying softly, "those who think of our culture as some kind of disease, who say we should hide and not inflict ourselves upon the galaxy . . . after all, look what we've done!"

The boy was looking. He didn't blink. Couldn't turn away. Couldn't belittle what he saw.

Beside him, Robert April smiled, let his voice go higher with excitement, and added, "If that was circling above your planet, wouldn't you *want* to talk to her?"

The four stood, two in front, two behind, as the stratotractor followed a prenegotiated path on invisible magnetic beams along the starship's port side. The cold-cream hide of the ship reflected the docklights in blurred pools and cast them back on their faces.

Then, there were voices again.

"This is Captain April, requesting permission to come aboard this lovely lady of ours."

A raspy but competent voice responded, one that seemed very used to the jargon of such moments.

*"Simon here, Captain. Permission granted and welcome back. We've got you on approach. You're clear for docking, port torpedo loading bay."*

"Thank you, *Enterprise.* Pleasure's all ours. April out."

Robert angled away from the viewport, and only then noticed George and Drake.

"Ah, gentlemen, you're back. That was my first officer. You'll like her. She's almost as old as Starfleet and twice as experienced. She's a grandmother too, so she knows how to handle peppery little boys!"

He poked Jimmy, but withdrew his hand quickly when the boy winced and smashed backward into the wall as though he'd been hit with an electric shock.

"Oh, Jimmy!" Robert said. "Sorry—didn't meant to startle you."

The boy gaped at him, seemed confused, then noticed his father and Drake, and fought to get control of himself again. Deliberately he did *not* look back out the viewport. He avoided watching as the vessel they were in approached the starship's gleaming secondary hull.

Now there was nothing but panels of hull material, faintly dotted with rivets and fitted bandings, little flashing lights, and the portal to which some part of this ship would go in like a foot into a shoe.

Then they would be on board the starship, and Jimmy wouldn't have to look at her from out here again.

He seemed to be holding his breath, waiting for that, so he could get control again.

"Jimmy, you all right?" Robert asked with a sympathetic grin.

Before their very eyes, the portcullis of resentment slammed down again between them and George's son. The sensation was so strong, so obvious, that Robert actually backed away a step and George had to buck an urge to leap inside before the gate came down.

He didn't make it. They could almost hear the *clang*.

"If I was all right," the boy snarled, "I wouldn't be here."

George felt his whole body tighten. "You watch your lip, buster. That's Captain April you're talking to."

If the reprimand had any effect on Jimmy, they couldn't see it—except that he didn't say anything else.

He held very still a moment, broiling, then stepped around his father toward the lift.

"Keep track of him, Drake," George snapped.

Drake nodded, but it was Jimmy who turned and spoke.

"Don't worry," the boy said. "He's got me in custody."

He stepped to the lift, the panel opened, he got in, Drake followed, and that was that.

Once the lift panel breathed shut, George sagged as though he'd just survived a bar fight.

Robert sidled toward him, both hands balled in his cardigan's pockets, his expression one of affection and even amusement.

"George, he's a wonderful boy."

"He's a brat!"

"Oh, yes . . . but he's a *wonderful* brat!"

# Part Two

———————— ☆ ————————

# THE BRIDGE

# THE BRIDGE

# SIX

☆

## USS *Enterprise* 1701-A

"Hard to think of *Bill of Rights* as one of a whole new breed of starship, isn't it?"

"No," Jim Kirk said. "It's hard to think of kids like Alma Roth commanding ships of their own. There's a difference."

"Well . . . that's what I meant."

Leonard McCoy kept his voice down as he joined the captain on the command deck. With everything going on, it was easy for him to remain ignored. Attempting to ease this awful time—the time that was always awful, the interim of travel between realizing there was trouble and getting to the trouble—he tugged the breast flap of his uniform jacket down from his throat into its informal position.

He thought he was helping the moment, but the captain's voice told him there wasn't any way to cotton-dab the sensation of dread they both had.

"Alma Roth's not a kid, Jim," he said. "She's thirty-six . . . thirty-seven, by now, isn't she?"

"A kid," the captain sighed. "They're all kids. All the midshipmen and ensigns who signed on my ships and let me risk their lives for them . . . they're all my kids."

McCoy grunted. "Maybe you've gotta be young to let somebody else make decisions for you. Beats me. It's not like I remember after all these years. Like you said, Jim, things change. Styles change . . . starships change."

"What is it you want, Bones?" Kirk said. "Want to hear me say I'm jealous of another breed of ship? All right . . . I'm jealous. I wish Roth was back on the engineering deck below just like she was for ten of those thirty-seven years, helping us get through this flushback. She gave me years of devoted service with no questions, and when she asked for a recommendation to command school, I gave her one. How many of those make it to a starship command? Two percent? Three? But she had the strong recommendation of a starship commander. I may have put more on her than she could carry. Now she's out there, in the middle of whatever's happening. Probably dead, along with four hundred and ninety other young crewmen. How many were mine, Bones? How many did I train to go out there and take these wild risks?"

McCoy squirmed self-consciously. "Didn't mean to bring up a sore subject, Jim."

"It's not a sore subject," Kirk said. "You know I don't believe in wishes. But she's out there, and her crew, and her ship, maybe in a million pieces, and that's what I hate."

His tone turned bitter, grinding, and his eyes grew harder. He glared at the screen, because he couldn't give another person this look that had a captain's despise at its core.

"They're telling me the *Enterprise* and the entire Constitution-class of starship is going to be decommissioned, eclipsed by a new breed of ship, new technology, new everything. They're saying skis can replace a toboggan. Or the other way around, for that matter. Depends on prevailing conditions. On who's traveling. And what the mission is. Every design of ship has a unique purpose, and a balance of ability all to itself."

McCoy groaned in some kind of agreement. "But you know as well as I do the Federation's dazzled by all the labs and science and fancy analytical gear on those big ships. They've got exploration on their minds, and not much else. I don't think they're remembering how flexible a starship needs to be these days. Some people don't want to face the facts."

"Federation delegates haven't been out in rough seas like we have,

Bones," Kirk agreed. "Damned few people see the back alleys of space. It took Starfleet to go out and get in the dirt. We were cavalry. We went out first."

The doctor tried to conjure something to say out of his black bag of psychological potions, but he was too set back by the captain's use of past tense. *Went. Were.*

Kirk broiled that hard glare of his at the panorama of passing space before them. He looked at nothing else.

"Not only Roth, but all the other people aboard that ship who started out on the *Enterprise,"* he said. "I owe them."

"I think they owe you," McCoy corrected.

Kirk tucked his lower lip and shook his head. "That's not the way a captain sees it. When crewmen give their youths to a commander and a ship, they're owed something back. Even if it happens later. No matter where it happens," he added, "or how much later."

Brow puckering with curiosity now, McCoy determined to fill in the holes that were still gaping for him.

"Do you know something about this place?" he asked. "I've never heard of Farmon."

Kirk glanced at him, annoyed, then away again. "Faramond."

"Jim, can't you take a hint? I've been inside kicking distance of you for twenty-five years and I've never heard of this place. If I had to testify, I'd say you've never been there."

"I never have been," Kirk said.

Yet, his old friend could read that it wasn't just evasion. It was some tainted sentiment at work. A memory of a burn.

"Never quite made it," the captain added.

"Okay . . . why not?" McCoy prodded. "What got in the way?"

In spite of the storm cones fluttering in their heads, the alarms and whistles and horns going off all over the ship that somehow they could hear right through the soundproof decks—because their years here had better senses than their ears did—both men had their minds on something else entirely.

It shone in the captain's hazel eyes . . . resentment of space, yet the inability to stay away from it. They had both been drawn to the fire. They had given up everything for it. Their youth. A chance for anchorage. Family. Home. Children.

Magnetism of space. Adventure always one light-year beyond wherever they stopped. Just one more light-year. Just one more after that.

The captain parted his lips and spoke to the flowing distance. "I was busy," he said, "finding out I wasn't perfect."

# SEVEN

☆

"Well, George? How did you like seeing the ship with all her decals and insignia and emblems in place? Her name on her bow, her lights encoded—"

"Great. Fine."

George tried to knuckle away a flop of his argumentative sienna shag as it fell in his face, but it wouldn't go. He felt his facial features stiff as rock beneath it. That was all he needed. To stalk around the *Enterprise* looking like a chip that fell off Mount Rushmore . . .

"Sorry," he said as they turned the corridor corner toward the turbolift.

"Not at all," Robert brushed off.

George stepped aside to let the captain board the turbolift first. "Where's the brat?"

"I believe Drake is showing him around engineering just to keep him busy. They'll be meeting us on the bridge." As the lift door gushed closed, Robert asked again, "Well? You didn't answer my question."

"What question?" George groused. "Oh—the ship. She looks different, Robert, real different. Gorgeous . . . kinda scary."

"Really? How do you mean?"

"I don't know . . . pretty, but . . . she's got authority now. She's got all that Starfleet makeup on her hull now, all those red streaks and blue things, and all those lights shining, and her name right out there, and her construction contract number . . . you know, I didn't remember her being so . . . so goddamned *big.*"

Robert chuckled. "You were right about letting Jimmy get a look at her in spacedock. A ship doesn't look quite the same from inside, does it? A wise sailor," he said, fanning his arms, "will one time stand upon the shore and watch his ship sail by, that he shall from then on appreciate not being left behind." He grinned and added, "Eh?"

George gave him a little grimace. "Who's that? Melville? Or C. S. Forrester?"

"It's me!" Robert complained. "Can't I be profound now and again?"

"Hell, no."

"Why not?"

"Because you're still alive. Gotta be dead to be profound."

"You're unchivalrous, George."

"Yeah, I know."

"All that savage Celtic blood in you. Same color as your hair. Good thing Jimmy looks like his mother."

"Mmm," George grunted. "He's still got the blood though. That's the problem. Winona gave all her nice pink civilized blood to Sam."

"Yes, how is Sam?" Robert asked affably.

"Qualified for the Science Academy in biosciences. Can you believe that? I can't even spell it."

"Same girlfriend?"

"Sure, same one. All the way through high school, two years of college, swears he's going to marry her after they both graduate. What I wouldn't give to see some of that consistency in Jimmy. Every *week,* a new scheme and a new girl."

"Ah, well," Robert sighed, "that's because he's—"

"A Casanova. I know, I know."

"No, George, no." Smiling and using that twinkle he kept in his eyes for just such moments, Robert leaned back against the lift wall and gave him one of those looks that made people think of him as a kindly uncle. "Not one of those at all."

"Okay. Don Juan."

"Oh, George, you're missing my point."

"What point? That my son's a wolf? I don't think he's seen me and Winn together enough in his life, Robert. She and I were better off apart, but I never thought—" Unexpected pain came into George's expression, and he sighed in a disturbed way. "I guess it's one of the ways I . . . butchered my family life."

"George," Robert uttered with scolding sympathy. "You're a bit clumsy at being a parent, but you want to catch the boy before he goes over the side."

"Can you blame me?" George tried to keep control, but his voice rippled. He sighed to cover it. "In space one time, and that one time he witnessed a mass . . . mass . . ."

"Execution," Robert assisted, "by a man who thought thousands of lives could be better run from a central power. The lesson was well taken by the Federation, at very least. We saw in a painful manner that no power at the top can do better than thousands of individuals all scrambling and deciding and trying and sweating for themselves, not even in a situation as desperate as Tarsus Four that day. Better to starve with a bit of hope than be marched off and slaughtered in the name of nobility."

Robert paused, stuck his hands into his sweater pockets, then pushed them out and poked along, gazing at his feet as though picking his way across cobblestones.

"Kodos the Executioner . . . they, um, never found him, did they?"

"No," George choked. *"I'd* like to find the bastard—what he put my family through, and me through . . . wondering if my wife and sons would be found among the survivors or among the charred corpses—" He crushed his eyes shut and winced. "Nobody—nobody—should decide what somebody else's sacrifice is going to be! Dammit, I wasn't going to think about this—"

"Didn't mean to fan an old flame, George, but you can't beat some things down."

"I don't want to talk about it, okay? I don't want to step out onto the bridge, talking about this."

"All right, as you wish."

The lift eased to a stop and the doors brushed open, and Robert stepped out first, but not before nipping, "We'll talk about it later."

George lingered in the lift until he gained control over his scowl of response. He was always surprised by that little bird of persistence nesting under the thatch in Robert April's country cottage. It inevitably came out and flitted by him at moments when he couldn't do a damn thing about it.

The lift's red doors almost closed again. The sound shook George out of his thoughts, and he jumped forward. The doors shot open again with a hissing automatic apology for almost closing on him.

Before him, Robert paused. "What's burning?"

Someone from the port side said, "We've got a bad circuit here, sir. Electrical problems with one of the overrides. Some dock turkey misconnected it."

Robert immediately stepped off in that direction.

Left alone in the "visitors' section," the porch in front of the turbolift, George drew a deep breath. It came out shuddering.

The bridge of the *Enterprise.* A place with a real, audible, tangible heartbeat. A living, breathing place that was the envy and desire of every cadet. The first of its kind.

Oh, there were other starships on the move out in space these days, or having their hulls laid even now, but this was the first. There wouldn't ever be another first starship *Enterprise.* There would never be another ship whose diagnostic panels pulsed back to the earliest date of starships, and at some point this ship would be known as the oldest of her kind. Someday . . . she'd be history.

Today she was the future. She seemed to know it too. Her diagnostics and subsystems monitors twittered and chirped and pulsed in beautiful but seemingly senseless patterns, like jungle birds singing. Little squares of red and blue, white and yellow lights and colored bands on black backgrounds patched the circle of black computer control boards all the way around the middle of the bridge in a big headband, flashing in happy nonsynchrony. Each pattern was reporting from some remote part of the ship, blinking diligently and waiting to be needed. Above them, mounted on the blue matte walls under soft ceiling lights, were displayed sectors of the known galaxy, known star systems and nebulae, anomalies and gas giants, maps and charts, prettier than any art.

There were shadows too. The lights here were deliberately subdued to allow for shadows. Shadows of overhanging panels, shadows of chairs, shadows of people standing, turning, walking.

Life-forms who grew up on worlds with trees and mountains liked shadows, liked a sense of depth, a memory of sunrise and sunset. The starship's designers hadn't ignored that. Because of the shadows, the bridge was a warm place that allowed for retreat and thought.

George figured there would have to be a lot of thought going on here over the next few decades. A lot of decisions would be made here, about many lives, and it was fitting that the place where those decisions happened should remind people about life. Shadows and soft lights could do that. The bridge did that.

As he watched Robert move around, George gazed at the luminous arena, the braintrust of the starship, and all the memories of trouble stirred up by this ship came flapping back at him. The ship's an example of how machines don't need humans anymore. It's too powerful. It's a big weapon that flies. It's a big computer that thinks. It's a flying bomb. It's a sign of mankind writing himself out. The wrong people will get their hands on it, it's too big to handle, it's going to get out of control, it can kill a whole planet on a whim, humanity's a kid and kids can't handle anything with an impact over two years, gripe, gripe, doom, doom, doom.

Hadn't happened. None of it. The ship had been out on a few trial stressing runs for spaceworthiness, and while the designers were at it, they'd executed a few darn nice missions and proven that humanity could make a wise decision, in fact a lot of wise decisions, and perfectly well understood the future impact of things present.

But today George wasn't concerned about the future of humanity. He was concerned only with the future of one boy on the edge. He shook all the memories out of his head and tried to focus.

The bridge had more people on it than the last time George was here—one, two, three—helm, science station, navigation, engineering, two guys at tactical, a girl up to both armpits in an access on the floor, and over there just a pair of legs sticking out of a hatch under the impulse propulsion systems console. Except for one man picking at the helm station, George didn't recognize any of these people at all.

They all looked so young. . . .

Suddenly he became aware of how long five years could be.

He stayed on the back of the quarterdeck, overwhelmed by his thoughts, watching Robert step down the two little stairs to the command deck. The captain caressed the parrot-red bridge rail, then the black and gray command chair. He looked like a visiting dignitary, his ivory sweater still hiding most of his command uniform.

Somehow it was comforting to see him down there.

Another deep breath let George inhale the crisp electrical smell, the scent of people at work, and he started to relax. In its way, it was a good smell. The smell of correction, accomplishment.

He hadn't expected to come back here. He'd been her first officer for a couple of minutes, but knew it was temporary and never anticipated coming back. He hadn't been ready to be second in command of a ship like this back then, and he knew he still wasn't—

A terrible thought almost knocked him over. He unclenched his fists, leaned forward on the red rail, and crouched to speak to Robert without anybody else hearing.

"Rob—Captain!" he snarled, just in case anybody *did* hear.

Robert turned, brows up. "Yes, George?"

"You haven't—I mean, you don't expect me to—I mean . . . have you *got* a first officer?"

"Oh," Robert said, and gave him a reassuring nod. "Yes, we have a wonderful first officer. You'll like her." He winked conspiratorially. "Don't worry. You're not on that hook this time."

"Who is it?"

"You don't know her. She's been out on policing missions between Federation colonies. You know, I thought she was here—" He glanced around the bridge, then finally addressed one of the men working at tactical. "Bill? Excuse me."

The larger of the two turned. "Sir?"

"Where's Lorna?"

"I'm under here, sir," a voice called from the floor. One of the feet sticking out of the impulse propulsion hatch rose and wagged.

Robert bent down and asked, "Getting the ship all natty and trim, are you?"

"Some last-minute trouble with the deuterium flow to one of the reactor chambers. We've almost got it, sir."

"Why are you in the hole instead of having one of the impulse engineers go down there?"

The engineers on the deck looked around guiltily, but the voice in the hole said, "Happened to be here, is all."

"I see," Robert droned. "I have someone for you to meet."

"Sorry, can't hear you."

"I have someone here I'd like you to meet!"

"Oh—"

"George, that's First Officer Lorna Simon down there. Lorna, Commander George Kirk."

The foot wagged again and a voice croaked, "How are ya?"

"I'm," George called from the back, "just great. You?"

"Arthritis. And I can barely breathe down here—"

Robert smiled and stood up again. "George, meet the rest of the officer complement and the bridge crew. Bill Thorvaldsen and Larry Marvick beside you at engineering subsystems, our chief impulse engineer and chief warp drive engineer, respectively. And you remember Carlos Florida, our helmsman since the beginning and still holding on. Carlos, look who's back."

The stout, dark-haired Latino fellow at the helm offered George a friendly wave of recognition and filled in, "How've you been, sir?"

George nodded uneasily, but he was inwardly damned relieved to see a face he recognized. "Great. You?"

Florida returned the nod, smiled, and made George feel a little more welcome.

"Over there is Ensign Isaac Soulian, our navigator." Robert gestured to a young skinny Arabic type, or Lebanese, or something, with one of those beards that wouldn't go away no matter how much he shaved. He nodded at George, but both hands were busy as he handed tools to—

"Ensign Veronica Hall," Robert went on, noting the young woman on the deck, "is our astrotelemetrist and communications officer."

"Hello, Commander," the girl said in her quiet voice, wagging a stylus-type instrument, then pushed aside one of a dozen blond braids—supposedly braided to keep the short hair *out* of her face, and apparently failing at that.

George nodded down at her, noting that she wasn't much older than Jimmy, and was assaulted by all the other why-couldn'ts that came with such a realization about young people. Three or four years ago, this girl hadn't been on the verge of criminal behavior, that was sure. Why couldn't—

"All our women seem to be on the floor today," Robert said. "Gentlemen, you're failing at your courtly duty."

Smiles rippled. The good mood started to seep over George and smother his doubts.

Until the turbolift doors opened again.

He turned, and was hit by a blast of cold teenager.

Jimmy Kirk stepped onto the bridge of the starship *Enterprise,* absorbed the active colored lights, the fog of shadows above and below, drew in a breath, and wrinkled his nose in contempt.

"It stinks in here," he said.

The deck turned to concrete. The words dropped and clattered.

Several members of the bridge crew heard. They turned to get a look at the jacketed, capped, eagle-eyed snot who spoke that way about their bridge.

Already they didn't like him.

A few paces away from his son, George Kirk felt his muscles turn to thread. He drew his brows together in a kind of warning.

"They're doing electrical work," he said. "You know . . . accomplishing something."

"Watch your tongue, son," a voice crackled from the lower forward deck. "Somebody might say the same thing about your ship someday."

For the first time since George came in, the first officer showed herself out of that hole in the deck. Lorna Simon let herself be hauled to her feet by Florida and Soulian, but her eyes were already on Jimmy.

She was a very stout woman with a shaggy hat of white hair and long time lines arguing between scowls and smiles etched into her roundish face. Everything on her was round, in fact. Hair, face, figure, fingers—a mushroom of officer material—and she would've had to tease that hair to make five feet.

George held his breath, terrified of what Jimmy might say to such an unlikely person.

Maybe there was a lingering resemblance to somebody he respected, or maybe Simon looked like a teacher he was scared of, but the boy clammed up suddenly and glared at her.

She didn't give him a second glance after that. She turned to the captain and said, "Permission to go below and adjust that thing at the source?"

"Certainly," Robert said. "I'd like you back on the bridge after we leave the star system."

"Aye, sir," she said. "I'll be back in time to spank any little ass who gets out of line."

She tossed a very short but puncturing glance at the somebody she had in mind, then toddled into the turbolift and disappeared.

Only after she'd gone did Jimmy muster the nerve to speak again. "What's somebody's grandmother doing on your ship?"

"That's Commander Simon," Robert said. "First officer."

"First officer? Seems more like first warden of the women's block."

"She's been offered a captaincy with a ship command nine times. Turned down every one."

Jimmy's expression changed from trying to gather up his spilled respect to real amazement. "Why would anybody turn down a chance to be a captain?"

Robert offered a supple librarian's shrug. "She didn't want it."

"That's stupid," the boy said, and was gratified to catch his father's wince in his periphery. "Why wouldn't you want to be in charge?"

"Charge means responsibility, Jimmy, decisions. Maybe lives on your hands. You could kill someone just docking a ship incorrectly. The prospect of command is enthralling, but there's a certain shine that comes off the function. Lorna's just smarter than I am," he added with a grin.

"Where's Lieutenant Reed?" George interrupted, turning to Jimmy.

His son shrugged, not in a polite way. "He sent me up here. I don't know where he went."

"He just sent you up alone?"

Jimmy ironed him with a glower that said he understood that his father didn't trust him.

"He said he'd sell me to a reggae drum section if I didn't come straight up. Whatever that means."

George set his jaw and tried not to snap back an answer, but it was Robert who took care of the ugly moment.

The captain didn't seem at all bothered by the boy's tone. He swept his bridge crew with a series of glances.

"All right, everyone, let's say we heave tight and fetch some headway, shall we? Bill, sound the farewell whistles in the dockmaster's office and request clearance."

"Aye, sir."

"Ensign Hall, get up off the deck, dear, and help us clear for making way."

"Yes, sir."

Hall clamped the access panel shut, squirmed to her feet, and wriggled over to the communications station, straightening her uniform girlishly as she went.

George tried to keep his eyes off her, but in spite of being very thin and small-boned, she was all girl. Seemed too soft and flowerlike to be in the service. Hard to ignore in this environment. He noticed Jimmy watching her too.

Behind him, the turbolift doors parted, and George stepped aside as quite another kind of woman stalked onto the bridge. This one was blond too, only straw-colored blond while Hall's hair was creamier.

Somehow it fit. George always thought that color had suited this particular lady from the moment he first met her.

"Robert!" the newcomer cried. "You're late!—oh, George. Hello. What in blue hell are you doing here?"

"Came to see you again, Sarah, why else?" George said.

"I know," the woman said. "It's always wonderful to see me. Robert, that sickbay's a mess! You said my surgical team was cleared for duty on this ship, and they're not!" She shook a yellow computer recording disk at him. "I've got four complaints from planetside Starfleet hospitals saying I'd appropriated their personnel without ample notice. They're bitching at me about the Third Interstellar Convention for Safety of Life in Space and quoting bylaws at me! What am I supposed to do at this late date? We're about to take off, for crying out loud!"

Robert turned a glad eye on her and said, "Ah, Sarah darling, yes. Veronica, would you patch my authorization through to those hospitals, please? And notify Starfleet Headquarters that it's all clear?"

Hall put out a hand for the yellow disk. "I'll take that for you, Doctor."

"Report for me, Sarah?" Robert asked. "All squared away in sickbay?"

"Well," the doctor grumbled, "I guess so. I just hate coming back to these details."

Robert stepped onto the upper deck and took both her hands. "Isn't she lovely, George? Gotten prettier every day since we welded the old nuptial bargain, eh?"

Sarah April softened visibly, sank against him a little, and lowered her voice.

"Cut it out . . . making me look bad."

"So lovely," he murmured, and pecked her cheek.

"That's not regulation, Captain," George commented from one side.

Sarah leaned back and cast him a casual look. "Who asked you, volcano? Hey—is that Jimmy back there?"

George stepped aside, but didn't look at his son.

Sarah backed away from Robert, though still holding one of his hands, and spoke to Jimmy. "Last time I saw you, you were sailing paper boats on the puddle behind your farmhouse. What are you doing here?"

"Not much," was all Jimmy said, and he put some space between himself and the adults.

"Well, let me know when you get spacesick." She pushed off her husband and headed for the turbolift without ceremony. "It's always like that when there's a young crew. Barf, barf, barf. I keep telling those idiots at headquarters that artificial gravity is never going to take the place of some nice chunky planet. I'm going to check the medical stores. I don't trust the manifests they sent me. And *please* be sure to have the department heads tell the new recruits where sickbay is, because I don't want to be running all over this ship, looking for some confused midshipman. You can get lost with a bad left turn on this monster. Don't forget!"

The lift doors almost cut off her last words, but she pushed them out in time.

"Oh, brother," George grunted. "One of the great universal constants."

"Ah, there she goes," Robert said, "twittering like a mistlethrush. What would I do without her?" He circled back onto the lower deck, turned the command chair, then settled into it and crossed his legs. "Short range scan, on visual."

There were responsive bleeps, and the big viewscreen before them came to life—a view of one open end of the box dock, the moon way out there, and after that . . . space.

Robert seemed notably more content at having had a few seconds with his wife. There was an extra lilt in his voice and a grin tugging at his cheeks as he casually said, "Batten down all external maintenance systems and confirm all running lights on, please."

"Confirming, sir," helmsman Florida said. "Battened and confirmed, sir."

"Thank you, Carlos. Let's get under way, then—oh, Jimmy, come down here. Want to watch?"

The boy stepped down as beckoned, but his attitude didn't improve. "What's to watch?"

"It's complicated," Robert said, "but very interesting."

"What's complicated about it? You just pull the ship out, and once you're out, there's nothing in space but more nothing."

"Seems like that," the captain agreed, "but you don't just bear off with a ship like this and assume everyone will get out of your way. Even on the ocean there are rules of the road. 'Pass port to port,' 'red right returning,' things like that. Aren't there?"

"Well . . . yeah."

"I envy you knowing about such things. I learned it all in space. Never spent much time out on the water other than the occasional fishing curragh in Ireland. I more or less cling to the land, myself. Never heard of a continent sinking, you know!" He swung around to the communications station and spoke to the young girl who looked so small against those controls. "Are we cleared by the dockmaster?"

"Clearance is coming in now, sir. All dockworkers and maintenance personnel are accounted for."

"Good, very good. Thank you, Veronica. Oh, Carlos, remember that we have to arrange our departure around the orbit of that new powerplant."

"Yes, sir, I'm working out a trajectory to avoid it," Florida said. "I'll be glad when they figure out a better place to hang that thing."

"What's a powerplant doing in orbit?" Jimmy demanded.

"Jimmy!" George spat from behind. "Don't interrupt."

But Robert tossed him a glance that said he had expected, and maybe even intended, this to happen.

"That's what he's here for." He looked at Jimmy and said, "It's a starship-type powerplant. There are several of them in orbit several thousand miles farther out than we are. The power is tight-beamed back to Earth. We have to be careful not to knock into them as we leave, and of course not to fly through one of those tight beams. That'd be spine-chilling, wouldn't it?"

He rolled his eyes, and the bridge crew chuckled and rolled theirs.

George was the only person standing stiff, almost at attention, consumed by nerves. Everyone else was hovering over his station with a hip cocked or a hand on a belt, poking at controls and overseeing monitors, every face showing a hint of satisfaction. Something about the launching of a ship, no matter where, no matter how long or how short a time she'd been at anchor—there was just something about it.

Their casualness made them seem particularly capable. They had the attitude of people who really knew the ropes.

George almost dared relax—but then—

"Why don't they just put the powerplant down on the planet?" Jimmy persisted. "That's where the power gets used, isn't it? Why bother to orbit it?"

"For one thing, they're ugly," Robert answered. "Who wants to live next to one now that we have an alternative? But most important, these are antimatter-type powerplants. We didn't dare use them for planetary power until we figured out how to keep them in orbit and funnel just the power down. Wouldn't want something like that sitting on the planet's surface, where all the people live, would we?"

"Why not?" Jimmy jabbed back. "We're sitting inside one, aren't we?"

On the quarterdeck behind them, George closed his eyes in misery and knew the nightmare wasn't going to end.

Below him, Robert was peering at Jimmy, trying to see under the cap's brim into that shadow where the eyes were burning, and he slapped the arm of his chair.

"By St. Christopher, everyone, he's right!" he said. "Let's turn back."

The crew laughed and made exaggerated nods and somebody muttered, "Too late. We're doomed."

George watched his son.

Suddenly a hillbilly at dinner, Jimmy's face turned hard and humiliation scorched his cheeks. The chuckles of the bridge crew made him seem dirty and oafish.

George couldn't help but empathize as Jimmy backed off a step, behind the captain's chair, and made a look that said he didn't want to be talked to. Suddenly, George felt bad for his son—then also remembered that this was why he had brought the boy here.

"Captain," Veronica Hall said, "the dockmaster's hailing with a correction from the barging port. He asks if we can wait for a hydrohaul to pass us."

"Of course we can. Signal affirmative. Jimmy, come here and look at what's passing by us," Robert called, seemingly unaware of the black cloud over Lake James. He pointed at the forward screen, paused a moment, and waited, then kept pointing as a long, ugly blue and gray ship came across the bow. "That's a barge, Jimmy, heading out to one of our colonies in another star system. Oh—see that little blue and white decal? That's a mail pennant. It means she's carrying mail for her port of destination, and possibly ports in between. That little sticker makes it a UFP offense to tamper with her in any way, rather than only a criminal offense. Quite a vision of accomplishment, isn't it? There's a whole stasis warehouse inside, with live fish and everything."

"Fish?" Jimmy snorted. "Why?"

"Watch."

As an answer, the big rectangular barge went out the other side of the screen and showed what it was towing.

Jimmy squinted disdainfully. "A block of ice?"

"Frozen saltwater. Several hundred thousand tons. Essentially an iceberg. They just beam it up, it freezes, they warehouse as many live fish as they can, and off they go to a colony. They're going to establish a saltwater hatchery."

"Don't they cover it up? Put it in a tank or something?"

The captain cranked around toward him. "Why?"

Unable to think of anything, Jimmy clammed up. After all, it was just ice.

"Doesn't seem to be any reason to go to all that expense," Captain April commented. "Nothing sticks to it in space, after all . . ."

Jimmy buried his bungle in another accusatory question. "They just beam up a couple cubic kilometers of ocean and take it?"

The captain looked puzzled for a moment, then said, "Oh, no, my boy, no! That would be a catastrophe! They have to beam it up a little at a time, in slices, essentially."

"Why?"

"Well, beaming isn't a net energy loss of zero, you know . . ." He paused again, surveyed his guest, then said, "No, I don't suppose you do know, do you?"

"Sure he does," the navigator grumbled without turning.

"Knows everything," somebody else underbreathed from forward starboard.

On the upper deck, George was beyond wincing. The heat flushed out of his body and into the deck. He'd made some mistakes before in his life, but *this*—

"There's a tremendous energy exchange involved in transporting," Captain April said, ignoring the comments. "We make the universe unstable for a moment. We take mass and move it. There has to be an equalization and absorption somewhere else. Theoretically the transporter takes a bit of where it's going and moves it . . . it's very complicated, Jim, and dangerous unless you know quite well what you're doing. That's why a transporter's not exactly a household tool. Perhaps your father back there can show you the ship's data on the subject after we get under way, eh, George? George, you still back there?"

"Yes, sir," George said, surprised. "Yes, I'm still here, I guess."

"Captain," Hall said, touching her earcom unit, "the barging port signals their vessel is cleared of our trajectory and they send their thank-you. Dockmaster confirms area is clear now."

"Acknowledge both of them."

"Aye, sir, acknowledging."

Robert turned his chair forward. "Carlos, clear all moorings, cables, and antigravity support systems."

"Moorings cleared, sir."

"Lay in standard angle of departure."

"Laid in."

"Move us out, one-fifth sublight."

"Point two zero sublight . . . here we go."

As if a drumroll suddenly erupted in all their heads, the bridge crew straightened their shoulders. No one wanted to slouch as the Federation's flagship embarked.

From deep within the heart of the giant ship, a low hum began. As a great sleeping swan raising her neck, stretching her wings, and pushing forward through the pond, the starship *Enterprise* glided forward and let the spacedock fall away at her sides.

Before them, the moon gave them a milky salute, then also slid away to starboard, and left open space before them.

The solar system was like a concert accompanying the swan, with subtle tones of the French horn and the bass, as she slid past each of the planets that happened to be in the path before them. The planets of the Sol system, particularly pretty to all humans because they were the first any human child learned about. They had been the first vision of "space" for everyone on the bridge right now.

George wished he could enjoy the sight more, but he was too aware of too many things.

Aware of Robert, who had stuck his neck out and pulled some very long strings to get Jimmy aboard, and who had bothered to take a mission he had intended to turn down just to do an old friend a favor.

Not even a Starfleet favor. A trouble-on-the-farm favor.

And there was Jimmy, clinging to the ship's rail and glaring at the planets. He looked like he was afraid he'd fall off.

Either that, or he hated all this as much as he pretended to.

Maybe he *wasn't* pretending. Maybe he really did hate it. Maybe he hated George all the more for dragging him up here. . . .

George felt himself start to sweat under his Security suit. He drew a careful breath and spoke quietly but firmly.

"Jimmy," he said, "step up here."

His son blinked a couple of times, then leered up at him. "Why should I?" he asked.

George gritted his teeth. "Get up *out* of the command deck, dammit."

Jimmy looked around, but his sixteen-year-old smart-ass fatalism prevented him from noting that he was the only intruder in what was traditionally and functionally the captain's private area.

He glared up at his father with that question on his face, and still didn't move.

George snapped his fingers and pointed at the upper deck, beside himself.

"Quit lipping off and get . . . up . . . *here.*"

Hard crust rose on Jimmy's face and his horns came up. He didn't like being ordered around in public. He barely put up with it in private.

He stepped up onto the quarterdeck, leering at his father.

"Fine," he said. "You want me out of there? How 'bout if I leave altogether?"

Without stopping, he stalked past his father and right to the turbolift, which opened accommodatingly and then closed as the boy turned and stabbed George with a final glare, the kind of glare that said he was a boy who'd been making too many decisions for himself in life.

Regret gripped George as he watched the lift doors close and swallowed that glare the hard way. He shook his head, touched his brow, and turned around again—

To find Robert gazing up at him. The captain was out of his command chair now, leaning on the bridge rail, framed by the outermost parts of the solar system as the ship cruised for open space.

"Ah, the rocketry of youth," the captain sighed. "Makes my heart swell."

George gave him a frustrated, embarrassed shrug. "He doesn't like being told to do something when he doesn't personally see a reason to do it. That'll get him killed someday, if he doesn't learn better—I thought maybe seeing the solar system . . . this was a mistake. I knew it. I should've followed my instincts when they told me to turn around and go back home."

"Really, my friend," Robert chuckled.

He grinned sagely and joined him on the upper deck, so they could have a semblance of privacy.

"Take that wasp out of your shorts and relax," he said. "It's going to be a charming little cruise, we'll do the Golden Shovel at Faramond, we'll cruise right back, and your boy will have seen things he never imagined. You see? Perfectly harmless. So don't get in a pucker. Whatever's into the boy, we'll iron it out. After all, he's only been on board an hour. Don't want to ask too much of him all in one dose of medicine, do you? He's only sixteen! He has *so* far yet to grow."

"I'm glad you can see something in there," George said, "'cuz I sure can't."

"Oh, I see lots in there," Robert agreed. "Take a little heart, George. Remember, it's the belligerent children among us who become the greatest leaders . . . Elizabeth the First, Alexander the Great . . . this kind of person naturally has conflict with parents. Sometimes violent conflict. Why, Alexander was suspected of conspiring in his father's assassination."

"Please, Robert!" George wailed. "Don't give my kid any ideas!"

# EIGHT

"Kirk here. Liaison Cutter 4 requesting clearance for launch."

*"Acknowledged, LC 4. Attention, all hangar deck personnel—clear the bay for depressurizing. Repeat, clear the bay and prepare for launch."*

Alarms began to ring, piercing the entire aft end of the starship's secondary hull, warning that the bay doors would soon open and any living thing left in the hangar deck would be blown to bits if he, she, or it were not inside the thirty-foot utility ship about to launch.

To some inside the small ship, those bells sounded like school was in session again.

To one in particular.

"Jimmy, are you strapped in?"

"I'm trapped, if that's what you mean."

George Kirk cranked around from the copilot/navigator's seat to look aft at his son, who was sitting behind Robert in the row of passenger/crew seats. Now in a Starfleet off-duty suit, obviously missing the jacket he liked so much and the cap he could hide under, Jimmy glared back at him. He was unstrapped and apparently intending to remain that way. Teenagers were indestructible, after all.

"Regulations," George said, somehow containing what he really wanted to say. "I know you don't care much for the law, but the rest of us do. Buckle up."

"Probably a good idea, Jimmy," Robert April said from his own seat in the crew section behind Carlos Florida's helm seat.

Letting them know with jerks and yanks that he didn't want to be doing this, Jimmy buckled up rather than argue with Captain April. Every little defiance seemed to have a limit after which it became impotent. He liked to make points one at a time.

Any point he wanted to make here, though, would have to be carefully measured. It was close quarters, and there were people here who wouldn't understand him.

There were only seven aboard. Jimmy, his father, and Captain April, of course . . . Ensign Hall, who was close enough to Jimmy's age to make Jimmy unexclusive in the young club; Lieutenant Florida, Chief Impulse Engineer Thorvaldsen, and a somewhat fleshy-faced engineering technician he had brought with him named Jennings or Bennings or Dennings or something. All here, in this cookie box with seats.

The two engineers were acting weird, Jimmy noted. Glancing at each other and grinning and whispering as though making plans. He recognized it, because those were the same motions and whispers his gang made before their attempt to escape from Iowa.

But these guys weren't going to run away, so there was something else they were excited about.

*"Hangar Chief to LC 4."*

Beside Jimmy, sitting directly behind Robert, Veronica Hall touched the comm and said, "Go ahead, Hangar Chief."

*"The bay is secured. You're cleared for launch. Commander Simon is standing by to verify your flight schedule."*

"Acknowledged," Hall said.

*"Depressurizing the bay . . . now."*

There was no sound or sensation except for the warning bells, but everyone on board tensed anyway. As the deck depressurized, even the sound of the bells faded away, to be finally no sound at all. The dead silence of space, where no sound can travel.

No matter how technology smoothed out moments like this, launch was still launch. Still a dive into a place that didn't want life. In a moment those hangar doors would slide open, and they would be in the unforgiving, inclement realm of space. They wouldn't have the advantage of a big ship, so big that the sensations of imminent danger seemed far away. This little ship was more like taking a rowboat out on the ocean.

Seated in the pilot's seat beside George, Carlos Florida powered up the cutter and placed his fingertips on the controls, just feeling them for a few seconds. He flattened his lips and shook his head.

"This new design," he complained. "Kinda clumsy on the power-to-thrust ratios. I can feel it."

"As long as you can steer it," George commented.

"I'm going to recommend they reconsider this in favor of the smaller design. They're calling it a shuttlecraft."

"Did they ask you?"

*"LC 4, Chief . . . I'm going to open the bay doors."*

"Chief, LC 4. Ready when you are," Florida said. Then he grinned at George. "Hell, no, they didn't ask me."

On the computer-generated viewing screen, which looked to anyone inside like a big window, the starship's dome-shaped hangar bay doors parted and showed the shocking emptiness of open space. It was black, it was big, it was diamond-studded—and it was *empty.*

Sitting inside his self-constructed shell, Jimmy Kirk kept the scowl firmly on his features as he felt the ship lift off the deck and move toward the great open space. To his left there was a schematic of the ship he was riding, and he tried to concentrate on it so his nervousness wouldn't show. Blunt bow, streamlined sextagonal body, probably flatsided for storage reasons—he remembered his father talking about Starfleet's attempts to conserve space by stacking utility craft. A detachable freight hold underneath made the ship look pregnant. On the top of the control section, outside, was a sensor pod for research purposes or something, so the ship looked like a pregnant whale with a tumor on its head.

An impulse engine in back, two low-warp engines on either side of it, the whole thing painted eggshell white—warp engines? How fast could this thing go?

A carnival-ride surge jolted him back to what was happening. His grips tightened on the arms of his seat and he tried to swallow but couldn't.

To know there was nothing between him and that deadly

depressurized eternity out there but the thin skin of this small ship . . . sure wasn't the same as chugging around Earth in some nice, safe orbital path.

"Feels funny the first time," Veronica Hall offered. Her enormous pale blue eyes flapped at him.

Jimmy looked at her and clung to what he saw. Better than a schematic, her features were very plain, except for the size of those eyes. She had almost no eyelashes, almost no color in her cheeks, and her lips were pale. Her blond hair was short, pulled back on top, and the rest of it was made into about a dozen little braids that brushed the nape of her neck. She looked to Jimmy like the medieval painting in the hallway of his high school, and he imagined her wearing one of those funny cone-shaped hats with a piece of silk hanging out of the point and a long dress with a high waist and no cleavage. Pretty, in a way. Different.

He clung to the sight of her and tried to imagine himself as a knight riding beside her, hired by the king to protect her.

Only then did he realize he was breathing too heavily, giving away his fear. And he was digging his fingernails into the arms of his seat now.

*I can't act scared. I can't be scared. I'm not scared.*

Yet he couldn't muster up a voice as the cutter bore off to the right at a notable tilt against its own artificial gravity. One of the smaller auxiliary viewers showed the *Enterprise* hanging in space behind them, getting farther and farther away. All they had between them and the cold of space was this thirty-foot city bus with impulse drive and another bus-size hold attached to its bottom. Not much to cling to.

He cleared his throat. "What kind . . . what kind of ship is this thing we're in?"

"It's a low-warp multiduty ship we use when we want to soft-land or do aerial mapping of a planet, or scout an area," she said. "Goes about warp two, max."

"I thought they could just beam down to wherever they wanted to go from a starship."

"They can. But a transport or a shuttlecraft or one of these cutters, they're used to take a controlled environment along with you until you see what you're getting into. Can't beam everywhere until you take a peek first."

"But we know where we're going," Jimmy countered. "Don't we?"

"Yes, Jimmy, we do," Robert said, twisting around in his straps. "This time, though, your father wanted you to see a few of the remarkable natural wonders of this sector. The *Enterprise* is going at high warp to settle a border dispute on the far side of the sector while we do our diplomatic tea party on Faramond. We'll rendezvous with them after—"

*"LC 4, this is the bridge. Do you read?"*

"Reading you, bridge," Veronica said into the comm.

After the acknowledgment, the voice changed to that of First Officer Simon.

*"Confirming your flight schedule, sir. Five hours at low warp on the set course, approximately forty-eight hours on Faramond Colony, and rendezvous with us in orbit at Faramond."*

"Confirm," Robert said.

Veronica tapped her unit, bothering to reach across with her left hand, which meant she had to lean forward. "That's confirmed, bridge."

*"See you in two days, then. Bridge out."*

Even as she spoke, the *Enterprise* veered smoothly off, and left their auxiliary screen.

"Liaison Cutter 4 out." She looked forward to the pilot station. "Cleared, sir."

"Okay," George said. "Let's get our bearings on the Rosette navigational buoy."

"Aye, sir," Florida responded, and told the helm what to do.

Using only the one hand again, Veronica tapped a record of the conversation into the cutter's log, then grinned at Jimmy and shrugged as though to show him how routine it all was.

He didn't like that. A girl trying to make him feel at ease instead of the other way around.

He hunkered down, wishing he could hide in the raised collar of his jacket, but the jacket was on its way to a border dispute. So he just clammed up and listened to the conversation at the helm. His father's voice, and Florida's.

"Searching," Florida was saying. "Got it. Wow, it's a real clear beacon."

"Position?" Jimmy's father asked.

"Bearing three points on the starboard quarter."

"Come about. Bring it two points abaft the starboard beam and take another one."

"Coming about, aye. Two points abaft starboard beam . . . stand by . . . mark."

"Log that, then keep going."

"Logged. Now it's broad on the starboard beam—correction—one point abaft starboard . . . coming on the beam now . . ."

Jimmy bit his lip unconsciously, trying to feel the ship turning. It had to be turning, unless that navy buoy out there was flying around drunk.

Staring at the readings, Florida went on. "Coming one point forward . . . two . . . three . . . broad on the starboard bow . . . three points, two, one . . . Rosette Nebula buoy is dead ahead, sir."

"Cross-sect and get a running fix by bow and beam bearings."

"Aye, cross-secting . . . three . . . two . . . one . . . mark. That's our heading, sir."

"Lock it in."

"Locked in."

"Ahead standard."

"Standard cruise speed, aye," Florida concluded. He gazed at the big emptiness on the viewscreen. "Here we go."

Amidships, Jimmy Kirk pressed his shoulders deeply into the cushion of his seat. There wasn't much to feel, but there was a *sense* of mechanical life coming up into his legs from the heart of the small ship. He didn't know how to measure it, how to judge it—

"Know what all that was?"

Jimmy shook himself and looked to his side at Veronica Hall.

He collected himself and answered, "I don't care what they're doing."

"Really?" She rolled her eyes. "You should. A small error in defining a fix can mean a large error in position."

"I'm not driving, so I don't care."

"Okay. That's you, I guess," she said. "Where are you from?"

"Riverside."

"Sounds pretty. Is it a Federation colony?"

Abruptly self-conscious, Jimmy realized he hadn't added the main part of his address. He was used to being with people who already knew.

"No . . . it's in Iowa."

"Oh! Sorry. The way you said it, I got the wrong idea." She shook her head. "I guess being out in space all the time stretches my perspective. You know what I mean? I'm from Minnesota, but I haven't been back in a long time."

Jimmy leaned toward her and quietly said, "We could go back together . . . just for a visit."

"Nothing to go back to," she said with a blush. "My family's scattered all over Federation settlements. What are you doing here?" she asked. "A term paper or something?"

Jimmy looked forward to see that the others seemed involved in getting the cutter on course, except for the two engineers who were tampering with hand-held equipment they had brought with them.

Lowering his voice to a grumble just above a whisper, he leaned toward Veronica. "My father dragged me here so he wouldn't feel so guilty about ignoring us."

Her pale, straight brows came together. "You mean you don't want to be here?"

"Do you?" he countered.

"I'd rather die than be anywhere else."

Skewering her with a courtroom glare, Jimmy lowered his voice. "Isn't that just a little crazy for a pretty, promising . . . officer?"

She smiled. "What's crazy about it?"

"You just said you'd rather be dead and I don't believe it."

Veronica settled her small shoulders against the back cushion of her seat. "I guess you don't have to believe it. I'm the only one that has to."

A fair point, as Jimmy sat thinking about it. He couldn't come up with any better argument than calling her crazy again, and he'd already used that one.

She apparently noted that he still didn't understand. She sighed and filled in. "I like the chance to see sectors of space like the one we're passing on the way to the Faramond system."

Hoping it sounded more like a dare than interest, Jimmy asked, "What's so fancy about this sector of space?"

This time he spoke loud enough to reach the front of the cutter. Even from two rows back he caught his father's glance and grimace.

"One of the most impressive natural wonders around," the fleshy-faced engineering technician provided. "A trinary star in the Rosette Nebula, neighboring Faramond. Most of the stars in the Rosette are fairly young, but it's got two suns orbiting a neutron star. Quickly! Who can tell me the gases? Quickly, now! Hup! Hup! Hup!"

Veronica spoke up before any of the men. "Green ionized oxygen, formaldehyde, ammonia, methyl alcohol, carbon monoxide, water . . . oh, no—that's Orion, isn't it? Darn it!"

"Yes, that's what makes the Orion Trapezium appear green."

The engineering tech chuckled and said, "Also why the Orions are so ornery."

"You would be too," Thorvaldsen said, "if you evolved in that mess."

The others chuckled too, sharing a mutual entertainment that Jimmy didn't understand.

He hunched down, taking it personally.

"We'll be going right past Orion," Captain April continued, "so we'll be able to take a good long look and compare it to the young stars in the Rosette Nebula. I never tire of nebulae . . . they're so particularly foudroyant . . . worth a voyage just to see one."

"Rosette's gorgeous. I've seen it once before," Carlos Florida said. "Glowing agitated helium. Makes it all red."

The tech added, "Hydrogen cyanide too."

"Nitrogen and sulfur!" Veronica finished with a lilt of victory now that she had the right nebula in mind.

"You guys are giving me a chemical headache," Jimmy's father contributed. "Why does every errand have to be a classroom?"

The crew laughed.

"Now, now, George," the captain admonished, "you of all people, now of all times."

Everybody knew what he was hinting at, and they laughed again.

Thorvaldsen glanced back at Jimmy then and said, "You're a lucky little bast—I mean, you're lucky to be here."

Then he and his assistant shared one of those so-are-we glances.

Pinched by the condescension he was getting from them, Jimmy shifted his feet and shrugged.

"Seen one star," he cracked, "seen 'em all."

He might as well have thrown liquid fuel on a fire. The entire shipload of eyes hit him. *Slap.*

Especially Thorvaldsen and his assistant.

They were looking at him as though he was turning polka-dotted in front of their very eyes. What had he said?

"Well, maybe you haven't seen 'em *all,*" Thorvaldsen commented with a mean glare.

Before things got out of hand, Captain April interrupted and dampered the response that pushed at Jimmy's lips.

"The neutron star," he said, "is a very massive sun that's gone through its supernova stage. It swirls so fast that it can't be seen. The little devil constantly sucks matter off the other two suns as they produce it. We're going to do some analysis as long as we're going right past it. Quite something to witness. Very rare in the known galaxy."

Calculating his response down to the last blink, Jimmy Kirk turned away and grumbled, "Yippee."

Because they had to go around a star system experiencing high sunspot activity that could even screw up a ship in warp, it was more like seven hours than five before the navigational beeper roused them all from an on-board nap. Carlos Florida was the first to rouse and wake up enough to decipher the flashes and notices on his controls.

"Coming up on the trinary, sir," he said to George.

"Take us off autopilot."

"Autopilot off, aye."

"Take us out of warp speed. Go to point five sublight."

"Point five sublight, aye. Reducing speed."

There was a notable whine, but almost no physical sensation as the ship dropped out of warp. Though Jimmy stiffened and waited to be pressed against his straps, it never happened. How could that be? How could they go from serious zooming to a crawl without feeling anything? What kind of compensators did this tub have?

"Well?" His father was leaning forward, scanning the upper part of the screen. "Where is it?"

Only then did Jimmy notice that the screen had changed. There was no longer the image of space matter passing by, but now the business of stationary nebulae and stars in the distance.

Then . . .

"There it is," Florida said. Awe closed his throat on his own words. "There it is!"

The two men in front had the best view, and they seemed suddenly hypnotized with appreciation. The engineers unstrapped themselves, got up, and went to look.

Before them, though the cutter was crossing laterally and not daring to get any closer, was the trinary star system.

Everyone but Jimmy was leaning forward. Somehow he was forcing himself not to do that. Even from inside his bubble of disinterest he could feel himself magnetized by what he could see.

Two suns, one yellow-orange, one scarlet red, different sizes, stood sentinel in space, burning hard and hot. Like two Irish women's long red hair in high wind, their heat was being sucked off and dragged in two great tails, swirling down into a dark central point, resembling the stuff that pours out of volcanoes.

Just above a whisper, Carlos Florida said, "It must be billions of years old . . ."

George nodded. "Must've been here already when the Rosette's baby suns started to form."

"Federation Astrophysics thinks it was a neutron star a billion years before those two other ones were even formed," Thorvaldsen was saying softly. "Probably a first-generation star, formed when the galaxy formed. Those two probably condensed out of the Rosette, and all three attracted each other and went into a mutual orbit. Jesus, it's really the last place a human being was ever meant to be, isn't it?"

The awe was uncloaked in their voices.

"Go ahead, gentlemen," Robert April said as he smiled at the engineers. "Have at her."

Thorvaldsen and his assistant almost giggled with sheer excitement. Their eyes flashed and they bit their lips and couldn't stop making victorious noises as they disappeared into the companionway aft. A few seconds—literally only seconds—later, they came up again, hauling satchels and containers of sensory equipment.

"Gonna get some readings, gonna get some facts," Thorvaldsen bubbled, "gonna get some readings, and take my star back! Do-ron-ron-ron, da-do-ron-ron!"

Laughter crackled through the ship. The excitement could've been planted and rooted.

Veronica Hall was already opening a sliding panel in the cutter's ceiling and drawing down a ladder. The engineers started handing her their equipment, and she stuffed it topside, into the sensor pod. One particularly heavy crate made her wince, and she stepped out of the way, favoring a hand and uttering, "Ow, ow, ouch."

The two engineers eagerly took her place.

"See you later!" the engineering tech said as he jumped onto the ladder and took it two rungs at a time, boiling to get up there and start looking at this thing.

Jimmy watched all this and tried to figure out why they were all so excited. Wasn't it just one of those space things? Just another nebula nobody could dare go into?

Thorvaldsen stood back briefly, held both arms open, and huskily propositioned, "Come to Papa, darlin'!"

Then he was on the ladder and up there.

"I'm next!" Veronica called, still holding on to her strained hand.

"You'll have to kill us first!"

The others laughed again. Jimmy just shook his head and kept wondering as the ladder disappeared topside and Thorvaldsen's hands appeared to tug the insulated panel shut.

"Ouch, ouch, ouch," Veronica mumbled as she plunked down across from Jimmy again. She was holding her right wrist. The hand was completely extended in a spasm, fingers out as far and straight as possible—even farther than possible. Out and bending backward.

She manipulated the wrist, then complained under her breath and . . . took the hand *off*.

Jimmy gasped, jolted against his side of the craft, and choked, "Wha—!"

She looked up. "Oh, I'm sorry. I forgot you didn't know."

As he gaped, horrified, she waved the disembodied hand. "The whole lower arm is prosthetic. Pretty good imitation, isn't it? You didn't notice I've been mostly using one hand, did you?" She nodded in agreement with herself and murmured, "That's because I only have one."

Gaping like an idiot, Jimmy choked, "How'd . . . how . . ."

"Oh," she groaned, "I just did something stupid, that's all, back when I was sixteen."

Jimmy struggled to shove down the quiver running up his spine. Sixteen . . .

She gazed almost sentimentally at her prosthetic and said, "I swear, it was another person entirely, sometimes. I went canoeing alone, after I promised my parents I wouldn't. I went over on some rocks and opened my arm pretty bad, then I didn't tell anybody. Tried to take care of it myself. You know, I knew everything, of course. Even when it got infected, I didn't tell anybody. I tried to handle it myself for over a week. Finally I got feverish and passed out, and nobody found me for almost a whole day. I was lucky to keep the elbow."

Trying to think of this soft-spoken, feminine, flowerish girl lying feverish in some back alley, Jimmy asked, "How'd you qualify for . . . I mean, with only one . . . uh . . ."

"Starfleet? By taking the requirements one at a time, that's all. I can't give myself a manicure and I'll never play a fiddle, but I can do a cartwheel, and I can even climb a rope if I have to. I just didn't want to give up my biggest dream. The prosthetic works all right, but I had to prove to Starfleet that I could do without it in an emergency. You know, prove I don't always need an extra hand."

While she busied herself getting the fake limb to relax its spasm, Jimmy sank back and cradled his own right arm.

"Extra—" he echoed softly.

"She's our one-armed bandit," Captain April interrupted. He

was looking back at them with mischief in his eyes. "You should see her manipulate a laser pistol and a communicator at the same time."

"Silly thing," Veronica commented, smiling at the captain. "State-of-the-science synthetic fingers. Sometimes it seizes up on me."

Gazing down at his two plain human hands, flexing his own fingers and making fists, Jimmy tried to think of one of his hands as "extra."

"Here." Veronica turned toward him. She seemed to be having a good time when she said, "Give it a shake."

He hesitated, but didn't want to insult her, so he twisted and gave the fake thing a good Iowa handshake—and it almost lifted him out of his seat.

"Wow! That thing's got a grip like a gorilla!"

"Sure does." She settled back and said, "Here. Hold hands with it for me while I get the seizure out of it, will you?"

Jimmy took the hand and held it open end out to her as she went to work inside the narrow little wrist that fit her so well.

"You make it all sound so easy," he said.

"It wasn't," she admitted. "I had sixteen years to get used to having more than one. I've had only since then to get used to having one to work with, but my mother always said easy things don't get any appreciation. That's why I appreciate Starfleet so much, y'know?"

"Yeah . . . sure, I know."

"They didn't hold it against me," she said as she worked, then emphatically added, "Of course, I didn't get any favors. I had to come up to everybody else's standards and meet the same requirements as anybody else."

Jimmy scowled and said, "That's not very fair."

She struck him with a wide-eyed look, pursed her lips, and admonished. "Then you don't know what 'fair' really means. It doesn't mean lowering standards to meet somebody's hopes. It means *you* raising your own hopes to meet standards. What if somebody's life depended on me someday? What if I could get along with the faker, but not very well without it? I mean, if one hand can get chewed off, there's no reason this one couldn't. Accidents happen, you know. Standards stayed up. I met 'em." Suddenly she smiled. "Preach, preach, preach, right? Well, I'm kinda proud of myself, I guess. How old are you anyway?"

"Si—"

*Sixteen. Sixteen. Say it, coward.*

"Seventeen."

"Oh, hey! Won't be long, then. You'll be in the Academy before you know it."

*Not if I can help it.*

"Right. Won't be long."

The words were barely out of Jimmy's mouth before he heard his father's voice in the forward section.

"Carlos," George was saying quietly, "would you mind . . ."

"Oh, sure. No problem."

Florida unstrapped, got up, and crouched back behind his own seat.

"Jim," George called.

Stiffening, Jimmy had to beat down a jolt of surprise and keep a leash on his tone.

"What?"

"Come up here to the pilot's seat and take a look at this thing."

Jimmy shook Veronica out of his head and fought to concentrate on his main message of the day.

"I can see fine," he said.

There was some shuffling on the forward deck.

"Not after I pound that snotty tone out of you," his father said. "Get up here, and I mean right now."

Jimmy thought about balking again. His father had never laid a violent hand on him, and they both knew it. The walls, the furniture, the occasional farm animal, yes, but his kids, no.

Something about being in front of these professionals, though, made Jimmy get to his feet so he wouldn't have to be groused at again. He could always count on his father for a second grouse. If only he could get up there and take a look at this thing without seeming too interested . . . that was the trick.

He collapsed into the pilot's seat so hard that the swivel mechanism shrieked. Then he slumped way, way down, still holding on to his right wrist. After a few seconds of calculated boredom, he looked up at the big main screen.

Before him, all of nature swirled.

The two suns, their hair streams being ripped off and sucked in two great gaseous spirals, the halo effect of three violent gravitational forces working against each other, glowing disks of residual matter spiraling slowly to a common center—what a mess.

But what a pretty mess . . .

"That's the neutron star," his father said. "The small dark area. It's a whole sun, millions of kilometers across, collapsed down to a rock only a few kilometers in diameter. All its elemental matter is crushed down that far."

"Son-of-a-bitch density," Florida murmured.

"Yeah, and it's spinning so fast it can't even be seen. Because it's still acquiring matter, taking it right off those other two stars, it'll eventually have enough gravity to collapse all the way down into a black hole. It could go at any moment."

Jimmy watched the churning, sparkling phenomenon out there, and half expected it to go and take all of them with it. Every time he saw a flash, his nerves jumped.

"We lost a good many advance exploration ships in storms like that," Robert added, "before we learned how to avoid them. Lot of decent people fell off that mountain so the rest of us could sit here and look without worrying. . . ."

His voice trailed off into respectful silence.

The neutron star twisted energy into tight braids as fast as the two suns could produce it, then ate it. The yellow-orange sun's orbit was elliptical and on a different plane from the red giant, and the red giant's higher gravity was also ripping matter off the smaller sun even as its own energy and matter was being sucked into the neutron star. A competition of the most primitive order.

All around the area was a blue haze that resembled fog, except that it sparkled with charged solar plasma. The whole thing made a wacky sight, and baffled Jimmy's imagination as he looked.

"What are those guys doing on top of us?" he asked.

"Looking at it," Captain April said. "Measuring it, analyzing it, and so on. The sensor pod has a retractable window with special screening. They're able to look at it with their naked eyes. They're taking readings of it in order for the Federation to justify posting long-term cameras and sensor monitors on buoys, in hope of witnessing the event when the neutron collapses into a black hole."

Jimmy's father mistily commented, "It could happen anytime in the next two minutes or the next thousand years."

"A thousand years?" Jimmy abruptly complained. "Then what's the big deal!"

"That's nothing in the billion-year life of a sun, my boy," the captain said. "The next thousand years is any moment. We stand a fair chance of recording the event if we can get sentinel buoys out here. They have an operational life of almost a hundred years." He leaned back in his seat and whispered, "Wouldn't that be something!"

"Thorvaldsen and Bennings are having kittens, they're so excited," Veronica said.

"But *you* aren't interested," Florida tossed back at her, grinning.

She shrugged and squeezed her shoulders girlishly. "Didn't you hear the meows from my seat?"

"This Blue Zone is a computer-enhanced image," Jimmy's father went on, pointing, "to show us the action of the energy out there so we can avoid it. It's not really blue. If you were looking at it with your naked eye, you'd see the suns and a hole, but all you'd see around them is a slight electrical discharge."

"You wouldn't even realize you were in danger until too late," Robert added.

"Right. But since this is a warp ship, the screen is computer-generated. The computer translates this according to temperature. So it looks blue from in here. No ship can go in there. Our science doesn't know of any shielding that can survive inside that. The high gravity and radiation and solar wind would even rip through the starship's shielding. Solar wind is made of charged particles of plasma shooting off from the sun itself—"

"How do you know?" Jimmy challenged.

"What?"

"How do you know a starship can't survive in there? That thing back there's the first starship, isn't it? Why don't you just go in anyway and try it."

His father drew his shoulders tight in anger and leered at him sidelong.

"Because we'd be dead, that's why," he snarled. "You can't get past that smart-ass fatalism of yours, can you?"

"Maybe I just have an adventurous spirit."

The collective annoyance could've been packaged and shipped. The idea that Jimmy would refer to the *Enterprise* as "that thing back there"—

Eyes suddenly hard as walnuts, his father turned more toward him and lowered his voice.

"Is it asking so much that you relax and enjoy some of these things we're showing you?"

Jimmy let his own expression go hard.

"You drag me up here against my will," he said, "and I'm supposed to enjoy it?"

"Can't you at least try? You're not here for *my* good, you know."

"Oh, right, forgot. I'm here for mine."

He got a mixed victory for his efforts to exterminate his father's efforts when George slumped, scowled bitterly, and jabbed a thumb toward the back.

"Get out," he growled, his teeth together.

Satisfied, but pushing down the nervousness that came with such a win, Jimmy took his time getting up. There was a certain stage timing to these things. The sooner he could manage to dismantle his father's hopes in all this, the sooner he could get back to Earth and get on with his life, his way.

He took care not to give that fantastic sight more than a passing last glance as he got up, crouching to keep from knocking his head on the low forward ceiling.

But that last glance . . .

He stopped short.

Staring—*what the hell!*

"What's the matter with you?" his father asked. "Go."

Jimmy tried to say something, but though his lips were hanging open, his throat was locked up tight. All he could do was blink, and point.

Point at the ship coming at them *right out of the Blue Zone!*

Even as Jimmy pointed, the cutter's sensor alarms went off—warning of intrusion into their flight space.

"Carlos!" George called.

Gaping, Jimmy couldn't move and was shocked when four hands grabbed him, yanked him away from the helm, and stuffed him behind the navigation seat. He had no idea who had grabbed him, and he couldn't take his eyes off the screen to check.

Carlos Florida slammed himself into the pilot's seat, gasping, "That's impossible! It's impossible!"

Two neon-orange glows appeared on the green/black hull of the intruder—and suddenly the cutter rocked under them and filled with the screams of electrical reactions.

Over it all, Jimmy heard his father's voice.

"They're firing on us!"

# Part Three

# FLUSHBACK

# NINE

## USS *Enterprise* 1701-A

"I ought to slingshot around the sun, go back forty-five years, and slap myself."

Leonard McCoy turned at the captain's grumble and asked, "Pardon me?"

Shifting uneasily, James Kirk drew a long breath. The taste of regret.

"I said . . . I ought to go back and slap myself for the first words I spoke on the bridge. They weren't exactly poetry."

"Why? What were the words?"

Smears of rosy humiliation ruddied the captain's cheeks. Kirk was a hard man to embarrass, but he could still embarrass himself.

He pressed his lips tight, then parted them, then pressed them tight again.

"I said the bridge smelled."

The taste came rushing back. Beside him, McCoy winced.

Suddenly they were both glad the yellow-alert alarms were honking in the background.

In spite of that, the two men might as well have been alone on the bridge. In spite of the bustling activity around them, the crew busy with a ship in alert, tense wth anticipation of horror and the

Starfleet officer's nightmare of antimatter flushback, the two felt alone in their reverie.

Even the concerned regard of First Officer Spock from the raised quarterdeck behind them failed to invade, and certainly failed to comfort. They knew why he wasn't stepping down. They knew he had picked up the captain's mood, but wasn't inviting himself into the conversation. Yet.

There were some moments only humans could understand—and only some humans at that—as they drew upon a common heritage, the special union with vessels that had carried them since the Vikings.

Jim Kirk's brow puckered, and he gazed forward at the vista of deep space as the ship raced forward at incomprehensible speed toward a place whose name made the years peel away at light speed. A place where another starship may have just died.

"Bones . . . do you know what it is to feel that a ship is alive?"

The doctor's silence prodded the captain further into thoughts that couldn't be measured. Kirk didn't look at him. Didn't really want an answer.

"When I took command," he said, "and came back onto the bridge for the first time as an adult . . . I wondered if she remembered."

He blinked, and looked around the bridge now, a superstitious seaman unable to throttle down those feelings about ships that somehow got into the blood of everyone who depended upon them. To depend on a ship for one's very life made it ugly to think of the ship as just parts and forms, wood, bolts, and mechanics. No one wanted his life clinging to heartless metal and wood. After all the years of vehicles in history, a pulse of the living had seeped into those manufactured pieces, and there wasn't a sailor alive who could deny it without being a liar.

The ship around him now wasn't that same starship, but her namesake and her design twin. Beautiful, yes, but not the ship to which he owned the apology. That ship—he had sent to destruction, spiraling down into the atmosphere of a hostile new planet, avoiding the necessity of bringing her home to be decommissioned after more than forty years of service. Shunted aside by new designs, caught in the spin of change, now destined to be brought home and picked apart in some drydock somewhere, like a whale decomposing out of water.

He had taken her out without permission, against orders. In some ways, he was pleased to spare her that fate. She deserved to die in space, where she had lived, where she had made it safe for countless millions to live.

Circumstance had forced him to send her in and let her burn, to let her go to sleep in space, where she belonged.

Almost as though the ship possessed a heartbeat—

Sailors . . . a little moonhappy, all of them.

Now this ship was being decommissioned too, and she wasn't that old. The design again. Everybody said the design was being superseded by a whole new batch of technology. Obsolete, supposedly.

Forty-some years was a long time, wasn't it?

"I was only thirty years old," he went on. "The Fleet's youngest starship commander. The ship was box-docked when I first came on board, the same as she had been when I boarded her at the age of sixteen. But the bridge looked smaller than when I'd seen it before . . . darker and quieter . . . and there was no one there but me. Only me and the bridge. It was like being alone with a woman I'd slept with but failed to appreciate. I felt guilty and unworthy of her. And I wondered if she remembered those first words."

He hesitated, his eyes fixed on the past, hands hanging just above the arm of the new command chair without actually touching it.

"I wondered," he added, "if she'd forgiven me."

Alert whistles chirped in the background, demanding attention like young eagles in the nest. Personnel ran on and off the bridge, each doing a small specific thing. Add the small things up . . . one very big thing. Survival in space.

Dr. McCoy shifted his feet, bobbed his eyebrows in puzzlement, and leaned back against the bridge rail, not exactly relaxed under these conditions.

"I used to think a person would have to be crazy to command a ship in deep space," he said. "Now I'm sure of it."

# TEN

*Forty-five years earlier . . .*

"Evasive! Get some shields up! Everybody take cover!"

"Astonishing!" Robert April's voice flushed between the crackling sensors and howling alarms.

Carlos Florida gasped, "They hit our pod!"

"Get the panel open!" George shouted. "Get those men out of there!"

"I'll get it!" Veronica yelled back, and vaulted to the middle of the ship, where she started working on the ceiling panel.

The control board sparked, knocking George sideways.

"There goes our hyperlight communications—" Florida said.

Robert crouched between George and Florida to see the chunky, unidentifiable black and green ship coming toward them out of the Blue Zone. "What kind of design is that? Looks like it's built of triangles. I don't recognize it at all—"

"Checking!" Veronica Hall called from behind. With her real hand on the panel she was trying to open, she reached down with her fake hand and poked in a code, then went back to the panel.

Her small computer screen went wild with diagnostic pictures, ship after ship, design after design, schematics and mechanical skeletons, picking out pieces here and there and putting them in boxes. Veronica finally frowned down at it, doing two things at once.

"No known configuration!" she said, shouting above the crackle as a laser struck their outer hull.

Florida transferred her readings forward to his own screen. "According to this, it's built piecemeal from several designs. There's at least one Starfleet thruster on it . . . a private-shipping cargo train . . . but according to the thruster-exhaust reading, their power formula appears to be what the Andorians are using."

"Are they Andorians?"

"No way to confirm that, sir." His voice cracked, but he kept control.

Jimmy felt his face turn parchmenty with terror. He was on his butt, on the deck, not even in a seat, and couldn't move, not even to crawl away. His eyes were big and hurting as he stared at the forward screen.

The intruder's gargoylish ship, green parts flickering bronze in the ugly lights from the trinary, was crowding down upon them on collision course. Its outer hull, shielded by a faint grayish outline that was apparently some kind of shielding, crackled with clinging energy from the Blue Zone.

"Damn! Where are our combat shields!" his father blurted out. He and Florida were frantically maneuvering back from the encroaching ship.

"We don't have any," Florida said.

"What do you mean, we don't have any! No combat shields?"

"Only navigational ones. Just enough to keep the space particles off us in low warp. I told you this model was silly! It's meant for peaceful, boring cruises in known spacelanes!"

"Warm up the lasers! Where are they! Where are the goddamn firing controls?"

Florida bent downward. "All we have is industrial cutting lasers. They're under here."

"What are they doing down there!"

"Open a frequency, George!" Captain April ordered. "Hail them!"

"Hall, do it!"

Amidships, Veronica scrambled to do that.

"Frequency open, sir," she said.

"George, take it. You're the captain here."

Jimmy looked at Captain April, then at his father in confusion. There was something both scary and odd about that realization . . . that his father was the captain in this vessel. How did these things work?

Another neon bolt shot from the stranger and hit the upper hull—

"I can't get this!" Veronica shouted, still yanking on the panel's manual latch.

Suddenly they were all thrown sideways, except her and George, who were still strapped in. Jimmy found himself folded up like an envelope against the starboard bulkhead, and realized the whole cutter was turning against its artificial gravity and whining in protest.

His father slammed a fist on his own control board, either in rage or tapping himself in, or both.

Probably both.

"Attention, unidentified vessel! This is Commander George Kirk of the United Federation of Planets Starfleet, goddammit! I demand to know the meaning of this unlawful discharge of your weapons! You're in Federation space and you're also in violation of about twenty statutes of the Interstellar Maritime Laws! Cease fire and identify yourselves!"

Sweat trickled down his face.

Sudden silence fell.

The green and black industrial animal out there stopped firing. Its laser ports glowed as though it were ready, waiting. Maybe thinking. Maybe something George had said was having an effect.

Jimmy knuckled his own face—and found a wet, hot film. Something had happened to the life support. The temperature control—

Smoke poured out of places where there shouldn't even be places. Instantly everybody was coughing.

The ceiling hatch! It was kinked partly open and smoke was billowing down from there.

"Dad! Up there!" Jimmy yelled.

George struggled to his feet, stepped over Robert and Jimmy, motioned Veronica out of the way, and yanked on the stuck hatch. "Thorvaldsen! Bennings!"

"Bill!" Robert called.

"Forward life support going on automatic backup!" Veronica called. She cleared her throat. "That last hit—oh, there goes the main-cabin oxygen!"

George didn't look at her, didn't take his eyes off the ceiling panel. "Seal off all sections!"

Carlos spoke from a dried mouth. "Why are they just hanging out there?"

"How's the cargo unit, Ensign?" Robert asked, twisting to address Veronica.

She fingered her controls with one hand while waving at the smoke with the other. "Secure so far."

"Seal that off too. Do whatever you must, but make sure it's not a target for their sensors. No point giving away information."

"Aye, sir, sealing off cargo level and shutting down activity there."

He got up and tried to help George get the pod's hatch open. "See if you mightn't be able to do something about this smoke also."

"Aye, sir, ventilating!"

The small ship's engines caterwauled with strain and the ship bucked. Veronica was thrown backward and landed hard, but almost immediately crawled back to her controls.

George hung on to the ceiling handle, twisting on his toes.

"Tractor beams!" he shouted. "They've got us!"

The cutter wailed around them with sheer mechanical effort, bucking harder and harder until everyone had to hang on to something, strapped in or not.

"Sir, our engines!" Florida choked out. He pointed spasmodically at the attacking ship with one hand and at the impulse systems monitor with the other. The indicator bands were washing back and forth crazily. "That monster's ten times our size! We'll overload if we fight a thing like that!"

"Cut the power!" George answered. "We can't afford a burnout."

Florida pounded his controls. The bucking eased and gave way to a nasty teeth-on-edge whistle deep inside the ship.

"We'll have to find some other way," Robert said.

Setting his jaw, George yanked open a wall panel, grabbed a piece of equipment that had a point, and started levering at the hinge. "Yeah. If we had a transporter, I'd beam over there and *explain* it to them. With my bare knuckles. Thorvaldsen! Answer me!"

His tool flew forward as the panel cracked, then opened with a godawful squawk. He yanked the ladder down, waved at the smoke, and climbed up.

Almost instantly he slid back down and landed flat on both feet.

Jimmy and the others stared at him.

George Kirk had turned into a ghost. Whatever he had seen up there took every cell of blood from his face, left his mouth gaping, his eyes wide, watering, stinging, and red. Robert and Carlos Florida caught his arms, because he looked like he was about to go over.

"George?" the captain dared.

Florida stepped past them and started to go up, but George caught him.

"Don't—don't—" he stammered. He shook his head and crushed his eyes closed for a moment.

Florida's round face crumpled. His shoulders sagged and he muttered something unintelligible.

Grief limned every face as Jimmy watched. Why weren't they going up there? Why weren't they making sure there wasn't a single thing left to do for those two men?

Florida pushed Jim's father back down into his seat, where he sat stiff as a mannequin.

Captain April clung to the back of that seat, hugging it. His eyes were closed too, and he was gasping in little breaths. After a moment he wiped his mouth with a palm and looked up at the screen again, at the ship that had fired on them.

"I simply can't believe it. How could they survive in the Blue Zone? How could they possibly survive? They came out of there like a trap-door spider!"

"Doesn't make a shred of sense," Florida filled in. His voice was quiet with fear. Perspiration burnished his face and plastered his black hair across his forehead. "As if any of this made a shred of sense . . ."

"Why do you think they ceased fire?" Robert wondered.

Florida trembled, but managed a shrug. "Suppose somebody staked a claim on this area and they think we're doing the intruding? Maybe they didn't know this is Federation space."

Rousing himself, George unpursed his lips and said, "Anybody who could get into space would have to be able to pick up transmissions. They'd know the Federation runs this sector. When's the last time you saw Aborigines inventing a space vessel? Communication always comes before space flight. I can't believe they didn't know."

"Right . . . good point."

"Whatever else they're doing, they're talking about us. That's for sure."

"You don't suppose you said something just right, do you?"

Still in a lump on the deck carpet, Jimmy stared at the adults and past them at the invading ship. How could they talk so casually? How could they talk at all?

He saw the fear in their eyes, but it wasn't coming out in their voices, not even when they shouted.

Not much, anyway.

What did come out was shudders of anger and grief. He knew what those sounded like.

He placed his shaking hands on the deck, flat, fingers spread. He shifted his weight and started to get onto his knees, pressing the carpet and using it for some kind of ballast. At least he was relatively sure where the carpet was.

And here was the bottom of the pod ladder.

With a glance at the others to make sure nobody was watching him, he used the ladder to stand up, then started climbing it.

The pod was still stenchy and filled with smoke, the atmospheric compensators whizzing a futile battle to save whoever was up there, and the seals frantically trying to keep open space out even as they cracked more and more.

Jimmy sensed the danger and forced himself in up to his shoulders. He waved at the smoke.

Something wet sprayed his face, then a flap of oily strings hit him across the cheek and mouth. He clawed at the strings, pulled them off, cast them aside wildly as he might cast away a big caterpillar crawling across his face.

And he found a hand!

"I got him!" he called over the whine and shriek of the ship trying to save itself. "I got one of them! Dad!"

He grabbed the hand and pulled, putting his thick arms to their best use. Save a life, save a life—

He leaned back against the hatch edge and drew hard on the weight of whomever he had hold of. Maybe the gravity was flooey in here because there wasn't much resistance. Maybe he could get one of these guys below!

With one more heave he could get this person into the hatchway —just one—

A wet mass suddenly released and flew against him, striking him and driving him backward against the edge of the hatch.

He choked. A disembodied arm, shoulder, and half a rib cage anchored itself around his throat.

Flailing senselessly, Jimmy felt his mind go numb and leave him to pure panic. His hands smacked wildly at everything, including his own face, his own hair, his own chest, until the gory mass fell off and was sucked back upward into the tornado of air and supplies twisting around the broken seals.

Jimmy lost his footing and dropped straight to the main deck, curling and gagging.

The cutter might as well have been on the end of a whistling string. Jimmy couldn't get up, couldn't get a thought, couldn't open his eyes. All he saw in his head was Thorvaldsen and Bennings and what was left of them. . . .

There were voices around him, but his brain was turned off.

Until that ship out there fired on them again.

The cutter rocked violently. Jimmy pitched and hit the nearest wall just as he heard his father yell:

"So much for saying something right!"

*WHOOP WHOOP WHOOP WHOOP*

"Hull rupture!" Florida shouted over the hideous alarm. "Sixty-four seconds to atmospheric zero!"

Even more hideous than the alarms was a telltale *hsssss* from somewhere in the superstructure of the cabin.

George made a sweeping gesture. "Go, go!"

"Aft, everybody!" Robert called at almost the same instant. The shouts overlapped, but the message was the same. "Open the seals to the hold!"

"They're open!" Florida responded.

"Get below! Seal off!" George shouted.

Jimmy felt his father grip his arms and almost instinctively pulled back from it, but there was no fighting the determined force above him. His father hauled him to his feet without even looking at him, because he was busy shouting orders to the others as they scrambled across the tilted deck toward the aft companionway that led down into the freight hold.

Staggering, Jimmy grabbed the seats for balance and hated feeling his father holding him upright, but he was too terrified and sickened to argue about it. When his father let go, Jimmy turned to see what was wrong.

George was half turned back toward the pilot station, yelling, "Carlos! Come on!"

"Take 'em!" Florida shouted back, waving. "I'll fire an SOS!"

"You can't! Communications are out!"

"I'll launch a buoy!"

"Hurry!"

"I will!"

Jimmy gagged a protest. "But he'll be—"

"Go!"

His father gave him a shove between the shoulder blades that sent him flying toward the aft companionway with most of his air knocked out of his lungs so he couldn't protest.

His hands bloodless and his breath coming in chunks, Jimmy fought to control the trembling of his thighs and shoulders as he climbed down the companionway tube after Captain April.

It seemed like a long, long climb. Eight feet? Ten?

The companionway was nothing more than a tube with a ladder in it and a hatch at the top and another at the bottom that could be shut and made into a contained airlock. It led down into the twenty-five-foot tin can of a freight hold attached to the underside of the flight section, but they might as well have crawled through a looking-glass into another dimension. The only company here was crate after box after stack of supplies bound for the colony at Faramond. Out of the environment friendly to people, with cushioned seats and carpet, warmth, lights, and fresh air, they crawled into a cold, echoing metallic rectangle whose minimalist control panels were meant to be used only in emergencies.

As Jimmy dropped into the hold, he heard his father shout above him.

"Carlos! Get down here!"

George's legs appeared, but he didn't come all the way down.

Stumbling aside, Jimmy found himself staring at a flashing panel bright yellow in the wall.

*WARNING–AIRLOCK AUTO SEAL–CLEAR PASSAGEWAY*

It repeated, but he already had the message.

"Dad! Get down!" he bellowed. Lunging forward, he grabbed his father's left leg and yanked.

Jimmy wasn't a skinny boy, so his weight meant something in spite of his age. With a gulp of protest George came tumbling down and crumpled on top of him in a heap.

Overhead, the secondary hatch slammed shut automatically. The bolts clacked—and that was it.

"No!" George howled. He shoved Jimmy off, but it was too late.

Barely five seconds later they heard the second automatic slam—and more bolts ramming home. The upper hatch!

"Oh, God—" Captain April gasped.

The panel on the wall changed, and flashed red instead of yellow.

*MAIN CABIN DEPRESSURIZED–DANGER–DO NOT OPEN SEALS–DANGER*

George vaulted to his feet.

"Carlos!"

# ELEVEN

☆

"It's wrecked! The sensor pod! Wrecked!"

With ten long fingers stabbed up against the viewscreen and his eyes in slivers, Roy John Moss spat saliva across his own knuckles as he shouted.

"Do you know how much that pod was worth? How many times do I have to show you porks how to aim these weapons!"

He took a breath to continue yelling—

But someone grabbed him by the ponytail and hauled him backward, then yanked him sideways and knocked him out of the way with a cuff across his cheek. He fell onto both knees.

"Down in front, bobbysox."

The drone was an insult in itself.

Roy Moss rubbed his slick raisin-brown hair now that his scalp was aching, and began again to despise.

He despised the captain for that tone of voice. Despised the crew as they gawked beyond him to their victims on the viewscreen. Despised himself for being only nineteen.

In the dark porchlike cubicle, which could only be called a bridge in a card game conversation, a piecemeal gaggle of racketeers glared out their own viewport at the sleek white cutter they'd just grabbed.

In the captain's seat, Angus Burgoyne chewed on the end of his long mustache and offered no more attention to the annoyance he'd just kicked out of the way.

At Burgoyne's left, old Lou Caskie clunked forward on two arthritic legs. "What you worried about? We're the Sharks, ain't we? We take what comes past here. Federation!" He spat onto the deck. "Probably got a woman running it. Deserve what they get."

"Daon't spit on moy deck, pig," Burgoyne commented.

His Australian accent clipped his words, left the ends off most of them, and changed the angle of all his vowels. He broadened his accent on purpose, to sound like a legend with an eyepatch and a hook. He had neither, so he relied on the accent.

Caskie leaned back and spoke past him. "Don't you think that, Okenga? Ain't I right?"

Behind Burgoyne, an Andorian engineer's two antennae turned forward slightly in reaction and his blue face darkened almost to indigo. His enunciation forced him to speak slowly. English was far, *far* from his native language, and his tongue didn't want anything to do with it.

"We take old merchant barges," he said, hitting the consonants too hard. "Cargo tanks, private sloops, transports—"

"That's no Federation barge, you lardhead," a heavy bass voice argued from behind.

Virtually the medical-textbook antithesis of his skinny son, Big Rex Moss turned his three-hundred-plus pounds and stabbed a fat finger between the Andorian and Burgoyne.

"We got a Starfleet reconnaissance cutter," he went on. "These people aren't gonna just die. We should drop this and beat it out of here while the beatin's good."

"And they will go back to say all about us," Okenga said with cold irony.

"I see no Starfleet signs," said a short, thick Klingon built like a New York City antique fire hydrant.

Burgoyne jabbed his finger forward and spat his mustache out so he could speak.

"It's roight theh, Dazzo," he said. "See it, mollyhead? 'UFP Sta'fleet.' Plain as bloody dayloight. That's what you get for spinding too much time behoind bahs."

Daring to wander forward again, still fascinated by the chemical destruction and the frozen atmosphere pouring out of the Starfleet vessel, young Roy Moss quietly mocked, "What's a 'baaaah'?"

126

Burgoyne ground his teeth and knocked the young man aside again, this time with a foot.

"Hey, Mr. Nobody! I said git your fracking becksoide outta my way! I can't frackin' see through your skinny butt, can I? The captain's supposed t'be ayble t'see, ain't he?"

Roy leveled a bitter glare on the back of Burgoyne's head, and felt his father's disgust from across the bridge. He enjoyed a moment of contemplation, imagining his father as a parade balloon and Burgoyne as Ichabod Crane. His father floated by, bumping into buildings, and Burgoyne, who was all neck and no chin, was constantly being suctioned from above. Eventually he would just suck all the way up and be gone for good, and Big Rex would be pierced by a flagpole and explode.

Roy fought a grin and waited until Big Rex lost interest in the altercation and looked forward again at the Starfleet craft slowly turning and gushing the last cloud of its frozen air into space.

"No," he murmured, "you can't see through me."

"Carlos! Carlos!"

George pounded on the locked overhead hatch.

"Dear God" was Robert April's shredded whisper. "Carlos . . ." He closed his eyes and brought a shaking hand to his mouth. "What shall I tell his poor mother . . ."

Jimmy stared at April and was suddenly aware of his own mother. He watched the captain and wondered if the line was some kind of joke or exaggeration. It wasn't.

Backing away until the cold metal wall stopped him, Jimmy shook until he thought he would shake apart.

His reaction was punctuated by his father's hammering on the hatch and angry shouts. Over that terrible noise there was another noise—the whine of lasers and the hum of that tractor beam.

"What are they doing?" Veronica Hall gulped as she huddled among the crates near the opposite bulkhead. "Why did they do this?"

Captain April finally stepped into the hatch cubby and took hold of the raging creature there.

"George, stop!" he said. "Stop . . . don't harm yourself. If we don't rock the boat, so to speak, they won't know we're here. This hold is sensor-immune for security reasons. They won't be able to read our life signs, and they won't notice us if we remain calm."

His soft English trill made the warning sound like a reading of poetry.

It had the right effect.

Swallowing his agony whole, George sank down to a crouch, gritted his teeth, and crammed his eyes shut to lock inside what he was feeling. He boiled and seethed, fighting for control. The single yellow utility hatch light, very small and direct, shined on his hair and turned it to copper. His features looked harsh in that light, skeletal, like a boy playing with a flashlight under his covers.

Finally he grated, "We've been losing ships in this sector for years! All the time we thought it was because of the Blue Zone. How many went to these bastards? How many good people! And three more today!"

He slammed his knuckles on the deck.

"George, your voice," the captain admonished.

Teeth still gritted, George crouched there, breathing like an animal, quaking with misery and rage.

"Everyone sit down," Robert said. "We've got to think. Is everyone all right?"

In the corner Jimmy Kirk sat, staring death in the face. His wits were in shreds. He barely understood what was happening around him and his limbs wouldn't move anymore. His own who-cares-if-we-live-or-die attitudes came rushing back to haunt him. At sixteen, he thought he had lived all of life. Lived it all, and none of it had been under his control.

His friends felt that way too. A friend had committed suicide last school year, and one more had attempted it.

Suddenly he felt foolish, having thought he understood their motivations and for mocking the adults who tried to save them. The paramedics, the police, the parents, the teachers.

He remembered standing on the school grounds with his gang, as though they had a secret language that no adult could speak, plotting subterfuge. Who wanted to live a life that was in some teacher's control, or some parent's, or some case worker's?

*"Better to control your own death, at least,"* he and his friends had concluded. *"Better to go out with your name in the headlines."*

It had sounded right back then. Somehow, he thought it might not hold today, though.

Seeing his father's reaction to the deaths of three people, two of whom he had just met, abrupt shame washed over Jimmy. The shame was a shock. He felt oxish and unfledged. Realized there was nothing *he* could do to change this.

He bent into a ball and stared over his knees down the fifteen-by-thirty-foot chamber at the aft bulkhead. Trembling. The metal wall was trembling. The thin doors on the storage closets and the cramped toilet were rattling. Something had the cutter by the throat.

For the first time in his life, Jimmy saw what it was like to *really* not be in control.

Thorvaldsen, Bennings . . . Florida . . .

"We'd better get our radiation suits on," his father said ultimately, "just in case."

He got up and nearly ripped the door off a rattly utility cabinet next to the toilet. Inside were eight white spacesuits, adjustable for size and loaded with hookups. On a shelf above were eight headpieces, and on the side were eight double sets of narrow oxygen tanks, each about the size of a woman's forearm.

He started pulling the suits off their hangers and tossing them across the deck.

"Everybody put a suit on. Never mind the helmets and tanks for now."

Halfway across the hold, Captain April caught his suit and Veronica's, then crouched near her, looked into her eyes, and was apparently satisfied at what he saw there.

Jimmy was barely aware of his father's approach until the off-white protective suit appeared beside him. Suddenly the twelve or so feet between them and the others was an ocean of separation, and the two were sorely alone.

"Here," his father said quietly. "Can you get this on?"

Fighting against himself, Jimmy grabbed the suit. He didn't meet his father's eyes, afraid the scared sixteen-year-old was showing through his protective shell as he made a Herculean effort to hide his fear.

"I could've been cut in half by that hatch," George said. He lowered his voice even more. "You probably saved my life. Don't worry. I've been in worse . . . I'll get you out of this."

Resentful of parent-to-kid lies, Jimmy crawled back into his self-imposed mental seclusion and saw lying there a prime opportunity to stab. His voice was stern, black.

"You got me into it."

A hit—low, sharp, and hard. The truth was a poison stinger today.

Jimmy watched in unanticipated surprise as his father failed to react the way he expected. Instead, George stopped in the middle of a step. He looked stricken. Instead of leaning closer, he leaned away, and turned. Put space between them. Slowly. The walk of a wounded man.

How could something that sounded so right feel so wrong? Jimmy watched and watched, perplexed. For the first time, he felt bad about getting a win. He'd been wanting to hurt his father for years. . . .

So why didn't it feel any better than this?

As though he'd smashed his own head against a wall, he realized for the first time that he wasn't the only one with feelings.

He kept watching, baffled, as his father wandered past Robert April and Veronica.

April was settling against the wall beside Veronica, glancing around at their makeshift coffin as they both pulled the safety suits on. With one leg in, he paused to listen.

"Do you hear that?" he said. "They're turning us for proper tractoring. They must think we're all dead."

Struggling to find the armholes inside her jump suit, Veronica took a deep breath. "Why would they tow the ship if they think we're dead?"

His face still puckered in distress, George Kirk took a couple of deep breaths, then looked up at the creaks and moans of their vessel.

"I think I know," he said bitterly. "I think we're being salvaged."

"We told you, don't get in the way, you skinny shit."

Big Rex Moss's voice boomed as he stretched his wide torso

forward, got his son by the ponytail—their favorite handle when dealing with Roy—and yanked him well to the side.

Offering his father only the smallest glance, Moss the younger didn't move any farther back than his father pushed him, and he kept talking, more to himself than to the others.

"It might still have decoders we can sell," he said. Then he plunged into thought. "Think of what those can be worth on the gray market. State-of-the-art chips . . . maybe a reaction-control magnathruster . . . just the hull and ducting material's worth salvage . . . we should move it out of the area and get it parted before its home ship comes back—"

"What home ship?" Caskie demanded.

"You don't think something that size got all the way out here by itself, do you? What am I saying? Someone like you *would* think—"

"Nobody asked you," Rex grunted in his very deep voice. He gestured at his son, then jabbed a thumb aft. "You go back and sit and mind your shields."

Roy stepped into the cabin portal, but didn't leave. He watched the adults and reminded himself that many a conqueror had been only nineteen. He sent them a mental warning and wished they were psychic.

But they were too stupid to be aware of anything but themselves. That was his safety net. They were all watching the screen as though they'd never seen a Federation ship before.

"Keep the tractor on," Burgoyne said. "We got no choice. Slice those ingines off the main body and bring 'em round to ayr hold. Caskie, you're gonna have to find the registry mahks and burn 'em off or nobody'll dare buy from us. We're gonna have to pynt the flippin' thing as well. Lookit all the trouble it's gonna cost us. What's Starfleet doing belchin' round in the Zone, innyway? Deadnecks dunno to steer clear or what?"

"Deserve what they get," Caskie repeated. "Deserve it, that's all."

He licked his thin lips and hungered at the idea of cutting and burning.

Behind the Sharks, Roy Moss rubbed the fuzzy juvenile beard he was trying to grow and imagined it as thick and woolly. Someday he'd be given that beard.

Someday he'd be given everything, by everyone around him.
Until then . . . he'd have to mark time, and *take*.

"Salvaged? Isn't that rather a leap of logic?"
Robert April rearranged his legs on the hard deck and glanced
around at his tiny audience.
"I'm in Security, remember?" George grunted.
"Oh . . . sometimes that does slip my mind about you. Sorry. Go
on."
"I'm talking about the gray market. It's a spaceborne black
market run by a mixed-bag splinter group. Klingons, Andorians,
Orions, Terrans, anybody. Usually people who can't even make it in
their own culture. They just band up together. They fence stolen
equipment or illegally salvage wrecks. It's called a 'gray' market
because it deals half the time in legal circles. It runs in such wide
boundaries it's almost impossible to crack down. Makes me sick."
George raked a fingernail on the deck until it hurt. Helped him
think.
"Until now I've never heard of them creating their own salvage
by attacking operational ships on the cruise. Makes me wonder how
many vessels are logged as lost for unknown reasons but are really
attacked, the crews slaughtered, and the ship ends up being parted
out so they can't be recognized, then sold back into legitimate parts
markets. Damn, it gives me the floods to think about it."
He choked on the last phrase and fell silent until he collected
himself.
They were all sitting now, conserving energy and letting their
environmental suits warm up so they could at least function in this
cold tank. The suits made them all look slimmer than usual, even
over their clothes—a pleasant illusion that came with the insulated
one-piecers.
When he spoke again, his voice was calmer, more insidious. His
eyes narrowed, and he looked up at Robert.
"It also makes me want to survive so they can't do this to
anybody else. And I've been thinking. If they think we're dead,
they're going to want to part out the electronics and hull of the ship.
If they drag us very far away, any hope for help gets pretty damn
thin."

"Have you got a plan?" the captain asked.

"I'm going to bet they've never stumbled onto a Starfleet ship before and they don't realize what they're up against. That was the pause after I hailed them. They realized they were in trouble and they didn't know what to do about it. Bet they were shouting at each other, too. Finally they decided they were committed, so they went ahead and knocked us out. They figure we're dead. They think they're towing a hulk, and that gives us a little time. If we can use that time to build weapons, just enough to disable them—"

"That's a big ship out there, sir," Veronica said.

"Size doesn't matter. The ship doesn't matter." George waved a hand and scooted a little closer, fostering a sense of conspiracy that was as good as an injection of vitamins right now. "It's the people inside we're fighting. This kind of group is hard to keep together. They're not exactly famous for loyalty to one another." He lowered his voice, then added, "I'm going to get them to fight among themselves."

*Tap.*

"The only catch," he added, "is that once we do anything, they'll know we're still alive."

*Tap. Tap, tap.*

Their heads swiveled, all in different directions, brows puckering.

*Tap . . . tap . . . tap, tap.*

Veronica voiced a near whisper. "What is that?"

"It's not mechanical," Robert offered, puzzled. "Too irregular. George, do you think—"

But George was already twisting toward the companionway. He gasped, "The airlock! Carlos!"

Vaulting to his feet, he was at the hatch mechanism in a second.

"George, no, wait!" Robert scrambled up and grabbed him.

"He's in there! He's gotta be in there!"

"Wait a moment," Robert insisted. They squared off in the cubby. "If you're wrong and you open that hatch . . . we're all dead."

Across the hold, Jimmy Kirk watched the expression on his father's face. Was the sound made by somebody in the airlock? One of the intruders boarding their cutter? Had the upper hatch been ruptured? If so, there was instant suicide in opening this lower hatch.

Was it just the quirky noise of the lasers or the tractor beam on the damaged hull? Or was it what his father thought it was?

Risk all their lives for one person? Was that how these things worked? He'd never heard of that before. He'd heard of one person risking everything for many, but never the other way around. That didn't make sense.

His father wanted to open the hatch. Captain April didn't. Who was the captain now that the mission had gone crooked? Which would prevail?

*What would I do?*

"I'm opening it," George said. "Everybody back."

Without further argument, Robert herded the two young people aft, handed them helmets and oxygen masks and helped them get those on. Then he put on his own, and nodded at George.

George didn't have his on, but he didn't care. He was fixated on that noise.

*Tap, tap . . . tap . . .*

He glanced back to see if the others were as far away as possible and had their units on.

Then he grabbed a basic wrench out of the tool caddy and banged on the hatch. Once. Twice.

*Tap, tap.*

Determination tightened his muscles. He pawed through the caddy for a magnetic lock turtle, found one, and clunked it onto the hatch, where it stuck like a trooper. A few seconds, and it had the right numbers. Then it flashed a tiny green light at him, and he cranked on the hatch handle.

The hatch opened so fast, it almost broke George's arm—and the weight that piled on top of his drove him to the deck and almost broke everything else. He shoved it off instantly, shot to his feet, slammed the hatch shut again, then bent over.

"Carlos!"

Lying in a heap under him, Carlos Florida tried to turn over. There was a small emergency oxygen mask strapped to his face, sweat pouring down his neck and saturating his gold uniform shirt, and he looked like he'd been beaten, but he was alive.

George turned him over frantically, and by the time he got him into a sitting position, Robert had tossed off his helmet and was kneeling there also and helping.

"Carlos?" the captain began. "Are you all right, my boy?"

Drained of every last thread of strength, Carlos forced his eyes open and tried to nod. He tugged weakly at the mask on his face, now probably doing more harm than good.

"I'll get it," George said, and pulled it off him. He dropped the mask and began rubbing Carlos's half-frozen arms and shoulders. "You okay?"

Carlos sucked air, nodded again, and whispered, "Thanks . . . thanks."

"Is the cabin blown?" Robert asked.

"No . . . still on . . . no air, though . . ."

"The airlock?"

"Okay . . . so far . . ."

"And you got in at the last moment?"

Veronica showed up with a blanket and handed it to Robert, who wrapped it around the shadow of a man.

"They . . . targeted . . . engines and life . . . life support," Carlos gasped. "Purposely left our main section intact."

While he stopped for breath, George said, "We know. We figure they're parts pirates. They're salvaging the cutter, but they don't know we're still here. Did you get the SOS out?"

Carlos shook his head. "They hit the . . . the SOS buoy . . . soon as it jettisoned. Knew just what to do . . . I guess they didn't like me swearing at them in Spanish. They hit the cabin and that was it . . . I saw the laser port heat up . . . barely made it in there in time."

He gestured sluggishly upward at the hatch.

Digesting everything, George sighed and grumbled, "No SOS."

"Nope . . ."

"Well, never mind. We're gonna find some other way. I'm sure glad you're here."

He rubbed Carlos's shoulders, stirring up that precious circulation, and venting some of his own frustration and relief.

"Damn, am I ever," he added. "Thought we'd lost you, pal. That's not what we came out for, y'know?"

Carlos blinked up at him and panted around a grin. "Thanks," he croaked. "I know it was a risk, opening up the hatch for me."

"Not enough of one," George said quietly. "Not even close to enough."

Still aft, still in his helmet, Jimmy stared. His father wasn't the tender type. So what was he looking at?

As he warmed up, Carlos reached out and offered a solemn handshake to George.

"What're we gonna do now?" he asked.

George Kirk straightened up, got right to his feet, and stood there like a gunfighter.

"I'll tell you what we're going to do," he said. "We're going to rip the wall off this hold and get directly into the engines and nav mechanisms, and we're gonna drive this beast from down here. They can tractor us all over hell for all I care, but you can bet your mother's silk underwear it's going to be the nastiest bitch of a ride those spiders have ever had."

# TWELVE

☆

"Can you make out a heading? Where are they dragging us to?"

Crammed into a rectangular hole in the wall sheeting they'd just ripped away, George Kirk and Carlos Florida muttered back and forth at each other.

"Laterally," Carlos answered. "They're dragging us across the edge of the Blue Zone."

"Probably to a place where they can dismantle us."

"Please, George," Robert April commented from outside the hole, where he was trying to hold a flashlight on the work they were doing. "Don't use phrases like 'dismantle us.' You may find it shatteringly accurate if we aren't very industrious."

If he was kidding, he was doing it dryly.

"Or damn lucky," George commented. "You know what's strange about all this? They came out of the Zone at light-speed. Why aren't they going at light-speed now?"

"Maybe their mechanical set-up is . . . I don't know what."

"I do," George said. "I'll bet their tech is so piecemeal, they can't work the tractor and the warp drive at the same time. I've heard of that happening. At least, not without a complicated warm-up process. Maybe that's what they're doing. Warming up for warp. That gives us a little time, but I don't know how much."

"I'll take it," the captain said. "It's all we've got. George, it might

137

also explain why we're being pulled along the edge of the Blue Zone. They may be giving themselves a way out in case any other ship appears."

"You mean if we get lucky and the *Enterprise* comes back to find out why we never showed up on Fara—"

"Yes. We'll be smartly pulled in there, merrily crushed, and no one will have a clue what happened. They might ruin their catch this time, but they'll remain on the hunt."

"Not if I can help it," George said. "I'm not going to wait for an opening. If they figure out at the wrong moment that we're still alive, it's all over. We've got to be in charge of that moment." He fought with a stuck cap on one laser emitter and groused, "Y'know, sometimes I'd be happier not being able to figure out how criminals think."

"Oh—we have something here," Robert said, squinting at a flicker on the bared machinery. "George, do you see this? They've shut down their tractor beam to twenty percent. We must be coming up to speed."

Confused, Jimmy spoke up against his own plan. "Why would they shut it off? I thought they were pulling us!"

"They think we're dead," Carlos pointed out.

"So what?"

"So they're conserving energy," Captain April said. "If they knew we were alive, they could keep the tractor on and prevent us veering off."

Inside the wall, George's voice snarled, "I'm betting they're taking the time to reroute their tractor from impulse to the warp engines, getting ready to go into light-speed. That's all the time we've got."

"I'm working as fast as I can, sir," Carlos added.

"I know you are. Shut up and concentrate."

What sounded like a reprimand to Jimmy apparently wasn't taken that way. Carlos was chuckling and muttering, "You're getting power crazy, aren't you, sir?"

Beside Jimmy, Robert April smiled.

A smile, at a time like this!

Jimmy shook his head and grumbled, "I don't get it."

The captain looked at him. "It's only at warp speed that one must keep constant thrust. At sublight you get up to speed and whatever you're towing will fly on in a straight line . . . oh, almost forever. Warp speed isn't natural, you see. Sublight and hyperlight are rather like the difference between rolling down and rolling up a hill. At sublight there's no resistance. Nothing to slow us down in the void of space. The only time you would use more power is to turn or stop or speed up. Until some force acts upon us, we'll coast at this speed indefinitely. I'm surprised you haven't gotten that in school. It's one of Newton's basic laws."

Jimmy clamped his mouth shut. All he needed was to blurt some comment about how seldom he paid attention in school. Or how often he skipped. What could he say? That he knew Newton's laws but hadn't bothered to think about applying them? Great.

"Don't worry," his father promised from inside the wall. "We're gonna get acted upon."

"I don't know what the big deal is," Jimmy said. "These are just stupid pirates. How come it's so hard to figure out what they're thinking?"

"Stupid people don't survive in space," his father cracked from inside the wall. "Never underestimate your enemy."

Beside him, Carlos sank back after failing to gain access to whatever he was working on, and sighed in frustration.

Pausing, George asked, "You all right?"

"Let me . . . rest my arms . . . I'll be—"

"Ensign Hall! Know anything about laser emitters?"

Beside Jimmy, Veronica got up, crossed the deck, and crouched before the opening. "Yes, sir, I do."

"Carlos, back out of here."

Jimmy watched from his corner as Captain April helped Florida out. Veronica crawled right in. The hole was small and her legs were tangled with his father's legs. Jimmy scowled. He didn't know why, but he didn't like the sight of it.

"What is it we're trying to do?" she asked, her voice muffled now.

"We're surviving, that's what. We've got to live long enough to warn the Federation about these snakes. Fries my fanny that our lost ships could've been pirated rather than lost fair and square in space."

"Sir . . . I mean, what are we trying to do in here."

"First order of battle, Ensign. Disable your enemy."

"Sir, they're about ten times our size."

"They're not ten times madder than I am right now. We're going to take off all the safeties and funnel all our power into one surge through these happy little chopper lasers. One blast at combat intensity, that's all I want."

"That's all you'll get," Carlos said from where he sat resting between Robert April and Jimmy. "These cutters aren't exactly the cavalry or even the covered wagons. These are the choo-choo trains meant to go in well *after* an area is secured. You can jury-rig until that star collapses, and there won't be enough juice on this whole ship for more than one combat blast. And, sir? We don't really know what it'll do to this ship, do we? Could knock out life support . . . the whole emissions systems might blow . . . who knows what we'll have left? After that—"

"After that we'll do something else."

The answer was accompanied by a shriek of mechanical strain— metal against metal.

Carlos let his head fall back against the wall and murmured, "He's not going to listen, is he, sir?"

With a glance back at the work going on, Robert April said, "Not if we're lucky . . ."

Sitting nearer to them than he wanted to be, Jimmy Kirk couldn't resist an urge that nipped at him when he heard that. He leaned toward them and kept his voice down.

"What's so lucky about it?" he asked.

Captain April pressed a dirty cloth against Florida's forehead and tried to mop up some of the sweat pouring off the helmsman.

"Those individuals in that other ship have their hands full," he said. "They did it to themselves when they turned us toward that Blue Zone. That's what changed everything."

He turned then, and watched as George Kirk cranked down on a bolt with both hands and double-barreled rage. Elbows shuddering. Muscles knotted beneath the red uniform tunic.

"A commander with nothing to lose," Captain April added, "is a very dangerous man."

\* \* \*

"'Ey! Bobbysox! Wot about them shields?"

"When I'm ready . . . I'll tell you."

Roy Moss lay lengthwise across the bridge floor, working upward like Michelangelo painting the ceiling of the Sistine Chapel. The work was almost as exacting and twice as hard on the arms.

"Well, wot's the rush?" Angus Burgoyne insisted.

Twisting until he could see the captain's face, Roy stopped working, let his hands and tools rest on his chest, and paused to speak as though addressing a kindergarten class.

"These shields," he said, "are not for rushing. They're not a wall against anything and everything. They take *very* delicate constant adjustment against anything trying to get through *second by second.*"

He lay back and gazed up at his microcircuits. For a moment he was a poet regarding a lake, a young man in passion.

"What we must look like to them . . . to anyone seeing us come out of the Blue Zone alive . . . our witnesses are nothing but primitive tribesmen watching in awe as a man in underwater equipment rises from the sea . . . he is a god. He is a sign. He is all-powerful. He is astonishing and indestructible. Yet . . . they can't possibly realize how delicate, how vulnerable, he is. They don't understand that he can kill himself in four feet of water if he's not very . . . very . . . careful. That's what we are . . . the delicate diver."

He touched both forefingers to the specialized maze above his eyes and thought about what it all meant to him. How long it would take to build up the revenue he needed for his long-term plans. Thought about how efficiently he was using these moronic toad pirates to his own purposes, and they were too stupid to realize it. Too stupid to see real threats coming. Too stupid. Period.

"These shields," he uttered softly, "these are not a shell. They're a mirror. They reflect the danger of the Blue Zone, but they can be so easily smashed."

Angus Burgoyne licked his mustache, used his tongue to pull the end into his mouth, and started chewing on it.

"Dreamy tail-headed runt," he said. "Some genius. Talkin' like a bloke on smoke. Just get'm goin' agin." He shoved out of his command seat and went to yell down the shaft to engineering. "'Ey, Dazzo! Cut the tractor beam a hundred percent. What is this 'eighty percent' bilge, anyway? We got that Sta'fleet rumrunner up to speed by now, don' we?"

Coming instantly out of his prayer, Roy wiped his bare brow with a wrist and cast mental disparagement onto Burgoyne, who was now bent over at the waist, yelling down the hole at the Klingon.

Roy raised his aching arms and got back to work with a final mutter.

"Deserves to drown."

"Here you go. Time to stop being a passenger."

Carlos Florida was still weak, but wide awake as he placed the last of eight mismatched monitors on the deck in front of Jimmy.

Jimmy frowned at the monitors lying cockeyed on the deck, and the wires and cables connecting all eight to different parts of exposed machinery in the torn-apart walls. Now there was a sea of cables and connections that everyone had to step through.

"You watch these," Carlos said. "Everything here is measuring something about that ship out there. That's your job, understand?"

"But I don't know what these are," Jimmy protested. "I can't read them."

He fanned both hands across the field of little screens and graphics and numbers, all flickering, flashing, distorted, competing for sparse power.

"We don't have automated equipment down here," Carlos said, "so we have to do it ourselves. This is the graphic image of the ship itself. That one is the distance from us and speed. Over there is energy flux by wavelengths . . . this one is the macro-diagnostic . . . this one is power-to-mass. . . . Over there is the energy measure—"

He stopped, read the display crystals on the monitor, and called, "Mr. Kirk?"

"Yeah?" George called from somewhere inside the forward wall.

"The tractor beam! Sir, they've shut it down completely!"

"Great. Thanks."

"That's the opportunity we need, George," Robert called from behind some crate somewhere.

Carlos shrugged and turned back to Jimmy. "The round one shows what I think is their intermix—listen, you know what? Forget what they're for. Doesn't matter. If any of them change, just tell us. Simple." He straightened up, obviously still uncomfortable. "You saw that ship first. You watch it. If nobody claims it in ten days . . . it's all yours."

He turned, winced, braced a sore hip with the heel of his hand, and picked his way between the cables.

Jimmy watched him, marveling that Carlos could joke at a time like this, after what he'd been through.

"What are you going to do?" Jimmy asked him.

Carlos gestured to a cracked-open panel a few paces from where the others were working. "We're trying to get maneuverability into our hands down here. There's no auxiliary control on a boat like this. We'll have to do everything from under the hood."

"Why do you call it that?"

"Beats me."

With a fatigued shrug, Carlos moved away.

They were all working, except Jimmy. He was supremely aware of that, and was glad to finally have something to do. He looked at the monitors one by one, and tried to rationalize what each one was telling him.

And might as well have been trying to read Egyptian. All at once he wished he'd paid more attention in advanced computer science class. He'd always figured the basics would be enough, and hadn't bothered paying attention to anything more complicated. Just as he could pilot a vehicle but not build one, he could make a computer go but didn't know why or how it went.

Suddenly he wanted to know how *and* why.

Across the deck Veronica Hall let out a yip of victory. "Mr. Kirk? I've think I've got most of the power diverted."

George wriggled out of a very tiny hole and grunted, "Percentage?"

"I'd say fifty-five percent of combat intensity."

"Fifty-five, fifty-five," George muttered, thinking. "Won't destroy them, but they'll be good'n shook."

He picked through the cables and wires, and knelt to look into the maze of machinery where Veronica was working.

"Show me."

"Here's where I got a connection through to our warp engines' power core. And up . . . *there* . . ."

"I see it. Don't strain."

"—is the utility laser housing—"

"Damn, is that ever small. Are you sure that's the right thing? Look at that little sucker."

"Yes, sir. If you follow this up to . . . right here, this is the trickle of power to the energy-focus matrix. We can do our beam-force heat adjustment from this. At least, I *think* we can. But I don't have any predictions about what it'll do to us."

"We're disabled," George said. "If they're disabled too, then at least we'll be on even ground with them. We might be trying to have a swordfight while we're up to our elbows in quicksand, but at least they'll be in the quicksand too."

Veronica accepted his help in slithering out of the hole—and Jimmy winced when he saw his father grab the girl's prosthetic hand to pull her up. He expected it to pop off and start running around the deck on two fingers.

"Okay, huddle," George said. "What do we shoot at?"

They collected around Carlos Florida, who was on his side, crouched in the exposed machinery inside another of the ripped-out pieces of hull sheeting, working on something.

Jimmy almost got up and left his gauges, until an overwhelming sensation pressed him down. He wasn't wanted over there. He wasn't welcome. He wasn't a member of the crew. They not only didn't want him . . . they didn't need him.

He drew his knees up tightly to his body, ducked his head a little, turned back to his gauges, and listened.

"What do we hit?" his father was asking. "Suggestions?"

"What about their warp engines?" Veronica said. "If they go to warp, we'll never get our shot."

"No good. We knock out their warp, they figure out we're still here, they turn and kill us, and duck into the Blue Zone to hide. Doesn't get us anything. Gimme this—"

He made a long reach, snatched one of Jimmy's monitors, and dragged it back to the huddle. Jimmy scowled at him possessively, but had no time to think of anything to say.

His father, Captain April, and the others peered at the monitor, which showed a flickering graphic of the spider ship. They were pointing at it and trying to identify what was what.

"Where can we hit that'll foul them up most smartly?" Robert April murmured, following Veronica's finger on the graphic display.

"An impulse hit?" she said. "Wrecks their maneuverability."

Robert nodded. "But nothing else, my dear. They could still turn on us."

Next Jimmy heard his father's voice. Very quiet. Not the usual grumble or roar.

"What's on the outside that affects the inside? Come on, people. Think."

"Sir," Veronica said, "I remember something from my Intro to Propulsion Engineering . . ."

"Well, don't make me tickle it out of you, Ensign. Shoot."

"Coolant? Isn't that right? Without coolant they can't run anything."

Robert clapped George on the back. "Coolant, by God."

George was gaping back at him. "Coolant compressors! That'll shut down everything!" Then he paused. *"If* we can shoot through their shields. That's the big question. Those shields can keep them alive inside the Blue Zone."

"Then what'll we do?" Carlos asked.

"We'll assume they think we're dead so they don't think they need shields."

"That's a devil of an assumption, George," Robert warned.

George flung his hands wide. "What d'you want? Shields like that have got to be a hell of a drain. I wouldn't run them all the time, would you?"

"No, I suppose not . . . but they're a complete mystery," the captain added. "We're guessing about how they do something they simply *can't* do. Heaven's sake, how do you fight something that's utterly impossible?"

"Don't confuse me. Okay, let's find that duct."

The finger-pointing on the monitor started again as they eliminated possibilities one by one and questioned others, while behind them Jimmy shifted his haunches on the cold floor and felt left out.

He frowned at them. They hadn't even congratulated Veronica on coming up with the coolant idea. Didn't anybody in Starfleet care how a person felt?

He watched coldly as they mumbled and pointed, using their fingers to follow the design, trying to eliminate the places where the duct couldn't be, then trying to conclude where it *could* be.

"That's got to be it."

"Starboard side, on the aft quarter?"

"What else could it be?"

"Mmmmm . . . I dunno . . ."

"It's got to be something important . . ."

"C'mon, it could be just an exhaust port—"

"Could be food storage. We'd be shooting at their dinner."

"A food port with signal lights for repair workers to see?"

"I don't see any lights."

"Right there. And there."

"That's static on our monitor."

"Steady static?"

"Listen, we've got to make a decision."

"No, *we* don't."

They all looked up, and Jimmy held his breath as his father's voice took on a sharp finality. His father was getting up and pulling Carlos up with one hand and Robert with the other.

"I'm the one who has to decide," he said. "On your feet, everybody. We'll knock out that port and hope it's their cooling system, then we'll move away."

Carlos struggled up and sighed, "If we can still move."

"We'll move if I have to get out and push. I intend to still be here when the *Enterprise* comes looking, and I want those greedy bastards to be here too." George stood to his full height in spite of the low ceiling, squinted in raw rage, and gritted his teeth. "I want to arrest them with my own bare hands."

Way, way down on the floor, down underneath the big red giant erupting at close proximity, the little yellow son blinked up and wondered if that was really his father talking. He was used to a scowling fellow who didn't have enough to occupy himself on leaves.

This wasn't the same man.

Lately it didn't seem so hard for Jimmy to keep quiet. He hadn't made a nasty crack for well over an hour. Not since that one he couldn't forget.

He saw it rolling in every one of his scanners. *You got me into it. You got me into it. You got me into it.*

"Shut up," he muttered, and raked both hands over his hot face. Since when did guilt have sweat glands?

"Robert," his father asked, turning.

Captain April looked up. "Yes, George?"

"Before it's too late, do you see any implications in this that I'm not seeing?"

"None at all, my friend," the captain said. Sad clarity swam in his eyes, which had long ago forfeited their sparkle for the reality he had to accept. "There is no excuse for piratical acts, and should be no leniency. We must . . . fight."

"Positions, everybody."

Jimmy watched from his seclusion inside the semicircle of monitors as the Starfleet people scattered to different parts of the exposed machinery.

"Oh, my friends!" Captain April said then. "We're forgetting one detail. We haven't the power to overtake them, and we can't strike that port from astern of them. How shall we entice them to turn and present the port to us?"

Immediately Jimmy cranked around to see what his father would say to that.

George Kirk was bent on one knee near the torn-apart access caves where Carlos was buried in the guts of the ship.

"You just said it. We're going to make them present it to us. Carlos? In position? Hall?"

Their responses were muffled inside the caves.

"Aye, sir."

"I'm ready, sir."

"Quite ready, George."

With a false steadiness George said, "Carlos, take a fix on that portal."

"Fix, aye."

"Robert, can you steer from in there?"

"I can do some lively guessing and generalizing, certainly, George."

147

"What?"

"I said I'll do my best!"

"Okay, this is it, folks. Robert! Turn us forty degrees to starboard and let's move! Full speed!"

"Turning." Robert's voice came up from back there. "Best speed is point zero zero four of sublight."

"Well, full crawl, then! Jimmy! Watch that monitor!"

Holding on to his skin somehow, Jimmy jolted up onto both knees. "Which one!"

Swinging toward him, his father bellowed, "That one! That one right there! Is it doing anything?"

"No—yes!" His mouth dried up and he choked, "They're turning!"

"They're coming about to fire at us!" Carlos confirmed. "I can see their starboard side! Sir, their laser ports are heating up!"

George swung away again. "Target that starboard compressor, Ensign!"

"I've got to eyeball it," Veronica warned, her voice muffled.

"Do your best. Funnel your power through the system. Give it everything!"

"Funneling, Mr. Kirk. Ten . . . nine . . . eight . . . seven—"

"Get ready—"

"Five . . . four . . ."

"Aim—"

"Two . . . one . . . full power!"

*"Fire!"*

# THIRTEEN

☆

"They're alive!"

Angus Burgoyne, without even leaving his captain's chair, reeled out to his right and smashed Okenga across the face so hard that the Andorian engineer went down on the deck, rolling. Electricity vomited all over the ship. The bridge was lit like the Fourth of July, and the ship was rocking and spinning off its course. Around him, members of his sparse crew were hanging on as the deck pitched. Sirens whined and sparks flew everywhere, on everyone.

"They're alive! You said they'd be dead! Damn your face, Okenga, you said they'd be dead! They're not dead! They're frackin' alive!"

Around them their ship rocked and tilted against its own artificial gravity as all systems went haywire. Alarms rang and rang, as if the living things on board didn't know they'd just been hit, and hit hard.

Roy Moss, unwelcome because of his age, unrespected because of his age, held in contempt for his abilities and kept around for the same reason, clung to a companionway rail behind the others, watching.

With his elbows against his ribs as he clung to the rail, he muttered, "I'd be alive."

\* \* \*

"Fire!"

"I can't fire again! There's no power!"

"Not *that* kind of fire! Get the extinguishers! Hall, get out of there!"

George Kirk pulled Veronica out of the wall only seconds before her mechanical cave flushed with smoke and sparks and flames. The gravity went crazy, and suddenly the ship was turning on its side according to the perception of any living thing inside. Open space might not care, but the crew sure did.

An instant later Robert was there with two small fire extinguishers, literally walking on the starboard wall. He tossed one to George, and both men stood with legs braced wide as the cutter tilted under them, spraying up a snowstorm.

Smoke billowed from a dozen cracks and three of the four peeled-back pieces of hull sheeting.

"Sir, you did it!" Carlos squinted to read the sensors at the source—with jabs of electricity, no screen. He poked his head out of the hole he was half in, wiped away the sweat-plastered hair. "They're disabled! It might be quicksand, but it's *our* quicksand! They're stuck, but good!"

Victory blended with pure hatred as George tucked his chin and growled, "I'd like to stick 'em somewhere. All right, crew—we're on a better footing, but we just gave ourselves away. They know we're here. It's a cockfight."

"You dirty son of a scarecrow, Burgoyne, I warned you! I *told* your dirty, smelly ass what would happen if we didn't move out, and now look."

"Watch'er mouth, Moss. I'm still in command."

"Command the warp drive back into place, then, since you can do magic! Command the weapons on line! Command this hulk back to full power. There's coolant foaming all over the lower level, for Christ sake!"

"Warm up the laser!" Burgoyne shouted. "Fire at them!"

"Laser with no coolant?" Rex Moss said through gritted teeth. "We'll go up like a nova!"

"Back your fat self away from me. And lookit who's talkin' about smell."

As the two powerful men thundered at each other, those of the crew still on the bridge now turned to their work, even if they didn't have any. Nobody wanted to get dragged in, to get in the middle of a dispute. Nobody knew which one would win, and didn't want to be attached to the loser.

Besides, if anybody got killed, there was more for the rest of them.

"Warp drive is forget it!" Okenga called from down inside the engineering area. "Weapons are very bad."

"How long?" Burgoyne called without taking his eyes off Rex Moss. "How long to fix the warp?"

"Five day. Six."

"What do we have left?"

Eager to throttle Burgoyne with bad news, the Klingon technician climbed up out of the companionway, waving at the reddish-yellow chemical smoke that puffed up before him, and leered at their captain.

"We can crawl around like a twenty-first-century tugger, doing a hundred thousand kilometers an hour. Half of one percent of light-speed. You can get out and swim faster."

Still staring at Rex, Burgoyne grumbled to the Klingon, "Go take a wizz, Dazzo. Nobody asked your filthy face."

At the back of the bridge, Roy raised an eyebrow and murmured, "The Sharks are now snails."

Burgoyne shot a glare at him and spat saliva. "Get back to your goddamned shields, boy!"

"You were so sure they were dead," Big Rex Moss boomed to Burgoyne. Sweat broke from his enormous bulk and added to the steam in the small, hot quarter. "So sure, so *sure*. 'Go aheeeeed,' you said. 'Smack 'em again.' Well, we smacked 'em, and they smacked back. Starfleet people don't roll over and kick like sailors on some merchant scow, but would you listen? Now look at us! No warp speed! No power! No weapons! You want to crawl out of here at a tenth of impulse? Go ahead, Angus. Let's see . . . how you crawl."

He moved closer in the cramped bridge, his last sentence a snarl of challenge.

Angus Burgoyne caught the serious note, the threat in that tone, and pushed out of his chair. He put his back to the viewscreen—

And a butcher knife in between himself and his hulking crewmate.

There had always been contention between them, always a tight string vibrating about who was the better to be in command, but contention usually faded in the light of money in their pockets and bourbon in their bellies.

Today they had neither. And their quarry was slipping onto a dangerously equal footing.

No one looked up. No one wanted into it.

Except a bony boy huddling beside the shielding portal where he was working.

Roy Moss watched his father from the side of one eye and judged the movements of Burgoyne with his pure senses. He could barely see the huge butcher blade flickering, glowing from the viewscreen's picture of the trinary. He dared not turn, for that would be uncalculated and unwise. He might distract them.

And he didn't want them distracted. He had waited too long for someone to legitimately challenge Burgoyne. If it was his own father, then it brought him closer to being in charge. If Big Rex was in command, then Roy knew he would get at least some respect, if only through fallout. No, Big Rex would give him none . . . but the other malletheads might.

Burgoyne turned the wide blade before his nose as he glared past it at his challenger.

Cloaked in fingers of steam and crackling electrical gushers from the shattered machinery behind him, Big Rex Moss was a monument to threat. He was big, he was hot, he was every bit as muscular as he was wide, as mean as he was heavy, and he cut a dinosauric figure with the nebula's lights and the bridge's darkness arguing in the folds of his neck. He never blinked. He took one step at a time. Almost a sense of music. A step for every sentence.

"We'll drag them in," he said. "Drag them into the Blue Zone and crush the life out. That'll give us time for fixing this hog."

Bending forward to put the knife closer to Rex, Burgoyne spat, "And no profit. We drag it in, we get nothing out. That's not wot I'm in this business fo'. But what do you know about business? You talked us into keepin' this snot-nosey whelp o' yours on board, gettin' a full share of our take—"

"That snotnose is the only reason we can go inside the Zone and come out alive," Big Rex said. Another step.

"He should be getting part of your share," Burgoyne insisted, "instead of a whole share of his own. You know it's true, that's why you're always kickin' the punk around. Admit it, y'grotesque maggot."

Roy listened, and this time he turned to watch. He stood up slowly. Since they were talking about him, they wouldn't be surprised if he took interest or notice if he moved himself into a better position. He enjoyed these little moments so. . . .

*Share. I should be getting their shares on top of my own. I'm the only one who keeps them in business. I'm the shielding genius. I'm the piloting genius. I'm the weapons genius. What could they do without me? Use this ship for a giant chamber pot, is all.*

Big Rex took another step. "We're going to drag them into the Zone. We're going to get out while we still can. We're going to hide and repair. You're gonna step aside."

That was when he brought out the Orion magnatomic pistol and pointed all twenty inches of it right at Burgoyne's funnel-shaped head. Where he'd hidden it until now, only his folds of flesh and shabby layers of sweat-stained clothing knew. Only the chains on his wrists really cared.

Burgoyne started to shake. His big blade wasn't big enough suddenly.

His lips peeled back and twitched. His lack of a chin began to wobble.

"Put the butch down, slug," Rex told him.

Hatred boiling through him, Burgoyne discovered he had no choice.

Roy held his breath and continued to watch without pretending not to.

Shaking so hard his bones almost rattled, Burgoyne slowly deposited the knife on what had minutes ago been his captain's seat. He knew it was the last thing of his that would sit there.

At least for now.

That was how fast things could change.

Big Rex never flinched. He didn't look at the knife, but waited until Burgoyne backed away from the seat.

Then, satisfied, Rex nodded and said, "Don't you ever pull nothing like that again on me . . . or you won't live to hear the echo."

Without the slightest regard for what Burgoyne might do to Roy, Big Rex chuckled to let them know he wasn't *too* mad, but that he was victorious for now. He tapped the barrel of the Orion pistol on his brow in a kind of warning, then turned and headed for the companionway.

Burgoyne let out part of a sigh of relief—

Only part of it.

Because Roy Moss saw his opportunity. He lunged forward, grabbed the butcher knife, and gave it a drastic fling toward the wide target of his father's shoulders.

Burgoyne's gasp of astonishment and panic was particularly satisfying to Roy, but Roy had his eye on the blade he had cast.

The blade turned sideways and didn't lodge, but hit hard enough at the right angle to take a slice out of the back of Rex's neck.

Rex grabbed his neck with his free hand and spun around at astonishing speed for a man his size.

Horrified, Burgoyne threw his hands out before him in a gesture of innocence, sucked in a gasp to explain that he hadn't done it—

*shhhhhhhwazzzzzz*

A scream of pure agony, a glowing pillar of heat and stench, and Angus Burgoyne was suddenly the stuff of legend. Literally—he was now a pile of black flesh flakes and scorched bones whose tendons had been incinerated, settling and sizzling on the deck.

"Always thought cremation was the best way to go," Big Rex Moss commented. He waved his pistol in the air to cool it, and turned away again. "All right, you Sharks! Guess who's in charge now?"

Behind him, his son licked his lips and smiled.

"This one's changing! Hey! Dad! Captain! Somebody! This one's changing."

Jimmy waved and pointed frantically until Veronica Hall dropped beside him and looked at the blinking numbers, reading

154

them through static on the screen. "They're changing course!" she confirmed.

"What's the new course?" George asked. "Carlos? Have you got it?"

"I was afraid of this," Carlos said. He stopped and swallowed hard. "They're trying to get back into tractor range. If they can get a grip on us, they'll drag us right into the Blue Zone. I'd bet on it."

"How long?" George demanded. "At this speed, how long have we got?"

"Well . . . I . . . wouldn't bother to start roasting a turkey, sir."

"What's that? Six hours?"

Carlos looked at him with a quizzical frown on his face.

"Sir," Veronica began.

She never got the chance to finish, because George blustered, "Well, how long does it take to cook a turkey? My wife always takes six hours!"

"Closer to four, George," Robert supplied. A sentimental grin tugged at his mouth.

Carlos nodded, but it was more like a hopeless shrug. "At the very outside."

Hands on his hips, George stared at the deck and paced back and forth between stacked and strapped supply crates. Four hours of disabled ship and disabled enemy.

Four hours to gain an upper hand. Four hours to maybe lose that upper hand.

Ultimately he stopped, turned, and faced them. His eyes were slim and angry, but a roulette wheel was spinning in them. There was a competitive sting in his voice.

"Then it's a race," he said.

Jimmy looked at him and almost—*almost*—smiled. "Thought you said it was a cockfight."

# FOURTEEN

☆

"Almost nothing left."

"Us or them?"

"Both."

"At least they don't have weapons yet."

"How do you know?"

"They're not shooting at us, are they?"

"Oh . . . right."

"*I'd* be shooting."

The voices of his father and Carlos Florida did little anymore to comfort Jimmy as he sat on the deck, getting stiffer and stiffer and more antsy by the minute. Forced to lean back on an elbow because the pitch adjusters were still broken and the ship was still tilted, he watched as the two men crawled around the deck from one exposed outlet to another, pushing wires out of the way and splicing cables snapped by the power surge when they took their one shot.

"We've got to keep them buffaloed," George was saying.

"Sir, we're moving away, but at a sick excuse for sublight," Veronica said from inside the same wall Jimmy was leaning against. He couldn't even see her legs anymore. Only the toe of one boot showed under a mass of disconnected chip shells. "Maybe one or two percent sublight. We're a mess."

"But so are they," Carlos added.

Jimmy craned his neck but couldn't see where Carlos or Robert April were at all.

The hold had gone from a neat garage carrying sealed crates to a hangar of parts and cannibalized goods. Crate lids now blocked most of his view, set aside so that any tools or parts inside could be put to use. Some had slid across the tilted deck and were crowded on one side. Edges of the lids had been torn off and were being used as knives or screwdrivers.

"They're dogging us at a little better than our speed," Carlos called over a snapping of damaged circuits. "Sooner or later they *will* catch us."

From the other side of an archaeology implements crate, Robert called, "Count your blessings. It's a *good* thing our propulsion's barely working."

"Why's that?"

"Because our navigational shields are down, my boy."

"Oh . . . right. Darn, that's right . . ."

"Hey."

Jimmy looked to his other side, where the "hey" had come from, but there wasn't anybody there.

"Hey, Jimmy? Jimmy."

He turned on a hip, then scooted away from the wall—

And there was Veronica's face, visible through a mailbox-size electrical-adjuster hatch.

"Can you push a vise-grips in here to me?" she asked.

He bent over, almost down to the floor. "I can't believe there's enough room for you to be in there!"

She batted those big pale eyes and grinned. "Barely. Could you get that, please?"

"You mean a regular old vise-grips? You don't want the one with the magnetic controls in it, or the timer, or anything?"

"No, I just need a grab-and-holder. You know . . . an 'extra hand.' Can you find it?"

Knowing he was being teased, he mumbled, "Yeah, sure," and got up.

Feeling green and raw, he ended up rummaging through four crates of excavation tools. His hands were scratched and lacerated before he found what she needed, and then it was too big. Eventually he had to lower himself to asking his father where he could find what she needed, and got little more than a finger pointed at a wall rack of hand tools.

Finally he was poking the correct grips through the tiny hatch at Veronica's face.

One of her prosthetic fingers caught it by its metal teeth and pulled it in. "Thank you very much," she said.

Jimmy got down on his stomach and peered in. "Can I ask you something?"

"Sure you can."

He lowered his voice. "How come it's good that we're not going very fast?"

"What? Oh . . . I see what you mean!" Louder than Jimmy wanted her to be talking, she asked, "Don't you know what navigational shields are for?"

He winced, knowing everyone else could hear her even though she was inside the wall. "Navigating, I thought."

"No, no. They're for safe travel at sublight," she said. "If we go much faster than this without navigational deflectors, any two molecules of space debris could slam through our hull like bullets through cheese."

Behind Jimmy, his father got up, stretched his aching legs, and stepped to them. "Hall, say that again."

"Pardon, sir?"

"The shielding."

"Sir, I don't understand. I was just explaining to—"

"Bullets through cheese . . ." George knuckled a lock of sweaty dark red hair over his eyes and gazed at the deck. "That gives me an idea . . ."

Suddenly the dim utility lighting flickered, just before they heard Robert's gasp from somewhere in the tumble of equipment toward the aft.

"Ouch! Oh, my lord!"

A second later Robert April tumbled from the open ceiling where he had been working, and landed somewhere back there on the cluttered deck behind some of the crates. Several pieces of small but heavy equipment fell out on top of him.

That sent Jim's father plunging across the tipped deck, around the crates, shoving aside anything that was in his way.

"Robert, what happened? Don't move—don't! Let me get this off you. What happened up there?"

"Bit of a backfire, I'm afraid . . ."

There was a shuffle behind the crates.

Then George lifted him to his feet. "You all right? Can you stand?"

"Just a twist . . . that's why I had to become a captain, I always say. I'm a country gardener when it comes to mechanics—oh . . . lord, the shoulder . . ."

Jimmy tensed and got up on one knee in case his father needed help with Robert. Losing the two engineers and almost losing Carlos had left them all on edge.

But his father's voice, when it came again, was heavy with relief.

"Go sit down for a few minutes. I'll do this."

"Oh, George, you're already trying to do so much—"

"Look, don't argue with me. I've got ten perfectly good thumbs to work with."

"Mmmm . . . suppose I can't challenge self-confidence of that caliber, can I?"

Over the crates Robert April appeared and straightened up. His gentle features were crushed in discomfort, brown eyes pinched and dull as he supported himself on the angled wall and moved away from where he had been working. His brown hair was mussed, but he was on his feet. Wincing several times, he managed to pull out of his smudged Irish cardigan and drape it over a piece of bent-back sheeting. Rubbing his left shoulder, he stepped back so that Jimmy's father could climb up into the ceiling—or practically walk up, the way the ship was tilted. George's upper half vanished into the ceiling right under the impulse engine, one of those places where mistakes really counted.

Huddling in self-imposed seclusion in the corner, Jimmy turned away and settled back to watching his eight disembodied monitors rather than having to witness the technical activities he couldn't help with.

The monitors—just as disturbing. They flashed, crackled, buzzed, and snapped at him, trying to get power from each other through the web of wires. Machines just didn't have it in them to cooperate or share, or work together in any way. There was something profound about that right now, but Jimmy didn't feel like being poetic.

He ended up staring at the monitor that showed the relentless pursuit of the spider ship, coming closer by the minute in the emptiness of space.

A glance showed him his father's legs dangling from the open ceiling, never quite relaxed, always with a strained purchase on the hold's flooring, and he glared with bitterness.

He turned away again.

*It's his fault. We wouldn't be here if he hadn't come up with this stupid idea. The captain wouldn't be here. Maybe Thorvaldsen and that other guy wouldn't be dead. They said they only came out here because April wanted to do Dad a favor. Give him an excuse to haul me into space. That's the only reason he's working so hard to get us out of this. It's his fault and he knows it.*

He talked and talked and talked to himself, feeling sorrier by the moment for the fellow he was talking to, but no matter what, he couldn't get past the fact that everybody else was handling the fear and working through it.

But here he was, stricken silent and unable to make himself useful, so he was blaming his father.

Useful? He couldn't even think straight.

"Jimmy Tiberius."

With a flinch, Jimmy looked up.

Robert April sat down beside him, holding his left arm and moving stiffly. "Feel all right?"

Jimmy shifted and wrapped his arms around his knees. "I guess," he said. Then he pointed at the captain's arm. "I should ask *you* that."

"Oh, I'll get along, never fear." He settled and tried to find the best position possible on a floor that was meant for crated cargo. "So . . . they've made you master of the hold, have they?"

"What?"

"You're in charge of the ship's hold." With his good hand he indicated the arc of monitors flickering around them. "Every ship must have a master of the hold, a ship's boatswain, chiefs of deck, people to whom responsibilities have been delegated. No duty is too small or too menial aboard a ship. If a chap fails to do his duty, then someone else *must* do it. Things can't go undone, not even the tiniest thing. Quite old traditions, and quite efficient."

"Even on a starship?" Jimmy asked.

"Especially," Robert said, "on a starship. You know," he went on, "your father came up with the name for the *Enterprise.* Did you know that?"

Perplexed by the change of subject, Jimmy tried to be cold. "No, I didn't know that."

"Oh, yes. He was involved in her first mission. We rescued a distressed colony from their disabled ship far within a very nasty area of space. I had been planning to name the starship *Constitution,* but after George risked so much, I thought he deserved . . . oh, a little reward, let's call it."

"That's some reward," Jimmy droned, trying not to be impressed while still at least being passably polite to the captain. "What was the big risk?"

The captain looked at him, brows up. "You mean he never told you?"

"Never told me. Surprise, surprise."

"I see . . . I suppose he took it seriously that some parts of the mission remain top secret . . . but not the part about the rescue. I went down with a head injury, and your father took over the whole operation. And it was a great deal dirtier than anything on the books, I can tell you."

Jimmy gave him a sly look. "But that's all you can tell me, right?"

"Well . . . yes."

"That's what I thought. What are they doing over there?"

He pointed to where Carlos was joining his father at the aft end of the hold.

"They're cannibalizing some of the interior flux conductors and rechargeable gadgetry in there."

"How come . . ."

"Beg pardon? How come they're doing it?"

Lowering his voice, Jimmy dared to ask, "How come . . . you're not in charge?"

Modestly, the captain tilted his head and said, "Oh, there can be only one captain to a mission, my boy."

"So what? You rank my dad, don't you? Why's he making all the decisions?"

"I do, yes, but this is his assignment, not mine, you see." Robert let his head drop back against the hold wall and tried to relax. "I appointed him charge of the cutter, observation of the trinary, and the voyage to Faramond. I can't arbitrarily take it back now, can I? We would lose the consistency of command. All sorts of things could go wrong. Someday I'll turn the entire starship over to someone else, and the future of Federation space will be in hands other than mine. There are styles of command as surely as there are styles of dance. Any good commander must understand that, as must any good crew."

Jimmy glowered and fixed his gaze on his father and Carlos as they tampered with the mechanisms.

After a moment he asked, "How are you going to keep other people from using the starship and all that power in ways you didn't intend?"

"Oh, I'm not!" the captain said emphatically. "Diversity isn't any good if it's only one man's diversity. Now, is it?"

Such a quick answer, so well thought out. Obviously this wasn't the first time such a problem had dogged Robert April's conscience. Yet he seemed utterly comfortable with what he had just said.

The idea settled softly around them, all its open possibilities and its inherent strifes gurgling with promise.

Unable to pop off a challenge—probably because there really wasn't a good one—Jimmy tucked his chin between his knees and muttered, "Guess not."

He felt the captain smiling at him. Maybe saw it out of the corner of his eye.

"You see, Jimmy," Robert said on a philosophical sigh, "I think humanity is all right. Mankind is cunning and artful, enthusiastic, and ultimately smart. Oh, we blunder from time to time, sometimes a bit butterfingered while we build on some unclear vision, but we always learn from our blunders and we rarely forget. And we never, *ever* . . . stop trying."

The enthusiasm in his voice, the faith in his tone, the ease of his posture, all belied this environment and the damnable hum of their straining engines.

"So we're stubborn," Jimmy said. "So what?"

The captain ignored all the so-whats coming out of this boy and smiled warmly again.

"There are a dozen other civilizations more advanced than humanity, just in known space," he said. "The Vulcans, Orions, Andorians, the Alpha Centaurians . . . a few others. Yet they keep to themselves while looking down their noses at us. What good is that? Humans have been the only ones to reach out, to ask others to join us in our common future. We're the only ones to initiate a galactic unity. Oh, how I love the sound of that. . . ."

Jimmy didn't want to look at him, but couldn't help sensing him there and feeling him there, and drawing strength from him. Somehow Robert April made the death around the corner seem a light-year away.

Just when Jimmy was thinking he might get out of this conversation with his ego intact, that gentle voice came back with a new suggestion.

"You don't trust others very readily, do you, Jimmy?"

Cold warnings flushed through him at the captain's statement. He swallowed hard.

Then he asked, "Who've I got to trust?"

A long, burdened silence picked at them. Jimmy's own words lay hard around him until he could feel the weight on his legs and his heart.

Then the captain asked, "What about your father?"

This was the question he dreaded most, and had known would inflict itself upon him sometime in this conversation. He thought he was ready for it.

"What about him?" he challenged. "I don't see him that often."

"Don't you? That's odd . . . I remember signing several leaves for him. How much is 'enough,' according to you?"

Embarrassed to find he had no answer, Jimmy offered a shrug as a miserable facsimile.

"He left my mother," he said finally.

"Ah, that lets a little light in," the captain said. "You've resented your father on your mother's behalf? Not on your own?"

"I can take care of myself," Jimmy indignantly verified. "She can't."

"Can't she? That's odd . . . she married him while he was a guard at Starfleet Headquarters. She always knew what it meant. There was some difficulty at first, of course—they were both so young . . . in fact, they were on the edge of divorce until he went into the Security Division. Their relationship has always been best off at . . . well, at a distance, if you understand." Captain April paused, thinking back with a puzzled nostalgia on his face. "As a matter of fact, I don't recall their having any serious strain between them until . . . oh, I'd say two years ago. Perhaps three."

Color raged across Jimmy's freckled cheeks. He didn't have to think back to realize who had been the cause of the two or three years of tension.

"He didn't have to drag me into space," he said. "I like Earth. I like sailing. On real water. It's always space with him. He can have it."

"Oh, yes . . . space is a jealous concubine, I know," Robert said. "It demands a whole heart from those of us who tend it. You see, the Federation doesn't have an iron-bound coast. It's incumbent upon Starfleet to constable the settled galaxy wherever we're called upon. Our colonists depend on us, as do our allies, and, frankly, anyone else who needs help, friend or foe. There's so much to be done, so many fragile details to tend . . . no one's life is perfect. If you're waiting for perfection, you're liable to spend your life deeply disappointed."

"I might never get the chance to get disappointed," Jimmy said. "Not if we're going to sit here and—"

"And get whitewashed, yes. I understand. But it certainly isn't your poor father's fault."

"He's the one who hauled me out here, isn't he? He's the one who had to be in Starfleet, had to go off to space. He's the one, not me."

Robert lay a hand on his own chest in a knightly fashion. "If you want to blame someone," he said, "blame me. I dragged your father kicking and screaming into Starfleet. Then I talked him into staying when he pondered going back to Earth. It's *my* fault, Jimmy."

He tapped his chest with the flat of his hand, as though to borrow a bit of his heartbeat to swear his oath upon.

Then he added solemnly, "Men like your father don't come out of every dozen. A man willing to gamble, willing to take his turn at the wheel . . . we simply need people like him so very badly."

They sat in silence for a few minutes, aware of the disembodied monitors flickering and burping in front of them. The captain leaned forward once, adjusting something he didn't like on one of the screens, then settled back again.

"A Security Division commander has plenty on his hands these days, with more and more interstellar traffic launching every day, every minute." He gestured forward, at the only screen that showed a staticky picture of the enemy ship closing on them. "These fellows out there, they know they're in trouble. That bit of hesitation after your father hailed them . . . they know they've stumbled upon Starfleet. That means they're not only in trouble for attacking us, but even if they can explain that—claiming they thought we were someone else or some such crockery—they're still subject to the theory of infection and contracts of affreightment and other laws of interstellar commerce . . . likely they don't have those things, so they can't let us go now even if they made some kind of mistake in the attack. It's like picking an argument in a pub and finding you've picked one with a professional boxer. All the little laws and regulations and treatises we've had to hammer into shape to form interstellar law—each one has been an adventure in itself. I'm sure your father's told you about some of them in his letters—that reminds me! Did your brother Sam manage to stick out those insidious ten-hour sessions in the lab and get his extra embryology credit?"

Irritated at hearing about his smart older brother, Jimmy hugged his knees and grumbled, "I don't know. I guess so."

"Oh—that reminds me about something else. How did the fishing pond work out? The one you dug out behind your barn? Quite industrious for a boy of fourteen. I recall George reading that and asking if I had a connection whereby he could get fish eggs to stock that pond for you. My goodness, seems like yesterday . . . did the eggs take? Did you get any fish out of it?"

Puzzled at the way the conversation had turned, Jimmy drew his brows together and muttered, "Got some trout out of it."

The captain chuckled softly and gazed at the deck. Finally he shook his head and smiled.

"Oh, the ribbing your poor father takes for those letters!" he went on. "For going to the trouble of sending real paper letters instead of transmissions . . . he's endured more hounding than a plebe at the Academy, but that connection is precious to him . . . to know that his family is touching the paper that he touched."

Sitting on needles, Jimmy fidgeted and stared past his knees to where his father and the others were working at such a fevered pace, but all he saw was the past.

"How do you know so much about my family?" he asked.

"How?" Robert raised his soft brows as though he'd been asked how fish swim. "My dear boy . . . you're all he talks about."

Those words floated around them like the last stanza of a patriotic song, carrying a sentiment above the ground and refusing to let it fade.

Troubled, pensive, and thoughtful, Jimmy found out what shame tasted like. His lips parted, dry. The moisture they needed was in his eyes.

For the first time since leaving Earth, there was no razor blade in his response.

"I . . . quit reading the letters."

He sounded like a criminal confessing a crime. Felt like one too.

Beside him, Robert April's soft voice turned bleak and disenchanted.

"Oh, Jimmy . . ."

"Where's my goddamned tractor beam, boy?"

Big Rex settled with appropriate grunts into a chair meant for a much thinner man.

The captain's chair. Though this was satisfying after all these months of putting up with a scavenging dog like Burgoyne, Rex had to do some down and dirty tucking to get himself between the chair's arms.

"Boy!" he called again. Now that he was in the chair, he couldn't turn any farther than the chair would turn, which wasn't much of a swivel on this model.

"I'm right behind you. No reason to bellow." Roy Moss buried his contempt in steadiness and glanced at the back of his father's bloated neck. "We have only ten percent tractor beam. We can pull them, but we'll have to get very, very close to get a good grip."

"Let's do it, then. Okenga! Dazzo! Can't you idiots get any more speed out of this hog?"

The Klingon poked his head up from the engine room.

"Not before the coolant compressor is back to twenty percent. You want to push it? Come and do it yourself, human."

Down he went, without waiting for a comment from the new leader.

Unlike Burgoyne, who would've demanded more speed at any cost and taken offense at being called "human" even though he was human, Rex Moss didn't argue. The engineers would want to catch that Starfleet ship as much as he did. They didn't dare let it go. They'd work hard enough without his hammering at them, and probably work better.

Behind him, his son noticed the silence and paused to cautiously evaluate it. After a moment Roy ventured, "Aren't you forgetting something?"

Big Rex tilted his large head without turning. "Like what?"

"Like trying a few . . . other things before we decide to drag them into the Zone. Things that may let us keep that ship and its mechanisms. Those alloys and the new programming . . . wait until the shields are usable—"

The captain's chair cranked to its full third around. Now Rex could glare at his son sidelong, hard, mean.

Suspicion and familiarity did mutual damage between them. Big Rex deserved every nickname he had ever been given, yet there was a keen, diamondlike edge to his sense of what others were thinking, especially when he felt threatened.

He could *smell* subterfuge.

His eyes carried an immutable dare as he looked at Roy now. In spite of the difficulty of getting into that chair, he grunted forward and levered his bulk out of it. He never took his eyes off Roy as he stood up and turned away from the main screen.

Backdropped by the flickering image of the ship they were pursuing, he moved toward his son.

One step, another.

Still holding his micromechanical tools, Roy didn't get up. That could get him killed, and he knew it. This wasn't a good time to be three inches taller than his father. The slightest hint of challenge, the wrong kind of flinch—

His father's wide shadow fell upon him, blotted out what pathetic light was left on the bridge. In the harsh threads of red and blue worklights stabbing from the deck rims and the garish contribution of the Rosette Nebula from outside, this massive man became a gargoyle in a burning temple.

"Are you telling me," he began, "that you agreed with that bag of kangaroo crap . . . and you didn't say anything?"

When Roy didn't speak, but only stared up at his father with a calculating eye, Big Rex took that as an answer in itself.

A yes.

The huge man's eyes grew even thinner. His face glistened with sweat under the tiny backup lights. He took another step, up onto the work level, butchering his son with his glare. Slowly, he grilled, "Why . . . not?"

Throat drying up, Roy knew he'd better come up with something —just the right something. His father wouldn't buy platitudes or tolerate lies, and knew what both sounded like. Roy knew better than to wave the bloody shirt of challenge when his father had his innate radar so obviously clicked on.

"You wouldn't have listened to me."

Roy took great care not to shrug as he said it. He needed to seem submissive without showing too clearly that he was pretending. His father knew him, but how well?

Well enough to know there was more to his motivations?

At moments like this, Roy Moss couldn't simply shrug off his father as the same kind of moron as the rest of the crew. He couldn't comfort himself with dreams of having been switched at birth and imagine that he was really carrying the brains of some unknown genius.

At a moment like this one, he could clearly see whose sense of self-preservation he had inherited.

The scarlet-blue mountain of skepticism moved another step closer, squashing Roy's drifting thoughts and yanking him back to the moment. If Angus Burgoyne had been dangerous because he was quarrelsome, Big Rex Moss was dangerous for a dozen better reasons, all subtle.

Below, Roy tried not to give away the fact that a parent could still terrorize, no matter how old a child became. All of a sudden, nineteen wasn't old enough.

Rex Moss glowered, grinding his teeth as he digested his own suspicions.

"You *wanted* him dead," he surmised finally. "You wanted that, didn't you?"

It was no question. He rolled his tongue inside a fleshy cheek and added two plus two. His eyes fermented as he leered down at his own son and asked the ugliest question of a voyage that was turning ugly.

"Who . . . threw that knife?"

# FIFTEEN

☆ ─────────

"They're gaining on us, Mr. Kirk. If they grab us with their tractor again—"

"Don't remind me," George snapped. "I've got an idea. Where's the jettison tube on this model?"

Carlos puckered his brow and said, "Abeam on both sides."

"Okay." Clearly hatching a plot, he stooped near Jimmy and looked at the monitors. "Which one of these is the mass-to-thrust ratio of that ship out there?"

Although Jimmy had been watching the monitors for a long time, he suddenly realized he knew nothing about them. With his father hanging over him, he felt particularly unfledged.

"There it is," George said, picking on one very small monitor with a divided screen showing two wobbling graphs. "Good . . . just might work. Heads up! Here's the project. I want you all to collect anything that's expendable. Anything broken, anything we don't need. What's in these crates anyway?"

"Archaeological implements for Faramond," Robert provided. "Toys for the children, farming and gardening tools, household appliances for the colony—"

"All of it, into the tube."

"I beg your pardon?"

"Hall! Get out of the wall. Carlos, come here! Jimmy, get up and help with this."

170

For twenty minutes they did the craziest thing Jimmy had ever seen. They ripped the bent-back sheeting right off the walls and stuffed it into the port side jettison tube. They stuffed everything in there from little bolts and pins to big saws, pitchforks, shovels, computer parts, spatulas, kids' toys, and even their garbage from lunch.

He only paused once to ask why they were transporting all these hand tools to a modern colony, and all he got back was Robert April's British lilt—"No one's ever improved on a good old shovel, dear boy."

So he quit asking questions.

All the time they were doing it, Jimmy was trying to *think*. This had something to do with those two molecules Veronica had mentioned, and something to do with the thrust-to-mass gauge. He found himself plunging whole-soul into helping his father peel back pieces of the ship itself and cut them off and stuff them into the tube. Somehow this wasn't the same as going through the motions of building a fish pond or stepping a sloop's mast, though he had done those things with his father too. This wasn't the same as his father doing something *for* him, or him doing something because Dad said so, or because Dad had come back from space to put time in with the family.

Suddenly he winced—and not because he'd scratched himself on the sheeting. *Is that the way I always saw it? Damn—did I ever say it to him that way?*

He glanced at his dad's face, blotchy with effort, hair shaggy as red seaweed, arms straining, and for the first time he saw some of himself—if only in the shape of his father's shoulders and the way the muscles knotted up. They had the same muscles, the same knots. The same furrow in the brow, the same mouth when it tightened with effort, with determination.

For the first time, Jimmy looked at his father and saw some of himself.

Always . . . always . . . "Jimmy, you look just like your mother!" "Why, Winn, he's the spitting image of you." "I don't believe how much you boys look like your mother. George, didn't they get anything of yours?"

There was always laughter following lines like those. Some joke between his parents and their friends.

Suddenly he wanted desperately to have something of his father's. A muscle. An expression. A bad habit. Anything.

*Our eyes aren't even the same brown—*

"Enemy ship is getting awfully close, Commander." Veronica's announcement cracked a diligent silence that had fallen as they stuffed anything and everything into the tube.

Jimmy paused, panting, and stared at her. Enemy . . .

"How close?" his father barked.

Kneeling at the monitors, Veronica said, "They're nine hundred sixty thousand kilometers behind us and closing at about three thousand kilometers per second."

"Damn! They're on top of us."

"Gives us about five minutes," Carlos added.

"Likely they're attempting to close in to use a weakened tractor system, George," Robert pointed out.

Jimmy was about to ask a question—probably a stupid one—when he pulled open a breadbox-size hatch in the forward bulkhead and found himself staring at four beautifully mounted hand lasers. He backed off a step and stared at them. Weapons . . . why was everything so new all of a sudden? Why were his knees locked and aching?

Somebody moved beside him, and without turning his head from the row of lasers, he asked, "Are these supposed to go . . . with the rest?"

*Please don't let it be Dad next to me—*

"Pardon me? Oh, Jimmy, the hand lasers, of course," Robert April uttered. "No, my boy, those we keep."

"But they're in a whole other ship. We'll never get to use them. Shouldn't we shuck all the weight we can?" Jimmy said.

"No, no," the captain said. "There's a spacefarer's rule of thumb that started, oh, a century or so ago, I believe, with our first establishment of space forts. We call it 'W and W' . . . water and weapons. At all cost, in a survival situation those two elements you must keep. You can do without food much longer than you can do without water, so you must keep water. Weapons can provide protection, power, and heat in space, which has no heat or power."

He wagged a finger toward the neat row of hand lasers. "Two ships or not . . . *those* we keep."

"Okay, that's enough!" George bellowed from behind them.

Jimmy flinched, thinking maybe he and the captain had stopped to talk too long. Then he turned and realized his father was talking about enough stuff being pushed into the jettison tube.

His father closed the double-thick hatch, shoving in the jagged corner of a cracked lamp lens before he could get the thing closed.

"It's a brilliant plan, George," Robert said as the hatch clacked. "The king would approve."

Jimmy cranked around. "What plan? I don't get it. Aren't we just shucking extra weight?"

The captain hung his good arm over Jimmy's shoulders, steered him toward the monitors and gauges, and pointed at the one with the shattery graphic of the enemy ship.

"Watch."

George Kirk straightened up in his son's periphery and said, "Carlos! A hundred and eighty degrees about."

"One-eighty, aye. Coming full about, sir."

The irritating hum of the strained impulse engine strained even more as thrusters pushed and burped against the natural course. That was the "force" acting upon the vessel—and it was turning.

The captain's arm over his shoulders was suddenly pitiful protection as Jimmy felt his jaw drop and his heart fall to his socks. He felt suddenly cold—he even shivered.

"We're going to play chicken," he gasped, "with a ship ten times our size?"

"Look at this. Hey, Caskie, get a blink on this."

"What?"

"The idiots are turning around."

Big Rex hunched forward in the command seat as much as his bulk allowed, and threaded his fingers as though anticipating a hot meal.

Beside him, Lou Caskie's nearly toothless grin broke wide as the old man gaped at the forward viewscreen. "Walkin' right into our tractor beam. Walk right in, walk right in."

"They know they can't outrun us. By damn, they're gonna fight."

Together, and knowing their Andorian engineer was standing on the engine room ladder, also looking, they watched the Starfleet hulk complete its turn and begin an approach.

Yes, it was a hulk—a wreck. The proud white neo-enamel coating on the outer skin was streaked with burns and ruptures now. A recognizable pennant that had once said "Starfleet" now said only "leet." The sensor pod on top was open like a used eggshell, still drooling threads of fluid and frozen atmosphere. A magnification inset showed the limbless gore left over from two, maybe three people still strapped into what might have been observation harnesses. The main cabin wasn't much better after a direct laser cut, with a surgical slit opening it from bow to amidships. Random electrical threads and sparks still searched for a connection.

Behind the captain's station of their own damaged ship, now filthy with scorches and oil stains, bleeding out the corner of his mouth, Roy Moss kept his voice low.

"We don't have shields," he warned quietly.

His father's glare burned into his back.

The young man turned.

Big Rex sat in the command seat, bulbous and huge and angry, still rubbing his knuckles from the little reprimand he'd given his boy.

Roy gazed back at him sidelong and touched a tongue to his bleeding mouth. Reprimands were such interesting times, such times of study. Would he ever be bigger than his father? He was already taller, but when Big Rex stood before him and said, "Come over here," there was nothing to be done but walk over there and be punished.

Roy knew about that. Once, he had refused.

Not anymore.

*Who threw that knife? Who threw that knife?*

They both still heard it in their heads.

Both knew the answer now. But the question still rang and rang, because there was defiance at its core. The real kind, not just the smart-mouthed kid snapping back because he was annoyed.

Rex glared and rubbed, and his son heard the message of the knuckles.

*Never again, tail. Don't manipulate me again. I'll find out.*

A shudder crawled through Roy. His sore, recently beaten thighs and shoulders told him to keep quiet and do his job.

His father turned away finally and squinted at the ravaged Federation vehicle.

"Whoever's left over there, they gotta be in the hold," he chewed out. "Driving the mechanics hands-on."

"Cannot be done," Okenga said from the ladder. "Must have computer control."

Still keeping his voice on low guard, Roy tried to get on his father's good side by saying, "He's not talking about Andorian scavenger engineers. He's talking about Starfleet pilots. They don't just steal technology. They invent it."

Without taking his eyes off the Federation's crippled ship as it hobbled closer on the viewscreen, Big Rex warned, "Back to your work, runt. I'm not through with you. Right now I want that tractor beam."

"You're going to need deflectors."

Lou Caskie dropped his rotted grin and advised, "Nobody asked you. Didn't hear nobody ask you."

He didn't turn around. Neither did Big Rex.

Rex's enormous body jiggled in a dozen places as he suddenly laughed at what he saw on the screen. "These weeners are going to play chicken with *me*. I love when suckers play my game . . . my way."

Okenga abruptly jumped, looked down, scowled, then climbed to the top of the ladder and made room for Dazzo to come up. But not enough room apparently. The two argued and snarled, each trying to get the best position to see the screen. When they noticed Roy watching them in contempt, the Klingon pushed Okenga aside, put his teeth together, and ordered, "Back to your deflectors, boy!"

Settling onto both knees and pretending to do as he had been told, the younger Moss reasoned not to argue aloud with these wastes of time. He spoke only to his tools and the quivering circuits in the open floor beneath him. "My name . . . is *Roy,*" he murmured.

He made a few halfhearted adjustments on the crashed deflector system—his perfect, beautiful, delicate, special brand of shielding program that let them go places no one else dared go. He would mend them, yes. But he would hold back. Make sure these porks kept on needing him. At least, as long as he needed them.

In the privacy of his mind he relegated repairs to one side and kept doing them, but indulged in adding up how much he'd skimmed off these porkers' stash. They were so mallet-headed, they didn't even realize he'd been stealing from them even while they were stealing from their victims. When he had enough . . . that would be a day with one sun. Himself.

No one was paying attention to him anymore. He slowly stood up and turned to the viewscreen.

On the screen, the Federation ship was heading straight at them, closing fast even for open space.

"What do you think, boss?" Caskie was asking. "What they doing?"

"Assuming we're stupid, that's what," Big Rex huffed. "They don't know how to think dirty. That's their problem. Always has been. Gonna be a bigger problem for 'em the further they fly."

"Farther," grumbled an unwelcome correction from behind.

"Warm up the pokers," Big Rex said, waving his right arm at the Klingon.

Dazzo limped to the shabby, pieced-together mass they called a weapons control board and checked their power. "Some. Less than one quarter."

Satisfied, Rex wobbled his head from side to side and grinned with one corner of his mouth.

"That's all I need."

They fell into a predatory silence. The ship out there looked mighty small.

Roy stood up and moved forward, his eyes, his mind, his sense of survival all on that screen.

"Back off," he said. "Stop us."

Big Rex said, "I don't back off."

"You'd better. Something's going on." He moved another step forward. "They've got something up their sleeves."

"Like what?" his father argued. "They know they can't outrun us, so they're turning and pretending they've got something left to fight with! It's that stupid nobility coming at us. Starfleet white knights."

"You'd better stop this ship."

"Shut your mouth or I'll shut it for you! We'll crumple them like a piece of paper!"

Abruptly Roy spun to his father and shrieked, "Don't you think they know that, you moron! This is Starfleet you're laughing at!"

Glaring up from his seat, Rex Moss slashed out so hard and with such impulse that he almost rolled onto the deck, and struck his son across the cheekbone. Reeling, Roy stumbled and caught himself somehow on Dazzo, who shoved him off, then slapped him hard enough to drive him to the deck.

When Roy turned over, bleeding and dazed, his father's wide shadow fell across him and he blinked up at a mountain of a man.

"What'd you call me?" Rex demanded. "What . . . did you call me? Call me that again."

The shadow fell darker, closer.

"They're practically on top of us!" Caskie called. "I got the laser locked on 'em. You want me to shoot?"

Big Rex ignored him and moved closer to Roy with a surprising sense of drama for a man his size. He glared down.

"I want to hear it again," he said. "Let's hear that word come out of your skinny neck again, smart boy."

Roy scooted backward, but dared say, "How did you survive before me? Don't you understand the physics of space?"

Rex paused. Anger gave way to experience with his son—he narrowed his eyes, thinking, sensing.

Roy took those seconds to crawl to the manual controls and get himself to his feet, never taking his eyes off his father.

"Hey!" Caskie called then. "Hey, they're doing something!"

Big Rex turned. "Doing what?"

"Opened their jettison tube . . ."

Shock breaking on his wide face, Rex lumbered around again, pointed at his son, and shouted, "Cover! Cover! Give me shields!"

Behind the command center Roy twisted a lean upper body so fast that his own ponytail slapped him in the face. Hands on deflector controls he knew were still useless, he skewered his father with a demonic glare.

*"There . . . are . . . none!"*

Finally, too late, it sank into Rex that what they really needed was protection and not size. Size had always helped him, and for the first time was failing. He pulled himself around, gripping the back of his chair so hard that it squawked, and howled at the horror on the viewscreen.

Suddenly the Federation ship ducked straight down and vanished from the screen at point-blank range. And in its place—

Pitchforks, jagged metal, jars, buttons, cans, broken glass, cracked parts—

"Turn!" Big Rex bellowed. "Evasive! Turn!" He plunged and got Caskie by the back of the neck. "Turn, goddamn you!"

"I'm trying!" Caskie howled. "Can't do it! Can't do it fast enough!"

Dazzo shoved away from his console and bellowed, "Debris! Still moving at their speed!"

"Lasers! Fire the lasers! Fire! Fire!"

"At what!" Dazzo demanded.

*Crrrraaackckclatatatatat*—

Big Rex's unintelligible bellow was sore accompaniment as their ship was turned into a dartboard.

Bits of junk moving at thirty thousand miles per second slammed into their hull like buckshot, puncturing it in dozens of places. Chemical fountains spewed and hot sparks erupted all over the forward portions of the ship, coughing smoke until they could barely breathe or see.

"Fire!" Big Rex kept choking. "Fire at those bastards!"

The ship tilted upward as though it had taken a punch under the chin, and started to spin. The crew shouted and blamed each other while desperately trying to get control back. Somehow, in the middle of chaos, Roy Moss dragged himself from the deflector access to the weapons panel and did what his father had instructed.

His hand came down on the targeting preset, twisted the beam-width to maximum, and slammed the firing mechanism.

Even as he went down on the deck hard on his side, as the ship buckled beneath him, he knew what he'd done.

He knew he'd made a hit.

If he lived . . . both ships were his . . .

# Part Four

☆

# COMMAND SENSE

# SIXTEEN

─────────── ☆ ───────────

"Spock, step down here."

When the captain called, the other captain—who was acting as first officer, science officer in his old, most familiar, most comfortable capacity—turned fluidly and stepped down to the center of the bridge as though expecting the call.

The two of them had been like that for a long, long time. Decades, now. Fluid together. Been like that through promotions and medals and commendations, even promotions that had put them up too high for a time, to positions neither wanted nor enjoyed. Flattering, but just not right.

Not right? How could anyone not want to go from commander to captain and take on the glory of commanding a ship? How could anyone not want to give up the day-to-day drudgery of ship command to be admitted to the Admiralty of Starfleet?

As the two men came side by side now, James Kirk silently reviewed all the reasons, and the fact that so few of those reasons could be effectively voiced. They'd both been asked, plenty of times, and both had stood blinking, looking for words that would make sense.

But this didn't make sense to any who hadn't been on a ship, in a trench, in a lifeboat, or clinging to a mountainside when flags were down and instincts were on line. Command through the ages had been tinctured by a tiny fact that some people were under- or overpromoted, and other than in the field itself . . . there was no way to know. How many sergeants had been followed by gasping lieutenants, frantic when the moment came down to decisions? How many resentful glances had he himself gotten when given not only a captaincy at the age of thirty, but command of the first *Enterprise?* How many experienced and deserving forty- and fifty-year-olds had wondered what connections he had—and whispered in dark corners about his father's friendship with Robert April? Why else would Starfleet hand over one of only twelve fabulous new ships to a thirty-year-old? Couldn't be any other reason. April's hand in the pie.

Oh, well, those were past whispers. He had gone past the *I showed 'em* stage, and into the *Who could blame them?* stage. Even the echoes were dead, killed by James Kirk's time-after-time survival, discovery upon discovery, and his bearlike parentage of anyone within the realm of his command. April may have pulled a string or two, may have steered the path to a particular ship because Robert April was a sentimental man as well as a wise one, but Jim Kirk had pulled mountains down in the course of proving himself, and April had been standing by for a long time. Nobody had whispered for years.

Through it all, even before they'd known each other well, Spock was the only one who had never questioned him, never pushed or pulled him, had stood silent behind his shoulder, right where Kirk needed him—in spite of the fact that Spock might indeed have made a more sensible and stable captain many, many times.

Spock had never wanted it. Still didn't. Some people just didn't.

And there had to be a little bit of arrogant *want* . . . Kirk knew the taste of it. There had to be a bit of grated jealously from somebody else's shelf on top of his Captain Cake, that was part of the recipe.

Captain April had told him something like that, way back then, hadn't he? The echoes started turning in his head.

He shifted from leaning on one elbow to leaning on the other, and looked at Spock.

"I've got a file," he said. "It's a technical file, high science section, half-century old. I need you to investigate it, analyze it, and get familiar with the science and the theories it's built upon. We may need you to recognize and extrapolate. I'll punch the recognition words right into my chairside, but you might have to do some hunting."

Spock, standing there as he had a thousand times, his hands casually clasped behind him, simply nodded, but also closed his eyes and opened them again as though in some kind of mellow salute.

"I shall do my best," he said.

Jim Kirk nodded back at him. *Permission to step back updeck. Permission to go up there and back me up.*

Spock turned to the quarterdeck again, then nested himself in the science cubicle and accepted the punch-in from the captain's chair computer access.

Just that simple. Ask, get. Spock knew there was something deeply significant to the captain about what he was doing, yet he would do it as though in a cloak, as though striding along the brick down a dark street after a rain at night. Why? Because he knew it was important and he knew it was private.

Spock and instinct.

"Logic, hell," Kirk grumbled. He twisted to the other side. "Commander Uhura?"

She turned and responded, "Sir?"

"Tie me directly into Starfleet's computer banks, historical section. Then notify Dr. McCoy that I'm going to want him to review something in a moment. Tell him it's private."

"Aye, sir . . . tied in . . . and . . ." *Bleep, blip, knock, knock, mutter, mutter.* "Dr. McCoy is standing by."

Then he punched the comm on the other armrest. "Dr. McCoy?"

*"I'm here, Jim, in my office. Privacy assured."*

"I've got a psychological file I want you to review and analyze."

*"Go ahead. Whose is it?"*

"You'll find out."

*"Oh—you want me to do the identifying."*

"Could say that. I want your unadulterated opinion, Bones."

*"Send it down, Jim. I'll do everything I can for you."*

"Uhura will send it as soon as we get it from the historical archives. Commander?"

"Aye, Captain," Uhura anticipated. "Receiving . . . relaying to sickbay. Completed, sir. Starfleet acknowledges."

"Acknowledge receipt."

"Aye, sir."

*"Jim? This is a half a century old!"*

"Darn near," Kirk said, leaning and lowering his voice a little more. "It was in the archives almost that long. Some of it is personal."

*"Oh . . . yes, I see. I'll keep it that way, Captain. Be right back to you. McCoy out."*

Kirk jabbed the comm off line, then looked forward at the helm of his ship, a ship that was highballing through open space at unthinkable, inhuman velocity, just because he told it to.

# SEVENTEEN

☆

*Forty-five years earlier . . .*
USS *Enterprise,* orbiting Vega 9 as Federation
presence to deflate a planet-possession dispute

"Commander Simon, message coming in over subspace. Priority two."

"Hmm? What?"

"Message, ma'am," Isaac Soulian repeated from his navigation console. He got out of his seat, went around her, stepped updeck to the unmanned communications station, and tapped into the signal. "Recorded message, sent via long-distance subspace."

"Oh, put it on, put it right on. Ought to retire here and now, go down to garden deck, put me up a little Mexican hammock, get a nice nap—"

"*Enterprise, this is Faramond Archaeological Sub-base, date April 27 on Earth-standard calendar . . . Requesting location of Captain Robert April and party . . . We expected the cutter to arrive twenty hours ago . . . Our Starfleet intrasystem cruiser has been unable to find them anywhere near our star system. Signal buoys have been posted, but we thought you should know. Please notify us if you have information and tell us what we should do. Thank you. Faramond out.*"

Lorna Simon shook off her doze and sat bolt upright—well, as upright as old bones would bolt.

"Verify that!"

Soulian tampered quickly with the console, then said, "Federation channel . . . an authorized signature numbers as required . . . and . . . the encoded identification checks out." He turned and added, "It's definitely them."

Simon pressed down a puff of her white hair. "Twenty hours—is that what they said? I didn't hear that wrong?"

"They said twenty hours, Commander," he confirmed. There was clear worry in his voice as he turned to face the command arena. "What could've stopped them from getting there? There's nothing hostile in that area . . . all they were doing was observation of the trinary—how could anything go wrong with something that simple?"

"Get Lieutenant Jamaica up here."

"Ma'am?" Soulian looked at her, puzzled, then said, "Oh! You mean Lieutenant Trinidad. I mean Lieutenant Reed."

"Whichever. Bring him up here."

*"Lieutenant Reed, report to the bridge immediately. Lieutenant Reed, report to the bridge."*

Simon stretched her short legs and got out of the command chair. She didn't like to sit down while she was trying to think.

"Dang arthritis," she complained. "Wide-range scan of space in the direction of the Rosette. Look for SOS signals . . . or residue of explosion . . . and send emergency calls to all bases and colonies in this quadrant to do the same. Hard telling how far a little ship like that can go off course. Don't want to take chances. Yeoman—I'm sorry, I forgot your name—"

On the upper deck, a very young science intern stepped forward to face the woman half his height and three times his age. He had a very high voice and hadn't yet learned not to stand at attention on the bridge. "Jones, ma'am!"

"Jones—seems like I could remember that. You don't look like a Jones. Duck down to my quarters and get the arthritis pills on my bed stand. Deck Nine, Cabin Four. And a glass of water."

"Aye-aye, Commander!"

"With a slice of lime in it."

He nodded, shouted, "Lime, yes, ma'am!" just before the lift doors opened, then he stepped aside to let Drake Reed onto the bridge. They changed places, then the lift doors hissed shut again.

"Lieutenant Francis Drake Reed reporting as howled at, madam."

"You always talk like that?" Simon asked. "Like you're directing a band while you talk?"

"There is reggae in my blood, madam. Not my fault."

"You men in Security, you spend too much time standing guard, I think. Step down here."

Drake's tawny face expressed surprise and confusion, and he paused up there. The walkway light overhead flickered on his curly black hair and made him look like a puppet about to dance.

Simon noticed the pause and didn't like it. "Well?"

"Oh—coming," he said as he stepped down to her. "Have I done something naughty?"

"No, no. You were assigned to watch the Delta-Vegans, weren't you? Where are they?"

"On the observation deck, in their eighth or ninth hour of spitting at the mayor of the settlement over the Federation adjudicator's head."

She waved her hand. "Kick them all off the ship."

Drake put a hand to his heart and grimaced. "Kick them? You did say 'kick them'? I don't think we are authorized for diplomat-kicking, madam."

"We're leaving orbit. If they can't solve their problem in the next five minutes, they'll have to find somebody else to transport them back to Starbase One."

"Eh, pardon me, but . . . is this a Starfleet Command order, madam?"

"No, it's my order. This ship isn't just a taxicab, you know. The starship program isn't meant for carting diplomatic baggage around. Today we're going to make sure that becomes a good solid precedent."

With a shrug Drake started to turn. "As you wish. I shall commence kicking."

"That's not all I called you up here for."

He turned again. "Sorry. My brain is soft from standing guard."

"I need you to tell me something."

"And that is?"

"How well do you know this George character?"

"George? My George?" Drake pursed his lips in thought, then something else came into his mind and he let go of any remarks that were about to pop out. He stared at her, buzzers going off in his head. "Why . . . do you ask?"

The old woman hesitated, but knew all along that there were some things that couldn't be eased into or made to sound nice. He was looking at her, so she went ahead and let some of the natural worry show up in her face. Human nature would take over—he would see the worry, and that would be the segue.

As his brows knitted slightly, she knew he was getting the sense of events.

"They never arrived on Faramond," she said. "They're twenty hours late."

The animation dropped from Drake's dark face.

She looked past him to the communications station and ordered, "Ike, tell the flight deck to warm up a transport. And tell those diplomats that they're having dinner on the planet instead of here."

Soulian nodded and sat down at the comm station to do all that. "Aye, Commander."

"And get somebody up here to man the communications. Just get the whole bridge crew. We need the duty engineer and helmsman back up here on the double."

Simon could tell she was making Drake nervous, ringing the chords no one wants to hear. Decades of Starfleet experience sent her instincts in a dozen directions at once. She wanted to protect Reed from what she was seeing in his eyes, but she also needed the raw truth on her side.

"I know Robert April," she said as she contemplated the cocky Security officer. "He's not given to bad judgment, or even bad luck. And now he's missing. That leaves something for you to tell me . . . what do you know about the luck and judgment of this George of yours?"

Swept by momentary flashes about what could have gone wrong, how the utility cutter could be stuck somewhere with a malfunction, or just off course, or trapped in a storm, or so caught up in viewing the trinary that they lost track of time, Drake found himself in a tornado of fears and imaginings and wishes.

His throat tightened up. He had to clear it and swallow a couple of times before he could speak.

"If there is a hornet's nest anywhere on the sugar plantation," he admitted, "George Kirk *will* step in it."

Lorna Simon's fifty-plus years of experience didn't like that answer, but she did understand it. She'd seen plenty of that type of person in Starfleet since the beginning—in fact, that was the very type Starfleet attracted with its thousand pretty flickers in the night sky.

"How is he," she asked, "at fielding a disaster?"

The choice of words wasn't exactly reassuring to anyone on the bridge.

Least of all, Drake Reed. Suddenly the lieutenant looked very young to her.

His expression crumpled with worry. "Usually he has me at hand, with whom he beats off the hornets . . ."

She distilled that comment, along with a sense that Drake really wasn't meaning to joke, but that some inner guard had clicked on to keep him from panicking.

She'd seen that before too.

She poked the comm panel on the captain's chair with a finger that hadn't always been so crooked.

"Transporter room, this is First Officer Simon. Tell the flight deck to forget about using the transport. We're in a hurry. Beam those diplomats directly off this ship and tell them they're on their own. Then advise Starfleet that we're warping out."

The bridge came to life as people and systems jumped to comply and calls for officers to report to the bridge thrummed through the huge white ship.

These were always the worst moments—between discovering a problem and being able to move on it. The moments of tidying up bothersome details that had to be swept off the bridge before action could take over.

It was during these tight few moments that Simon allowed herself to look again at Drake Reed.

She watched him for a long time, because he didn't notice her. He was staring at space beyond the planet, on the big forward viewscreen. His dark eyes had no glint in them now, and even failed to reflect the distant stars.

His whisper barely surfaced over the bridge noise.

"George . . ."

# EIGHTEEN

───────── ☆ ─────────

"Lock it down!"

"They did the same thing! They hit our coolants!"

"Are the failsafes coming on?"

"Where are they down here?"

"Port aft control access!"

"Stay out of the stream! Carlos, get your head down!"

"I'll get the environmental support—"

"Why aren't the emergency lights coming on?"

"Cryogenic environmental—backups—"

"Just do it!"

"Stay down, Jimmy, stay out of the way."

"Failsafes coming on!"

"Get out of that smoke, Ensign!"

"Life support on secondary backup—switching priority to respiratory systems . . . grav generator is down to one-eighth. Inertial potential varying—"

"See if you can't bleed it for stability."

"Aye, sir!"

"Robert? Where are you!"

"I'm starboard of you, I believe."

"Are you okay?"

"I believe so."

"Can you reach the ventilators?"

"Ah . . . yes."

"Be careful of your arm. Don't hurt yourself again."

"Thank you for thinking of that, George."

"Everybody sit down till we can see."

"I feel like I'm floating—"

"Well, hang on to something until he gets over there."

*Click—*

Little frantic ventilators began to whine in three places, and grayish-brown smoke piled in those directions. It never did clear completely, but in a few seconds the crew could at least make each other out in the near darkness and move without tripping over one another.

A moment later a few of the last-ditch emergency lights flickered on in the forward side of the hold.

None of them was spared the shock of what they looked like to each other after the laser hit. They were smeared with filth, coughing, beaten, and bruised, as though they'd spent a month in the woods without a decent meal. The hold around them had erupted into a junkyard of detached plates, burn streaks on the walls, crates turning lazily on their edges as though floating along a streambed, and squirts of fluid, gas, and sparks from a dozen broken conduits and power veins.

Carlos and Veronica immediately started pushing around the cabin, closing off whatever they could.

Jimmy was clinging to a loading dock utility handle when his father pulled himself around a smoldering crate, lowered his voice, and asked, "You all right, Jim?"

Blinking the sting out of his eyes, Jimmy hoped the moisture wouldn't be mistaken for tears. "I guess. Got something in my eyes."

"Chemical fumes. We'll put the air on priority as soon as we stabilize the gravity."

"The gravity's out? Is that why I feel like I weigh thirty pounds?"

"It's on, but not much," his father said.

Jimmy managed a shrug, and only then noticed that his arms were trembling. He tried to ignore that and said, "Well, it's one way to lose weight."

His father looked at him, paused, wiped a dirty hand across his own mouth, then said, "Great—great. Try to hang on. You're doing fine."

He moved away, toward where Carlos was shoulder-deep in the open wall.

Jimmy blinked after him and wondered what he was doing fine at. Not panicking? He didn't dare. Nobody else was.

*Guess we'll all panic later. Maybe that's how it works. Just keep putting it off.*

That had to be it, because he sure wasn't being much help.

Great. He was doing a fine job not being an annoyance. There was something to take home.

If they ever got to go home . . .

Home. The place he'd tried to get away from.

He shoved himself away from the handhold. "Dad?"

George turned. "Yeah?"

"Do you want me to try to stop some of those coolant leaks? Maybe I could plug them up some way."

"No," George said. "Only trained personnel are allowed to tamper with exposed coolant tanks. You just sit tight. But . . . thanks."

Frustrated, Jimmy settled back and realized that all he was good for was staying out of everybody else's way. Not a very noble way to go. Not much of a story to tell later.

Maybe he could help Veronica.

More swimming than walking, he bounced awkwardly across the cabin and took a hell of a lot longer than he expected to get to her. Halfway there, he felt like something was pulling him back, and two feet later felt like he was being tugged upward. Nauseating, but he ignored it.

"Can I help you with anything?" he asked when he finally got over there and pulled himself down to where she was working inside a hole in the flooring.

Veronica looked up at him, managed a halfhearted smile, but immediately went back to her work. "Oh, I don't think there's room . . . well, know what you could do? Hold my legs down, can you?"

"Oh . . ." Hoping for something more glamorous, Jimmy started to feel disappointed, then decided not to, and put himself to use where he was needed—ballast. "What is it you're doing down there?"

"Trying to stabilize the gravity."

"No, I mean what are you . . . y'know—*doing.*"

"Can you see this saucer-shaped thing under my elbow?"

"Uh—the red and black thing with the manufacturer's name on the side?"

"Right. That's the superconductor. A gravity generator. Inside, there's a pressurized gas. It spins around and provides a gravity field. Basically, it's not able to spin fast enough to give us what we need to feel normal. All I'm trying to do right now is make it work enough so we don't get smashed up if we manage to get the cutter moving."

"Why would we get smashed up just from moving?" he asked. "Wouldn't it make more sense just to turn it off completely and float around, and put all our power into life support? Or the engines?"

"Gravity *is* life support," she said. "If Florida gets even part of the propulsion going, we'll need artificial gravity or our acceleration would have to be so slow that we'll never get away."

Jimmy frowned, annoyed that these things weren't making sense fast enough for him. Any other time he would have just ignored whatever he didn't understand.

This wasn't any other time.

"Gravity has something to do with acceleration?"

"Artificial gravity is what compensates for acceleration," she said, wincing as she tugged on something down inside the hole. "If you accelerate in a matter of moments even to something like one percent sublight, you'd be slammed through the back of the ship. Unless gravity is tugging you in the other direction, compensating like crazy, I mean. Even in airplanes a long time ago—jets—they could turn so fast that the pilots would black out. So they wore special suits that squeezed the body during a banking turn and kept the blood pushed up into the brain. And one percent sublight is a lot faster than they went. Artificial gravity is just something we've got to have. If this thing isn't generating at minimum rpms, we might as well hand ourselves over to those people out there."

All of a sudden a bit of reality that Jimmy had almost ignored turned on him and got particularly unignorable.

He watched her work with the generator, and noticed he was listening to his father, Robert, and Carlos talking behind him as they surveyed what few were left of the monitors and gauges.

"Life support's on secondary backup. I wish we had more light—"

"We've beastly little technical integrity left to be repaired."

"And nothing to repair it with . . ."

"We can pick at things indefinitely . . . but not if there's no air to breathe."

"What condition are our friends in? Can we tell?"

"Look at this screen. They're barely two kilometers away. I'm not even using the magnification. They're right *there,* hanging off our bow."

"And they're still alive. Some of them, at least."

"How can you tell?"

"They're not spinning . . . their failsafes are coming on. See the spurts cutting off one by one? Some sections are ruptured, but their automatics are still protecting somebody."

"There've got to be places to hold out on a ship like that."

"We're both floating hulks. Can't seem to get an upper hand, either of us."

"And they've got a lot more to work with than we do."

"Hall? How're you doing over there?"

Under Jimmy, Veronica pushed onto an elbow, rested a moment, then said, "Nineteen percent, sir."

She nodded at Jimmy to let her up, but suddenly Carlos Florida pointed at one of the gauges and yelled—

"Mother a' God, the compressor! It's not holding! It's gonna blow! It's gonna blow!"

Drowning him out, a plume of supercoolant broke from the burned upper part of a port side sectional tank and turned loose a solid blue-white sheet of spray, cutting Jimmy and Veronica off from the others and splattering them all with what felt like needles of ice. If it filled the cabin—

Frantic shouts erupted almost as loud as the dangerous gush.

"Lock it down again!"

"The discharge buffer grip's on the other side!"

"Veronica!"

But Jimmy realized he was still lying on top of her, holding her down against the minimal gravity, and that put him in the best position to move. He held an arm near his eyes to take the spray and looked for the discharge cutoff next to the tank. Was that it? That red handle under the two blue ones? Had to be!

SECTIONAL COOLANT GRIP – AUTHORIZED USE ONLY

Made sense—if he could pull that handle down, the sections of the tank would seal off. At least, that's what he figured would happen, and things couldn't get any worse, so he determined to take the risk himself.

"I'll get it!"

He pushed off Veronica, forgot all about the gravity, and virtually flew toward that handle—almost flying into the spray. He caught the handle with one finger and kept himself from plunging right through the spray, and levered himself back.

*"No, no!"*

Was someone shouting at him? Was it the hiss of coolant spewing six inches from his head?

He fumbled for a grip and to get his feet against the wall for leverage. Something hit him from behind just as he got the leverage he needed and cranked down on the handle. A force hit his shoulder, shoved him sideways, and at the last second he glimpsed Veronica's synthetic hand close around a bright orange compensator fishtail and crank it sideways.

The plume of spray turned into an umbrella and enveloped half of Veronica's body!

She screamed—it was a horrid, gulping scream—as she was blown in a heap toward the opposite side of the hold. An instant later the spray dropped to a bitter hiss and the last of it was slurped back inside the tank's cracked shell in some kind of automatic suction.

Jimmy pulled himself over the top of a seed storage box and tried to see through his watering eyes.

The girl lay on her side in a puddle of expended coolant fluid that was quickly changing its chemical composition with exposure to air. It changed, as they stared, from ice-blue to a wine-pink as the supercold crystals melted. In moments, even before anyone could move, it would be inert.

But not soon enough for Veronica.

She lay with her pale hair soaking up the fluid.

Stunned, as they all were, George Kirk was the first to move to her, to touch her. Carlos stepped in behind him and knelt there. Pushed her over, gently . . .

Her prosthetic hand stuck to the frozen metal floor—and tore part of her arm off with it. Hair on the right side of her head snapped like dry straw. Her right thigh tore almost in half lengthwise, clothing and all, leaving a gaudy section of torn muscle on one side and a patch of gore on the other.

George sucked a breath through his teeth. Carlos shuddered, fighting not to throw up on what was left of his crewmate.

They hovered over her, helpless, as the torn thigh and arm crinkled with crystallized blood and skin cells.

Mind empty, hands spread, legs bent, breath coming in puffs, Jimmy hovered a few feet away, staring in some kind of automatic disbelief.

He barely felt the hands on his shoulders.

"Jimmy," the captain said, "come away from there. Come with me."

"She—she's—"

"I know, my boy. Come with me."

"But that's not . . . that's not how it's supposed to be . . . the girl's not supposed to . . . it's supposed to be the guys who—who—get—"

"Our poor Jimmy," Captain April sighed, "you're an old-fashioned lad, I'm afraid. . . ."

Letting himself be led away, Jimmy went on mumbling over and over.

"That's not right . . . it's not right, it's not the right way—that's not supposed to be how it is—" Then he suddenly gasped, "What happened? What'd I do wrong?"

"You didn't understand."

"Tell me . . . I've gotta know . . ."

"The pressure compensator has to be in the on position before the safety buffer is activated. Or the whole tank could blow up under the pressure of sudden cutoff."

*Only authorized personnel are allowed to tamper with exposed coolant tanks.*

"I didn't know . . ."

"We realize that, my boy. We understand. Sit down . . . that's right. Don't move for a while. I'm going to see to the others."

Trembling so hard he thought his bones would fall out, and only vaguely noticing Robert moving away from him, Jimmy stared across the deck at Veronica Hall's mutilated form. His mouth hung open, his throat drying.

He wanted to make this feel unreal, like a dream, that's how it was supposed to feel—

But it didn't.

It felt damn real. Damn real. She was *dead?*

And all for him. She'd knocked him aside so he wouldn't be lying on the floor, half frozen.

Until now, giving lives for others had always been song lyrics. He'd never seen a group like this Starfleet bunch. They weren't losing their heads. They weren't giving in to the terror chewing at them all. They were obeying orders one by one, step by step, to accomplish something very specific. They even obeyed orders when there didn't seem to be a reason to do a particular thing. They didn't ask why. They asked what, but never why.

*When are you going to realize that rules exist for a reason?*

The echo of his father's voice . . . he looked for his father, needing to see him.

And there he was.

Crumpled in a corner with his back against the hull and his knees up, his arms braced across his bent knees, his head down. The perfect quintessence of misery.

Robert April was kneeling beside him, touching George's shoulder, gripping his friend's trembling wrist in a simple human bond, ready to listen, since there wasn't much to say that would help.

Before long a pathetic sound rattled from George. He didn't look up.

"Robert, what've I done?"

In a soft, scolding, troubled tone that couldn't nurture away the guilt, Robert simply murmured, "Oh, George."

George shook his head and pressed his other hand to the back of his neck.

"I can't do this . . . Robert, I can't handle this . . . she's just a kid . . . it could've been Jimmy . . . it could've been *my* kid . . . what the hell have I done?"

There wasn't a sliver of hardness or rigidity left in him. His saw-file temper was utterly gone, invisible. His face was parchment, his eyes glass, ready to shatter. Insufficiency weighed him down.

"There's nothing left to fight with," he said. "Nothing we can do is enough . . . can't save ourselves . . . can't stop those bastards from doing this to anybody else . . . ."

His voice fell away as though expended, and he closed his eyes, consumed by the impoverishment of hope from the bottom of his soul.

Even in the big hold, even with broken machinery hissing and crackling and spitting, Jimmy heard his father's voice as though tuned specifically in.

"What'd I drag him out here for?" George Kirk murmured.

"You couldn't have known," the captain said. "There could be accidents on Earth just as easily."

"This isn't an 'accident.' This is plain wrong. You and I know the risks. We chose this for ourselves. He didn't want to come and I made him. I chose for him and that's not fair. He's right . . . I got him into this."

His heart twisting, Jimmy heard his own words and felt them rush back to bite him, to infect him. *"You got me into this."*

When he'd said those words he was after the quickest, sharpest hurt he could inflict. He hadn't given a thought to how long words can last. The future had always been ten or twenty minutes. He rarely considered that something he said could come back to do damage later.

At a moment when there might be no "later," he was finding out how long words could go on hurting. As he saw how bad his father felt, he realized that he would have to learn when *not* to talk—when things he might say could last a hell of a lot longer than the anger or passion that made him speak.

He knew he'd lied in that old fit of anger. He knew he'd gotten himself into this.

Yet never once had his father said, "I wouldn't be in this mess if you'd behaved yourself."

He gazed at the two men who had tried to change him against his own will and suddenly saw a vision of his father that was utterly new.

*I thought he was goofing off on some pretty planet with some pretty technician . . . I thought he left us and went off for fun and games and irresponsibility in space . . . I thought space was easy for him.*

But his father hadn't been out gambling or taking dips in an alien lake or schmoozing on some cushy starbase.

He was out here. Doing hard, hard things.

Staying on Earth would have been the easy choice.

*The easy choice . . .*

It left a bad taste. Jimmy bit his lip and tried to get the flavor of cowardice out of his mouth. These people—people he'd come to admire—Captain April, Carlos Florida, Uncle Drake, First Officer Simon, the engineers, Veronica . . . his dad . . . all said they wouldn't want to be anywhere else, in spite of the risk.

*They can't all be stupid. For all these people to go out so far . . . there must be a lot out there.*

Robert was holding on to George as though one of them were going over a cliff, and it was hard to tell which one. His expression ran through changes, from pain to empathy, to a sad, regretful Mona Lisa smile that had some true misery behind it. Somehow right on Robert April's gentle face, it still wasn't even close to what smiles were for.

Finally he regained control, patted George's shoulder as though to awaken him, and asked a question both official and personal.

"Would you like me to take command, George?"

Jimmy's attention snapped around. He held his breath and stared at his father. What would happen?

He never found out.

Carlos's sudden cry was both dream and nightmare. "George! Come here, quick! She's alive!"

Jimmy sucked in one sharp breath, then quit breathing until his chest started hurting and reminded him to start again. Two shocks hit him—that Veronica could somehow still be alive, and that Carlos was so moved as to call George by his first name.

George scratched to his feet and shot to Carlos's side with Robert right behind him.

"She's got a heartbeat," Carlos gasped. "Let's do it. Can we do it?"

They were all trembling, breathing in little gusts, trying to think straight, trying to stay calm.

"We have no facility to treat this," Robert said. "Supercold burns . . . blood cells crystallized . . . detroyed . . . ice crystals in the cells themselves—exposure killed the flesh and muscle . . ."

"She'll never use the right eye again," Carlos added.

The tones of voice were recognizable on almost an instinctive level. No hope—but responsibility to try? Try to save her under these conditions, only to die later *because* of the conditions?

"What should we do?" George asked.

Jimmy winced. He felt crushed between the half-dozen terrible answers to that question. History class. World War II. Troops struggling on foreign soil, behind enemy lines, in the middle of battle, when choices were nightmarishly few. Soldiers so badly mutilated that their unit mates gave them morphine—then more morphine—then all the morphine—until death came to help them all.

Decent people forced to do these things—

Was that what the question meant?

To face death . . . to see someone mutilated nearly to death— two different things, two distinct horrors, and a weird sense of choice.

Then he heard his father ask, "What would Sarah do?"

"Oh, Sarah . . ." Robert murmured his wife's name under his breath as though wishing she were there at the same instant as being glad she wasn't. "Immobilize that arm, wrap the leg, stabilize the vitals, first-aid that facial burn. Make her comfortable."

"Thermal sheets?" Carlos suggested.

George swallowed a clump of frustration. "We jettisoned them. Damn, that was stupid!"

"Maybe the pressure suit. We can warm her up, strap the wounds, keep her from bleeding to death, but . . ."

*There's nothing we can do, not here, not like this.*

The unspoken truth dangled around them, twisting with residual puffs of electrical smoke.

They felt a jolt from outside the ship—a yank that almost would have thrown them off their feet if they hadn't already been down.

Without being asked, Carlos crawled toward a monitor that was sitting on the deck with its own cable twisted around it. He studied the grainy image, then frowned and spoke as though he couldn't be surprised anymore.

"Tractor beam's on us again . . . only about one quarter its original power." He turned to the others. "But I don't think we've got anything left to break it with."

George blinked painfully, his eyes creased. "They're going to pull us into the Blue Zone. They're going to crush us once and for all."

Beside him, Robert April touched the forehead of the injured girl as she began to move her head and to groan faintly.

Gently he said, "We must face facts . . . ."

# NINETEEN

☆

"Jimmy," George called. "Jim, can you give Robert a hand?"

Maybe they were trying to keep him busy.

Jimmy wasn't interested in reasons anymore. He pulled Veronica's spacesuit back out of the locker, along with two of the personal emergency medical kits, moving like a zombie in a strictly-for-scare campfire story.

Elsewhere in the ravaged hold, his father and Carlos Florida were doggedly trying to repair their haven before the atmosphere all leaked out, plugging holes the autosealers couldn't handle, welding torn sheets of the inner hull in case there was another laser hit, generally seeing what was left.

Moving numbly and without thinking, Jimmy felt as if his mind was on magnification 10. Details, exaggerated before his eyes, possessed him as though crowding out the encroachment of bigger truths. As though dressing a doll, he helped Robert draw the suit onto Veronica's body, over the wrapped remains of her leg and the tourniquet on the stump of her right arm, now destroyed almost to the shoulder.

By the time he and the captain closed the suit over the girl's chest, taunted by her shallow breathing, too steady because of the painkillers they'd given her almost to the point of overdose, Jimmy couldn't even remember putting the suit on her legs and arms.

The suit had a built-in retractable cervical collar that the captain gently tugged out to hold Veronica's head immobile. He had to be careful around the right side of her head—her fluid-caked hair and what was left of her eye now covered by one of several patches on that half of her face.

The patches didn't look right. This wasn't the way a hospital would put them on . . . no one here was a doctor. . . .

Dulled by shock, Jimmy just watched as Robert broke the silver seal marked "Emergency Only" and poked at the tiny controls that put the suit into medical mode. Jimmy heard the captain's calm explanation of what the suit was doing every step of the way—automatic monitoring of her vital signs, ongoing intravenous feed of medications, and anything else the captain put into the suit's medi-guard brackets. From the medical kits he took several finger-size vials and attached them to the brackets. One of them was anesthetic, one was blood coagulant, one was antibiotics, another was something else . . . Jimmy heard, but couldn't listen.

"If her heart or breathing stops," Robert was saying, "the suit will even do cardiopulmonary resuscitation. There are pumps and respirators built in. They have a limited functional time once on the go, of course, but they've saved plenty of lives in space during these critical first few hours."

Jimmy nodded, but most of it went around him. The suit would take care of her.

*Hours. We don't have hours. . . .*

"Captain?"

"Yes, dear."

Feeling his forehead crinkle, Jimmy blinked and shook himself. He hadn't said anything. As he opened his mouth to ask what was going on, he saw Robert April's pliantly animated face easing the moment, gazing downward, touching the girl's left cheek—

—as Veronica blinked up at him with her remaining eye.

An electrical flinch went through Jimmy's body. She was awake! She was not only alive—she was *awake.*

His mouth dried up as he realized he might have to talk to her. What could he possibly say?

Veronica's undamaged left eye was slightly dilated, and she focused with some effort on Robert as he pampered her with his gentle expression.

"I got lucky again, didn't I?" she murmured.

Robert managed a very peaceful grin. "Veronica," he coddled, "brave as ever."

She swallowed with great trouble and licked the side of her mouth that wasn't taped under the patches. "What've I . . . got left?"

Even through his shock Jimmy could tell that Robert was battling to press the misery out of his expression.

"Mmm, yes," the captain began, "your right thigh is a bit torn up, and part of the same hip. I can't tell about your eye, but I'm certainly no expert. However, there's . . . not much left of the right arm, darling."

She digested his expression through the fog of medication. "That's okay," she whispered. "It's . . . still under . . . warranty."

Robert chuckled, but he was fighting himself. Several moments went by as he gathered his composure and fought to keep his expression benign. He leaned a little closer and brushed her one bare cheek with his knuckles, clearly frustrated that it was the only part of her that he could touch. He couldn't even dare hold the hand she had left.

"Is it any wonder," he said finally, "why Starfleet wanted you so badly?"

He wiped a bit of moisture from her left eye, and her cheek puffed into a little white ball as she tried to smile.

"At least," she began, "it didn't get my good arm."

Jimmy sucked a painful breath as his chest tightened. How could she lie there with half the cells in her body killed, the ship around her falling apart, and say something like that?

"How do you feel, dear?" Robert asked her.

"Don't feel much," she said, as though she knew that was what he wanted to hear. Even in that condition she was trying to make the captain think he'd done enough for her.

Incredible.

A clatter rang through the metal walls from forward, and he flinched out of his thoughts and turned to look.

Under the forward airlock his father and Carlos were doing something to the hatch that had apparently just fallen off.

Jimmy shook himself and forced a lucid thought out of the cotton wadding in his head. Fallen off? The hatch wouldn't fall off. They must have taken it off on purpose. Maybe they were going to use it for a big bullet. He couldn't guess anymore. He'd never imagined all the bizarre jury-rigging they'd done in the past few hours, or the strange ways they'd found to use seemingly ordinary things that were lying around. When he first came down, he'd have sworn the hold was barren of anything that could be used in a fight, yet here they were, hours after the first deadly attack, still alive, still picking their way forward, and they'd even managed a couple of counterattacks.

Maybe not enough, but it was something.

"Jim," Robert said, "stay with her. I'm going to help your dad if I can."

Jimmy scooted a little closer to Veronica and said, "Yes, sir."

In a moment he and Veronica were alone. She was trying to turn her head, to look at him now that the captain was gone.

Sensing that she needed a human face to cling to, Jimmy moved even closer and leaned over her, no matter how it squeezed his heart to have to look at her damaged face.

"Hi," he began.

She whispered back, "Hi."

When she smiled at him, he almost choked. "I'm . . . I'm really sorry . . ."

That was all he could get out before his throat knotted up.

"Oh," she murmured slowly, "they'll fix me. One arm . . . one eye . . . just call me Admiral Nelson."

He frowned. "Who?"

Picking back through endless classes he'd sworn were too boring to commit to memory, he sifted out the lesson about events in history that changed history. If this hadn't happened, that never would have. If so-and-so hadn't been decisive, or had lived two years longer, or had given up when he lost that battle or that argument, or that arm or that eye . . .

"Yeah," he uttered, "Horatio Nelson! I remember that! The ship—my dad wanted to take me to see that ship of his. It's still sitting in cement in England! God, I remember that—"

"Classic navy," she said. "He was . . . always my inspiration . . . at the Academy. You know . . . one arm."

"That's right," Jimmy breathed. "He lost an arm in a battle at sea. And then he lost an eye, and he still commanded the whole British fleet. Hey!" He snapped his fingers. "Trafalgar, right?"

"Right," she gurgled. She drew several long, even breaths, mercifully dazed by the medication, but wasn't fighting what the suit was doing for her.

"I can't believe I remember that," he went on, fixing his eyes on the medical cartridges but seeing something else. "I failed the stupid test . . . how come I'm remembering it now?"

"'Cuz you need to," she said. "Makes all the difference."

She pulled the answer out as easily as drawing a business card—as though she kept it handy in the emotional survival kit she'd built for herself.

She licked her swollen lips again. "Did you get to see it?"

Jimmy came back to the present abruptly. "See what?"

"The *Victory?*"

"Oh," he uttered. "No, we never made it. Kind of a . . . busy summer that year."

"Maybe we'll go sometime," she said.

He shook off the self-embattlement and forced himself to look squarely at her. "If I have anything to do with it," he said, "we sure will."

Her sore mouth tugged into a smile again, and her whisper had a tiny, courageous lilt.

"Hey . . . something to live for!"

So much bravery in such a weak noise. The steel rod of it went through Jimmy, and he clung to it and determined that it would straighten his spine and that the fear would be backpocketed from now on.

Used to thinking of himself as the only person bearing a load, he was suddenly aware of the banging and creaking behind him as his father worked to save them all. There wasn't anything in his father or in any of the others that was concern for themselves. He had blamed his father for this tragedy, for the deaths of the engineers, and been completely wrong to do that. These were Starfleet people and they all knew their chances of dying in space. They were doing what they believed was best and right, death or not.

*All these other people—they left their families too. Maybe he thought that was normal . . . or worth it . . . all he saw around him were Starfleet people doing the same thing.*

Jimmy knotted his fists, and relived the awful lesson that things he said didn't necessarily go away thirty seconds later and he couldn't do damage control on whatever popped out of his mouth when he wanted a fast sting.

*You got me into it.*

"I'll apologize," he muttered, eyes wide and fixed again on the survival cartridges.

Veronica blinked her one dilated eye at him. "Mmmm?"

"I'll find the time," he said. "There's gotta still be time—there's gotta be a couple seconds. I'll get him alone for a couple seconds and just say it."

"Jimmy, come here for a minute."

His father's voice was a trumpet out of the night, and suddenly Jimmy couldn't wait to do anything they asked him to do—anything. They needed him! They needed his help! He still had a chance.

He spattered an insensible phrase to Veronica, and she uttered back that he should go without worrying about her, and he was on his feet, scrambling his way forward to where the three men were huddled under the open companionway.

"What can I do?" he asked.

Robert April took hold of Jimmy by an elbow and said, "It won't be easy, my boy."

"That's fine," Jimmy shot back. "I'll do anything."

Hearing that seemed to disturb them more than reassure them. Just as he was wondering what to do about that, his father sighed and said, "Well, okay . . . Carlos, explain it to him."

Obviously on edge, he gestured with the screwdriver in his hand at the hatch they were just now reattaching to the bottom of the companionway, and he busied himself working on it. His lips flattened with effort and his elbow went up and down as he put his strength into what he was doing.

Carlos faced Jimmy and pointed up at the companionway. "This tube is airtight, and it's detachable for easy maintenance. We're almost done jury-rigging a portable life-support system—I don't guess you need to know all the details . . . but it's kind of a lifeboat now. Kind of an escape pod. We hooked up an automatic SOS beacon, and emergency flares. We also attached several little candlepower thrusters which we pulled off the docking directionals of this hold we're in. I'm trying to get them to work."

"They'll work," George ground out with determination.

"I think so. It'll be a decent lifeboat if we can just find a way to clamp that respiratory support unit onto the regulators."

"There's got to be some way to do it."

Carlos turned back to Jimmy. "The *Enterprise* should be back in this sector in about thirty hours, and they should be able to pick up the beacon—"

"You're sending me out?" Jimmy choked. "You're ejecting me in that thing?"

"It's your best chance to survive," Robert said sedately. "You'll have to accept the chance, my boy."

Frantic that they didn't understand, Jimmy said, "Oh, I'll do it! I'll bring them back for the rest of you! I can do it!"

He almost bounced on the hope of it. Finally—something he could do right!

Then he paused in the middle of his excitement and jabbed a finger upward. "But what about those outlaws? Are you going to be able to hold them off till I get back?"

Nobody answered him.

He looked at Robert, then Carlos, then back again at Robert. Why weren't they answering?

The captain seemed thinner and emotionally drained, his brows moving like soft caterpillars, his maple-sugar hair glittering with metallic dust under one of the meager utility lights that was still working. He looked at George, eyes full of something that only George Kirk could decide, commander or not.

Only then did Jimmy notice that the cranking of the screwdriver had stopped in the middle of a crank.

His father was kneeling there under the hatch on one knee, elbow up, where it had stopped, the glow from that same little light turning his hair a dirty terra-cotta, and he was looking at Robert from underneath that arm. He resembled a bad boy who'd been caught breaking into the toy chest.

The arm went down. His shoulders sagged. He tapped the palm of his bruised hand with the screwdriver and struggled through some inner argument with himself.

Then he said, "Tell him the truth."

Senses suddenly on fire, Jimmy started to pull away. His shoulder bumped an open panel and stopped him. "No . . ."

"They're pulling us into the Blue Zone, Jim," Robert said. "We've barely two hours before we're swallowed up."

"After we eject you in the airlock," Carlos said, "we'll flush the impulse drive with any power we've got left and blow off the aft end and slam forward through their tractor beam right into that ship. The explosion'll take care of them." He tipped his head toward the outside, where their attackers chugged relentlessly through space. "And us too."

"No—" Jimmy repeated. "I can—I can bring the starship back!"

"There won't be time," his father said. "As soon as they pull us into the Blue Zone, we're all dead anyway."

Robert nodded and patted Jimmy's shoulder. "It'll be your job to advise Starfleet of what's happened here."

Seeing the protest rise on his son's face, George went on. "We're going to do what we have to do. As soon as you're out of range, we'll blow the aft end, ram into that ship, and demolish them so they don't have a chance to throw another tractor on you. We'll all go up and that'll be that. At least they won't do this to anyone else." He stopped, took a harsh breath, collected himself, and added, "You'll understand someday."

Jimmy stood before them with his mouth gaping and nothing coming out of it. Thoughts clogged his head, excuses, arguments, defiances—

But nothing that would make any sense.

Two hours. The *Enterprise* coming back in thirty.

As soon as they entered that Blue Zone, they were dead. Even if they managed to launch him in the airlock, the others were still dead. Captain April, Lieutenant Florida, Dad . . . Veronica, who had already paid her price . . .

He licked his lips and could almost taste the nobility with which the others were facing death for his sake. His sense of obligation started to scream. If anyone should sacrifice, it should be him. He was the only one who hadn't given anything yet.

Forcing himself not to stammer, he asked, "Why don't you send Captain April? He's got a better chance than I do. He knows more about—"

"Jimmy, we don't have time for this," George said. "You're just going to have to do what I say."

He stuffed an O-2 canister into Jimmy's hand.

Standing there holding the canister, Jimmy squinted at him. What had just happened?

There was something seriously different about his father's voice. A no-kidding difference. A this-is-it difference.

"We'll be ready in about five minutes," Robert said, steering Jimmy away. "You go and get into a pressure suit. You'll need to have it on as a backup. Go ahead . . . see if you can't get used to the idea, eh?"

Just like that. Get used to it?

He stood a few steps away, holding the canister in one hand and nothing in the other, without a clue what to say to make the situation any better.

Someone handed him a pressure suit—he didn't even notice who. Limb by limb he pulled it on, staring mostly at the deck.

The others were back to work, as though they'd just told him he was going to have to be late for team wrestling practice.

"I still need a clamp."

"Where are those vise-grips Veronica was using earlier?"

"Welded into the wall, holding the ship together."

"What about the other ones?"

"In the walls."

"Damn."

"Gentlemen, there must be one last bit of resourcefulness left between us to hold this in place, surely."

"Can't we tape it into place? Medical tape, maybe?"

"Wouldn't hold. The unit vibrates."

"Maybe it can free-float."

"I wouldn't trust it. One bump, and it could start leaking. Cut his survival time in half."

"There's gotta be something left. There's *gotta* be something."

"Sir . . . sir . . ."

Out of the jumble of voices Jimmy found himself roused by the weakest one. He spun around, and saw Veronica blinking at them from across the deck, where she lay in the puffy white spacesuit.

Surprisingly, it was George who pushed his way past the others, past Jim, and knelt at her side.

"Yeah, honey? What do you need?"

"Use my hand," she said weakly. "You know . . . as a clamp."

George gazed at her.

Not four feet away, the disembodied prosthetic hand lay on the deck in the puddle of pink fluid, looking pasty but too human, right down to the end of the wrist, where the attachment cowl showed its synthetic muscles and connections still partly attached to the torn-off piece of her forearm. The fingers were still spread in that position of shock and surprise, reminding them all of what Veronica must have felt as the coolant blew over half her body. The ring finger was even twitching a little.

No one else moved.

Veronica seemed to sense the reluctance, and she was ready. She blinked up at George.

"It's just a tool," she murmured. "Let me help save him."

A few feet away, listening, Jimmy Kirk grew up ten years in ten seconds.

He watched as his father flattened his lips in a regretful excuse for a grin, brushed Veronica Hall's bangs out of her remaining eye, then made very little ceremony about doing what she asked. He simply reached over her, scooped the prosthetic hand from the deck, shook the pink fluid and torn muscle tissue off, and got up.

"Good suggestion, Ensign," he said.

"Thank you, sir," she gurgled up at him. "He's . . . a good shipmate."

George nodded awkwardly—the moment was very hard for him, hard for them all. Then he hurried toward the airlock.

As he passed, he took Jimmy's arm.

"Come on, pal. Let's do this."

Carlos Florida strained to point into the two-foot-diameter airlock at what he was talking about, without crowding his student out entirely.

"You've got these little candlepower thrusters here, here . . . there, and up there. They swivel, like this. I've got them set to steer you away from the trinary and back toward the spacelanes. Here's the light. Sorry there isn't any more than that. It's on a very small battery, but I know nobody likes to sit in the dark. Up there is the observation window. It's narrow, but it goes all the way around, although I don't know what you're going to have to look at. On the bottom left is your SOS attachment. It'll automatically broadcast on subspace, and you don't even have to touch it. We couldn't get it to fit very well, so try to not bump it or anything. Somebody'll spot you easy. The *Enterprise,* or somebody. Think you understand everything? The SOS? The flares? The distress signals? And how to alter your course?"

Carlos wrapped up his crash course in survival, and couldn't keep his emotions from bumping up against a touch of pride that they'd managed to do this.

Unable to speak as his own throat dried up, Jimmy managed a nod. He knelt there at the bottom of the airlock, holding his survival helmet, all the lessons about how to work it still floating loose in his brain. Pull it on, yank this latch, it'll automatically attach itself to the suit's cowl, the airlock could rupture, the suit'll offer another ten hours of such-and-such. The whole contraption, airlock, suit, and all, the whole plan wasn't exactly foolproof. The whole thing assumed their attackers were too damaged to throw another tractor beam on the airlock as it puffed merrily away from the scene of their crime.

Carlos fidgeted. All these things were going through his head too.

"Now, you realize . . . could be days before anybody spots your signal . . . right?"

Obviously he was afraid a sixteen-year-old who'd never been hungry might not understand.

Determined to make him feel better, Jimmy said, "Well, you know how teenagers are always trying to get time alone."

There was some ballast in seeing that Carlos seemed reassured. "Wish you luck," Carlos said. He offered a handshake. "You're a good shipmate, Jim."

The handshake was surprisingly soulful in this chilly, struggling environment.

Jimmy started to point to Veronica and stammered, "That's what she—"

He cut himself off and just returned the handshake as warmheartedly as he could, not wanting to diminish Carlos's compliment. He was absolutely set on not complaining or arguing or saying the wrong thing, or doing more than he already had to make anybody feel bad.

That effort almost twisted his neck off as they led him to the airlock and prepared the vaultlike panels that would come down just before the airlock could be detached.

As Carlos and George worked on the vault panels, Robert April collected Jimmy to one side and plied him with that soft-spirited gaze.

"Best of British luck, old fellow," the captain said. "Brace up, be stalwart. Just do your job, no questions . . . it's all that's asked of a member of the crew, eh?"

Jimmy cleared his throat and said, "Yes, sir . . . I'll do my best."

"That's the spirit."

Dauntlessly, Robert didn't make a scene in spite of the sensibilities bubbling on his face. He offered an emboldening handshake, just as Carlos had, then patted Jimmy's hand once he got hold of it.

"Proud to have had you aboard, my boy," he said. "You've been a good shipmate."

Jimmy couldn't manage to respond. Was there something about that phrase?

Or maybe just the idea . . .

Shame chewed at his ankles. What if they were just being nice to him so he wouldn't feel bad that they were all going to die for him?

Worst of all was the half-truth. He sure hadn't started out to be a very good shipmate. Suddenly all he wanted was to *really* be one.

"Panels are set, sir," Carlos said from the port side.

George nodded and simply said, "Thanks." Then he motioned Jimmy toward the airlock hatch.

The others left father and son to do this alone.

Typically a man to whom tender moments were faux pas waiting to happen, George Kirk simply pressed his lips tight, furrowed his brow, and when the right words eluded him yet again, called upon the simplest ones.

The two stood simply looking, as though trying to memorize each other's face.

He swallowed, parted his lips, and said, "I just want one thing."

Jimmy squinted in empathy, shrugged, and uttered, "Guess I can handle one thing."

George blinked at the floor, then found whatever he needed inside himself to look up again.

"Promise you won't watch."

As though caught in two nets, neither moved. The sound rolled and rolled. The idea haunted their imaginations.

Then George added, "I'm sorry, son."

A sound of pain. The words hurt him, simple or not. The pain showed in his face.

Helplessly, he motioned Jimmy up into the companionway.

Perhaps a kind of shock took over; there would never be a satisfactory compilation of the emotions gripping either of them at that moment, but Jimmy found himself up inside the tube, where there was room to turn around, but not much more. The ladder had been padded into a kind of cot, and he was lying on it, wondering how the longest hours of his life suddenly seemed to have flashed by. Wasn't he going to get a few more minutes? He needed only a couple more—

Below, George reached up, rubbed his son's knee the way he used to when little Jimmy was afraid at night.

He tried to speak, but couldn't.

Jimmy gazed back at him from the top of the tube.

Then someone said something. Robert April's priestly voice. The captain's hand came into the picture, and George stepped away.

His father's face . . . the last thing Jimmy saw before the hatch bumped closed and the vault panels were drawn to make the hold safe once the airlock was blown.

That was it. That was the difference! The new thing he heard in his father's voice—a tone that said they would never see each other again. The past no longer mattered, because now there was no future for them together.

In the nearly dark tube, lit only by two small orange backup lights, Jimmy touched the inner skin of the airlock. "Dad?"

They couldn't hear him. They were right out there, inches away, but they couldn't hear him. The airlock was soundproof, airtight—

"Dad?" he said again, louder.

*"I'm sorry, son . . . I'm sorry, son."*

Jimmy stared at the tiny thruster switches and the blinking lights. Right, left, up, down, reverse. Like a child's toy.

He stared and stared.

For the first time in his life he saw a true choice of paths—and he had his hands on the controls.

# TWENTY

☆

"They're launching something!"

"You're spacesick. That's a research cutter. How can they have anything to launch?"

"You come and see for yourself, then."

Big Rex took a long time to hoist himself from his seat and appear at Lou Caskie's side and shove him away so they could both see the secondary screen. The crackly main viewer in front of the command station was now showing only a corner of the Starfleet ship, enough to prove it was still being pulled along behind them.

The little viewer, clearer than the main one, showed a little blue and silver tube slowly moving on its own.

Big Rex squinted at the frosty screen. "Maybe it's another SOS buoy. Split the main screen and stick it up there."

Caskie swore at his controls as he pecked and pulled at them. The main screen fizzed, flashed, then divided to show a poor view of the ejected tube over the partial view of the cutter.

"How big is it?" Roy craned his neck and called from where he was feverishly trying to restore their shields.

Caskie shrugged his knobby shoulders. "Size of a coffin."

"Oh, that's all," Big Rex said. "They're giving themselves a funeral!"

Laughter rolled around the dark helm area.

217

Behind Big Rex and Caskie, the Andorian engineer and a handful of the crew from below decks had come up to watch the win—a kind of tradition among thieves—and now they laughed and shook each other's hands. Big Rex's body wobbled like a pile of water balloons as he chuckled his way back to his command seat.

Behind them all, Roy hunkered at the deflector auxiliary, tight-lipped with sequestered rage. Progressive stupidity had allowed them to damage their prize, and now he had to get the shields back before they could go into the Blue Zone and finish wrecking it. Just to survive. That was all they'd get out of this one.

If these fools had listened to him, they'd have hulled the Starfleet cutter in several small places with a surgical laser, let the crew die, then collected their "salvage." Instead, the morons were laughing and backslapping each other and celebrating a disaster as though they'd won something.

But this. This.

Pushing his moment of control further and further into the future, just as he had drawn it to his fingertips.

Keep the goal in mind. Do whatever it requires. Tolerate anyone.

He felt the future ticking. This Starfleet cutter must have been a supply ship for Faramond. Nobody would come out here just to look at a couple of stars immolating each other. They were going to poke around Faramond with the rest of those archaeological bughunters. They thought they were just looking for artifacts and small cultural revelations from an old civilization.

How long before one of the fools found out what he had found out?

A race against time and chance, but a race that he could run just so fast. Maybe a year. Maybe six months. Everyone would get out of his way.

He crawled out from where he was working, unfolded his legs, and looked past the back of his father's fleshy neck at the viewscreen.

"Hit it with the laser," somebody from the crew said.

"Coolants are blown," the Andorian engineer said. "All we can do to make the tractor work."

Lou Caskie dabbed at the open cut on his head from the buckshot hits they'd taken before. "Why don't we dump the cutter and suck on that little thing? They're dead in space anyway. Ain't going nowhere."

"Even a rabbit can smell a trap," Roy spoke up. Contempt dripped from his tone. "They could want us to bring it on board."

Before his father could snap an insult, a skeletal human from the crew, whose name Roy didn't even know, blurted, "A bomb? You mean it's a bomb?"

Roy lifted one shoulder. "I might do it if I were them." Then he eyed the mob he was reluctantly running with, and added, "Considering."

"Let's push it away, then!" The bony man twisted around, looking from one to the other of the crew, trying to find somebody to agree with him.

"If it's an SOS," Big Rex said, "they could be wanting us to push it away for them."

"That's right," Roy said.

He enjoyed how everyone stared at him, surprised. Defending his father? Ah, to keep them guessing, to remain unpredictable—a good game.

"They hit our coolants," he added. "They know we have tractors but no lasers."

Their cook, a mask-faced, pug-nosed Tellarite, asked, "How do they know?"

Roy's delight fizzled. He glared at the Tellarite and spelled out, "Are we shooting at them?"

The Tellarite blinked around, trying to see through his receded eyes, which Tellarites couldn't do very well, and was typically insulted just by being answered in some other way than he wanted, but said nothing else. He was new enough in the crew that he hadn't started an argument yet, though he and the Klingon had been spitting at each other so much, the rest of the crew wouldn't even walk between them unless they had their backs to each other.

"If it's a bomb," Big Rex went on, "it'll just blow up out in space. If it's an SOS, it would take fifty years just to get out of the solar system on those tiny thrusters. They're betting we'll get nervous and spin it out of the area and do their job for 'em." He hunkered down and glared at the split screen. "Why don't we have a backup tractor beam?"

"Why use up time and power?" Dazzo rumbled from the port side controls. "We never needed backup tractors before. We attack only one thing at a time."

Big Rex slumped forward, shook his head, and complained, "Can't you measles ever think ahead?"

Staying where nobody could hear him, Roy arched his aching back. "Question answers itself."

When nothing happened in the next few seconds and that small blue and silver tube just puffed and turned on the split screen, their unappointed new leader shoved out of his chair and lumbered toward the aft of the bridge, one eye on the forward screen as he made his decision.

"We'll be in the Blue before that little turd gets ten thousand miles out. It'll be a hundred years before anybody stumbles on a pea pod that size in a sector this wide." He waved his sausage-thick fingers at the screen and added, "Just let it float away. You slugs get back to work. We've got a sucking mess to repair all over this crate. We'll go back and blow that thing up later."

He hoisted himself to the upper gallery, where his sparse hair brushed the ceiling and made him feel taller than he was wide for a change.

There, he stopped.

He glared at his son's face.

At the grayish eyes of a woman he'd sworn he would forget. At the tag-along hatreds he'd run away from.

Suspicion, which to Rex was the same as knowing, had told him his son had manipulated him into killing Burgoyne. In an odd way, he was proud. He'd have had to ax Burgoyne sooner or later anyway. The ponytail had just provided the right excuse.

*If he wasn't my own kid, I'd be scared of him.*

Roy was glaring back in that silence he did so well. The kind that whined in everybody's ears. That said he was thinking about whoever he was looking at. Making decisions. Judgments. Plans. Calling them names in his head.

Big Rex balanced most of his considerable weight on one foot.

Sweat tracked his wide face in two places. Acrimony crusted his warning.

"You can stay right there," he said. "We don't need your help."

The airlock turned slowly. The tiny thrusters alternately puffed and then shut off, seeking their prerecorded heading.

Through the clear band of unbreakable aluminum that made a window, a boy's eyes creased.

As his tiny metal prison turned in space, he lay on his back against the padding, arms down, fingers closed on the sides of the ladder so hard that his hands were cramping. How far away would he have to be before his father would blow the cutter into a million pieces?

Were they waiting until he was on the other side of the cutter, so the explosion would push him in the right direction—away from the Blue Zone and toward the spacelanes?

The thoughts were ugly, unavoidable, and persistent. He didn't expect to see beauty ever again.

Yet there it was.

It came to get him as his tube stopped turning and found its course.

Came even in the middle of tragedy. A savage beauty, but a beauty he could finally see. Glazed fire in space, pearly in the centers, licking outward at each other, then braiding and twisting toward a common center.

His lips tugged apart, and he breathed, "Wow . . ."

The trinary.

The hungry neutron star pulled and sucked at its two companions, and would keep on even after its witnesses were long gone.

In the core of crisis, Jimmy discovered in himself the ability to pause for a few seconds, suspend all worries, and appreciate beauty.

Better to have had those few seconds, in case things didn't work out.

"I'll remember," he whispered. "Dad, I see it now . . ."

He stared at the gorgeous fire of the trinary and wanted desperately to tell somebody. He didn't want to have his father die without knowing that his son finally *saw*.

He didn't want to have his father die. Period.

The first time, he had run back home and cowered on Earth and in his unconnected, irrational fourteen-year-old mind had blamed his father for his having to see what happened on Tarsus.

Now he was two years older, and this time he felt different about what was happening. He'd once thought all his growing up was done, except for getting a little taller. He'd seen an execution, so he'd seen it all. He'd seen space. There wasn't anything more. Go back to Earth and act damaged.

But this time he was two years older and knew this was the fault of those pillagers out there and not his father.

Two years, that was all. Two years, and he saw everything differently than the last time. He'd never noticed before today, but he was changing with every month that went by.

What would be the difference between sixteen and eighteen? Eighteen and twenty? How much would he change?

Why had he always admired the pioneers of the American West but not the pioneers of space? Too close, probably. Too familiar with people who'd been there. History tended to make heroism bigger and cleaner.

But it was the same thing. His father and the others—would they retreat? Veronica sure wouldn't. Jim had seen that his father wouldn't. Because they were Starfleet, and this was their reason.

Starfleet smoothing out the rough spots in space, the U.S. Army setting up forts and hammering out the American frontier for the pioneers, the Canadian Mounties—all the forerunners going out in remote areas, into the spines of danger, insisting that even way out there the laws of common decency and individual rights should be adhered to. He realized how easy it had always been for him and his friends to crow about being advanced, but somebody else had gone out before them and taken the big risk, stood up, and demanded that civilization be civilized. They'd gone out and done the hard part of their era. They'd averaged a grave every hundred yards, but the pioneers had never stopped pioneering. They hadn't run home and acted damaged.

Where would humanity be otherwise? If not for the Robert Aprils and George Kirks of Earth's past?

Still shivering in the alleys of Europe, probably.

And here he was, holding a chance to do the hard part of his own era.

What if he'd been two years wiser and two years angrier and had been there to take some wild cowboy action against the executioner on Tarsus?

What would he do today?

"Something, that's what," he said aloud. "I'll be a stampede of one."

He didn't know, and neither had the others known, whether he could survive at all in this tin can, so why waste the chance he might have to change the moment? He'd seen their faces when they told him he'd be all right in here, that it would all hold together. Then they put him in a pressure suit and gave him that kind of handshake that everybody recognizes.

One plus one equaled four of them and one of him, which didn't add up.

"It's not right . . . it's not *right.*"

His own voice buzzed in his ears like something coming over a speaker, but he clung to the sound.

Moving in the cramped space, under the tiny faint lights, with Veronica's disembodied hand clamped onto the respirator unit an inch from his face, he nudged the thrusters and turned his capsule until he could see the ship that had attacked them. He saw its engines. Not so different from any he'd seen before. He knew what engine exhausts looked like, impulse or warp. Those were basically the same anywhere, anytime, any ship.

And being basically the same, *any* engine could build up to explosion . . . especially with a detachable airlock crammed up its back end.

He didn't listen to the little voices shrieking in his head. The voice that made him always protect himself, always consider himself first—he wasn't going to listen anymore. He was ready to give.

In spite of the clumsy work gloves attached to the pressure suit, he got his hands snugly around the thruster controls. This was going to take more than just puffing and turning.

This would take steering and ramming.

"Well, Dad," he uttered, "I promised you I wouldn't watch, and I'm not going to. I'm too busy."

He aimed the capsule as best he could using only his hands and eyes. When he thought he was pointed right and trajectory was right, he fired up all the thrusters.

Suddenly the crawly green and black ship in front of him was very big and getting bigger damned fast.

The engines' exhaust expanded before his eyes as though made of rubber, stretching in all directions. Inside, there was the Hades of violent energy popping and boiling unsteadily. That unsteadiness was the destruction his father had done to their enemies.

Wider, hotter—closer—

Jimmy crammed his eyes shut. He was two years older, yes. But still not old enough to want to watch death coming.

"No! Jimmy! No, no!"

"George!"

Robert April held on to the bigger man and dug his heels into the deck, trying to prevent this unthinkable turn of events from killing the father as well as the son, and called across the darkened hold.

"Carlos! Are you sure?"

Carlos Florida gripped the breadbox-size monitor with both hands as though about to crawl into the screen. "He's turning—he's under power and heading right for their engine exhaust!"

"My God, I gotta stop him!" George bellowed, yanking free and plunging for the gaping exposed machinery in the forward hull.

Robert scraped after him and got him by the arm again. "You can't! You'll tear us apart if you counterthrust that tractor beam! George!"

"Let me go!"

Then Carlos's voice, heavy and beaten, cut right through them both.

"It's gone."

Locked in a grapple, the other two men froze and glared at him—two distinct expressions, the postures of devastation.

"I can't see it anymore," Carlos said. He couldn't look up. "I

can't see it at all . . . might have bounced off and disinte-
grated . . . crashed . . . or it could've gone into their engine core
and—"

The captain cut him off by simply saying, "Carlos."

Carlos let his shoulders sink and dropped the officiality he was
clinging to. "Sorry, sir."

Robert wanted to be in two places at once, but George needed
him more than Carlos did.

George Kirk's face turned almost as red as his uniform. His hand
bit hard into the bent-back hull sheeting, so hard that the ragged
edges cut him. Blood broke between his knuckles, slowly traced his
fingers, then gathered and trailed down the gray metal.

"Why'd he do that?" he gasped. "Why'd he do that . . ."

"For us, I'm afraid," Robert balmed.

As George sank to his knees on the deck, doubled over by
anguish, Robert forced him to loosen his lacerated hands before
permanent damage took over—as if it hadn't already.

George never even felt his hands being cut, or the cuts being
wrapped with gauze. He sat slumped on the deck, filthy with dust
and metal shavings from the drills they'd used to try to save
themselves, and he stared at his own bent knee.

Past it, he saw Veronica's supine form lying in its white survival
suit, mutilated for the sake of Jimmy.

"His mother'll never even know what happened . . ."


"Where the hell is it!" Rex Moss thrust his huge body forward to
the edge of the creaking command seat and bugged his eyes at the
screen. "Where'd it go? Caskie, find out where it went!"

"Got no sensors on that side!"

"It bounced off and fell apart," Dazzo cracked from the port side.
"Sensors are not working on that quarter."

Big Rex twisted against his own bulk. "No viewers? No nothing?
What are you pigs good for?"

"We're so banged up," Caskie said, "beats me we can move at
all."

"Keep looking for it."

"How? A little thing like that?"

Dazzo backed off from his controls a step and kicked the housing. "Half our sensors down and no shields! How can we tell you where it went?"

"I'm the captain," Rex said. "I ask, you find the answers."

"Captain the sensors back on line, then."

"Drop dead."

He stood up. Not a castaway task.

The forward viewscreen was his enemy. He stared it down. His voice was smoke.

"I'm done putting up with this bullshit," he said. "Screw the Blue Zone. Get me some engine power and let's turn this crate around."

Caskie and the Klingon both turned, glowered at the unexpected order, and didn't move to follow it. Caskie asked, "What're you gonna do?"

Sour red and yellow lights cloisonnéd Rex's domineering mass in the center of the control room.

"I'm gonna do what I should've done in the first place," he said. "I'm gonna put the construction claw on those suckers, rip the sheets off their hull, and kill 'em all right now."

"Jimmy, what were you thinking . . ."

Unshrouded agony pressed George Kirk to where he sat on the deck and held him down. His surly talent for digesting the unthinkable almost immediately betrayed him this time just by existing.

No shock. Just raw, unpadded devastation.

At his side, demanding composure of himself, Robert April labored through his own grief, clutched to the core by the sound of his friend's misery.

He arranged himself off his aching knee and sat down beside George, against the tilted wall.

"Jimmy didn't want to watch the game from the bench," he said pacifically. "He knew we meant to sacrifice ourselves for him and for any who might stumble this way in the future. He's the same blood and thunder as you are . . . a prodigality you should be proud of tonight." He swallowed dryly and added, "We must be proud of them both tonight."

Together he and George gazed across the dim hold at the white spacesuit and the motionless girl whose face was fortuitously turned away from them. Her chest moved up and down in carefully regulated shallow respiration.

At least she wasn't awake to know what had happened to Jimmy, to know that her sacrifice had been for nothing.

Across the deck, Carlos Florida looked also, then turned away and huddled even closer to his monitors, doing a job that a few small hours ago had been Jimmy's.

The hold divided into private places.

Robert allowed himself a cemetery sigh. "He knew Veronica risked her life for him, and perhaps hoped to return the gesture. At least he believed he did that much. Our two young people . . . both valiant under fire."

"Both dead," George trembled out. "Like us."

His face felt like shriveled fruit. Pain drummed behind his eyes, and around his heart, which his son had thought was made of marble.

Robert let his own throbbing head drop back against the hull wall. A ruddy British pink appled his cheeks, and his otter-brown eyes filled with warm esteem.

"When an officer disobeys direct orders for the sake of his crew, he's either hanged . . . or promoted. That's because of the character of decisions made in the unkind arbiter of the field. Jimmy chose to march into a cannon's mouth on our behalf. And he knew we could see it all happening . . . perhaps he left a message for you in his final defiance. He wanted to show you that he'd learned what you brought him here to learn."

Despite the timbre of his words, his Coventry accent painted a quiet English lane for them to stroll, made sparrows sing where there were only sparks, made a lake with reeds where there was only puddled lubricant, and flew flags where there was no wind.

"You understand, don't you, George?" Robert hoped. Salient emotion rose on his face, drew him through a half-dozen expressions, any one of which might have been a tearstain upon a letter home. He turned and pliantly gripped his old friend's hand, in spite of bandages, in spite of blood, to put to flesh the precious thing for which a boy had sacrificed himself. "He was thinking like a man."

# TWENTY-ONE

☆

He tensed. He waited for it. Wondered if it would hurt much.

*Brrrraaackkk—*

Were all the superstitions and wishful thinking right? Was there life after death? If he opened his eyes, would he see heaven?

*With my record? Better keep the eyes closed.*

He'd felt the strike, the airlock hitting the enemy ship, felt the muscles of metal give, then the jolt of hitting something tougher than the thing he was in, and a sudden stop. No sound other than the shriek of his tiny, pressurized tomb as it was crammed beyond its capacity to withstand. Just a hard hit, and a hard stop.

He opened one eye.

And found himself alive.

That didn't make any sense. How could he still be alive inside a big hot engine?

There was only one answer to that. So he opened the other eye and looked around.

Both boots smashed against the inside of his tube.

"A garbage dump!" he grated. "I killed myself in a garbage dump!"

Looked like a junkyard with walls. Except that the piles of junk were strapped to the walls and the floor and the ceiling with elastic straps and industrial webbing, and anything else that could hold it. His voice rang bitter and ugly in his ears.

"Great job. Now we know what legends are made of."

Another failure. He'd failed *again.*

He grumbled at himself, giving himself a sound to cling to, and a sense that maybe he wasn't as terrified as his insides were telling him. He was cold and realized he was trembling within his survival suit, his spine straight and locked, his legs the same. Hard to breathe . . . his chest hurt.

He'd missed somehow! Missed the engine exhaust entirely, and smashed through one of the gashes in the ship. Probably one his own father had put in this ship with his buckshot trick. Through his narrow viewband he could barely see the ragged edge of torn metal and shredded insulation and layered hull material, now a colorful mess like a club sandwich with a big bite taken out of it and the mustard leaking.

Now what?

Color—there was some light in here.

Jimmy craned his neck and spotted two small intermittent docking lights or maybe loading lights, both yellow, both blinking sluggishly. Between them, they made some light most of the time.

That was why the hull insulation looked like mustard. Yellow lights.

*Hsssssssss*

Jimmy heard it—but only for a few seconds. The sound was fading away. The sound of leakage.

The tube! Leaking!

He scrambled for his helmet. Hadn't even bothered to put it on—he hadn't needed a helmet on to go blow himself up.

Where was it? Mounted behind his head. Right. He cranked backward, arching his spine, which ached and told him how tense he'd been until now, how tense he still was. Clumsily he pulled the helmet on and yanked the thing Carlos had pointed to. The cowl activated itself instantly with an airy *thok,* and the suit sucked tight on his body. All at once he had oxygen-rich air to breathe and a sensation of lightheadedness. Pressurized.

Now what?

They were going to barge in here, find him trapped inside a stupid-looking cocoon, and they were going to slaughter him.

"Well, they're not gonna kill me in here," he snapped. He

pounded the viewport material and shouted, "You're not gonna kill me in here!"

Was there a way out from the inside? There hadn't been much to work with. What if there were no way out? They'd be down here any second—

He looked up at the vault hatch. No handle. The original had been cannibalized for the propulsion unit—there hadn't been anything left to make another one. He tried to bend, but there was no way for him to reach the bottom hatch. With boots on, he had no way to pull the latch off its housing with his feet.

That meant . . . no way to get out.

The pirates were on their way down, and he was a sitting duck!

In anguish he hammered his fists against the sides of what could very well be his coffin, even now—and his right knuckles bumped what felt like flesh. It startled him, and he looked. Beside his face, valiantly clamping the respiration unit, was Veronica's pale hand. Yellow lights from out there buttered the skin. The crafted finger-nails looked like hers. Unpainted and slightly tattered. The fingers were long-boned and waxy, knuckles pronounced and a little pink.

"Okay, all right," Jimmy huffed.

Even with gloves on he was bothered by the idea of touching the hand. If it hadn't been attached to a friend once, things might be different.

He forced himself to grab the bare wrist. Lubricant squirted back on his glove and he flinched, but didn't let go. Holding the wrist with one hand, he reached inside the open end with his other fingers and tried to find whatever mechanism made the limb work like a real hand. There had to be something mechanical. It couldn't all be computer signals. Somewhere inside, there had to be strings that acted like muscles and a structure that pretended to be bones and joints. He had to find those—fast.

"Uch . . . oh, this is sweet . . ." He winced as though it were his own hand being violated. "Sorry, sorry, sorry—"

All at once the hand unclamped, fingers flying as though startled, muscle reaction thrust it backward into Jimmy's face shield, and he batted it off in a childish reflex action, then barely managed to catch it before it got knocked to the other end of the tube, where he couldn't reach. That would be too stupid. Then he'd have to kill himself again just to avoid letting the story get around.

Bending upward, he arranged the hand's fingers on the housing where the vault latch had been taken off, then stuck his own wet, gloved fingers back inside the wrist and hunted awkwardly for those contracting muscles. A moment later, the strong mechanism so daintily disguised as a woman's hand was doing a great imitation of a pipe wrench.

"Please hold, that's all," Jimmy muttered as he grasped the wrist firmly with both hands. "One, two . . ."

He cranked hard. The delicate-looking hand held, but so did the latch housing. Sweat broke on his face. He kept cranking, his legs braced against the inside of the tube until he thought he was breaking his own kneecaps. His teeth grated fiercely, but he didn't stop. More and more muscles in his body knotted against the strain. He had to get out. He had to. Any minute they could come in and hit him with a laser. If he could get out, he might still die, but he wouldn't die idle.

His arms suddenly flew sideways as though he'd thrown a punch at a bad dream and missed. His entire body twisted, and half his muscles pulled. There was fluid on his face mask.

The latch! It was down!

Without pausing, he put his shoulder to the vault hatch and shoved—

And found himself flying across the open area, right into a pile of garbage.

Then he bounced off that pile and flew sideways into another pile, then a wall, then caught himself with one hand on a parted-out tail fin from some kind of atmospheric aircraft.

He hovered there, panting, sweating inside the suit, gathering his wits, trying to figure out what had just happened. Across the open area he saw his tube, stuck halfway through a horrible gash in the skin of this ship.

"Weightless," he gasped. "Why didn't I think of that? Why don't I *think* of things?"

Made sense. Why waste energy putting gravity and pressure in a storage deck used for storing salvage? This way, all they'd have to do was open those big segmented folding doors over there and swallow up any ship they . . .

Suddenly his arbitrary analysis turned deeply personal. Resentment surfaced, and anger came close under. Anger made him determined.

He let himself be angry. It was easier than being afraid and made him want to do something.

Trying to assess where he was, he forced himself to calm down, to breathe deeply and slowly in spite of the claustrophobia of being inside a helmet, and to look around.

On two sides of the big, dirty, cluttered area were stenciled the words TRUNK DECK. Clear enough. Below that were handwritten numbers on a board, the words *LOAD DRAFT, HEATED CARGO AREA,* and the letters *L. D. P.*

Familiar words, but didn't apply to what was being stored there. This might once have been a Federation loading deck, though nothing around indicated Starfleet. Probably an Earth merchant vessel. Probably old.

Old, and full to the gills with parts of hulks, whole engines, entire computer cores and pieces of others, struts, sheeting, ribs, rolled insulation, small warp nacelles from little interstellar ships, generators, jacketing, coils, frames, shield grids—almost anything, in no particular order, most of it broken.

So his father was right. This was a salvage ship that attacked ships, wrecked them, killed the crews, and thereby created its own salvage for a melting-down market with no questions.

All around the trunk deck was the evidence. Jimmy pulled himself slowly along the industrial webbing, and discovered a tragic gallery opening beneath him.

Pieces of vessels, torn apart so they couldn't be identified, huddled against each other, cold and shamed, stolen from the dignity of transportation and shoved into the realm of contraband.

Jimmy touched the ripped side of a personnel transport—he knew that's what it was because there were two windows still in it and a bolt where a seat had once been attached. A seat where a living person had been sitting. A seat where terror had gotten somebody by the throat.

He turned above the blackened, scorched transport section and floated to the other side of it, and there he held himself still for a moment, his heart beating in his throat.

Blood was smeared across the broken part. Some of it was just a grotesque spray. The rest was even more gripping, for it was smeared into letters, drawn by a human finger.

HELP    SOS    ATTACKED    OR- ROS    AX-8
DEC 4    HELP

Jimmy shuddered and sucked his breath as though he'd run a mile. The reality of danger and the violence around him plunged back on him and made him cold again. This was real blood. The blood of a slaughtered crewman. Maybe a family member . . . a mother, a child, a father. It was all they'd possessed with which to write a message no one would ever be able to answer. December 4. Which year?

No year. Of course not. Nobody would put a year on an SOS. Whoever they were, they'd hoped to live longer than another month.

Nauseated, haunted by thoughts of what he'd been wasting his time doing back in December, Jimmy dug deep through regurgitating fear for that anger he'd had a few minutes ago. He needed it.

With his gloved hand he touched the long-frozen, crusted plea for help, and drew the anger from there, from the blood of those he hadn't been there for. Maybe all they'd needed was a quarrelsome plain dealer with a good right hook.

They'd needed him, or his dad.

They handed him their hope and their strength through the connection of crusted blood. He hovered there and got angrier and angrier, adding their loss to those he'd already endured. He would need this rage to get out of the trunk deck and do something for his own people that had come too late for these.

In his heart he made a promise to the blood people. They were part of his crew now, and they hadn't died for nothing.

Through his anger came another sensation. One that filled him up, one that helped. If only he had been there for those others, he could have changed everything. He was glad he could be there for his father and his friends, and suddenly wanted to be there for any who came after. A glimmer of why they had all come to space, why Starfleet was here at all, expanding like crazy, flashed in his head, and warmed him up fast.

In fact, he was hot now. Good and hot.

Hot to get at the targets of his anger—the foul lowlifes who didn't even have enough dignity to wipe up the blood of their victims.

He could still change everything! He had a chance to survive! If he did things right, maybe they could all survive! Dammit, they could all still live—he might still have the chance to make everything up to his father, make it up to his mother, tell them what a jerk he'd been . . . go back to Tom Beauvais and Quentin and Zack and Emily and all the others, and tell them everything, go back and show the whole world that he wasn't an idiot after all! He had to survive, and he had to make sure his father survived.

But the Blue Zone burned too close. The cutter was going to be blown up any second.

He pushed himself off with a snap of aggravation, and determined that if he didn't find a door, he'd chew his way right through the wall and teach these scavenging maggots a lesson.

There it was.

His way out. A man-size vault door, a big version of the hatch on his tube. A conventional airlock—a way out.

With a shove he flew off the plundered pile and back past his tube, where he caught hold long enough to retrieve Veronica's prosthetic hand from the hatch housing. He wasn't going to leave any part of her in this dump, and if possible he was going to give the hand back to her. This sorry excuse for a voyage wasn't going to cost her any more than it already had.

Tucking the hand into the straps that would ordinarily be used for tools, he yanked a jagged piece off an unidentifiable piece of junk and swung it like a bat a few times. He now had a weapon.

"That'll work," he breathed.

It would have to work. They must be waiting for him to come out. They must not have pressure suits, so they were waiting outside that airlock for him to come dodging through.

Preparing himself for the street fight of all street fights, he shoved off again for the vault door.

Expecting trouble with the door, he got a surprise when the thing

234

opened with a simple one-two-three combination that was right on the wall beside it. Apparently these pirates didn't expect problems down here. Probably they'd just never thought about it.

Jimmy paused, glowering inwardly, his eyes tightening to crescents.

"I can use that . . . I can *use* it. There's got to be a way to use that."

There was only one of him. He couldn't punch them each in the face—well, he *could*—but there had to be a better, smarter way. He decided to start collecting anything these guys didn't think enough about.

It had no pressure, but there was gravity activated in the airlock. He knew, because he stepped through the vault door and fell flat on his butt. His weapon clunked over his shin, and he found out it was doggoned heavy.

He sat on the floor of the airlock, gasping and trying to remember what it was like to weigh this much. He hadn't felt his normal weight since the laser attack. This was like dropping onto the dock after being stranded in water for a day.

With arms heavy as iron bars, he crawled to the trunk deck hatch and put what felt like tremendous effort into yanking it shut. The gaskets compressed, and he hauled down on the locking handle. One down.

On hands and knees he turned around, pulling his weapon along with him, and crawled the four feet to the inner vault door that he hoped led to a pressurized deck or a corridor and not out into some ripped-open section. This ship was almost salvage bait itself, thanks to Dad and Captain April.

He hesitated. Once he opened that door, he'd have to be ready to fight. There had to be somebody out there, setting a trap, and here he was with bricks for arms and legs.

He struggled to his feet, then lifted his jagged piece of metal into swinging position.

"What the hell," he grumbled. "Been dead once already."

Feeling as though there were a buffalo corpse on his back, he got a one-handed grip on the other hatch handle—a bolt of shock went through him when the handle snapped down and the gaskets expanded!

"What the hell—" he gasped.

Open! The vault door was open! Why hadn't it waited for him to tap in the open signal?

He looked accusatorily back at the other airlock door. Why hadn't the safeties come on? One hatch open should automatically prevent the other from being opened without proper pressurization. Any decent airlock had double and triple backups! At the very least, both doors wouldn't be allowed to open at the same time. He could just walk back there and open up that trunk deck door, and *whooosh*—depressurization. The whole section of the ship would collapse on itself.

Either this ship was busted up bad, or these jerkweeds didn't even bother with safeties on their airlocks.

Shivers numbed Jimmy's arms, and he called these guys names in his head. He knew the type a lot more intimately than he wanted to recall right now. He could too easily look back, not very far, and hear himself saying, "Forget the safeties. Who needs 'em? We know what we're doing."

*Rules exist for a reason.*

*Authorized use only.*

With his hands on the heavy white latch handle, Jimmy closed his eyes for a moment, drew a steadying breath, and demanded of himself that he not forget.

He shoved the flat of his upper arm against the vault door, raised his jagged bat, pushed—

And spilled himself out into a dimly lit corridor, legs spread, weapon back, and yelling, "Hah!"

Holding his breath as he waited to be hit by a guard or caught in a trap, he looked from side to side.

Nothing. Not a thing. Nobody.

No safeties. No warning lights. No red alert. Big ship, little tube, no pressurization backups, no shields, no alarms. No organized damage control, nobody here to attack him . . .

The revelation went up like a flare.

"I don't believe it!" he choked. "They don't even realize I'm here!"

Possibilities spun in his head. This was a whole new game all of a sudden, with new rules.

This meant he could make setbacks for them, provide unseen chances for his own team. He could be *tricky*. His dad and Captain April would figure out ways to take advantage . . . sure they would!

As long as they didn't blow themselves up or get dragged into the Blue Zone before he could do something—he suddenly had double the chance.

*The stupid pisspots don't even know I'm here! Don't do anything, Dad! Don't blow up the cutter! I'm working! I'm working!*

He started thinking ahead. What could he do for his team if they did get dragged in? He'd have to be ready for that.

A click, and his helmet dropped to the black deck. He glanced one way, then the other. A triangular corridor with a black floor of some kind of hard rubber, ribbed with red structural members whose padding was sparse and worn, and lit from a single long panel in the bottom of each section. Some of the panels were flickering. Some were completely dark.

"It's going to get a lot darker," Jimmy promised through gritted teeth. "These pigs got a hundred-sixty-pound worm in their apple now."

Cradling Veronica's disembodied hand to his chest, he picked a direction and ran off down the narrow corridor.

"We're going to do it."

"I beg your pardon?" Robert blinked himself out of his sad reverie about Oxford and Coventry and fishing in the Cotswolds and Jimmy and never being able to show his godson a few simple things before life got too complex. He looked again to his left, at his greatest immediate concern. "Sorry, George?"

George didn't look back at him. He thrust himself up on numb legs and wavered, but there was nothing unsteady in his face.

"We're going to do what we planned to do. We're not going into that Blue Zone. We'll blow the whole sector apart if that's what it takes, but my son's not dying alone out here. We're going with him, and we're taking those black-hearted bastards with us."

He gathered every ounce of fury to push down the grief so he could function, and crossed the deck.

Carlos was lying prone on the deck, his head resting on one outstretched arm as he watched the monitor with reddened eyes.

Kneeling beside him, George touched him and said, "Still with us, pal?"

The other man flinched, glanced at him, regained control over his expression, and sat up. "Oh, yes, sir . . . I'm with you all the way."

Warmed by the devotion on Carlos's face, the willingness to go with him into the fires of hell if that's what he chose as their leader today, George had to swallow a couple of times before he could talk.

"You know what we have to do, right?"

"Yes, sir," Carlos said quietly. "Sure do."

"Want help?"

"No, sir. I think this is one I'd like to do by myself. I don't want to have time to . . . ask myself any questions, if you know what I mean."

Solemnly, George nodded. "Yeah. I know what you mean."

He helped Carlos to his feet and only then noticed that the starship helmsman was still limping.

"You okay?" George asked.

Carlos hesitated, almost answered, then gave him a quirky little smile of all things, and commented, "What difference does it make?"

Something about that smile, without a touch of irony or resentment, made George's own mouth tug upward on one side. "Not much, huh?"

They chuckled briefly, then moved to two different parts of the hold deck.

George joined Robert at Veronica Hall's side. The captain was running his finger pointlessly along the medical cartridges that were trying so hard to keep the body inside alive. Other than her chest moving slightly up and down, there were no signs of life from Veronica now. She was pale and clearly on the edge.

"I was about to change the life-support cartridges," he said, "then I realized . . ."

"Just be glad she's unconscious." George gazed at the girl, let his eyes go out of focus, and thought about Jimmy, who'd been wide awake at the worst moment. His chest squeezed hard.

He felt Robert watching him. They both knew there was nothing more to be said.

They got up and started to walk together, but George paused, looking at Robert.

"Something's wrong," he grumbled.

Robert's brows popped up. "Excuse me?"

"Here." George reached over an open crate and retrieved the Bainin cardigan that was now dusty with insulation fuzz. "Put your sweater on."

"Why?"

"I don't know. Just looks right."

"Oh . . . of course. Thank you, George." The captain winced as George slipped the cardigan over the injured arm and up onto his shoulders.

"There," George said. "That's how I want to—" He made a feeble gesture, but stopped talking, not wanting to sound as if they'd have a chance to remember this. "It just . . . looks right."

But Robert grinned that sentimental grin of his, and took the moment to appreciate that he meant so much to George. He patted George's back as they walked together across the tipped deck.

Carlos Florida sat cross-legged before the open panel where double insulation had been cut away to expose the critical machinery to the engines' reaction-control flow. Though he had his fingers on the mechanisms, he wasn't doing much. Most of the work had already been done and was waiting for them to make that final decision.

He knew George and Robert were behind him, but didn't look up at them.

"All set, Commander," he said. "On your order . . . I'll flush all our power trickles into the impulse system and overload it. They're small engines and they're pretty sick right now, but they've got enough juice to make a nice big boom. All we have to do is point at them and follow their own tractor emission right up to the source." He shrugged, then sighed. "Wish it sounded a little fancier, but I guess . . . ready when you are."

George nodded stiffly. "Thanks, Carlos."

He and Robert retreated into a slow, solemn handshake that lasted a few seconds longer than either intended.

Soft brown thatch on one side, a whip of oxblood red on the

other, one face made of pipe smoke and tweed, the other of hatchets and hammers, brown eyes, both, but not the same. They stood there, the extract of the Federation dream—different people, different goals, different ideas, different styles . . .

Diversity.

Still holding Robert's hand, George put his other palm on Carlos's shoulder.

Simply and firmly, he said, "Blow 'em."

# TWENTY-TWO

☆

Raise hell. Rattle them at every turn. Make them mad. They couldn't think if they were mad.

That was the theory, anyway.

Of course, Jimmy was mad and *he* was still thinking.

Sort of. In a panicky, press-lipped, nose-breathing sort of way.

He had to get as far from the trunk deck as he could without being found. That meant keeping low, ducking past open or broken door panels, not making noise any louder than the bangs and shouts of these sidewinders as they fought to keep their ship in one piece long enough to win.

The amount of damage over here was staggering. A few little Starfleet cowboy tricks, pulled off with rubber bands and finger-nails, had knocked these people on their ears and bashed this ship into a knot of gasping sections. As Jimmy dodged and sneaked and ducked around, half the doors and sections he passed were bolted off and red-flagged for nonentry. Probably breached to open space, or contaminated.

Some of the smoke was rancid and chemical. Some of it was from simple burning. That meant two kinds of damage. If only he knew about chemicals . . . he'd heard engineers and mechanics talking about being able to smell what was wrong, but he'd always figured they were nuts.

He rounded a corner, filled up with conflicting thoughts, and tripped on something big and thick. Before he even realized what had happened, he was lying on his side on the deck, wincing and confused.

Turning over, he found himself staring into a pair of bugged eyes and a mouth open in shock.

Stunned, Jimmy jolted backward, away from the corpse. Human or humanoid—he couldn't even tell. The body was too battered and too burned, stiff and pasty. In death it had released its bowels. He'd heard of that. The smell almost sent him retching.

He held his breath, stumbled to his feet, and ran.

How many were left? How many people were still alive on this ship for him to face? How many thieves were in the den?

Again he wished he had paid better attention at the important times in his life. How many people did a ship this size and type take to run?

"What difference does it make?" he sputtered as he skidded around a corner and paused, glancing back and forth along the groaning walls. "Ten or ten thousand. They're just second-story burglars. Doesn't take any brains."

Even rough and grumbling, his own voice was an anchor line and he hung on to it in spite of the hurricane he'd steered into.

Again he ran through the twisting, smoky corridors, then slowed to a tiptoe stride when he thought he heard voices—too close. Imagination?

No—definitely voices.

And coming closer!

He ducked into a bulkhead crack under the strut that had fallen and cracked it.

Two aliens and two humans ran toward him, involved in their own argument, shouting at each other about repairs and calling each other names while they came closer and closer.

Panting, Jimmy flattened himself behind the shifted strut and tried to get control over his breathing. Didn't want to be heard gulping for air, and wanted to be ready if he had to fight. Behind his strut, as his breathing fought him and his heart throttled against his ribs, Jimmy realized they couldn't possibly miss him. They'd see him, and he'd be dead, just like that.

He balled his fists. Maybe he could just take one of them before—

"Hey!" a voice shot out of the creaking, moaning ship. "You savages, where do you think you're going?"

As Jimmy peeked down the smoky corridor, the four men stopped running at a T-intersection with another corridor and looked down it. The voice was coming from there.

"Why do you care?" one of the men responded.

"I care. Why is none of your business."

The voice materialized into a young man—very young in fact, fairly tall, with brown hair sloppily yanked back into a ponytail. A kid! Hardly much older than Jimmy. Maybe eighteen. Maybe a little more. A kid, barking at these pirates as though he thought they should be listening to him.

"Why won't the tractor beam release?" he demanded of them.

"It's locked on, that's why," one of the thieves said. "Locked on and jammed."

A Tellarite poked a finger up at the kid and snarled, "What difference does it make? Where we go, they go!"

The kid wasn't intimidated. "We're going to come about and smash that ship up right here and now. It's going to be a starboard turn, so get your flabby thighs moving and secure that tractor beam."

One of the humans held out a hand and asked, "Why don't we just turn around and smack 'em?"

The kid cocked a hip, annoyed. "Because our maneuvering thrusters are damaged. We're going to have to push out and come around in a wide arc. Want me to draw a picture for you and your little buddies, McKelvie? I'm going back to the bridge, and you better be ready to recalibrate when I get there. Go on."

Nobody moved. They didn't seem to like taking orders from him.

The kid paused as they stared fiercely at him, then drew a harsh gust of breath and shrieked, "Go . . . *on!*"

Jimmy felt his skin contracting at the kid's tone of voice and the undisguised insane flare in those eyes. The kid wanted to be listened to, was frustrated that the men might not listen, and there was a dangerous intensity about him.

Not in charge . . . but someone to watch.

The four criminals glanced at each other, then two of them about-faced and headed back the way they'd come; one of them went with the kid down the T-angle, and the Tellarite headed toward Jimmy.

A Tellarite. They'd fight at the untying of a present if it wasn't untied their way. Jimmy would have his hands full if he didn't get the jump.

So Jimmy ticked off the paces, then flew out of his hiding place and yanked the broken strut down on top of the stumpy alien. They both went down.

The Tellarite sucked a gasp, reared back, but too late. The strut hit him in his squared chest, and he was pushed down backward. His furry head hit the deck, and he was out before Jimmy could even get back on his feet.

Jimmy scampered to the alien, yanked the Tellarite's braided belt from his thick waist, and wrapped it around the neck. Then he started to twist it, tighter and tighter.

And . . . gritted his teeth, then stopped.

*Kill him, you idiot.*

He tightened the belt again. The unconscious Tellarite started to gurgle through his porkish nose.

"Aw, dammit!" Jimmy thrust the ends of the belt down on the Tellarite's masky face. "I've got no guts!"

Life-or-death situation or not, he pushed off the deck and stood staring down at the unconscious alien, not knowing whether to be proud or ashamed.

Should he waste precious moments tying the Tellarite up and hiding him, since he didn't have the nerve to do what he knew he should? Confused, he grabbed the belt from around the Tellarite's throat—then changed his mind again. There wasn't time.

As soon as they could get this horse and buggy turned around, they were going to kill the Starfleet ship. He didn't have a week to pick off these guys one at a time. He knew he couldn't just run, hide, and run.

Stuffing the leather belt next to Veronica's hand in his shoulder strap, he dashed down the corridor again, deliberately not going in the direction that kid had gone. That was the way to the bridge, and he didn't want to get trapped up where the command center was.

He had to stay down here, in the core of the ship, and *do* something. Hurt these people.

Gas? Poison the air? Kill them all?

"Damn," he snarled. "Why didn't I keep my helmet—"

Starboard turn, starboard turn . . .

His cold hands and the shuddering in his thighs told him he wasn't as ready to die as he thought when he touched the thruster controls in his tube. He'd accidentally lived, and now simple animal fear was ahold of him again when he thought about dying. Funny how nerve could come and go.

On the defensive—hiding—wouldn't do him any good . . . he could stow away all year and it wouldn't help his father and the others. He had to do something, anything, now, before these dirty dogs could act on their plan to slice up the cutter.

Anything. Anything to throw these quarreling animals off their track.

Something his father and Captain April would be able to see on the little screen. Something, something—some—

ENVIRONMENT MAINTENANCE CELL

Gas 'em . . . poison 'em . . . black 'em out somehow . . .

Maybe if he could get in there, an idea would surface that he could live through himself. He had to survive. There were people to talk to and a hand to return.

He scooted across to the environmental cell door. It swung on a full-length metallic hinge, or should have. Stuck, jammed, bent, jarred slightly open—he put his shoulder to it and summoned his strength. The door budged a couple of inches, hinge squawking like an alarm, but then Jimmy was plunging forward. He landed on his forearms and knees on top of the collapsed door inside the garbling, noisy roomful of struggling equipment.

Pain dazed him and he stayed down too long. The survival suit might be happy to keep him breathing out in the vacuum of space, but it sure didn't do anything against bruises. Both elbows throbbed, both knees were jarred, and the outside edge of his hand was lacerated on the ripped hinge. Blood splattered when he shook his hand as though to push away the wound.

Trembling, he rose to his knees and looked. The side of his hand was gashed open the long way. A garnet flow ran down his arm. He was used to blood coming out of the corner of his mouth after a fistfight, or the side of his head after a scrape, or a kneecap after a fall, but not this.

Brash understanding struck him of how slow and gruesome a death could come his way here. He might not get that sudden heroic way out that people would want to write stories about or tell their children. He could die here in a way that nobody ever wanted to describe to a child. If he was having even the tiniest shred of fun or adventure underneath the danger, that shred dissolved now and suddenly.

His heart pounded fiercely. He could feel it in his head, neck, and chest. What looked like a lot of blood was dripping, smearing all over the floor. They'd find him if they saw. He was leaving traces of his presence, his whereabouts—

His heart throttled harder. Breath came in gusts. Do something, do something . . .

He shook his hand again. Blood splattered on the scuffed floor, and spotted the red base of a cylindrical mechanism and the black polymer legs that held the housing in place.

Saucer-shaped. Red. Black . . .

Pressing his cut hand against his thigh to slow the bleeding, Jimmy gathered his wits and crawled closer. Was this what he thought it was?

Looked the same . . . bigger, but in general the same. Even the same colors. Probably contracted by somebody in the Federation.

On the far side was the stenciled word SUPERSTATOR.

Stator, stator, super . . .

"Superconductor!" he blurted out. "Veronica!"

With his good hand he gripped the synthetic hand tucked in his shoulder strap and offered a victorious squeeze.

Smaller stencils said ELECTROPLASMA, CRYON GAS, something about dampers and conduits and wavelengths, and lots of hands-off warnings and maintenance directions.

Veronica's voice tickled his mind—what gravity compensators were for . . . why they needed this during acceleration and deceleration or . . . a turn . . .

"I'm no environmental engineer," he rasped. "Guess I might break something."

All he had to do was *hurt* it.

Lips pressed flat, eyes kinked into knives, he looked around the small room as though suspicious of the walls themselves. He needed something that could hurt.

How long did he have before they turned off the tractor beam and started to turn? What was it Veronica had tried to explain to him about physics and gravity?

For the ship to accelerate or turn, this would have to be working. He had only minutes, or only moments.

As if to taunt and call him, the gravity compensator began to hum, then hum louder. Glaring at it, he gritted his teeth and narrowed his eyes in bitter rage. The turn!

Staggering to his feet suddenly, Jimmy pushed off the floor, slipped on his own blood, but in seconds he had a wall-mounted hand-held emergency fire extinguisher in his grasp.

Simple, basic, easy. A heavy little canister that shot stuff out of it. Hadn't changed in a couple of centuries. Science had come up with a dozen fancy chemical mixtures to put out more fire, faster, with more damage to the flame and less to the thing that was burning, but the stuff inside still had to come out of one end of a canister and come out fast. That meant pressure.

Pressure. Enough of it could keep delicate life-forms alive where they were never meant to live. Too much of it could melt steel into putty. It could save or destroy. Depending on how it was used.

And Jimmy Kirk had a handful of it.

With that and a hatchet, he could save the universe.

A tremor of anticipation almost knocked him off his feet as he stumbled over the collapsed door to the opposite side of the cell.

He needed a tool. Heavy, preferably with an edge.

The best he found was a set of antimagnetic screws. Not enough.

Slumping back against a heating system, Jimmy shuddered and closed his eyes as he dealt with the pain in his hand and both arms. Injuries he hadn't felt happen were starting to surface. His body ached until he couldn't tell the difference between what he was feeling and the constant throb and hum of struggling environmental systems that confused him and clouded his thoughts. Fatigue made him dizzy, demanded that he rest.

No time. He forced himself to his knees again and ignored the aches that twisted down into his calves. There was some way. He had to find it. Or make it.

All he had to do was cut the valve off the top, and he'd have a little rocket.

"Cut it off, or knock it off." He chewed his lip as he fought to keep his head clear. "Where's a rock when you need one?"

He looked around again, and reset his thinking. He wasn't going to get the right tool. He'd have to settle for a wrong one. What he needed right now was a Frenchman with a portable guillotine in his pocket.

There had to be something in there that he could use. Sure couldn't risk tiptoeing all over this ship, hoping to find—

A maintenance dumbwaiter!

With a door that slid upward. A *heavy* door.

Heavy enough?

Jimmy shot across the environment cell again, shoving piled parts aside to reach the wall and the dumbwaiter. It was mechanical, not meant to be hand-hoisted, and so the door was solid as a frontier iron stove.

"Perfect," Jimmy gushed. Ignoring his injured hand, he forced the thick black door up a few inches, enough to cram the fire extinguisher under it and keep it open. The door squawked and moaned as though to complain that it hadn't been used in years. A puff of dust came out and choked him.

He backed off and paused to gather the strength he would need, then used the time to overturn a little portable light stand and rip one of its three legs off.

Leaning the leg against the wall under the dumbwaiter, he ignored his own huffing and puffing and once again put all the power he had into raising the dense door as high as it would go. More dust and cobwebs wheezed out and clouded around him. He coughed, tried to find clear air, then held his breath. Using his shoulder to keep the door up, he struggled to grab the leg—not knock it over and have to do this again—then he crammed the leg under the door. It had to go in at an angle because it was a little too long, but it did keep the door up.

Not for long, though—under so much solid weight, the hollow rod was already bowing under the strain.

That meant he had only seconds more before his own time ran out, as well as his father's.

Confiscating two insulation pads from a tool locker, he dragged them back to the dumbwaiter and put them to one side, where he could reach them. Working so fast his fingers tangled, he positioned the fire extinguisher with the valve facing into the dumbwaiter shaft and the bottom of the canister facing the gravity generator housing. Then he tied one end of the Tellarite's belt around the light stand's leg, and backed off to the other end.

If only he could feel the ship turning . . . but there was only the taunting hum from the stator spinning in its casing. A starboard turn. He had to brace against—that wall over there.

Using one hand, he put the insulation pads up against the wall to his right, the starboard wall, toward the back. He could barely reach the back part of the cell. He'd probably be crushed a few paces in that direction, but it was best he could do.

The stator was still humming. Now it was working for him instead of against him. They were still turning for the kill.

He closed his eyes briefly, then gasped, "One . . . two . . . *three!*"

With both arms he yanked the belt.

The leg shrieked and popped out. The dense door panel came down—yes, just like a guillotine blade—and smashed the valve.

The extinguisher canister jiggled crazily for an instant, then shot across the cell like a missile, spraying a yeasty mist all over the cell and Jimmy.

Flattened against the insulation pads, holding his breath, Jimmy saw the canister hit the gravity casing.

A giant fist hit the ship.

A seizure of raw natural power smacked the vessel bodily in the gut with cyclone force. Its whirlwind outbreak made a mockery of technology and turned the universe into a senseless lather.

Nausea flushed Jimmy a fraction before he was pulled off the wall by a sucking force and propelled across the cell and right out the open door, angled upward toward the corridor ceiling, helpless even to pull his arms and legs forward. Pieces of the ship went with him—anything that wasn't tied down flew for freedom, heedless of its path, or whether or not there even was a path. Bolted-down equipment ripped right off housings and hurtled in the most direct line, smashing through the walls as though everything had been changed into a bullet.

Whatever couldn't smash through was destroyed by the walls. The weaker force was destroyed, whatever it was, alive or not. Sounds of smashing and crashing, breakage, explosion, and screams erupted all around him, but he was caught like a leaf in the cyclone.

The door frame whipped past. All the lighting changed. The corridor wall rushed at his face, struts spreading like the arms of a great black bear.

The last thought Jimmy had was about the physics of a starboard turn, that the wall rushing at him was the one he should be braced against, and how this was a really pointless way to die.

"They're on to us! They're moving off!"

Dripping sweat, Carlos Florida raked a wet hand across his forehead.

"Now, Carlos!" George shouted. "Blow the engines!"

Carlos gritted his teeth and winced as he hit the switch.

Nothing happened.

George shoved past him and slammed the switch with his fist. And again. "What the hell's wrong! What's wrong with it!"

On the small screen before them, the enemy ship was already hundreds of kilometers away and coming around in a wide semi-circle.

Carlos frowned and said, "They're coming about."

"I don't believe this," George groaned.

Despondent, Carlos shook his head gravely. "There must be a leak in our system. The buildup's being purged somewhere. It won't blow up."

George plastered a palm over his eyes and battled the sudden draining weakness that made him lean forward on Carlos and groan. Unfulfilled anticipation sucked the strength from his back and down into his legs and right out the bottom of the cutter. His head sagged and breath came in shallow gusts.

"God," he wheezed. "I can't even commit suicide right. . . ."

This sorrow-sick noise was the voice of the brokenhearted. Worse than the concept of sacrifice and dying for this cause was the prospect of somehow surviving a situation that had taken the life of his youngest son.

Burdened and guilty, driven spiritless by the failure of their final act, he knew none of them would get back the strength to do this a second time. Such resolve was hard to stoke and almost impossible to rekindle. Could he ask of Robert and Carlos to try again?

The enemy ship was racing nearer with every second, and was again practically on top of them. There was no more time, no chance to do anything else.

"They've got us," he murmured. "We've lost."

He felt Robert's hand on his elbow and a squeeze that was meant to be some kind of support or sympathy, but there was nothing to say that would wipe away the fact that they'd failed. From now on, when these criminals attacked any other ship in the future, it would somehow be Commander George Kirk's fault. He and his son and his crew, and his friend Captain April, the founder of the Federation Starship Program, would simply disappear and become a mysterious statistic in the history of space exploration. This area of space would become known as some kind of quicksand, but nobody would know why.

Under his wet palm, Carlos suddenly stiffened. "Look!"

Before their eyes the attack ship buckled against itself in the middle of its swing around, spitting flotsam like an animal vomiting bones. Crystallized air sprayed out of scissures all over, and in other places the hull material caved in even as they were watching. Slits opened up along seams, and some chambers blew open and spewed everything inside.

"Good God!" Robert uttered as they all leaned closer to the little staticky picture. "What on earth—?"

"Right in the middle of a turn!" Carlos choked out. "Their gravity compensation went!"

And a hideous sight it was. The enemy ship spun sickeningly on a point, pocked with holes torn by entire consoles that had come off their mountings and smashed through deck after deck to shoot right out the hull. Whole sections were blown open. Atmosphere sprayed in frozen funnels from a dozen places. Squinting in empathy, they watched the backups shutting off portions of the ship where atmosphere spat. Some funnels puttered and closed off quickly, but others sprayed until the atmosphere in that area simply petered out. The two circumstances looked different somehow to trained eyes . . . one had a little more control than the other in a situation where control was a shabby wish.

Chunks of ship and machinery, tools and parts, food and lamps and boots and bottles, flew outward from the enemy vessel, small, large, and even the grotesque remains of crewmen slaughtered by the impact, some blown out holes while still alive and then torn apart by the vacuum of space, others crushed by flying machinery, then driven through the shattered hulls crammed into open space. Headless bodies, bodiless heads, limbless torsos—all had a sort of expression of horror endemic to living creatures, bodies in a state of surprise, the last second's emotion recognizable by anyone who lived and breathed and saw.

A wild, demonic ship's nightmare. A tempest of physics. A ship with its gravity shut down in the middle of a turn.

"What happened?" George rasped. "What happened to them?"

Robert April closed the few inches between them. "I'll tell you what happened, old boy—"

He coiled an arm around George's shoulders and howled enthusiastically.

"Your *son* happened!"

# TWENTY-THREE

─────────── ☆ ───────────

Klaxons honked obscenely, shrieking what the crew already knew. Alarms demanded attention that wouldn't come soon. Nerve-ripping screams and frantic shouts from below shot up through the crawlways.

"What happened! Caskie! What stopped us!"

"How d'I know?"

Lou Caskie spat broken teeth out of his mouth and fingered his nose and a cheekbone, both broken. Smoke poured from somewhere and nearly blinded him. The bridge stank and the heat was almost unbearable. Through it all he heard Rex badgering him again.

"Ask Okenga, then!"

"I ain't asking him!"

"Why'n hell not?"

"'Cuz he's . . . ask him yourself."

"Aw, Jesus Christ, why can't that blood-sucking yorker stay on those engines, where he belongs! Okenga! Get up off your back, son of a bitch!"

Big Rex Moss stumbled forward, off balance because the deck was hoisted up to nearly a twenty-degree angle, which made him virtually lift his own bulk and pull himself along the destroyed control panels. He skidded on something slick and looked down to curse the flow of lubricant.

253

But it wasn't lubricant under his shoes. It was Okenga's innards.

The Andorian wasn't on his back on the deck. In fact, he was still standing, fitted grotesquely into an indentation in the side-mounted starboard control center, a dent that was form-fitted because his form had crushed it in. Across his lower body lay a three-foot shard of torn computer casing, half of the navigational console torn right out of its base and thrown across the bridge into the consoles on the other side. Only Okenga had been standing there in the way.

He looked sag-eyed at Rex with a perfect opera-house stare, waiting for the music to start. His blue complexion was pasty, stumpy antennae shifting slowly, lips hanging open and oozing fluid, but moving—open, shut, open, shut—as though trying to form a sentence.

The alien reached out toward Rex. Beryl fingers gnawed the air. A plea, an accusation—all this was on his mottled face as it rapidly changed from blue to bleached white. On his hand, tangled in fingers that should have been mending machinery, hung a vine of intestine.

Open, shut, open, shut.

"Christ!" Rex gagged. He staggered backward, away, wagging his hands. "Don't touch me! God!"

The whine of the ship trying to keep itself from falling apart, blowing up, or blowing out smothered his shouts.

He dragged himself past Caskie to the crawlway, straddled it, and shouted down into the billowing smoke and fumes in the engine room.

"Dazzo! Munkwhite! Smith! Gowan! Get up here! Clear out this junk and get this corpse off the bridge!"

There were no answers. Only howls for help, groaning, panicked accusations, the crashing of broken machinery and whole sections collapsing fifty feet below him.

From the deck, a voice cut through him, quiet and stable.

"At least give him a chance to die first."

Purple with rage, Big Rex thrust around to snarl at his son. "If we had those shields, none of this would be happening! We'd be in the Blue by now!"

Lowering his voice, though he was in no position to challenge,

Roy had to ask, "What've my shields got to do with this? The *gravity* went haywire!"

"Find out what happened," Big Rex snarled. "You, boy, you find out. They did something to us! I don't know what and I don't know how, but they did something! They made the gravity turn itself off."

Panting as if he'd run through the ship, Roy pulled up from where he lay with legs curled under him and his knuckles crushed against a spurting vein in his left calf and gave his father a you're-stupid look.

"Gravity doesn't turn itself off," he said. "There's compensation as long as the stator is spinning. Either plasma power has to be cut or the housing has to be ruptured. The power wasn't turned off. The backup compensators are still working, since we have some gravity left, but the main system—"

"What's all that mean?" his father bellowed. "Quit sucking your tail and give me an answer! What does it mean?"

Shuddering under his father's vast shadow and the form that cast it, Roy licked at the salty taste of blood in his mouth before he could answer.

Then he said, "It means we've got a worm."

George Kirk stared at the small screen. His legs were thready, eyes red and moist, his voice heart-pricking.

"He's . . . alive?"

The pathetic whisper wanted desperately to be an answer and not a question, but there simply wasn't enough assurance in it to carry beyond the small sound of a parent's hope. His hands trembled and had nothing to do. He opened and closed them in nervous spasms.

"At least," Carlos said, "he was a minute ago."

The fact struck them all as they pushed for a view of the tiny screen and the sickening picture of the ship.

Robert uttered, "Somewhat of a determinist, isn't he? My Lord, look at it. They must've had a shattering blow . . . perhaps they're ready for a stand-down."

With a taste of irony in his mouth, George complained, "What're you gonna do? Swim over there and say, 'Checkmate'?"

Indulging a passive grin, Robert said, "Wouldn't that be a jolly moment. Well, we can't destroy ourselves in such a way that we would take them with us, and we can't cross the little mile between us and board them, so what can we do? We'll have to reassess the situation, gentlemen, but I warn you, we're still dancing on a hot griddle."

"Sir?" Carlos grunted as he stood up and faced them. "If there's a purge in the power system, that means there's enough coolant left in the system somewhere to keep the failsafes on line so we couldn't overload."

He looked from one to the other of his commanding officers, and knew his analysis hit its mark when Robert strode off a pace or two and muttered, "Oh, dear."

"So," George said, looking at Robert then back at Carlos. "What's that mean?"

Carlos shifted nervously. "Well, it means I might be able to find some electroplasma in the system and funnel it into the cutting torches. I might be able to get you a couple of low-power laser shots. At this distance," he said, pointing at the very close enemy ship on the monitor, "even industrial lasers'll slice that ship in half." Knowing what he was suggesting, he paused then and spoke more quietly, only to George. "If you . . . want to, I mean."

The moment's irreducible weight sat again on George Kirk. He breathed heavily through cracked lips, and stared at the cluttered deck. Wrapped in the thorns of his problem, he felt his two shipmates' sympathetic eyes, but couldn't force himself to look up and meet them.

Cutting lasers at less than two kilometers. It'd kill everybody over there, no question. One last-ditch hair-brained idea. One last chance—again. How many last chances would they get before their deadlock was broken and they started backsliding? How long before somebody else would pay the price?

"Get on it," he said. "Get me a shot before they get their shields back up."

His voice cracked. His expression was heart-melting, crusting over quickly as he summoned his saw-file temper to protect himself. Putting space between himself and the others, he warned them with his posture to leave him alone.

"Aye, sir," Carlos said sadly.

Robert saw the dark wall descending, and stepped across the deck. "George—"

But the other man didn't look at him. Words snapped between them like the crack of a leather whip.

"Don't talk to me, Robert."

The galaxy moaned in the rapture of unconsciousness. Pain misted its stars. Plenty of stars, everywhere.

Vibrations tortured the vessel. A relentless force, wave after wave.

Jimmy swam back to awareness through a contaminated sea. He groped through darkness, stroked for the surface, lungs crying for relief. Salty bubbles clogged his mouth and nose. He moaned aloud and nearly choked, but the sound gave him something to swim toward.

A relentless force held his arms and legs down. His muscles were helpless to do their jobs, and they whined with frustration and effort. Paralyzed?

In a daze, he moved his head from side to side. His tongue worked inside swollen lips. Moisture squished between his teeth.

The bubbling, and the warm, salty taste, was blood. Internal damage. Maybe his lungs. Maybe his face or his head. Why couldn't he feel the pain? He had a moment ago . . . he felt his eyes blinking now, but though vaguely aware of straining lights above him, he couldn't see through a pinkish blur.

Was he blind?

If Veronica could take being ripped in half, then he could take being blind. He made that decision before he even attempted to sit up and account for his injuries. Whatever it was, he would get through it.

As thoughts about Veronica and his father and the others came back, so did the pain.

Nothing to worry about. Dad would take care of it.

The thought bulldozed him. He hadn't had a thought like it for years . . . this idea that he was being taken care of . . . that he was better off than somebody else might be . . . that he owed anyone anything . . .

His chest pounded. He groaned aloud again. The sound pulled him up fast, like being pushed upward out of a grave into the light of consciousness. Lying on hard rubber . . . faint bands of light, in no particular direction. The smoke. The smell—

The corridor. The enemy ship. The gravity compensator!

What a mess he must have made. The whole ship was whining, groaning, hissing spray and smoke from ruptures up and down the adjoining corridors. His chest pounded from inhaling whatever gases and fumes were spitting out.

"God . . . damn . . . was . . . that . . . *stupid* . . ."

He had pinpointed the gravity thing, tried to imagine ahead of time what would happen to the ship, tried to recall everything Veronica had explained to him so that he would get it right, and kept the presence of mind to brace himself against the wall.

"The wrong wall," he sputtered. *New rule . . . always, always, always keep a mental map of your ship. Three dimensions, jackass. Three of them.*

"Wait'll I . . . tell Dad."

Jimmy laughed at himself as he lay there, fighting delirium. He laughed first at his mistake, then laughed again at the anticipation of telling his father, so they could laugh together.

The ship whined beneath him. The ceiling creaked and sounded as if it wanted to cave in on him. He'd done it. He'd hurt them. The confusion was palpable right through the hard rubber deck, and announced itself in a dozen alarms, crackles of shattered machinery, warning whoops, and howls of life-forms in agony.

All around him, the trumpet of destruction proclaimed his win—at least, for the moment.

He'd bought this moment for himself and his shipmates. What could be done with it, he hadn't the slightest clue. His plan hadn't gone into the what-next part of the tourist map.

And he was still flat on his back, gasping. He felt his own weight, so the backup gravity must have come on already. But the ship— he'd made a mess.

Air raked in and out of his damaged innards, each breath a shudder. He felt the stretch of every muscle and the expansion of every rib, then each contraction. The heat here was like a closet in

August. Stuffy, hot, moist. Feeling as though he were being cooked inside his survival suit, he began senselessly clawing at the straps and closures until the suit relaxed its grip on his chest. Without complete awareness of what he was doing, Jimmy clumsily peeled the suit off. He was on hands and knees in drenched off-duty clothes, his head sagging. Blood pushed into his head and rolled him toward blackout again.

Consciousness surged, faded, surged. Jimmy fought to keep it when it surged, and to stay on his hands and knees until the waves passed and he thought he might be able to get up.

The survival suit was puddled under him, a moist, shimmering white rag. In a fold, Veronica's hand waved at him, fingers out and thumb folded in as though showing him the number four. It must have been crushed between his body and the corridor structure when he hit, he figured.

Four . . . four seconds . . . four minutes . . . no, that didn't make any sense. The hand wasn't telling him anything. But did remind him that he was on borrowed time now. These outlaws would struggle to recover from the damage, fight to put themselves and their ship back together, and they would come looking for the saboteur.

Jimmy Kirk, worm in the apple.

He had to move. Get away from here. This was where they'd look first.

Determined not to make the kind of mistakes he'd been making, Jimmy crawled to a crack in the corridor wall sections, dragging his survival suit with him, and stuffed the suit into the crack. He wished he'd had the presence of mind or the experience to have done the same with his helmet. If they found it, they'd know what to look for. He could only hope they wouldn't be looking down in that unpressurized storage section until later. He hoped they wouldn't have time.

As he got to his feet, he recognized the sensation of weighing less than he was used to. That made sense—he'd blitzed their gravity system. Probably relying on partial power, or backups, if these morons had any backups.

Supporting himself on the wall, fighting to ignore the pain in his chest and legs, Jimmy scooped up Veronica's hand and tucked it into the elastic belt of his trousers. At least if they found him, they'd wonder for a minute what kind of mutant they'd picked up.

What the hell . . . maybe it'd give him a moment's advantage.

Flushed with fever, limping, gasping, fighting blurred eyesight and a foggy, thunderous pain in his head, Jimmy struggled down the corridor. He had to get as far as he could from this section of the enemy ship.

He had to hide.

"Dad," he gurgled, "we'll laugh together about this . . . even if it kills me. . . ."

# TWENTY-FOUR

———————— ☆ ————————

"George, turn around."

"I'm serious! Don't talk to me."

Gnawing dread crawled through the hold. The sense of backsliding offered an almost physical pressure.

Not even hotheaded petulance could hide a father's anguish under a commander's responsibility, nor could it disguise the ruptures and fissures of simple human doubt.

George's hands dug hard into the edge of a crate lid. His cheeks were blotched and ruby with heat, his hair clawing his forehead in damp claret thorns. He didn't look up as he felt Robert's unwanted attention and responded with another snap.

"Don't look at me either."

But Robert April was a commander of souls as well as ships, and he wasn't about to turn away from this. He did not, however, come any closer.

Before him, George boiled like stew. His bandaged hands clenched hard and his knuckles went as white as the gauze. His shoulders and ribs constricted within the scarlet Starfleet tunic with such exaggeration that the tunic itself seemed alive and writhing.

A wrong moment. Perhaps the moment would never come right for them, but Robert stepped off to the side, knelt beside Veronica, and consumed the moment by replacing the spent medical cartridges.

The girl was unconscious, pale, and breathing very shallowly. Her face was clammy and cool, her eyebrows slightly raised as though dreaming. The survival suit in its medical-nurse mode struggled visibly to keep her alive, applying doses of whatever was needed to counter losses it read in her body, keeping dabs of silver nitrate on her slaughtered limbs to reduce bleeding. In spite of all that, the right side of the suit was beginning to turn cherry as blood defied effort and soaked slowly through.

As he stood up again, Robert noted that Carlos was deep inside the mechanics again, applying himself to his purpose, only his legs showing as he attempted to follow an order that had them all by the throat.

There would be no good time, so he turned again to the surging lava.

"You're not thinking, George."

"That's a lie," the crust shifted. George pushed off and paced the length of the hold.

Robert watched him but made no attempt to close him in. Seconds ticked away. Both men were barbed with awareness of each other.

"There's only one way out of some things," George finally said. "We've got a responsibility to people who come after us. If it were anybody else on that ship—"

"It's not anybody else," Robert said forthrightly. "It's your son. No one would ask you to do this."

"We're not sure he's alive."

"We're fairly sure. Don't ask more of yourself than anyone else would ask of you."

"I don't have a choice."

Passively, Robert repeated, "No one expects you to kill your own son. It's not part of the oath."

"Yes, it is."

"No . . . it's not. Now, listen to me."

"I can't listen to you, goddammit! These people are dangerous! They've killed before and they'll kill again if we don't stop them now. If that gravity slam didn't kill Jimmy, they've probably found him by now—how long do you think they'll let him stay alive on their ship? I can't make this decision based on . . . on a guess."

His throat almost twisted apart with the emotion surging through it. The words came out skinned and raw.

Robert pushed his hands into his cardigan pockets as though to supplement the tension with a dose of calm. "You're over-compensating, my friend. If he weren't your son, you'd be clearer-headed. You're trying too hard to go by the book—"

George wrenched around, one hand out in a bitter plea, his brows knotted into a single copper pipe.

"What do you want me to do? Let those bastards live because I *hope* Jimmy's still alive? What if he *is* alive? You want me to leave him over there and ignore what they might do to him? Torture him? Murder him? We don't know who or what's driving that ship! They could be slave traders! They could be cannibals!"

"George, stop that kind of talk!"

"Why are you making this hard on me? You know I'm right!" A bandaged fist slammed into the hold wall, and way down the deck made Carlos's legs flinch. "If I could, I'd stand in front of them myself, and you know it!"

"I do know it, yes."

"Then don't get in my way. Carlos, what've you got?"

From the wall, the answer was "Maybe one blast, maybe a third power, sir. This close . . . it'll do the job."

Robert shook his head slowly, firmly, and moved closer. "George, you'll have to pay attention. If it were me over there or if it were a stranger, you'd consider another option. You're not allowing yourself that. Your judgment's clouded. You're not even giving Jimmy the consideration you would give a stranger."

"Don't you get it?" George jammed a finger toward open space. "He's probably dead! One of those"—he couldn't say the words, but waved his hand frantically—"was probably him!"

"We don't have those facts. We're guessing. You're so aware it's your boy that you're afraid of making a decision based on that fact. You're afraid others might die in the future, but we're not liable for the future at moments like this. You must make yourself understand, George. Some junctures have no precedent to call upon. We have to make one to fit—"

"Fine! *You* invent how we're going to get across the mile of vacuum between us and them! Out of all of outer space we've got this one little mile, and we can't do anything about it except fire at them!"

The subject was shifting, becoming confused, garbled. Science and physics were sneaking in where Robert didn't want them. He lowered his voice to a tone that said he wasn't going to argue.

"No, George," he said gravely. "Jimmy's not only your son. He's an underage civilian who swore no oaths of risk or enlisted with reasonable perspective. He's not Starfleet. You can't apply the same articles to him. As your commander, I'm not letting you sacrifice an innocent civilian, and as your friend . . . I'm not letting you kill your son."

"Carlos! Get the laser on line and bring us around to firing position!"

The exhausted helm engineer crawled out of his hole, sat sweating on the deck, and looked with dismay at them both. He'd heard it all, of course. He looked from his captain to his commander, then back again.

"Carlos," Robert overruled, "get the laser on line, but there will be no firing yet."

George spun at him and whined, "Don't put him in the middle! That's not—what—what're you doing? What kind of behavior is that?"

"Mine, I s'pose."

"This isn't a joke!"

"Believe me, I am *not* joking." True to his words, Robert was uncommonly grim as he lowered his chin to schoolmaster level and added, "It's not up for debate."

Undeniable plangency gave weight to his tone, his years of experience rising as they rarely did even at such times. His eyes were utterly still.

Astounded and speechless at what he was hearing, George gawked at him.

Only after seconds of disbelief, he stammered. "Are you . . . are you pulling rank on me?"

"That's right. Sorry."

It seemed absurd, with Robert standing there on a cocked hip, hands pocketed in the much-beleaguered Irish sweater, the cream wool collar bunched up around the back of his neck and his brown hair just brushing it. His natural probity stood behind him like an army of trees that refused the storm. He might as well have been standing on a reedy shoreline holding a fishing pole, saying "sorry" for having put the wrong bait in his creel.

Battling astonishment, eyes ringed and glaring, George shook with frustration.

"You—you don't have any right!" he breathed. "There's no regulation that lets you take command at this point!"

"I don't care about that."

"I'm not injured, I'm not irrational, I'm not—"

"Regardless," Robert said. "You can keep command, but you simply may not make this decision. I won't allow it."

George aimed a shoulder at him and mocked, "What're you gonna do? Duke it out with me?"

"We're not *doing* it, George. Find another option."

The grist of their problem gurgled and broiled, and refused to be dismissed. The worst of all moral dilemmas crushed in on them from two directions. Not a right and a wrong, but two wrongs. Kill Jimmy, or leave him to these people to kill him and chance these criminals killing others in the future.

Two terrible options, knocking up against each other, both relying on guesses and hopes.

Now what?

Soulsore, George cranked away from the others and found a corner. There were no rules to fit this situation. The rules that did exist were inadequate to the grave emotions and plagues on him now.

"Captain!" Carlos called suddenly. "The energy readings—"

He was squinting through the dimness at the monitors on the floor.

"Yes?" Robert asked, turning. "What is it?"

"The sensor screen, sir! Third from the right. I think their shields are starting to go back up!"

A lead ball landed in the pit of every stomach. If those shields were going up—

George plowed out of the shadows. "Fire! Fire, Carlos!"

"No!" Robert challenged. "I told you, we're not doing it."

Carlos had his arms inside the wall, hands on the connections to make a laser bolt happen for them, but he looked back and forth at them, baffled.

"I said fire!" George called.

Robert was damningly calm. "Absolutely not."

"Sirs, their shields are activating!" Carlos cried. "I've got to know for sure what to do! We've got just a second!"

"It's not for you to decide!" George bellowed down at him. "This isn't gonna happen to anyone else! You're under my command here!"

"No, Carlos," Robert said, "you're not."

"Oh, God," Carlos moaned. "Please . . . I . . . I can't—"

George rounded on the captain. "I told you I don't want him in the middle! You don't put your crew in the middle of something like this!"

"There is no middle," Robert reminded sternly. "We're not firing to destroy a ship where an innocent child has been captured. I'm not doing it. Nor are you."

Sweat pouring down his face from the effort of the decision itself, George panted out a savage frustration. It had to be now—now or—

"That's it," Carlos said, crawling to the row of monitors and tampering until he was sure of what he saw. "Yeah, that's it," he sighed. "They've got a higher level of screening back on line than we've got laser power. Wouldn't do any good to fire on them now, even with full torches. We just . . . waited too long." He looked up at them both. "Sorry, sirs."

Lips pressed like two parts of an iron pot, George glowered at him, then at Robert. His eyes could have lit matches.

Hounded by the loss of a chance, he gestured at Carlos, glared at Robert, flopped his arms in anger, and stormed farther away from them, all the way to the other end of the hold again.

No matter how many simulations Starfleet gave its trainees, they never had to kill more than numbers going up and down on a chart. Training told *what* to do, but never could say whether a person had the mettle to actually do it.

Robert saw that unfortunate kink in the noble armor right before his eyes today. Here with him was a man who had the mettle, and whom fate would test if allowed. Now they had lost their chance to know which was the better answer.

To prevent fate from getting its way, Robert had stepped in, and now they might never know. He had learned a long time ago that he could turn comets if he stepped at the proper moment. Even if the comet was about to self-immolate.

He glanced back and tactfully said, "Carlos, see what you can do about rerouting what you had there and gathering us a little maneuverability, as long as we've found some power in the system."

Uneasy, Carlos hesitated, and grumbled, "Aye, sir."

He drew a couple of weak breaths, then disappeared inside the wall again.

That element taken care of, authority in place for the moment, Robert strolled across the deck to where he was trying to mix oil and water in a very hot caldron.

With that truepenny candidness glowing in his eyes, he leaned one elbow on a crate, hands still balled in his pockets, and hoped the subservient position would give him a tad of an edge as he gazed at the man he had just shot down.

"George . . . please try to understand. We're not merely commentators to how life and law will be in space," he said. "There are no precedents, because we're the ones out here first, making them." A humane pause gave a lift to his condolence before he softly added, "That's why you don't know what to do."

Seconds broiled past in silence.

Anxiety chewed at them both, each feeling at some distance the soldierly stoutheartedness of the other, yet neither able to give in, until George found it in himself to speak the most bitter sentence he had ever tasted in his own mouth.

"I *did* know what to do," he ground out. "I managed to make the hardest decision of my life . . . and you stopped me."

# TWENTY-FIVE

☆

He pressed his cheek to the quivering metal and wept with joy. The metal moaned and shuddered as though responding to his nearness and his touch.

Beneath his outstretched body, the ship was staggering, limping, dazed, but *his* part was right again. They had come back to him and were ready to give again. Joy came back, because his personhood was knitted to these coils and conductors.

"Oh, my shields . . . my shields . . ."

Tears broke from Roy's closed eyes and dripped the few inches to the deck he lay upon, and he murmured senseless blessings to his machines for their coming back to life. He had suckled and cooed them back, in spite of the invertebrates around him and their weak-minded shilly-shallying, in spite of the victims fighting back this time and the worm in the ship.

His guardian angels were back. His Blue guardians that made his future surge and swell. He would have all these jugsuckers indebted to him someday. Soon—months, perhaps weeks. They would all rely upon him and speak well to him and call him "sir." There would be shameless extravagance of gratitude to him.

He felt tired in his mind. Tired of somebody else being in charge his whole life.

"I'll get it," he whispered.

The deflector mechanism hummed softly back at him as it

268

pressed into his cheek. He heard a corresponding velvet bip-bip-bip, and knew the beautiful blue light on the control panel above was going on, off, on, off, its activity proof that there were shields again. This was the only beauty on the bridge of the *Shark.*

The *Shark.* As if this was one ship, and not a stitched-together Frankenstein without a soul. That's why nobody knew for sure what the ship looked like—because it was constantly changing, weekly added to or subtracted from, built upon or repaired. None of their victims had survived so far, and even if they had, there would be no describing the *Shark,* because the looks of the ship kept changing.

So his shields had to keep changing. Bigger, smaller, angled beam fragments, intensified here, reduced there. And no one knew how to make it work but him.

"You can get what I need," he murmured. "We'll have a reputation of our own. Our destiny will arrive."

"Who you talking to, tail?"

Big Rex's bark bit off the moment of adoration. His vast form loomed overhead, carrying with it its own smell and a corona of heat. "Don't you know how freakish it looks to other people when you talk to the scrap? There's always been something wrong with you. Swear I'd pay to fix it if I knew what it was."

He backed away, since he was too big to turn in this cramped section of the bridge, then lumbered away on his tree stumps.

Roy ticked off the paces until he was safe, then grumbled, "Devotion on the hoof."

Having his father in charge had rallied him the resentful silence of the others, but not the respect he coveted. No one seemed to realize that his shields were the only reason they could hide and pounce as they had, make careers for themselves rather than shoveling manure on some subsidized colony, which was where most of them belonged. They *knew* his special delicate deflectors were their lifeline, yet they didn't quite *realize* how heavily they already relied on him.

Nothing else had gone right this trip, and they were back to relying on him, whether they knew it or not. The ship was stumbling around, blown open in a dozen spots, a third of the crew dead or dying on the deck. They were back to relying on him and his shields to pull the Starfleet cutter into the Blue Zone and crush it.

They should realize their dependence. He shouldn't have to tell them. He shouldn't always have to remind them, "It's all because of me, and only because of me."

The words buzzed on the end of his tongue day after day, and especially at moments like this, when he could still sniff the essence of Big Rex lingering on his own clothes like smoke. He'd stopped saying it out loud long ago. Ever since he was fourteen he'd said it, then somebody would hit him. So he stopped saying it aloud.

Five years . . .

He lowered again to his task, his body stretched out on the deck as he shouldered his way deeper under the cracked and chipped control panel, and parted his lips against the cool, murmuring deflector mechanism.

"Sooner or later," he whispered, "we'll convince them they can't survive without us. They won't have any choice. It's on our calendar . . . it's fate. It's destiny." A squint through damage haze showed him the sweaty, stubbly rolls of his father's neck. "He'll learn. Even he can learn. We'll convince him . . . to let *me* be in charge."

Pure common sense, after all. At barely nineteen, he had more intellect and better brains than any ten of these others. They just didn't know brains from beans, or they'd put him in charge right now. Everywhere, it was like that. Recognition. That's all he needed. The whole Federation would be indebted to him someday.

"It's on my calendar," he murmured, and turned back to his fine-tuning.

"Shut up, I said!" Rex glared at him with one eye, because he couldn't turn all the way around in the command chair. The eye was glistening grotesquely in the bad light from the main viewscreen, on which the ravaged Starfleet cutter hung helpless. A handful of other men on the bridge twitched when he waved at them also and blared, "Keep working!"

Lou Caskie interrupted as he appeared in the open crawlway and cried, "We found blood!"

Coming up the rest of the way, he showed Big Rex a piece of shattered plastic with blood splattered diagonally across it.

"We found it in the E-cell. He was there! The main stator casing has a hole in it!"

"Can you patch up the hole?" Big Rex asked.

"Well, yah, but all we got is backup gravity, backup respir—"

"Do it, then. If you can't live on backup, get out of space."

Behind them, the voice of aggravated youth clipped, "There was a hole?"

The two antitheses turned to him. "Said that, didn't I?" Caskie lisped at him.

"No weapon," Roy muttered. "What kind of blood is it?"

"Who cares?" Big Rex huffed.

"Maybe it's his," Caskie bug-eyed, then laughed, showing where some of his teeth had been knocked out—the ones he'd had at the start of this, at least.

"Go retch," Roy snapped back as he got to his feet and tried to see through the stinking tendrils of smoke. "Is it red?"

"Red," his father said, "pink, green, who gives a rat's ass."

"Dark red?"

"Here!" Big Rex held the plastic out at him. "You wanna lick it and see what it tastes like too?"

Roy screwed his brows together, looking at the splatters. "Red . . . dark red."

Caskie gurgled another laugh, but Big Rex paused. "Mean something to you?"

Straightening his tortured back muscles, Roy paused too, enjoyed the moment, and let it go on as long as he could. When he spoke, he did so in such a way as to make theatrical use of the curling haze and the silence on the bridge.

"It means," he said, "we're looking for . . . a human."

Big Rex threw his arms up. "Well, goddamn! Think of that! We're looking for a human! And to think we've got only thirty-nine people on board and only thirty of 'em are human! Why, hell, why didn't we think of that! What were the odds! I'm surprised enough to shoot my cookies! Damn, boy, damn."

Burning under the sarcasm, Roy felt his face go hot. The other workers paused, and were looking at him.

He shifted uneasily, bitterness rising in his mouth.

"It means we can flush him out," he attempted. "We know what air he needs to breathe, and how often he needs to eat, and what will kill him."

The strategic line of thinking didn't impress Big Rex at all. "If we were a shipload of Tholians, that might do some good. What do you want me to do? Let all the oxygen out and see who chokes? That's great."

"It's great," Roy responded, "considering there are only sixteen of the thirty-nine left on their feet since you took command. Don't you even know your manpower numbers?"

Heavy silence erupted and held them all hostage for a few seconds—the terrible kind of silence that says throats are being held the hard way.

Lou Caskie backed off a few steps, just in case. The other crew barely breathed. Some were poised in the middle of carrying a part or twisting a bolt, but they had stopped and were watching to see whose orders they'd be taking ten minutes from now. On this ship—ten minutes was about average.

But Big Rex only glared at his son for a beat, then said, "Thanks for telling me. Couldn't keep your mouth shut, could you? Had to blare it all over that we're down. Yeah, boy, that's command material. I ought to just step aside, eh? Hand the old crown on down. People used to say you were a smart little kid. I'd like to have 'em here now and let 'em listen."

Roy flinched so violently that the clipping tool in his hand bit his thigh and drew blood from the big muscle.

Human blood.

The pain gave him purpose.

"I'll find him," he said. "I'll find him and show you."

The hand-held tracer wasn't exactly state-of-the-art, but it had been confiscated from one of the less sophisticated ships they'd plundered a year ago, and he'd been tampering with it. He had it set to pinpoint blood of the type found in the E-cell, and project the find visually on a small screen, with the blood showing up as green on the black and white screen. Worked fairly well.

Well enough, since he hadn't showed anyone else how to use the tracer and they'd all have to tell him he was smart for knowing how to track a chemical compound.

He looked forward to that. If it didn't come today, it would come months from now, when he took over and they thought back on these events. Sooner or later, it would come.

He moved one step at a time through the ship, having started at the place where the worm had done the sabotage. Not easy—the crew were already repairing the G-stator, stomping their big fat feet all over the traces of evidence. Good thing he'd gotten there in time to get a big enough sample for his tracer to read.

Then he found lots more of the same blood anyway, out in the corridor. The tracer lay in his palm, happily displaying chartreuse smears. The worm had taken a pounding out there. Caught in his own gravity trick.

Roy snickered and enjoyed, thought about how he would have avoided the same mistake, then turn his tracer on the corridors. Three directions, one at a time—

There was a dot. Very small, but very green. Roy followed it.

No weapon, and injured. So the worm would want to stay low, probably the bowels of the ship. Probably engineering. Clever enough to use the fire extinguisher to smash the stator housing, but not smart enough to hide the pressure suit helmet they'd found outside the trunk deck. Forward thinking only.

That meant . . . more destruction. The same trick twice, that's what people with forward-only thinking would do. Not a takeover attempt, or a capture or a trap, but destruction. Physical damage to stall the ship. What this worm had done once, this worm would try to do again. *What* would he try to damage?

Engineering.

Roy licked his lips with anticipation and let his logic guide him to choose the right corridors when there was no dot, no smear of blood for his tracer to pick up. His intellect served him, as always. Where there were expanses with no blood, he would aim for engineering, and ultimately there would be a dot or a streak of green, and he would know he was right.

The bowels of the ship. That's where a saboteur who had no weapon would go. Wounded too. Time might be a factor, weakness, fatigue, success the first time . . . all these were elements to consider. Roy had a good time considering them and playing his game of plot and stealth, until it paid off.

He peeked into an eight-inch-diameter porthole in the door of an engineering subroom, and there was his—

A kid? A curly-haired teenager with dirt on his face and a crowbar in his hands, working at ripping and smashing the mechanics in there? A squirrel storing nuts.

"Oh, this is too easy," Roy mouthed in near silence.

Also in silence, he reached sideways to the door panel controls and very quietly turned the locking mechanism. Then he fingered the intercom.

"If you had any brains at all, you'd realize there's no power in there. We already rerouted."

Inside the subroom, Jimmy Kirk slammed backward with shock and dropped his crowbar. It clattered as though to call attention to the smug face in the eight-inch window. He knew that face already. He knew the two wings of brown hair flopping from the middle part. He knew those eyes.

He knew he was sunk.

"Disorderly conduct," the face said snidely. "Just pranks. I realized I could take your one little naughty as a pattern, and it worked. I found you. Here you are, trapped like a bug."

"Who are you!" Jimmy demanded.

"I'm Roy John Moss and I'm about to kill you. Say good-bye."

"Oh, yeah? Well, I'm Jim Kirk and I'm about to spit in your face."

And he did.

Saliva dribbled on the window, mixed with blood, illustrating how it would have gone right into Roy's left eye if he hadn't been cowering behind glass.

Jimmy sheered with satisfaction. He'd seen this Roy flinch when he spat. There wasn't as much confidence on the other side of the wall as the bluff pretended.

Maybe he could stall.

"I had a good time," Jimmy said, and waited to see if curiosity popped up in the face.

Roy frowned. "Doing what?"

"Being a worm in your apple."

"Worm?" Roy shorted. "That's what I called you."

"Guess we think alike."

Roy grimaced with true distaste and muttered, "Oh, go retch. As soon as the engines have enough maneuverability, we're going to pull your pals into the Blue Zone and crush the guts out of them. Then I'm going to open up a solid waste chute and flush you too, maggot."

"Come on in here and we'll see who's about to kill who," Jimmy added. *"You* . . . have picked on the wrong people."

A match flickered in the other young man's eyes. Brown brows closed together.

"Just say good-bye," Roy insisted.

Fear crept in on Jimmy and squeezed his throat shut so he couldn't say anything else. He was trapped, and there was no fixing that fast enough.

The face, Roy John Moss's face, was still steaming up the window, but Jimmy could see the shoulder moving out there and knew Roy was doing something with the controls to this subroom.

When it got hard to breathe, he knew what was being done.

And his pressure suit was gone now. And he'd left his helmet in the back alleys of this ship.

Pressure . . . he felt it now . . . the air was slowly being sucked out of this room.

In his mind he imagined the dial on the side of the wall there, outside the door, and Roy's hand on the dial. It was an old-type mechanism, meant for a medical unit, and made to fit onto this engineering cubicle. So was the door, and the porthole. He could scoop up his crowbar—break the window—then came the realization that a confiscated medical pressure-chamber door wouldn't have a breakable window in it.

Mustering his most defiant expression, he tried not to show how much the effects of depressurization were starting to hurt. His ears popping and crackling . . . his eyes hurting, starting to push out . . . head pounding . . . his lungs crying, expanding . . . like flying too high, too fast . . . it was getting hard . . . to breathe . . .

Black barn doors closed slowly in on his vision. At least he would be unconscious when the truly gruesome part came and his body was blown apart from the inside.

As the blackness engulfed him, he focused through the strip of vision on the face of Roy Moss, and his last thought was to curse himself for having been predictable.

"George?"

"Hmm."

Robert knelt beside his personal thundercloud, but made no such commitment as sitting down, for both their sakes at the moment. Mellowed by his natural Lake District affability, he gazed at George in genuine concern, and tried to read an expression that to a stranger would be simple crankiness served on a slab of crust. Robert knew George Kirk, and knew there was much more going on behind that ruddy face.

Ultimately he asked, "Are you all right?"

George didn't look up. The answer was a rasp. "I guess."

"Awfully quiet, is all."

"Yeah, I'm quiet."

"Any reason?"

"Because there isn't much left to say, Robert."

"Oh, now . . . mustn't pout. Why don't we stop all this crepe-hanging and say our sorries, eh?"

"Because I was right."

The ramrod statement hit hard. Hit them both. Robert's forbearant grin dropped like stone.

After a pause he did sit down, for they were at least back on some common ground.

"Never said you weren't," he offered, and quirked a scolding, amused gaze that didn't really fit the moment, then a sigh of regret to show he knew it didn't fit. "Now, did I?"

"Guess not."

"Listen, old boy, Carlos has a new twist for you. He's found that he can turn on our tractor beam, what's left of it, and in combination with theirs it might pull us closer to that ship out there without their realizing it straight off. We can move in on them slowly. What do you think?"

"How slowly?"

"One to one and a quarter meter per second. We should close the distance between us in roughly—"

"Twenty minutes."

"That's *if* they don't happen to notice our closing in."

"How the hell can they *not* notice?"

"We'll do whatever you want, George," Robert said, "although I'm not certain there are many cards left to draw."

They fell back into the pitiless, unyielding silence neither of them liked. There wasn't anything to like. It wasn't really a lack of words, but a silence of the soul.

"Well?"

"Well, what?"

Robert smiled, though not at ease. "Shall I tell him to do it?"

A half-dozen snide replies flashed on George's face as he ran through childhood tantrums, the strain of puberty, and the ground-work of what it was to be an adult all over again in about four seconds. Maturity forced him to be more resilient than he either felt or looked at the moment.

After an uncomfortable few more seconds he sighed and simply said, "Yeah, tell him to do it."

Relieved, Robert raised his head and waved a hopeless hand at the smoke that still snaked around the hold as though confused by one-third gravity.

"You have the go-ahead, Carlos," he called. "See if we can't get up against them. Perhaps we can find a way to disentangle ourselves from this yet."

"Aye, aye, sir," Carlos called back, then retreated somewhere among the machinery behind the shattered and scattered crates.

So the two of them were alone again, listening to Carlos clacking and tapping back there.

Robert perfectly well knew from experience that there was more than just cantankerousness keeping George silent. Though disturbed, the captain couldn't bring himself to regret his decisions or his actions.

Somehow, he knew, his lack of regret was coming across in his tone, and he tried to curtail it as he turned to his old friend and again tried to douse the burning thatch.

"George," he prodded softly. "George, we've known each other a long while. Your sons are my godsons, our wives have become friends because they both knew they couldn't pry us apart . . . you and I have trod together through passages I wouldn't wish on a pair of geese slotted for a harvest table. Please let's not have this one be our tide level from here on in, eh?"

He waited for a response, but received only blustering cold, so he shifted, wrapped his aching arms around his knees, and tried again, lubricating the moment with that poet's touch he kept in not very tight reserve.

"Oh, don't do this, George," he went on. "You'd have put a staying hand on me as well, had the score been reversed. Isn't it better, after all, to err on the side of caution? Be a bit canny on these things?"

"There's a difference between being canny and being downright tentative," George chopped. "Everybody out in space is somebody's son or daughter. Jimmy's probably dead, and I've accepted that, whether you have or not. If the situation was reversed, I'd be advising you, not taking over, even if sometimes I advise with my fists instead of my head. Advise is different from what you did to me. Everything's different now."

He stood up in a manner clearly abortive, then loomed down at Robert.

"From now on," he finished, "I won't know which decisions you're going to allow me to make. It's dangerous, Robert, damn dangerous. And I don't know what to do about it."

*"Hey, Dad! Got the oars?"*

*"I got oars, I got sandwiches, I got the rods and reels, you name it, I got it. You, me, Sam, the Upper Peninsula, Hiawatha National Forest, canoeing the Millecoquins and a whole lot of places with really old names! What d'you say we hit the skylanes and get there before noon?"*

*"I say go, go, go!"*

*"Get your brother out of his book and let's fly."*

Go, go.

Warm rubber underneath. Fresh water lapping on the canoe's side. Dunes backdropping the fishing trawlers. Then home again. Always home again too soon.

*"Sometimes I think you're all better off without me than with*

278

*me . . . Sometimes I think I can be a better example for the boys at a distance. Sad clowns don't look very good close up. . . . I know I'm rash and brusk—"*

*"And temperamental."*

*"I just admitted that, didn't I?"*

*"And caustic, and unsatisfied, and always on a slow burn—"*

*"Thanks, Winn, I got a faceful of it tonight. I don't need to hear any more from you. I always take care of the three of you, don't I?"*

*"Yes, you do. You always have the boys' best interest in mind. I tell everybody that, George. I can't help it if you take every glance and look from our family and friends and my colleagues as some covert attack. If we didn't live in such a rural place, you wouldn't notice. It's just that almost everybody here is home most of the time—"*

*"And everybody out in space leaves their family to go do what we do out there! When I'm in space, I feel like I should be home. When I'm home, I feel like I'm dumping my duty on somebody else. How come I don't feel right in either place?"*

*"Shhh. The boys'll hear us."*

It was a hot world with cold sheets to lie on. Acrid smells rolled in the air, confusing the nature of dreams and guiding them in wrong directions. Was he at home? Was he canoeing in Michigan?

*Sam? Mom? Dad . . . Dad? Are you there? . . .*

*"Did you see the look on Jimmy's face today? I never saw that look before."*

*"George, you're imagining things."*

*"Like hell I am."*

*"Will you at least keep your voice down?"*

*"What difference does it make now what he hears? He hates my guts, Winn . . . my own son hates my guts."*

Air clogged in his throat.

He choked.

*I don't! Dad! Dad!*

Had he yelled the confession out, or was it still itching in his throat?

*Dad, we're not better off without you—*

Now there were more voices, the voices of strangers, and Jimmy knew he wasn't at home.

279

"He's coming around. Back off."

"What do you drag him around the ship for? Why did you fail to kill him when you had the chance?"

"We need a hostage."

"We need no hostage! We have shields and in minutes we'll have engines again. We'll haul the Fleeters into the Blue Zone and crush their meat."

The venom of contempt dripping through Jimmy's veil made him rouse to reality. The veil was unconsciousness again. He recognized it from the last time. He was still alive?

A bestial growl and a dirty body odor told him there was a Klingon bending over him. The other voice, unsolicitous and grim, was the one he'd heard before. Roy John Moss.

He didn't open his eyes. He just listened to the acrimony in the voices and made his deductions. A plan started to form in his clearing mind.

"Well, I'm glad you're here to tell me all about dinnertime on Klingon, Dazzo. How many times have we said that, only to have them pop up with some new trick? Oh! I forgot. If you learned from mistakes, you'd still be in the Klingon fleet instead of scraping a living off the Federation's garbage pail lid, wouldn't you?"

"You smell, boy."

"Lick it, Dazzo. You can't do anything to me and you know it."

The contempt wasn't just for the Starfleet people who had foiled the scavengers' plans. These two had open and obvious contempt for each other. A sour excuse for crewmanship.

Jimmy hadn't heard anything like this from anyone in Starfleet, so he clung to it as something he might be able to use.

As he breathed and his battered ribs expanded and contracted, he forced himself to deduce where Veronica's fake hand was pressing against his breastbone, inside the partially open front of his suit. Where were his own arms?

Eyes still closed, keeping his face passive, he twitched his fingers imperceptibly, just to see where they were. Right arm almost straight out to his side, left arm kinked between his side and the Klingon's boot.

On his left. He made calculations in his mind. Rehearsed his plan a couple times, then—

"Yaaaaaaaa!"

His shout took the two other by complete surprise—and there's nothing as grotesque-looking as a surprised Klingon.

The Klingon, the one called Dazzo, was a lot more surprised when an Earth teenager vaulted at him from flat on the floor, drove him back against the wall, and clamped an artificial hand at his throat.

With all the force of his legs and body driving against the shocked alien, Jimmy gritted his teeth, thrust his bent elbows forward on either side of the Klingon's head, pushed his hand into the fake hand's wrist cowl, and cranked.

The Klingon's wolfish howl of shock and fury was cut into a gargling choke as Veronica's fingers popped the skin of his throat and clamped together on the inner side of his esophagus, then clawed it apart.

Air and pink blood sputtered and spat all over Jimmy Kirk and the astounded Roy Moss behind him. He knew Roy was there, but he also knew he had a chance of fighting a human close to his own age, and no hope of fisting down a Klingon in a fair fight. The Klingon simply had to go first, and he would take his chance with the other one.

The plan was pretty good, and Jimmy missed only one element that didn't hit him until the splatter of blood hit him too: He hadn't ever killed anybody. Certainly not with his bare hands.

The blood surprised him almost as much as he had surprised Dazzo, and he thrust off the Klingon's sinking form. Dazzo scraped down the wall, clutching with frantic ferocity at the artificial claws deep in his throat, but there was no getting the thing loose. He reached toward Roy for help, but the other teenager did nothing but stand a few paces back in nothing but mild disgust, watching the Klingon gag to death.

Gasping, Jimmy also sagged against the opposite wall, and let his best chance for another surprise sink away. His hands, his bare hands . . . Veronica's wonderful miracle, used to murder . . .

Roy moved a few steps closer, as though fascinated by what was happening to Dazzo. The Klingon lay in the crease between the wall and the deck, gawking up at Roy and reaching for him with one hand, while the other hand clawed uselessly at the thing at his throat. Every time he pulled at Veronica's hand, his ripped windpipe bowed out and gurgled.

This didn't go on very long.

Roy enjoyed every second and all but licked his lips when the last rattle came out of the Klingon and Dazzo's pleading arm fell to the deck.

Finally, Roy backed off a pace.

"Hmm," he huffed. "Darwin would understand."

Jimmy collected the bland profundity of it from Roy's smirk and the fact that these people weren't willing to put themselves on the line for one another.

Roy watched a few seconds longer, then without taking his eyes off Dazzo's intriguing remains, he drew an electrical stunner from his belt pack of tools.

Even though Jimmy hadn't seen one like that before, the shape of the little weapon and its pronged business end had a very obvious purpose.

"This'll knock you buzzy," Roy said, "so don't try anything. You might not have the rocks to go through with what you start, but I do." He looked up and down at Jimmy's now-filthy suit, with its burgundy trousers, white shirt, and brown waistcoat, and said, "What do you call that Star-fancy-fleet uniform? Doesn't look like one."

"It's an off-duty uniform," Jimmy said caddishly. "You wanted me in standard issue, didn't you? So you could show me off? Tough luck, bub."

With only a rude glower, Roy snipped, "It doesn't matter! Now, turn around. Walk in that direction. I'm going to parade your little Federation butt in front of my father."

# TWENTY-SIX

☆

"That ship's getting closer."

"No, it ain't."

"Like hell it ain't," Big Rex Moss insisted. "Look at that screen!"

"You're lookin' at magnification," Caskie told him. "It's all bollixed up. Visual's banged up inside."

"Get Dazzo to fix it, then!"

Jimmy heard the voices and measured them as argument long before he was forced up the ladder at the point of that stunner of Roy's, through a hole, and onto what was apparently the bridge of this Frankenstein ship. Unlike some of the other parts of the ship, the bridge hadn't been taken off any type of vessel that he recognized, and it was manned by a mismatched gaggle who had nothing in common but the dirt on their clothes.

Roy Moss shoved up behind him and pushed his way in front.

"Dazzo's dead," he said.

The gaggle of subhumans all turned to look at him.

The announcement was taken with accusative glares that made him shrug and add, "Death by stupidity. It was just evolution at work."

By their expressions, the others let out the little secret that they were pretty sure he was crazy.

An enormous man, enormous in every possible direction,

grunted out of the command seat and hoisted around to glare at the chunky boy who had just stepped out from behind Roy.

"Who'n hell is that?"

"Prisoner," his son crowed. "I found him. Said I would, didn't I? I can find anything. See what he's wearing?"

The big man lumbered a step closer and bellowed, "What about it?"

"That's a Starfleet off-duty suit."

"Looks like a who-cares suit to me."

Ignoring the sting, Roy pointed at the Starfleet cutter on the screen. "That ship *is* getting closer."

"It's not getting closer. We've got malfunctions."

"Picture, but bad readings," a wide-shouldered man on the upper deck grumbled down.

Keeping to one side in a place where the odds were too much against him, Jimmy bit his lower lip to keep his mouth shut, but noticed that the ship did look awfully close.

Could've been just enhancement on the flooey, but . . .

The bridge seemed undermanned by the five hands on it, and he assumed they were down on manpower and couldn't watch everything. The way this tin can was put together and the way it had been torn apart in the past twelve hours, nobody could watch enough to know what was really going on inside the mechanics.

Over to one side, at what might be part of the engineering section—never mind that the whole console was smashed in and stinking with moist gore from some poor dead stooge—Jimmy shifted his eyes to the submonitors and tried to read the ones that were still working.

Picture, but no readings? No numbers? He tried to add up what he knew about graphic readouts to what was going on around him, tried to remember the hours he spent reading the monitors Carlos Florida had given him to watch, and tried to pick out which of these just might be the distance between this ship and the Starfleet cutter.

Could have been either of two, he decided. One of them showed no changes at all. But the other one . . . the numbers were slowly decreasing. A few decimals per minute.

Maybe the cutter *was* getting closer. How? Had his father and

Captain April figured out something new? Found a way to make use of the extra minutes he'd yanked out of nowhere for them?

Maybe his father was trying to get over here!

A father whom he had once thought didn't care.

Everything he'd done, and his dad was still taking crazy chances, risking everything to get to him.

If it was true, then these people were misreading their own gadgets—or maybe they just didn't trust one another to know what was going on. He thought he heard that in their voices. If so, was there a way to keep them guessing? Prevent them from trusting one another?

Possible with these others, but Roy Moss was smart enough to notice the statistics sooner or later. Roy was definitely the smartest kid in class.

*Not if I keep him distracted. Needle him, irritate him, don't let him think—*

"Well, kill him. Break his neck."

Jimmy snapped back to the moment as he heard those words, because he knew they were about the wrong "him."

"You'll like it," the huge man said. "It feels great to break a neck with your bare hands."

"We haven't won yet," Roy argued. "Until the Starfleeters are dead, we might need a wild card!"

"The tail might be right, Rex," the wide-shouldered man said. "Keep the punk around. Hostage."

"Mind your own party, Munkwhite." The man called Rex didn't even turn around to toss the comment back. He glared at Jimmy with the look a hungry bear gives a turkey with a broken leg.

"Fine," Munkwhite gruffed. "Do what you want."

He turned back to the battered controls.

Jimmy felt as if he'd been abandoned, even though he would gladly have stuffed a shoe down any face in there, including one that suggested they keep him alive.

The man called Rex, the one apparently in charge, had to use both hands to hoist himself up the step to Jimmy's level.

"Yeah," the big man said, "I think I'll exercise my grip. C'mere, kid. I want to teach my boy something."

Jimmy backed up, but there was nowhere to back to. The head of this crew was enormous, outweighed him by two hundred pounds easily, and intended to use him to show Roy how to murder.

"No!" Roy stepped between Jimmy and the approaching mountain.

Rex Moss jolted. "What're you doing?" he bellowed at his son, jowls shaking.

"It's too good a chance!" Roy countered. He extended a hand toward Jimmy. "Look at him! He's a snot-nosed whelp! He's a cherub! A kid! They'll try to save a kid! Don't you get it?"

"If you're not man enough to do it," the father said, "then move aside, ponytail."

Roy did step aside, but only as far as a particular panel with an open mechanical cave under it. He reached down under there without taking his eyes off the big man, and did something with his fingers.

*Plink—*

"Deflectors just went off again!" Munkwhite wailed. He spun at Roy. "You peach-ass punk! We're almost into the Blue Zone!"

Then, from the hole that led to engineering, an Orion popped up and hoarsely howled, "What happened to deflectors! Get deflectors back! Blue Zone is right here! We'll crush!"

"Turn 'em back on, tail," the man called Rex said. "Don't you defy us."

"Not until I get my way," Roy countered. "I'm not giving him up. He's my prisoner. He's *mine*. I found him. If you kill him, fix the shields yourselves."

Rex's small eyes turned catlike, and he leered at his son.

Even from the side Jimmy recognized the kind of anger. He'd seen it broiling under his own father's skin—but there had always been control.

There was no control here.

"You pick a pretty piss-poor way to try to be a man," Rex rumbled. "I'm not gonna forget this."

Roy twitched, but didn't back down.

"We're getting awful damn close to that Zone," Munkwhite ground out. Again he glared at Rex. "He's your kid . . . you do something about him!"

Apparently affected by the hint that just maybe some of this was his fault, Rex forced himself to back off a step. But he never took his eyes off his son.

"Keep your pet hamster if you want to," the huge man said, "but you mind him and keep control of him. Now, turn your shields back the hell on."

Jimmy caught Roy's eyes at the last second as the tall young man stooped enough to put his hand under again, and did his magic.

A few things changed on the bridge—lights here and there, buzzing and humming that hadn't been there a moment ago, and that Jimmy hadn't noticed until now.

"Hey!" Munkwhite shouted again. "Look!"

They all turned.

On the main screen, well beyond the possibility of screen illusion, the Starfleet cutter appeared to be flying into their very faces.

"It's not the magnification!" Munkwhite spat out. "I tried to tell you it wasn't! They're getting closer! They're trying to dock with us!"

"Speed up!" Rex blasted. "Get us into the Blue! If they get aboard this ship, we'll have a goddamned civil war on our hands!"

"Everybody secure? Suits? Helmets? All secure? Carlos, you got Ensign Hall?"

"Affirmative, sir! Ready when you are."

George yanked his own helmet over his head and secured it, then waited the longest four seconds of his life while the suit pressurized and became independent of the ship they were about to abandon.

"Robert! Distance?"

"Twenty-eight meters and closing! We're almost on them, George!"

"Get ready!"

"I don't believe they let us get this close," Carlos muttered as he pulled Veronica tight against him and made sure her helmet and suit were properly pressurized on top of trying to keep her alive medically. That suit had a lot to do.

George flashed him a glance from inside the helmet's shield. "I don't believe we found a way to use our hand lasers in a fight out in space. Okay, Robert, you give the word at ten meters. I'm going to pop the hatch. You stay at least fifteen feet behind me."

"Affirmative . . . twenty . . . eighteen . . . fifteen . . . ten . . . eight —six, five, four—"

"Here goes!"

They were hit by a tornado of spinning crates and monitors and general trash from their troubles as George dropped the hatch where once his son had been imprisoned in a removable airlock, and let the pressure out into open space.

They huddled until the hold equalized—equal to the vacuum of space—then George climbed up.

But now there was no airlock. There was nothing but the shattered, open area that a few hours ago had been the pilot cabin, now torn to the point of the unrecognizable. Even the observation pod was entirely gone, along with most of the upper half, and in its place, looming bigger and nearer than George ever hoped to see it, was the spider ship that had pounced on them out of the impossible.

And there was a tractor beam—wide as a tree trunk, gory, ugly, a gigantic klieg light of contracted phosphine yellow, the beam spilled like arsenic over the cutter's magnetic center, making the hulk shimmer and tremble—and right there was the port where it emitted from.

The only place on the spider ship that wasn't covered by impenetrable shielding.

Without pausing to be scared or impressed, George crawled out of the ripped hull, grabbing for sparse and unforgiving handholds in the zero-g, and trying to keep himself from floating in the wrong direction. He made his way toward that beam, carrying with him an industrial extender claw and a neat little grenade cannibalized from the four on-board hand lasers. What people couldn't do when they got desperate enough . . .

He edged closer. The beam would happily, hungrily, crush a living body, or anything without enough tonnage or the right alloys in its construction to fight back. Too close . . . hard to move . . . even through his pressure suit he felt the tractor beam licking at him, sucking for him, tasting him. He edged closer as the last few inches closed and the two ships physically bumped.

A shower of electrical reaction rained over him as the cutter rubbed against the enemy ship's special shields. Suddenly it was like fighting with a prisoner and bumping up against the brig shielding.

The cutter waved off a few inches, but kept brushing those shields, kept throwing electrical spray over him every few seconds.

He moved sideways against the ravaged hull of his own ship, or what was left of it, trying not to touch the shields of the other ship. Who knew what would happen to an environmental suit if it rubbed up against those shields?

It took him an eternity to reach the tractor beam source, but he did reach it.

Then he stretched toward the emitter port and pushed his industrial claw outward, with the makeshift grenade in its teeth. For a horrid few seconds he could barely hold on—and he had to. He had to make sure the grenade went deep into the tractor beam, not just caught in the edge.

"All the way," he grunted, teeth clamped, "all the way in—"

His arms were almost yanked out of their sockets as the tractor got a good grip on the banded laser weapons, and suddenly reality turned a bitter yellow. George let go not at the last second, but during it. The claw went too, and almost took him with it, striking his rib cage as it flipped and was yanked into the emitter core.

An instant later the laser grenade ignited, ruptured by the tractor beam and the impact of being sucked in there.

The explosion blew outward like a giant's last gush. What had been an orderly, if fuming, yellow tractor beam now became a savage red hell. George felt his body lifted and slammed to the opposite side of the cutter's remains, then sucked back again into the core as energies conflicted.

In a flash of irrationality he tried to signal to Robert to follow him into the two-meter rupture with the others before the deflectors closed over the hole, but he was thrown forward hard into a wall of smoke and shattered inner core.

There was a tremor of activity around him—the others? He couldn't see, couldn't feel anymore. He groped his way forward before automatic shutdowns in the tractor mechanism took over and trapped them all outside.

Like a fireman moving through the visionless void of a burning building, feeling and groping and hoping his way, George stumbled forward until the tug of outer space left his body and he thought he might be in a pressurized area. How could that be? In a vacuum one moment, inside the ship in another—

Was that what Jimmy had gone through? Thrust by violence into more violence?

A great shudder rocked through the skin of the vessel around him, and his instincts started ringing. The Blue Zone!

It had them! They were in, they were committed. The cutter was a crushed pancake, just a few feet back there. That was the crunch he'd felt through the deck—

Robert! Had the others made it in? They were just a few feet behind him—but a few feet in a situation like this . . .

Had they gotten Veronica in?

All at once a force grabbed him and pulled him down.

Gravity!

It drove him to his knees. Frustrated at not being able to see, he tore off his helmet and collapsed, waving weakly at gushes of smoke.

He waved and crawled, or at least he thought he was crawling. He felt pressure down there on his knees. Where was the ceiling? Which way was up?

"George! George!"

Robert's voice . . . Robert's hands . . .

"George, you all right?"

"Are we in?" he choked. "Are we inside?"

"Yes, we got in! We got in a few seconds behind you, just as you calculated. The shields closed right behind us. Look at me—are you all right?"

With both arms coiled around his plundered rib cage, George sucked at air he couldn't get enough of and shoved himself up on one elbow. He was lying on his side, his eyes focusing on a sheet of black deck insulation.

"Robert, quit—asking me that—will you? I'm a wreck—that's how I am. This whole—situation's . . . a wreck. What happened? Why is there air in here?"

Robert knelt beside him and held on to him. "I told you. Because the shields closed as soon as our ship was destroyed by the Blue

Zone, and this ship repressurized. It was a remarkable lesson in timing, old boy! Just remarkable."

"Great—let's get moving."

"No, don't move! George, you're hurt. You can't ignore it."

"Wanna bet? Don't make me feel fragile right now! I wanna feel mean."

Taking that as hopeful, Robert hoisted him to his knees, then to his feet, and managed to keep him up by leaning him against a scorched wall. Unable to stand without the wall, George blinked and tried to get his burning eyes to operate again.

Robert's helmet was off too. How long had those few seconds been?

Out of the brownish-green billows Carlos Florida stumbled at them, yanking off his own helmet, and grabbed George by an arm and gasped, "George, you all right, sir?"

"Oh, for cripes' sake!" George pushed off from between them and staggered away.

Gaping helplessly at him and then at Robert, Carlos babbled, "Wha—what'd I say wrong?"

"Nothing at all we can help, my boy," Robert soothed, stepping close to look him over too. "How about yourself? Hurt anywhere?"

Ignoring what was going on behind him, George winced his way out of his survival suit.

"Damn, I hate these constricting things," he groused as he stomped the suit to a shimmering lump under him. "Is Hall in here?" he called. "Is she safe?"

Carlos turned. "Over there. Still alive, sir."

"Where are we?"

"Inside, someplace. And we better move out. If they figure out what we did, all they have to do is turn off their deflectors and all our air is gone."

"They can't," Robert said. "We're inside the Blue Zone. The deflectors have to stay up from now on. It buys us a few moments, at least."

"If this ship's designed anything like a Federation ship," Carlos said, "the tractor emitter core would be on the lower decks, forward of impulse, but topside of warp drive."

After clearing his throat, George said, "I'm not making any assumptions. Look around. Find out for sure where we are in relation to . . . anything we can use."

"Aye, sir, I will."

George pointed a warning finger at him. "You be careful."

Smiling hesitantly, Carlos muttered, "Thanks . . . I'll do that too."

Limping back to where Robert was just peeling off his own scorched pressure suit and confiscating its reserve packs for Veronica, George breathed heavily and winced out his words.

"Well, that took care of our hand weapons. We're down to thumbnails and spit."

Robert nodded and straightened up to eye him. "You sure you're all right, George? You don't look good."

"I don't feel good, okay? I might be horn-mad and jaundiced, but at least I'm consistent. We're on level ground with these ax murderers now, and I intend to make use of that."

"Let's think calmly, shall we? See if we can't get ourselves disentangled from this after all. Perhaps we should find a place to hide and rest for a few moments."

"I'm not waiting a few moments. They've got my son. And nobody . . . takes my son."


"That's your father?" Jimmy asked, leering at his captor.

Roy Moss gritted his teeth. "Let's just say I came out of a woman he used to know."

Now, with his hands tied, Jimmy had only his best cold-teenager particularization to aim at Roy Moss as they climbed down to the lower decks. "What kind of a woman would get close to that?"

"Shut up!" Roy roared. "I might have to drag you around, but I don't have to listen to you."

"What're you going to do? Stick a shock collar on me?"

"I might," Roy grated. "Just shut up. I'm busy."

"Busy keeping those deflectors up, right?" Jimmy nagged. "We hurt you, didn't we? We smashed you up. Now you've got to tamper all the time to keep the shields up. Glad I'm here to come along and watch. Maybe I'll learn something."

Below decks, through the dimness and the smoke, Jimmy allowed himself to be shoved through the scavenger ship, all the while memorizing the layout and counting whatever pirates were still walking around. When his father and Captain April needed information, Jimmy was determined to have it. Those oxygen-deprivation dreams had reminded him of things bitterness and selfishness had caused him to forget—that adults had a life to live too. That his father hadn't come home and spent his leaves sitting around, relaxing. He'd come home armed with outdoor gear or a ticket to an adventure park or a new museum. Always doing things with his boys, that was George Kirk . . . until his oldest boy grew up and his youngest boy decided to count only the hours apart.

Guilt burned under his skin.

But now he knew the key. The memories were helping him. He understood Roy Moss as though looking at a horror story that flashed his own future. Roy was provokable, and Jimmy set out to heckle the skin off him.

"You'll learn something," Roy grumbled. "Your shipmates might be on this ship someplace."

"They're aboard and you know it," Jimmy crowed, hope rising in his heart. He pushed it down and kept his tone belligerent. "And you're all dead."

"Maybe they are! Fine! I've still got you! I don't intend to run into them and have nothing to bribe them off me with. You're my personal little shield. So shut up and shield!"

"Why should I shut up?" Jimmy kept pestering. "Why do anything you say? You're just their hatchet man. I can go back to Starfleet with my father. At least he's a commander and *supposed* to tell people what to do."

"Mine's a captain!" Roy shot back.

Through a grinding pause, Jimmy actually smiled. The right kind of smile, the dissecting kind that everybody told him he would outgrow.

"A captain?" he snorted. "Your father's no captain."

Teeth on edge, Roy bristled. "He's . . . in charge . . . of this ship."

"I used to be in charge of a gang too. Didn't make me a captain," Jimmy said, "and it didn't make them a crew. I found out what a real captain and crew are when you insects swarmed us. You people have the ethics of swamp lice." Fulfilling his role as Roy's personal fault-finder, he ticked off a couple of seconds, then added, "Guess I should thank you for that."

They went down the next corridor to the engine with Jimmy heel-nipping all the way and Roy snapping more than once, "Leave me alone! Leave me alone, I said."

Finally he shoved Jimmy aside in an engineering subroom, aside, where he could keep an eye on him, then knelt under a console and tried to work.

"Captain April called you trap-door spiders," Jimmy badgered. "He was right. That's all you are. A shipload of dirty dealers."

"April?" Roy blurted. He suddenly stood to his full height and stiffened. "Robert April? Founder of the starship program?" He thrust himself closer to Jimmy, armed with a rude glower. "Are you off a starship? Are you off the *Enterprise?*"

Realizing he'd said too much, Jimmy kept red-flagging the bull in a different direction. "Aww, what's the matter? Miss your chance for cushy duty like that? Talk to your father, why don't you? At least my father came out here to make things better for other people. Yours came out here to make things worse."

"At least mine kept me with him. Yours was just another Starfleet widow maker. I know the type."

Jimmy bristled at Roy's intuitive pinning of the truth. "We were all right and he knew it," he said. "He went out where he was really needed. He didn't have to provide a perfect life for me. He was out here trying to build something better for everybody. Me . . . you . . . we're the same kind. We're the cause of our own problems."

"Don't try to distract me! I know that's what you're doing." Roy stumbled past him and hit a wall comm unit with his fist. "Bridge! Bridge! Does anybody hear me up there?"

*"What d'you want?"*

"I think there's a starship after us!"

# TWENTY-SEVEN

## USS *Enterprise* 1701-A

James Kirk got up and paced around his command chair. Damn, if only he had more to do than just stare into that screen.

He opened and closed his fist. Nothing to do with them.

That was Command's biggest problem—no *job* to do. No hand on the wheel. No hand on anything, really. On a ship with a crew bigger than ten, the captain really didn't touch anything. Been like that for centuries . . . so why wasn't he used to it?

"Captain?"

He spun around, toward Spock. "Yes?"

The arrowlike eyes were reassuring. Spock didn't come down. "I've analyzed this entire file, and reviewed all encyclopedic files related, and found I had to trace it through fundamental Starfleet Engineering archives. This is a basic anchor in exploration, and aggressive and defensive engineering science for starships. It is the main reason starships can broach areas impenetrable for other types of craft, and endure situations of violence intolerable to lesser mounted vessels. It is a structural member in Federation expansion."

"I realize that," Kirk said. "Do you understand the science itself? The deflector technology and everything else that came out of those incidents involving Faramond?"

295

Spock nodded. "To the molecular level," he assured Kirk.

Kirk sighed with relief. Having Spock *know* made a big difference. It would continue to do so when things got dicey.

"Captain." Pavel Chekov spoke up in a tone that said he could
tell he was interrupting private thoughts.

Kirk nodded to Spock, then turned to Chekov. "Report."

"Reading the planetary system of Faramond on the long-range
sensors, sir. No reading of the *Bill of Rights* yet."

"Secure from warp speed in five minutes," Kirk said. "Ahead
standard sublight."

"Secure from warp speed in five minutes, aye," the new helmsman said. "Ahead, point eight sublight . . . arrival at Faramond
Colony is approximately twenty minutes to orbit, sir."

"Keep the crew at stations at least until we come within hail of
her," Kirk said, "assuming we find her."

"Aye, sir," Uhura responded from behind him. "Maintaining full
alert and emergency stations," she echoed.

Then the disturbing quiet fell again, and the high-speed waiting
resumed.

Kirk wished there were more to be said. Getting used to the few
words required for efficient command of a ship had been one of the
hardest lessons Starfleet had taught him. What was he about to find
in that solar system? Was he about to discover that he had failed to
be there when Roth needed help? He still saw Alma Roth as an
ensign . . . and he still felt parental.

He rubbed his palms. They were moist. Cold. The palms of a
frustrated man whose arms were never quite long enough.

Trying to compose his dread, he turned away from the main
screen and found himself once again looking updeck.

"What am I going to find, Spock?" he asked quietly.

Spock stepped closer, lowered his voice. They both knew how to
converse in such a way that no one else heard, even in the confined
environment of a ship's bridge. And there was something about a
conversation between anyone and the captain that made others turn
their faces away and allow the privacy. Any ship was like that. Crew
learned this one thing fast—there were some moments the captain
didn't want to be approached.

"I have been isolating and arranging scattered data on Faramond, sir," Spock said, his tone even and perhaps sympathetic. "It is an archaeological dig of an ancient culture which was highly advanced, far beyond us, but they are extinct . . . or have gone away. It is a multispecies dig, quite a vast project, in fact, and—"

"And Captain April is supposed to break ground with the Golden Shovel," Kirk murmured.

Spock's brows gathered like two fireplace pokers falling together. "I beg your pardon?"

"Nothing. Go on."

"As in most archaeology," Spock continued fluidly, "writing is a critical link. Any recording material that survives is considered valuable. Commonality is the key. Discovery of the same language on two continents is an indication of seafaring, and on two planets is an indication of possible space travel, yet raises endemic questions. For instance, discovering Sanskrit on Mars . . . did we go there, or did they come here?"

"We went there," Kirk prodded, intolerant of illustrations today. "Go on."

Something in his voice made Spock pause, then step down to the lower level with him. The Vulcan's posture was relaxed, as though to silently comment on the captain's impatience, and that some things would have to be explained point by point, slowly.

"Not everyone carves on stone," he said. "Some people write on the backs of envelopes, or jot notes on table napkins. With the advent of computers into daily life of the average person, such things tended to lessen with time, but use of paper, as you know, has never lost its appeal and tends not to in societal cultures. This is fortunate since formal records are rare in archaeology."

"I know," the captain said. "What do we have from ancient Crete? We have inventory of the king's olives and oils and breads. We don't have the letter the king sent to the high priest of Jupiter."

Spock frowned, this time for a different reason. "High priest of Jupiter, sir?"

"It's a joke. Move along."

"Yes . . . you have the essence. We have political graffiti, but we do not have Sophocles's plays."

"Are you being facetious?"

Pausing, Spock appeared to understand the accusation without

297

understanding how anyone could possibly have any good reason to be facetious. "Not at all," he assured Kirk. "You must understand that volumes of poetry are nearly unheard of in archaeology. Library material is simply not found. Archaeologists build their careers upon the middens of vanished peoples . . . refuse heaps . . . things in intestines of mummies. That's why finds such as the Fabrini Lexicons or the Rosetta Stone are considered so precious."

"I get it," Kirk said impatiently. "We have the scratchings about who to elect and how they were going to liberate one another from whatever religion had hold of them, and my ancestor invented the wheel but unfortunately he didn't leave me a note. What's your point?"

Spock shifted and rearranged his hands behind his back. "At Faramond, the archaeologists have been working for forty-five years, and last year reported a major leap in the dig."

"Which was what? A shoehorn with the manufacturer's name? The word for 'toilet bowl' is the same in two places? Don't make me beg, Spock."

Spock stepped closer. He dropped his attempts to preface and simply blurted out what he had to say.

"They think they have discovered a basic chemistry book," he said. "Perhaps a children's text."

Kirk paused to remember his grade school chemistry and get an idea of what might be in the book, then forced himself to sound more patient. "What does that mean to them?"

"It means we can begin to read the language. We are now on the way to translating the language, by way of universals."

"Universals," Kirk interrupted. "The laws of gravitation, physics —simple science?"

"Yes, sir. Water is water, hydrogen is hydrogen. That is the key to an alien language . . . there are no metaphors for the laws of physics and chemistry. Newton's law of gravitation cannot be described in a parable. We know this Old Culture was a spacefaring culture, and a people who can't communicate in basic science terms can never get into space. With science, we can communicate brilliantly without a single vocalized word."

"So we're on the verge of discovering what was the big attraction on a cold planet." Kirk paced a step or two away, then back. "Always wondered myself."

"Yes." Spock seemed somewhat relieved. "The planet has long been inert. Any settlers had to bring their own heat and respiration, which lessens its appeal for any kind of work. We have been baffled as to the reasons the Old Culture settled there at all, and especially how they left. There is no evidence of ships. No fuel or lubrication residue, no vessel technology, no docks, no markers for spacefaring, no maintenance facilities, and no remains of workers or farers. That has been the standing confusion of Faramond for nearly half a century. We know they departed in a single exodus, but we do not understand how. An enduring question for Federation archaeologists, Captain."

"I have a different question," Kirk said, pacing again. "What happened between the discovery of that chemistry book and the *Bill of Rights'* arrival? A cold planet, in a cold solar system, that had to have domes built on it before a single pick could be stuck in the ground, that wasn't used for farming or mining, but was developed. What's there? What's there that caused antiproton flushback, when the only thing known to our science that causes flushback is the explosion of warp engines? I hate it, Spock . . . I hate asking myself what's on Faramond that could've caused the *Bill of Rights* to explode. An Excelsior-class starship doesn't . . . just explode."

He knew he sounded angry. He'd been through this before—the death of an entire ship, of an entire planet, or a solar system—but that didn't make it any easier for him to swallow or even to comprehend. Not even forty-five years' experience could sweeten that poison.

He knew it showed on his face, and didn't care.

"You may have to make a bet, sir," Spock said.

Kirk paused, turned, and squinted. "You're telling me to make a bet?"

His Vulcan friend gazed at him steadily with a reassuring quiescence.

"Yes," he said.

He didn't have to say anything else.

More than logic was at work. Hope was at work. Defiance of hazard was at work. Belief in the skills of Roth and those young people who had trained under Jim Kirk was at work. Serving with Kirk and these humans over the decades had taught Spock to do the one special thing that humans did better than anybody else in the known galaxy.

Gamble on themselves.

Abruptly the main bridge entryway hissed open, and something told Kirk to swing his chair and look.

There stood a presence of glowering weight. Skinny, but glowering.

A moment, and McCoy had brought his glower down.

"Bones?" Kirk prodded.

McCoy closed his eyes in illustration, shook his head, then opened the pale blue glower again. "Biggest psychological spider web I've stumbled into in years," he said. "I think you'd better fill me all the way in. And at this speed, you'd better talk fast."

# TWENTY-EIGHT

_Forty-five years earlier . . ._
USS _Enterprise_ 1701-A

"Picking up body parts, Commander Simon!"

"Specify! Human or what?"

"Difficult to specify, but definitely organic tissue masses in small amounts. Some of it could be legs or arms. Also getting debris that's nonorganic . . . hull material . . . mechanical parts, including some pieces that are clearly identifiable as Starfleet issue."

"How clearly, Jones?"

There was a pause. One of those that anybody can read.

Then . . .

"Stake my rank on it, ma'am."

Lorna Simon, under any other circumstances, would have enjoyed pointing out how that wasn't much of a testimonial coming from just an ensign, but this time there was more on her mind than a cheap joke.

"Order battlestations," she said.

The bridge jumped to action at key points, and an instant later, the entire starship echoed.

_"Red alert. Red alert! All hands come to battlestations. Battlestations!"_

The starship *Enterprise* hovered just outside the Blue Zone, her red sensor disk washing the area down, her crew disturbed by what was coming out in the rinse.

None more than Drake Reed, who had watched his best friend and a boy he felt he'd raised go out into this bizarre area of space only a few hours ago and was wondering if he would be able to see them come back. Now came the bad moments of imagining how long his friends had suffered—or how short a time—and if they were still suffering just out of his reach. Or if mankind should stay out of space unless there was a starship like this around them. But how many of these special ships would there ever be to go around? And not even a starship could be in ten places at once.

He'd been through times like this with George Kirk before, but this time . . .

"A ship! Commander! I'm picking up something just inside the Blue Zone!"

Simon cranked her ancient frame around with notable difficulty and more than a little cantankerousness, and barked at the cub minding the science station. *"Inside?* Repeat that!"

"Affirmative—inside! And intact! Moving under power, I mean!"

"Impossible."

"Correction!"

"I thought so."

"It's not one ship! It's two!"

"You sure you're reading that thing right, son?"

"Clearly power-regular . . . not just debris."

"You're telling me they were just pulled into that mess?"

"It reads as the cutter and some other . . . thing. It's just pulling them along in there."

"Are they docked?"

"Appear to be docked, yes."

"Oh, that's enough! Let me have a look at that." Simon hobbled to the upper deck, peered into the submonitor, then shook her head. "I'll be slam-dunked . . ."

"Tremendous interference," Ensign Jones said, "but regular

signals. I don't know what to make of it. Maybe leakage . . . but it wasn't just torn apart in there. I don't know how," he added, "but they're still in there."

"Pinpoint the source."

"I tried. It won't pinpoint."

"Hey, Trinidad. Step up here."

Drake spun around from his hopeless gaze at the natural terror on the main screen, the trinary and its dead zone, and knew his friends were in there and that nothing could survive in there. Reluctant to move backward instead of forward, even though that made no sense at all, he did as he was bade and joined Lorna Simon on the quarterdeck. He felt the sensor readout making odd lights on his tawny complexion.

"Madame Simon, ma'am?"

"This loose screw George of yours."

"Ah . . ."

"Troublemaker?"

"Oh, tut . . . not maker, per se . . . attractor, perhaps . . . handler, possibly . . ."

"He's good at handling trouble?"

"Oh, better than handling normalness, I might say! A good rascal to have on your side."

"Doesn't give up at the drop of a hat?"

"Ma'am, this George of mine doesn't give up at the drop of an anvil."

"Even to finding a way to survive inside the Blue Zone?"

Drake put a hand on his chest and said, "Commander, you ask big questions for a mere continental like *moi*. But I see these screens, and I see something pulsing in a place where nothing should pulse." He hesitated, measured his chances of finishing the next sentence, then said, "George Kirk would be out here betting on us with all his credits if the situation were backward."

The weathered woman glared at him for a long count to see if he would back down in his faith, and he didn't.

She nodded once, then stepped down to the command arena.

"Here's what we do," she said as she settled back into the command chair as though she'd been there for decades. Which she had. "Channel as much of the warp-drive power as you can through the tractor beam."

"Warp drive?" Isaac Soulian raised his head from the science station. "You want us to reroute it?"

"Engineering'll know how. Get Marvick on it."

Ensign Jones gave her the kind of look nobody should ever give an officer. "Just ask the circuits to do something they weren't made to do?"

She cast him a glance. "We're not under drive, are we?"

"No, Commander—"

"Then use the power for something else. Just do it, son, they'll figure it out downstairs. I want the strongest possible traction with the best possible beam integrity."

"Yes, ma'am . . ."

"I want you to start 'plucking' at the Blue Zone." She used her craggy old hand to pick at the air as an example, although their faces said they all had the idea. "See if you can . . . *grab* anything."

"Florida! What've you got?"

"We've got a one-way ticket, sir," Carlos said as he joined George Kirk in an isolated corridor. They were both scouting ahead while Captain April stayed behind with their injured Veronica. "Our ship reads as falling apart. What I wouldn't give for a ten-second glance into the formula for these shields—"

"What about the recon?"

"The what?"

"Reconnaissance. Looking around in here. What've we got here?"

"Half the compartments on this ship are open to space, so they're blocked off. We'll have to find our way around indirectly. It's a pretty sizable ship, but it's all battered up. We'll have to be careful . . . not open any locked panels or hatches. A lot are sealing off ruptured areas."

"We also have to be careful not to damage the ship itself too much. Hurt these shields, and we're all dead."

"Oh—that's true . . . and also they know their way around, but we don't. Those are our disadvantages."

"And no hand weapons."

"Oh . . . right. Sorry, Mr. Kirk. I'm just not used to this kind of thing."

"After serving with a luck-buster like me? Sure you are."

Carlos smiled, shrugged, and turned a little red at the reminder that his only forays into near-death had been at George Kirk's side.

"Here's how it goes," George told him. "I scout ahead about fifty yards at a time. You come next, and fifty yards later, Robert'll do his best with our little girl. Got it?"

"Got it, sir. You can count on me."

"Let's get the captain and the girl, and find my son, and get our behinds out of here."

"Fine. I admit it. There's a starship coming after you. You're sunk. Starfleet's coming after you now."

"What do you know about it?" Roy snapped at his prisoner's relentless picking as he prodded Jim Kirk to walk in front of him through the ship.

Why did the ship seem so empty? And it was too quiet for a full ship with a lot going on. The damage was obvious, but where were all the men? Where were all the white and black and brown and blue and mottled faces he usually found handy to cuss out?

"I don't have to listen to you," he said to his only company, grabbing for a moment's assurance. "You're going to be dead and I'm going to still be alive."

They stepped over two badly burned bodies. Roy tried not to be affected by the bodies, though he was noticing there were fewer and fewer of the crew visible in the corridors. Where was everybody?

"No," Jim Kirk tossed over his shoulder, "not this time. You've blown it this time. You attacked a Starfleet research cutter. You got caught—you're in the brig or dead. And there's not any border patrol coming after you. There's a starship. They won't buy guesses about ships getting lost or sucked into the trinary. They know a Starfleet crew doesn't just 'get lost.' What can a pack of racketeers do about it? You're thieves. You're nothing but pirates."

"We're *not* pirates!"

"Why not? Because you don't call yourselves that? You only do everything pirates do. Sorry. My mistake."

"We're Vikings."

"And murderers. You justify your actions by convincing your-selves that your victims deserve what they get. You're smugglers. Hoods."

"Leave me alone! Or I'll take my father's suggestion!"

Roy's shout stabbed through the barren, smelly corridor as he forced Jimmy to walk. Jimmy did as he was bade, walked where he was told, climbed whichever ladders were put before him, stood aside and worked at the tough vinyl bindings on his wrists when Roy had to stop and fix something, but he wouldn't shut up. He wouldn't quit picking at the malignance he'd seen between Roy and the others on this ship. Unlike those moments on board the *Enterprise* or the cutter, here he knew what to do. These people were people he understood—too well, he was ashamed to realize. These were what he had been headed toward becoming until a few short hours ago.

He could still get out of it, and get his father and his friends out of it with whole skins. To do that, the one to watch, the one to manipulate, would be Roy Moss.

Following a few classic moves of strategy and some not so classic, George Kirk sneaked through the enemy ship one corridor at a time, doing everything possible to annoy anybody who might go before or come after him—anything, at least, that would not damage the outer protection of this ship. That had to stay.

But everything else—he turned off lights, he dried wet areas and wet down dry ones, broke every corridor access control panel he passed, and when possible he locked any doors and panels. Maybe he couldn't fight every one of these people, but he could sure lock them in and hinder their paths and keep them from talking to one another.

He kept the others moving about a half corridor behind him, and made them duck and hide frequently while he scouted ahead. Ordinarily that wouldn't have been necessary, but they had Veroni-ca Hall to carry and to protect, and that meant being more responsible for their own well-being. A man could always be more reckless when he had only himself to care for.

He had scouted the upcoming corridor and was about to wave a come-ahead to Robert and Carlos, when he suddenly found himself waving them back and ducking for cover himself. He heard voices.

One . . . two voices.

He ducked under a piece of collapsed ceiling, then craned his neck to see if the others had managed to double back and hide. They must have—he couldn't see them.

"You know, I never used to get mad just on principle," one voice said, "I always like stories about the Old West—"

George almost shouted. Jimmy! His son's voice!

Alive! Jimmy was alive!

He forced himself to remain hidden until he could case the situation . . . now he heard footsteps!

"Goody," a second voice spat out.

"—people stumbling on each other and clashing," Jimmy went on, "border disputes, culture wars, conflicts over law and land, the way the future's going to be etched out and whose rules are going to be the best for everybody . . . but is that what you're doing? No. You lowlifes are just trying to make a few coins for your pockets. This is no interstellar dispute, no encroachment on somebody's space. It's just brainless piracy."

George ducked and held his breath. He had no weapon other than a short pipe. All he could do was peek out and see—

The tall, thin man shoving Jimmy around a corner!

No—not a man. Another boy. Hardly older than Jimmy, at second glance. Maybe a year or two older, with the teasings of a mustache that hadn't really grown yet, shoulders that would be wider by the month, no waist at all, and long brown hair pulled back in a ponytail. Both boys were battered and looked as if they'd been picking through a junkyard for parts.

A knot twisted George's heart. Jimmy's hands were tied, his clothes filthy and bloodied, his face smeared with blood too, and the tall boy was holding some kind of palm weapon on him.

"I'm warning you," the tall boy said. "Keep your mouth shut."

"Take it, then," Jimmy whiplashed. "Why are you hanging around with these people? Ever since we left the bridge you've been steaming and spitting about these lugheads you have to yes-sir.

They're just a gang. No purpose. Just ganging together because nobody else in a civilized place'll take 'em. Not what I'd want to do with my life. These dumb funguses around you—they're not a team. They use your talent and your inventions, but they don't give you any respect. What are you really getting?"

"But . . . out!" Roy breathed through flaring nostrils. Suck, hiss, suck, hiss. "Nobody'll ever tell me what to do again. That's what power gets you. You just shut up and . . . shut up."

Jimmy knew he was hearing just the right level of annoyance in Roy's voice, and stopped dead in his tracks. As George watched, not daring to breathe, his son turned on the other young man and stood him down right there in the smoky corridor.

"You resent that you're not in charge, don't you?" Jimmy challenged him. "You don't like following rules you didn't invent or don't see reasons for yourself. You can't get anything past me. I know all the excuses by heart. You're annoyed with life and you want to get on with it. So why don't you?"

Backing off a telltale step, the other boy demanded, "Why don't I . . . *what?*"

"You want something. You want more than this," Jimmy badgered. He felt his hazel eyes burn in a glare. "What are you doing here with these idiots? Anyone who would hang around here has to be an idiot himself. I don't know what you want and I don't care, but I know you'll never get it here."

He paused after the last statement to see the reaction to it.

And there was one. A good one.

Jimmy's eyes narrowed, and he was reading the other boy's face.

"I'm using these people!" he insisted. "This is temporary! It's just bad luck that I'm here for the moment!"

"I don't believe in luck," Jimmy said. "Show me 'luck' and I'll beat it."

"What about you!" Roy accused Jimmy. "What're *you* doing here? You could've escaped in that pod! You think those idiots in that other ship appreciate what you did?"

Jimmy pushed forward so fast and so suddenly, with eyes so enraged, the other boy stepped back a pace.

"Those people were willing to lay their lives on the line for me!

They're not perfect, but at least they're trying! They have as much in common with you and your crew as a stallion with a cockroach!"

George clamped his mouth shut tightly and begged for the situation to change so he could go out there and grab his boy and hug him. The words warmed his aching ribs and made him grin in spite of what was happening.

Jimmy had paused and realized he was losing control, and quickly changed to get it back. He lowered his voice for a touch of drama.

"Then there's these pigs you ship with," he added. "Ever dawn on you they might be using you?"

The tall boy stood there stiff, boiling, staring, with the hell being annoyed out of him.

As George hid and watched, he tried to deduce what was happening so he could help his son, and figured that Jimmy was jockeying for position.

And not just position for fists and kicks—position for a psychological advantage!

"I'll be damned," George whispered as he skewered the tall quarry and tried to analyze that face.

Whoever the captor was, he wasn't a happy captor. Jimmy was getting to him.

George watched as his antagonistic son wagged bound hands in front of his captor's flaming eyes.

"Never thought of any of this, did you?" Jimmy persisted. "How much have *you* gotten out of this? I can guess that you invented those shields, not these other clowns. You're so stupid, you don't even realize what you've got. You've found a way to survive inside the Blue Zone and you're trying to pick parts of a salvage and sell them? You're the only one who can work on them, right? What's it gotten you? The pennies you can scrape up out here in deep space? You know how much that's worth? Talk about stepping over dollars! You could've sold that science and had anything you want! Not only could you have had anything you want, but you'd have been Roy Moss, the hero!"

George almost got up and applauded. He had to fight the inclination and force himself to keep hidden and keep collecting information.

So *that* was the story—this kid had invented the special shields.

The one called Roy Moss stood there, virulent, jaundiced, gawking at a brutal fist of reality that had bruised him square in the face. His eyes went glassy—this meant something to him.

A hero . . .

George saw Jimmy grate his teeth with satisfaction, and realized his son had this other boy figured out. This pony-tailed wetsock wanted people thinking well of him. That was the key.

Jimmy had the key in his hands.

Dig, dig, dig—

"You've been with criminals all your life, haven't you?" Jimmy picked at him. "It never occurred to you to go legitimate, did it? You could've had people thinking well of you all over the galaxy! What are you instead? A common crook. Now you'll be lucky just to live long enough to grow a beard."

Roy Moss looked like a child about to have a panic attack. He seemed to know the other boy could read his reactions, and looked as if he were fractured in a dozen places. He aimed a finger at his antagonist's freckles.

"Look, razormouth," he growled, "someday they're all going to owe me! I'm just making sure I get what I deserve."

Jimmy retreated into satisfied silence, but not before George heard him mutter, "So am I."

George twitched until his legs hurt. His teeth ground and his jaws ached. *Jump them! Go on—one, two, three. . . . Do it right now. . . . Nobody takes my son.*

His legs wouldn't work. Training had drilled bolts through his knees. He couldn't go up against a wild-eyed kidnapper with a weapon after finally seeing proof that Jimmy was all right.

Down the corridor where the two boys had gone, doors swished and squawked. His chance was gone.

Now what? Had he done right?

This scouting-ahead business had its drawbacks.

He couldn't be just Jimmy's father right now. He couldn't suspend Robert and Carlos and an injured girl who were trailing a corridor or two behind him. There was a job to do, four people under his command, not just one.

And Jimmy . . . wasn't exactly whimpering and crying for Daddy.

George backed up a step and forced himself to think. Keep gathering information, get familiar with the terrain, find the point of command and the points of weakness, don't leave anything unchecked—

"Hold it! Freeze!"

Including the corridor behind him—

Damn!

Caught off guard, George did as he was told—froze solid in the middle of the nasty, broken, smoky, damage-littered corridor, just as he was ordered by the sizable individual of questionable planetary background who spotted him.

There was proof. Thinking too much about one member of the crew instead of the whole plan—and he'd let himself get spotted.

Okay . . . shift to plan two.

He turned slowly, hands up.

In front of him was a craggy human holding some type of mean-looking hand laser. George didn't recognize the make, but the weapon made him hungry.

He wanted it.

He'd burned his up in the tractor beam, and now he wanted that one.

His son was on this ship, working on weakening a key mind; it was up to George to weaken other things.

Ticking off five seconds, he hoped Robert and the others were using the seconds to hide. Then he put both his hands up and said, "I give up."

The crag lumbered toward him.

George put all his experience to work and tried to look submissive. He dropped his pipe and put his hands on the wall and spread his legs, just as he liked his own prisoners to do.

"I give," he repeated. "I'm lost. I can't find my way around your ship."

"Yeah," the large, dirty man said. "We like it that way." As he approached George, he paused and poked a wall communication panel. "Bridge! This is Munkwhite. I got one of 'em! They're down here on the anchor deck!"

He waited, but there was nothing but static responding. He punched the buttons harder.

"Bridge! This is Munkwhite! Somebody answer me!"

Static. Crackles.

"Damn it, what's the matter with this thing?" He kept an eye on George while cranking on the tuning knobs for a few seconds and cursing.

"I busted your system," George offered, peeking over his own shoulder. "Didn't want you creeps talking to each other."

"Sure you did! Shut up!" The man turned his frustrated attention back to his captive, came toward George, and started patting him down for weapons.

George didn't resist. In fact, he held his breath, hoping—

*Pssshhht*

Munkwhite's expression of anger turned to one of surprise. His eyes went wide, he staggered back, gasping, "That's not fair! That's not f—"

His eyes glazed over as he stared at the hand he'd been using to pat at George's clothes. He staggered back, legs spread, then fell over like a stone and hit the deck full-length.

George drew a long breath and pushed off the wall, wincing at his own wounds and trying to control his limp.

"Good idea," he commented. "Always pat a prisoner down."

From his pocket he'd pulled his booby trap: one of Veronica Hall's medical hypodermics. He expended the used cartridge which Munk–what's-his-name had so accommodatingly injected into his own hand, then replaced it with another dose, just in case somebody else got a jump on them too.

Of course, now he was armed . . . with the laser weapon he had so recently coveted. Then he opened a wall storage panel and ungraciously crammed Munkwhite into the wall to sleep it off where he wouldn't leave a trail, and with a few not-very-kind shoves managed to close the panel almost all the way and get it nice and jammed.

"Don't worry," George added. "Three or four hours and you'll feel . . . just terrible. Besides, nobody promised you 'fair.' Robert! Come on! I'm going to corner these bastards on their own bridge!"

\* \* \*

312

When Roy Moss dragged Jimmy back to the bridge to report to Big Rex that everything was broken or sabotaged and a lot of the crew were missing or unconscious, there was a distinct difference in the tone of voice from the nineteen-year-old knot of frustrations. Jimmy deduced it might be one of the first times, if not *the* first time, that somebody had gotten the best of Roy in an argument without using fists. These deadnecks around here had never been any competition for Roy, and he didn't like being told he was an idiot by somebody smart. His intellect was all he had to hold over these other bandits. He wasn't big like his father, or tough, or powerful. He was used to being the smartest kid in class. Everyone else had fallen easily under his "everybody else is stupid" catch-all.

Now Roy had this Kirk kid around, who might not be a science wizard, but who knew how to plumb for feelings and annoy them out. He wasn't used to having someone around who could smell traps and figure things out and anticipate trouble. This Jim Kirk had an amazing survival instinct and was trying to get under his skin and find out *why* he was doing what he was doing. Whenever Roy had said anything, it hadn't gone over Kirk's head like it did all these brutes around them. Jim Kirk caught and deduced everything. Not just words, but glances, looks, grunts, grumbles, posture. Figuring out mechanics was one thing, but being able to sift motivations . . .

"The whole ship's falling apart!" Rex Moss was howling as the two boys came back onto the bridge. He rounded on his son. "Haven't you got the intercom mended yet?"

"You said it yourself," Roy grumbled. "The ship's falling apart."

"Well, get it back together!"

Roy had started to pick at the control boards, but now turned to look past the frantic bridge crew, what few of them were left, and glared down at his huge father.

"Don't you understand?" he accused him. "It's *them!* They're sabotaging the ship! I warned you every step of the way, but you didn't listen! They're on board now, and I don't know what I can do for you!"

"Nothing," Jimmy piped up. "You can't fight Starfleet on equal terms and win."

Both Mosses turned at the same time and howled, "Shut up!"

Jimmy settled back in satisfaction, one eye on Big Rex Moss, and one eye on Little Roy Moss, and enjoyed the steam coming from both. The malignance between father and son was like a sumptuous appetizer, and he wallowed in his talent for siccing them on each other. There was enough antagonism on this bridge to stoke and light, and Jimmy felt strangely at home in the odium. He felt an evil side rising in himself, a side that knew just what to do, just how churlish to be, and just how to tease acrimony into erupting. There was a brute inside him, a cad who seldom got the chance to fledge, and now was its perfect time. Pick, pick, pick—that's what Jimmy Kirk did well.

Suddenly somebody screamed, "Antimatter leakage!"

The alien who had yelled was down the deck from Jimmy, arms stuck halfway into an open wall panel and reminded Jimmy of the jury-rigging and faking-it that had gone on between himself and the others in the cutter's hold. He remembered Carlos Florida's phrase —under the hood.

He recognized the alien as an Orion, and knew better than to get close to an Orion who was panicking.

And this one was.

So was everybody else. Antimatter leakage? Bad?

He kept back as the thieves dodged this way and that, shouting down crawlways and pounding on unresponsive panels, then dodging again.

"What can we do?" Big Rex Moss shouted. He turned from one crewman to the next, grabbing them each by the collar or the sleeve as they scrambled past him. "Stop the leak! We'll blow up! Do something!"

Jimmy surmised that the best he could do was stay out of the way and let them panic. He surmised maybe his father was doing something to fake a leak or create the illusion of a leak. If so, it was to his advantage to stay calm. If the leak was real, it was to his advantage to stay out of the way and let it get solved.

"The port warp engine!" the Orion shouted into a small screen that played erratic lights on his face. "Detonation thirty seconds! Twenty-nine! Twenty-eight! Twenty-seven!"

"Do something!" Rex Moss called.

"Twenty-six!"

314

All at once, everybody on the bridge turned not to Rex, not to the Orion engineer, but to Roy Moss.

Big Rex himself lumbered toward his son. "Well?" he bellowed.

Roy straightened and looked down at him.

There was something different. For the first time Jimmy noted that his words from the corridors hadn't gone unrooted. There was something distinctly changed between Roy and Rex Moss. Something beyond a son's fear of a brutal father.

This was a coarse glare of challenge and offense.

Roy glowered down at his father and rancorously said, "Yes?"

His father looked like a man about to have a heart attack.

*"Do* something!"

Tension broiled raw on the grill of the Mosses.

Finally the son shifted his weight and asked, "Why should I?"

# TWENTY-NINE

☆

"Reading antimatter leakage!"

"From inside the Blue Zone?"

"Affirmative! Heavy waves!"

"That's what we've been waiting for, kids."

Lorna Simon tried to make her voice sound calm and reassuring for the young folks aboard, and especially for this Drake Reed, who had the look of a man watching his best friend walk up the guillotine ramp.

She couldn't help standing up. There were times when even the command chair of a ship like the *Enterprise* wasn't enough.

Not when antimatter leakage came out of a place where some of her children were lost. And she'd been thinking about retiring again . . . just couldn't make herself do it. Times like this kept pulling her back.

"Get your sensors cracking!" she snapped. "Pinpoint it! Reed, get down here and take the navigation chair! Let's put our tractors into that mess and get our people out of there!"

Nobody was moving. All sweating, but nobody moving. All stared at Roy.

He let them sweat. His advantage reaching its strongest moment, and he used it to add friction. Not even his father knew what to do.

"Fifteen! Fourteen! Thirteen! Twelve!" the Orion engineer shouted.

Roy stepped down to his father's level. "Get out of my way, you imbecile."

Big Rex Moss had no choice, and apparently he knew it.

Hating the universe, he stepped aside.

On the port side, the Orion's voice cracked. "Eight! Seven! Six!"

Roy stepped past Big Rex as though he were nothing.

The effect was astonishing for Jimmy as he witnessed the other things that can happen between a father and son. His young captor, who just minutes ago had been so surprised at the idea of taking over, now seemed to figure that his father wasn't worthy of respect or fear any more than these other low forms of life.

With one hand—as though to make a point—Roy reached into a section of the open port side mechanical panels and worked some unexplained magic, then yanked on something.

They had only two seconds to spare when the countdown stopped and the Orion choked on the phrase, "Port engine is ejected! Starboard engine is still stable!"

An instant later the ship shifted under them and knocked them off their feet. Jimmy grabbed for balance and realized that the discarded engine had just blown up and knocked them with backwash. He struggled to keep himself up in spite of his hands being tied and curtailing his balance, and only when the ship settled again did he realize he'd missed a chance. He should have hit somebody or kicked something or jumped somewhere.

Another little lesson to log away for the future.

Roy enjoyed—as much as that hideous, spiteful expression could be called enjoyment—having gotten his father and the others out of a situation that would have killed them all if he hadn't been here. He straightened, and faced Big Rex.

"I'm going below," he said. "I'm going to secure the shielding and do whatever else needs doing so that doesn't happen again. You . . . just stay here and be the big man."

Rancor dripped from his tongue.

He stepped aft, scooped up a utility tin marked CHEMICAL RINSE, and gestured for Jimmy to lead the way out.

Below, once again in the corridor, Roy fell into a callous silence that Jimmy read with all but obvious glee. Finally Roy took one too many of his captive's snotty glances and said, "You're pretty cocky for a noxious runt with his hands tied up."

Jimmy cast him a glance of pure flint. "I'm not the one considering patricide."

"Oh, shut up! Where'd you even learn a word like that?"

"Heard it in a play."

"Well, keep it to yourself. You don't know what you're talking about."

"Yes, I do," Jimmy insisted as Roy shoved him into one of the engine rooms and pushed him off to a safe distance.

Roy grumbled something unintelligible, then crawled over a dangerously jagged pile of electrical parts and circuit boards that had fallen from the ceiling. He ended up on all fours to get over the pile, then crouched in a corner, opened the tin he'd brought from the bridge, and began selecting fine pieces of equipment and dipping them one by one into the chemical cleaner.

Between them, the pile of shattered boards crackled and occasionally snapped with live electricity, as though laughing at the two human boys trying to keep their noses above the water in a very serious adult business.

Jimmy stayed aside. He didn't have duking it out with Roy Moss in his plan—yet. He'd used his fists enough in his life, and this was a new adventure. He was going to see how far he could annoy this one.

Tenacity kicked in again. He discovered he was pretty good at reading other people, but until today, until now, he hadn't read himself very well. He determined to survive, not just sacrifice himself, but live through it, and let his father know.

He erupted out of his private thoughts and glared at Roy.

"I can't figure you out," he said. "You're obviously brilliant, and your father thinks it's some kind of parlor trick. When it gets him something, maybe then he'll respect you. Until then, you're nothing. If you don't realize that, you're stupid too."

Roy buried himself in his dipping and cleaning, mumbling incoherencies, not really conversing at all, but just growling out his frustrations.

It was working, Jimmy knew. He could goad Roy by making him feel stupid, because that's what he knew would work on himself. He felt the whole future was lying out before him in Roy Moss—the perfect example of what his father had been trying to avoid happening to Jimmy in two or three years. An angry young man who wasn't sure about the rightness of what he was doing.

"Stupidity . . . stupid people can make a living . . . undisciplined people can't . . ."

Roy was muttering louder now, and Jimmy was catching some of the phrases.

"Idiots claim part of it . . . never give it up . . . mine and all mine . . . scratching Faramond like lice . . ."

"Faramond?" Jimmy went so straight against the wall that he hit the back of his head. "What about Faramond?"

Roy looked up, eyes wide. A tiny electrical chip dripping fluid from his fingers to the floor. He looked like a trapped squirrel.

"What interest have you got in Faramond?" Jimmy badgered.

"None of your business! Who do you think you are—Sherlock Holmes?"

The look on Roy's face said it all again: that he wasn't used to having somebody around who could figure things out, smell traps, make deductions.

He tried to go back to dipping and cleaning.

Jimmy pushed off the wall and pointed his bound fingers. "You've got something on Faramond that you aren't telling your father about!"

"He's still my father!" Roy bellowed. "Shut up!"

The guilt came back to prick at Jimmy as he read the other boy's face. Roy had shown him what it was like to have a *really* bad father, yet Roy was showing more loyalty to Big Rex than Jimmy had shown to his own father.

"You know something nobody else does," he kept on. "That's right, isn't it? Sure! Why else would you put up with this shipload of maggots? That's why you keep your mouth shut, isn't it?"

Roy's arms shook violently, his face turned red, and he visibly broke. "I don't need them! I'm well on my way to taking over! I've been funneling off my own stash, stocking for my future! *My* future! Which isn't going to include these cretins!"

BEST DESTINY

Jimmy edged along the wall, forcing Roy to turn away from the main corridor doorway. "What is it?" he teased. "Bet you've been dying to tell somebody. Why not me?"

"I don't need to tell anybody! It's mine! When I get all I need, I'm going to take what these fools have stolen and blow them all out into space! They wouldn't be alive anyway if not for me, so it won't really change anything! I'll get everything I want! And when I do, I'll get rid of these people! They don't mean anything to me, and I'm not going to feel bad after I do it! Darwin would understand!"

"What about your father? That include him?"

"Look, he's my father! I'm stealing from him for his own good! Doesn't mean I have to kill him! He'll understand when the time is right for him to understand! He won't have any choice! You saw what just happened on the bridge! I'm in charge now! I've got something on Faramond that's worth a lifetime's work, and it's all mine! It'll make me an emperor!"

Jimmy didn't say anything.

He didn't have to.

The shadow being cast from the meager corridor light said everything. Roy spun around.

Big Rex Moss stood in the anteroom doorway.

And there was nothing fatherly left in his eyes.

# THIRTY

Young Roy Moss transformed from a dominant bastion of the future to a shriveled victim in three seconds. He even got shorter. He shoved upward against the wall, an electrical piece in one hand and the tin of fluid in the other. The tin was heavy, and dropped the few inches to the floor, sloshing, but landing upright.

"I'll share everything with you!" he whined as his father moved slowly into the anteroom. "You heard me tell him that! It was going to be for us! The two of us!"

The offer came too late. The idea alone that Roy had been stealing from his own people kept scorching the air.

But Big Rex Moss wasn't in a mood for teamwork.

"I shoulda killed you a long time ago," he grated. "I'll do it now. I'll kill you just like I did your mother."

Rex Moss never took his small, hot eyes off his son. He started climbing over the hill of collapsed parts and conduit boards. The pile crunched and snapped as his feet pressed down, then his hands, one by one. Parts groaned under the weight as he crawled closer and closer, giving him a platform from which to lunge down upon Roy.

Jimmy was ranked by the very presence of the enormous man, but he knew an opportunity when he saw one, and started sidling toward the doorway. If he could just clear it—

A hand caught him at the throat. Or was it a catcher's mitt? So big that the palm alone spread from his ear to his shoulder, the hand

321

drove him deep into the room and slammed him into the side wall so hard, it left him dazed and numb.

"Siddown!" Rex Moss roared. "You're next!"

The voice echoed like a kettledrum.

Cut down to size, Jimmy Kirk realized he was being given a crash course in the anatomy of open murder, and there was nothing he could do about it. Big Rex Moss could reach the width of the anteroom to either side without even leaning. There would be no getting past him.

Tyrannosaurus Rex was going after his own son again. He climbed right over the pile of trash and snapping parts in the center of the room and got Roy by the throat.

"Where's my stash?" the father demanded. "Where've you been putting it?"

Rex was choking Roy to death. There was no doubt for any of them. But he was so enraged and choking Roy so hard that Roy couldn't have answered if he'd wanted to.

Terrorized into action that had never been raked up out of him before, Roy suddenly raised the electrical chip in his left hand and raked it across his father's flabby cheek as though scraping paint.

Rex bellowed in rage and pain, hoisted Roy clear into the air overhead, and pitched him across the room.

Dizzy and tingling, Jimmy struggled to get to his knees and keep aware of what was going on, but he couldn't muster enough dare to challenge the giant again. Not just a giant, but an enraged giant . . . one who had been personally betrayed.

Rex came again over the pile of half-connected machinery, crunch by crunch, grab by grab, ignoring short circuits snapping right under his hands and knees.

"Where's my stash!" he demanded. "I want *all* of it!"

Before him, Roy shook and moved his mouth, but no sound came out. Bruises were already forming on his neck.

"Steal from me?" Rex went on, coming closer and closer.

Roy tried to maneuver away, but there was nowhere to go other than along the wall back toward where he had been before. He edged sideways, confused and unable to think, eyes flashing from side to side, fixing on his father every second or two, for Rex was almost over the pile again, almost to him—

His boot bumped against the tin of chemical cleaning fluid and almost knocked it over. The liquid splashed.

Roy grabbed for it and, miraculously, he got it.

Perhaps he meant only to discourage his father, perhaps to splash some of the fluid in the hideous face coming nearer and nearer, but the tin had other ideas. The top came off completely, and the entire contents of the tin, a half gallon of chemical fluid, fanned out across Rex Moss, and across the pile of parts under him.

The pile of charged and connected parts, half of them still flowing with power.

A funnel of sparks went up in a giant short circuit. Big Rex bellowed to a pitch no man his size should be able to hit, and he froze stiff, then started to shake.

His eyes bugged out, then out farther. Electricity broke into jolts through his arms and legs and set his hair on fire.

Sizzling like an ox on a spit, Rex Moss started to fry. His clothing burst into flames as though someone had cast a spell on him and was burning him in effigy somewhere. Locked by ugly science to the material under him, Rex grabbed convulsively with both hands at the mountain of metal, eyes still fixed on his son. Lightning surged through him and left scorch marks on his forehead as wave after wave permeated his enormous body, the soaked clothing and wet metal conducted electricity with nothing short of passion, and he started to cook.

There was nothing for him to do but hang there, and fry . . . and fry . . . and fry.

Jimmy dodged for cover, betrayed by his tied hands, and barely got under a broken chair as the sparks rained and splattered around him. He glimpsed Roy dodging for cover too, his face redefining astonishment.

The stink of burning chemicals and blistering flesh was nauseating as the liquid soaked in and crackled viciously. The big man collapsed, his body poaching where it lay, flabby face bubbling as though it had been blow-torched, eyes wide with pure horror, but still fixed on his son as the life seeped out of them.

Ultimately, the last grab fell from his fingers. He lay there, a sizzling heap on top of a sizzling heap, slowly being cauterized by electrical heat.

Overcome by terror and scalded by splashed fluid and sparks, Roy lay almost on his back and stared through his knees at his father's broiled body.

Suddenly he cringed against the wall, slammed the wall with his fist so hard his fingers could have shattered, and he shouted bitterly.

"Why did you make me do that? Why'd you make me kill him! That's not supposed to happen! He was a big man! Now, look at him! Look at him!"

Rex was still staring at his son, and neither of the boys could tell if he was even dead yet.

Suddenly Roy jolted to his knees and closed the distance between himself and Jimmy with staggering speed and held the stunner at Jimmy's head—the stunner that Jimmy didn't even realize Roy still had.

"You'll pay for this! I'll make you pay!" Roy spat, half sobbing and half enraged, unable to take the blame for his father's death himself.

The fried junk under Rex Moss shifted abruptly and the huge body shifted too, drawing Roy's attention again.

He turned away from Jimmy and spoke to his father's gawking, blistered face.

"Not my fault . . . not my fault . . . it's not . . ."

Jimmy came out of his hiding place and looked, but not with the regret or compassion that Roy demanded. There was simply nothing left in him for these people, who had possessed chance after chance to mend their mistakes and hadn't done it.

"Now you can render him down into soap," he droned. "Get some use out of him."

Shuddering, Roy leaned against the wall, both knees bent, breath coming in sucks and blows through his nostrils, his teeth gritted, lips closed tight. Every cell in his body was shaking with palsy, as though he were ninety instead of nineteen, and he couldn't stand up without leaning.

Expression after expression came and went, none of them particularly rational, but Jimmy could see that Roy was rallying his mind and trying to get it to override his emotions—of which he had plenty.

An interesting process to watch. Insanity taking seed.

"Destiny," Roy said finally on one of those gasps. "Makes sense . . ."

Scooping his ever-present nerve stunner from where it had fallen beside him, he pushed himself off the wall and stood over his father's body, shoulders tucked down and inward, feet out, knees in, trying to keep balance. He still looked old.

"It knew," he murmured. "Forced me to take over . . . grow up before I was ready . . . it knew maybe I *am* ready . . . I just didn't believe it. Destiny . . ."

He straightened a little, seemed to be gathering his inner strength, almost against his own will. Being in charge was something he had thought about all his life but had never considered within reach.

Unwilling to walk too near Big Rex's body, he sidled along the wall until he could extend a long arm and get Jimmy by the collar.

"I've got to get to the bridge. Get moving."

Veronica Hall let out a bone-shattering groan as her shipmates dragged her through a jarred door panel, then lay her down in the corridor as they gathered their wits and their options.

George panted, sweated, and tried not to let his hands clench too tightly as he watched Robert and Carlos replace Veronica's medical cartridges for the fifth time since coming aboard this vessel. A strange ritual, this lurking about, covert, dangerous, in danger, all the while hauling an injured girl who needed nursing as diligently as if she were lying in an infirmary.

While watching this again and feeling the acid of responsibility and inadequacy peeling the paint off his heart, George made a decision that tasted bitter as he forced himself to speak up.

"Robert," he began.

"Yes, George?" Robert responded with monklike calmness.

"I'm going to go on ahead."

"Yes, I understand."

"Can you hold out here?"

Robert looked up at him, pale and gathering all the will he had left. He glanced at Carlos in a comradely manner, then back at George.

"We'll do whatever is necessary," he assured him. "You go take charge and find your son."

"Where *is* everybody?"

Roy ground out his words while pulling at a drawer of circuitry in the corridor wall.

The circuitry was dead, the intercom didn't work, the sensors didn't work, a good seventy percent of the doors didn't even open anymore in the passages leading to the bridge.

Off to one side, just out of kicking distance, Jimmy clamped his lips shut, rubbed his hands to keep the blood circulating in spite of his bindings, and didn't respond. The ship did seem peculiarly, eerily, empty. The crew was missing, communication was down, everything was down except those special shields.

"What are your people doing?" Roy demanded. "Do you know what they've done? Do they have a plan? Do they follow a policy? If you tell it to me, it may help keep us all alive."

Bobbing him a glance, Jimmy shrugged. "How should I know? I'm just a kid. Besides, how can a few Starfleet gorillas compete with an intellect like yours? You know . . . Darwin would understand."

Roy actually growled at him, teeth locked and nose wrinkled, and threatened him with the stunner.

Jimmy had been proud of himself for one or two good jabs, and here was his father in eight places at once. His father and Captain April—he tried to imagine Captain April clunking somebody on the head, and just couldn't see it. Robert April would sit them down and give them a good talking-to, and the guys would feel guilty and give themselves up.

*Then* George Kirk would hit 'em.

A main insulator door opened before them and they went into the upper level of the ship, and came around a corner to a horrid sound of pounding and banging, easily traced to a torn-up section of corridor wall. There, right on the wall, a line of locker-type doors were rattling, which they traced down to one particular locker.

"Stand back," Roy ordered, gesturing Jimmy well out of kicking range. Keeping one eye on his captive, his "personal shield," he traced the banging to what could have been a locker or a control panel with a hinged door.

Whatever it was, the door was ajar and somebody was in there, rattling like crazy and trying to get out. Roy grabbed the door and tried to pull it open, but only the top quarter would budge.

"Open it!" a voice roared from inside.

"Munkwhite?" Roy attempted. "Is that you?"

"Get me out! Get me out of this hole!"

"It won't open."

"Open it!"

"Would you like me to spell 'won't'? It's jammed. Who did this?"

"Those Starfleeters! They're here! They jumped me! Just get it open!"

Roy rattled the door halfheartedly, obviously thinking more of himself and the fact that several Starfleet people were loose on his ship, then gave it a final kick and said, "Well, it's your tough luck for being stupid." He turned to Jimmy again. "Come on, you. Let's make hay while the sun shines."

Nervous and ready to use his stunner, he yanked Jimmy in front of him again and off they went, with Munkwhite hammering away in the background almost until they reached the bridge itself.

There, Lou Caskie was alone, wide-eyed, frozen with pure terror. He looked twenty years older—and he was already old—and on the ravaged bridge, with chunks of machinery the size of sofas and chairs collapsed across almost any sensible path. What Roy had inherited was a miserable ruin now, a hulk of hissing parts and spitting leaks, and one old man who was panicking.

"What's left?" Roy called over the crackles and noise.

"Where's your father!" Caskie shrieked, his voice snagging. "We're gonna get killed in here! We're gonna die like rats!"

"Where's the rest of the crew?"

"I don't know! Nobody answers! The sensors don't work anymore! Intercom's down! Crew don't answer! They're all dead!"

"They're not dead," Roy droned, climbing over a big chunk of junk and going down to the bridge center. "But they're going to be." He gestured to Jimmy. "You—get down here too. Stand over there where I can see you. What are your friends doing? You tell me!"

"How should I know? Just a kid, remember?" Though he did as he was told, Jimmy had no cooperation in his voice when he taunted, "Ship sure is quiet, isn't it?"

"Shut up! You shut up!"

"What're you gonna do?"

"I'm going to play my last card, smart-ass. I'm going to turn off the heat everywhere but right here."

Jimmy felt the cockiness drop from his face. "You can't!"

"They'll all freeze," Roy said with flaming satisfaction. "And we'll have Starfleetsicles."

"Keep talking," Jimmy antagonized. "Sooner or later you'll believe yourself."

Enraged, Roy turned on him and started closing the space between them, using his nasty little nerve-stunner to bridge the gap.

"I've had it with you!" he grated. "I don't need you anymore. This'll shut you up!"

From behind them—

"Stop right there, bud."

Jimmy thought it was his own voice, but he and Roy turned at the same instant and found themselves staring down a laser pistol barrel and over that toward one of the engineering crawlway openings—

At George Kirk.

Clamping his lips, Jimmy had a flash-thought about not giving away his dad's disadvantage—the fact that the kid was *his* kid— but from a low point behind the crawlway Lou Caskie appeared on the other side of the bridge, brandishing a sharp piece of metal.

Without even thinking, Jimmy shouted, "Dad, behind you!"

His father reacted almost as spontaneously by putting his foot in Caskie's face. Clearly, that's how he had been explaining his way through the ship. An instant later, the old man was out of the picture.

But while George Kirk was occupied with Caskie, Roy wasn't standing idle.

He dove for a panel and put his hand under it—the shield controls—

"You can't fire that faster than I can move my finger!" he shouted, trembling. "You can kill me, but not before I turn off the deflectors and we're all dead! You can't put me down fast enough! You can't!"

He was right.

"You'll die! Your son'll die! Your friends'll die! I'll do it! I'll do it! Give it to me!"

"All right!" George barked.

"No!" Jimmy interrupted. "Don't do it, Dad. He'll kill us anyway. That's the way he is." With a dissecting glare at Roy he added, "We can't let him win. You were right. This shouldn't happen to anybody else. Better we all die here."

His father straightened and stared at him. "No kidding?"

Jimmy offered a duelist's nod. "You bet no kidding."

"Shut up! Shut up! I'll do it!" Roy howled.

With eyes made of smoke, Jimmy took a step toward Roy. "Then *do* it. What's taking so long?"

On the upper deck, separated from the two boys by a huge chunk of collapsed machinery that he would never be able to get over in time, Jim's father said, "No!"

Jimmy stopped and looked at him with a "but" in his eyes.

"Back down, Jim," George said firmly.

Roy crouched there with his finger on the switch, watching the two Kirks and trembling so hard his teeth clattered.

Broiling, Jimmy felt a hundred arguments rise inside him. He wanted to be defiant, but somehow defiance didn't fit the bill anymore. It wasn't real. It wasn't right.

Both hands out in a subservient posture, George lifted the hand laser's barrel a few inches, raising the aim off Roy, then stepped forward just enough to lower the weapon and set it on the chunk of machinery.

"Get it," Roy snapped, and waved at Jimmy. "Pick it up by the barrel and hand it to me."

"Get it yourself, chicken," Jimmy snarled. "I got my pride."

"You get it for me or I'll do this, I swear I'll do this!"

"Jim," George said steadily, "do what he says."

Perplexed, Jimmy frowned.

"Do what he says," George repeated.

He connected looks with his son in a manner so honest and so private that both felt the magnetism.

Jim said, "He won't do it, Dad. He won't kill himself."

On the upper deck, measuring his options in inches, George Kirk studied his son's face. There was a certain quiet communication going on between the two of them that hadn't been there in years—and he was sure he wasn't imagining it. He could see just *looking* at Jimmy that there had been a change. Jimmy had a look of confidence—confidence in *him.*

Slowly George added, "Orders."

Without understanding why, without waiting until he saw the reason, Jimmy simply said, "Yes, sir," and followed an order that he disagreed with.

With a winning smirk on his face about having somehow pulled his tail out of the fire again, Roy Moss was closing his white, cold hand around the laser. He licked his lips, stood up, and aimed the weapon squarely at Jimmy's head.

Roy was knotted from head to toe, keyed-up and nervous, excited, scared, and elated to the point of giddiness that he'd won, and he had to rub their noses in it.

"I knew you couldn't beat me! Nobody beats me. You thought you had me. I know you did. People think that all the time about me, and they're always wrong. Now everything's going to be mine and you're just going to be dead. You should've listened to your son, Mr. Kirk," he said. "Now you can watch him burn."

The weapon leveled at Jimmy's head, and Roy squeezed the molded firing handle.

Jimmy didn't wince. He was ready for any scenario, and his trust in his father was riding an all-time high. If he had to catch a laser beam in his teeth, he'd do it just to make the point. He'd learned.

*Ffffssssst . . .*

The weapon whimpered.

Horror dawned on Roy's face that he'd been gulled into taking a useless weapon, that he'd been made a laughingstock—the one thing he couldn't stand. Being suckered by ordinary idiots was too much.

He had barely realized the weapon wasn't working when he heard Jim Kirk's father let out a yell.

Abruptly the whole ship was yanked sideways—everyone, everything, was thrown. The Kirks hit the same wall at the same time, and Roy turned, saw something flying at him—and part of the collapsed ceiling glanced off his chest and knocked him sideways.

Though Jimmy was pressed against the bulkhead by gravity and by shock, George had the advantage of knowing what was happening to their ship. He thrust himself against the whining new gravity and got his hands on Roy, and threw him as hard as he could.

George Kirk's attack drove Roy toward his shield controls. With a shout of pure, incredulous fury, Roy dove for the panel that controlled his shields again, but that card had been played and the Kirks weren't going to let him table it a second time. This time Jimmy had an extra second in his own favor and used it for a headlong plunge, tied hands joined in a hammer.

He knocked Roy to one side, then tackled him and laid him out flat. They ended up lengthwise on the littered deck, pressed against the bulkhead, George Kirk knee-down on Roy's spine, coiling the boy's hands with a discarded length of insulation tape—

Then George grabbed for leverage and shouted, "Hang on, Jim! Hang on!"

"What is it!" Jimmy yelled over the whine. "What's happening to us?"

"You know what it is, pal! It's a starship!"

# THIRTY-ONE

☆

"Ah, here's our Artful Dodger even as we tickle his ears."

Robert April's charming voice took the entire hospital deck of the starship *Enterprise* and somehow made it a stage play, complete with popcorn and curtain calls.

The popcorn smell came from the eight or ten different medications being pumped into what was left of Veronica Hall's body as she lay on a complete life support diagnostic bed. The curtains— they were everywhere, blue and white, some for sterility, some for privacy. All for Veronica.

"Sir," Jimmy began as he limped to where the captain sat in his best British visiting position. "You all right?"

Captain April wore a sling on one arm and a notable bandage on the other forearm, which made Jimmy remember the condition April had been in when they'd last seen each other.

And that voice, which could make any situation a poem.

"I'm quite fine, my boy, thank you," the captain said. "How are you doing?"

"Bad leg and about forty bruises," Jimmy said. "One cracked rib."

April nodded. "You must be disenchanted such that we'll never entice you back toward the service. Twice in space, and twice attacked. However will we convince you to stay?"

Jimmy dropped him an aweless look and grinned. Somehow he felt on more equal footing than he ever had before with this man. "What's the big deal about making me stay?"

Robert smiled. "Oh, let's just say there's a certain martial tradition I see fledging in the Kirk nest . . . a rare muster of those who will stand on a volcano if tactics beckon . . . hmm?"

"Hmm," Jimmy grunted back. "How's Mr. Florida?"

"Carlos? A bit stretched in the pinfeathers, but we're all here, Jimmy, we're all here . . . not without due commendation to you."

Jimmy found himself blushing, and turned to Veronica. "Can I talk to her?"

"She's been waiting for you," the captain said civilly. "Then I'll take you to your father."

He approached the diagnostic maze with the cold fear of those who still have all their limbs. It was like suddenly joining a silent guilt society.

The girl's skin was glazed white—from the inside or outside, he couldn't tell—and made him think of the girls he'd been drawn to before, in better situations, and the moon under which he'd been drawn to them. Every vein that could be reached in her body was attached to a tube, a tape, or a bag. Her right arm and leg were missing, those arteries and sterilities taken care of artificially. Everything looked blue. Her skin, her curtains, her hair, her eyes as she blinked at him—

He flinched. It was like having a corpse blink at him.

"Hey, crackerjack," she murmured.

Wasn't much of a voice. He just hadn't expected to be talking to her.

Veronica smiled a tiny little smile. "Heard you used some top-notch stopgaps when you got on board their ship."

"Bet you can't say that twice," Jimmy said. "Bet I can't either."

"Just old-fashioned," she said. She stopped to swallow, and her eggshell cheeks grew more hollow. "Captain April always talks about old-fashioned ways getting us through . . . guess he's right."

"Yeah, I guess he is," Jimmy uttered. "How do you feel?"

She seemed to think the question was funny. "You mean with one less arm and one less leg? I feel okay, considering . . . I'm alive,

333

aren't I? Lucky to be here. That's the bottom line . . . don't worry, Jimmy, they'll fix me. . . . Starfleet knows how to fix anything . . . the big bird pulled us out, after all, right?"

"The *Enterprise,* right," he said quietly.

"Jimmy, you did great. Captain told me what you did . . . how you didn't let them take you easy . . . thanks for giving me a chance to live."

A grilling guilt overwhelmed Jimmy as he frowned at the reflection of himself in her respirator. Bad enough he felt this way because she was lying there after saving his clumsy life—bad enough he'd blundered his way to somehow getting out of this—but here she was, thanking him. Thanking him. He was getting glory in a cheap way. He was getting it through those who had done the real giving.

Touching what was left of Veronica—hopefully a wrist and not just a main umbilical—he scooted a little nearer.

"Veronica," he began, "it wasn't me who was the hero. Look at you. You're the one who sacrificed. You're the one who really gave."

"But I couldn't be here to talk about it," she whispered, "if not for you . . . I know . . . they told me everything . . . solves a lot of questions about this area . . . now we can clear up the Interstellar Maritime Laws for this area and rules of the road . . . rights to search . . ."

"What?" Jimmy leaned over her and tried to find the focus of her eyes.

"Signal a merchantman to lay to . . . leakage and break-age . . . apply the negligence clause . . . according to the Interstellar Code of Signals . . . two intermittents . . ."

"Veronica?" Jimmy stood up and leaned closer, but there was a hand on his shoulder, drawing him back.

"She's dreaming, Jim," Captain April said. "She's taking her Academy tests over again. Let's leave her alone to study, shall we?"

Jimmy straightened, and sought comfort in the captain's gentle face. "She won't have to, will she? In spite of . . . ? She'll still be in Starfleet, right?"

Robert April's soft features turned into that pondside smile he gave when he needed to be believed on an extraordinary level. He slipped his good arm around Jimmy Kirk's shoulders and walked the boy toward the intensive care door.

"Starfleet never abandons its own. Once commissioned, always commissioned. All rights and privileges ascertaining thereto . . . no matter how much of the dirty side that person may carry, and indeed sometimes because of it."

"Sir . . . you lost me," Jimmy said. "You might have to put that one in English. I mean—American English."

April smiled, sought help at the ceiling, then drew a long, contemplative breath.

"Trapped me," he murmured. Hanging a hand on Jimmy, he said, "You survived because you have a bit of the dirt in your soul that let you understand those men."

Jimmy rolled his eyes. "Gosh, thanks."

"Now, I'm sullenly serious and you'll just have to bear it. That's why I laugh when your father frets that you'll turn out to be a hoodlum of some kind. I tell him he's seeing only the streak that will save you some day—may save a lot of people. Who can tell the future? You see, Jim," he said softly, "a clean soul can't fight a dirty one and win. I couldn't have, and I've always known it. That's what you have, and men such as I lack. This isn't the kind of advice I'd ordinarily offer gents of your age, but, Jimmy, keep that bit of the gangster in you . . . you may need it to do things that men like me can't find the grit in ourselves to do. Know the rules, my boy, but know when to break them."

Captain April's words lay before them like a carpet as they walked the corridors of the great starship. They looked at each other, and each knew the other understood—everything. All the ugly everythings that life was really made of.

"There," the captain went on, "isn't that a naughty bit of advice for me to give you, officer and gentleman and Englishman that I am? You won't tell a soul, though. You're one of mine, I know. Now, let's closet that and go see how our favorite copperhead rattlesnake is interrogating your prisoner."

The interrogation grid down in detention was a lot different from intensive care. Just as ugly, but with a clearly less noble purpose.

Jimmy had heard the phrase "rogue's gallery" somewhere before, but until now he'd never limped the halls of one.

The two of them had to go through four separate levels of security before they were allowed to open the door of the interrogation room.

There, inside a small cubicle, the first thing Jimmy saw was the old family friend and general pest, Drake Reed.

Drake was doing his see?-I'm-a-Security-guard-of-the-first-order imitation in a corner. His brown face was stoic, brows up, collar just a bit raised, sidearm pushed forward on his belt, and his hands behind him in the at-ease position.

In spite of all that, he flashed Jimmy and Captain April a Caribbean smile that was all teeth, then instantly fell back into the on-guard face.

Jimmy hoped that meant things were going all right. Sure meant Drake Reed was glad to see them both as they came in slowly and heard the door panel lock behind them.

They stayed very quiet.

At a small, plain black table, wearing a gray Security prisoner suit and looking spookily correct, sat Roy Moss. He bore damnably few scars from the ordeal he and his father had put others through. His hair was even combed and his ponytail nice and neat.

Across the table, also sitting in deference to a bandaged left calf and the narrow sling on his own arm, was George Kirk.

As Jimmy first saw his father, he felt guilty again. He had a few bandages of his own, but he suddenly wanted to take on some of the wounds others had taken and deal with those for them. Suddenly he was aware that he was limping, but that was all that showed. His father had both hands bandaged, and even a small one on his right cheek. If his dad had a sling and Captain April's shoulder was in an immobilizer, why couldn't he get a sling or a crutch or something?

Just as he was realizing how stupid that sounded, Jimmy was pressed by the mood of the room and by Robert April's firm hand to stand silent against the closed door panel.

"You better start opening those pretty lips, boy," George Kirk was saying in a growling tone. His bandaged hands gripped the edges of the black table as though in pain. "I want the names of the ships. Every last one."

Roy not only didn't respond, but didn't react. He shifted casually, seeming not to understand that he was expected to participate.

"We've downloaded most of your computers," Jim's father went on, "and I just got the list of most of the ships you've attacked, and it's incomplete. It's damaged. You can complete it. You're going to if I have to peel your face, and I wish to hell I was joking. These mysteries that just got solved . . . have you got any idea of the pain . . . the strain, and the anguish you've caused? The people who didn't know what happened to somebody they loved? Don't you understand why we want to know?"

He leaned forward toward his prisoner, and the interrogation lights fell on his red hair, there dividing into tiny strand-by-strand spectral patches. His hands gripped the table so hard that Jimmy and the captain winced with empathy.

George shook his head and stared downward, dizzied by the pain he described.

He looked up again.

"Don't you get it?" he demanded. "It's one thing to have a person die, to have a memorial service and know what happened . . . but do you know what a mystery does? What *not* knowing feels like? Have you even bothered to keep track of the people you've killed? The families you've tortured?"

There was nothing in Roy's face. The most excoriating nothing imaginable. A *nothing* that could be boxed and preserved.

Roy Moss was the box. A professional nothing holder.

Jimmy glared at the nineteen-year-old statue and saw what he had been aimed toward, what he could have become. Not only could he have died on one of his crazy rebellions, but he could have done worse. He could have turned into this. Mr. I'm Right. At the expense of any—

A sharp cackle of furniture broke Jimmy's self-recriminations. The chairs crashed to the sides. The table struck Jimmy's leg and drove him back into Captain April, and suddenly a carrot-topped thundercloud was crushing the shocked prisoner up against the closest wall.

"Dad!" Jimmy plunged in before his father could hurt himself or his reputation, or even hurt Roy. He had his fingers around his father's knotted arm, tangled in the sling that was being ignored right now.

Drake Reed flew out of the at-ease position, leapt right over a spinning chair, and suddenly became a fully functional Security man. But, surprisingly, he didn't push George Kirk away from the attack—in fact, he helped smash Roy Moss flat against the wall and made sure it didn't turn into a brawl. He held Moss's wrist and knee against the wall and waited to see what would happen.

Jimmy was trying to figure that out when something pulled him all the way back until he had to let go of his father. Captain April's voice brushed his ear.

"Jimmy—let your father handle this."

What? Passive Robert April stopping him from letting his dad peel Roy's face?

But adults didn't understand reality—no . . . he knew better than that now. Those old traps wouldn't catch him anymore. Smart people weren't that simple. There weren't molds or forms for men like Robert April or George Kirk.

*I'm going to be a man who didn't come out of a mold. I'm going to be like them . . . like both of them, somehow.*

His fists had been twisted in his father's uniform shirt, but now he backed away. With a small nod he let Captain April know that he understood.

Some things just deserved doing.

The room was small. The table and chairs were on their sides now. All the action was happening near the door panel. All the tough decisions. There, under the ugly and unforgiving entry lights.

George Kirk's face was as red as his hair. He pressed his prisoner tight to the wall, eyes watering with pure sore fury, not just for the dead but for those who had lived with the mystery. His throat muscles twisted like the cords on a sailing ship hard to the wind, and his teeth were gritted and bared all out.

Held by both men, spread-eagled against the wall with George's fists under his jaw, Roy Moss didn't want to be hit, but there wasn't anything else there. No appreciation for *why* he was being hit, or for the emotions that were driving him to be hit. He was just Roy, all out for only Roy. The pressure of gauzed hands against his esophagus put only the fear of street bruises in his face. He backed tight up against the wall, an inch or two taller than his assailant. George's forgotten sling batted casually against both their elbows.

Drake didn't move, but didn't relent in holding the prisoner from making any countermoves. He waited. Jimmy connected a glance with him, but everyone was waiting.

George saw the fear in Roy's face. Didn't bother him. But he also saw the silky skin and hairless jaw, the smooth brow and the eyes without lines, and that he had knocked loose a few strands of lush brown hair to fall forward with youth's bounce. He saw a tinge of what might be genuine scare. The kind that truly doesn't understand because there's not enough experience. He didn't know the boy.

The boy, the boy.

"I can't," he gagged suddenly.

He pushed backward, still holding Roy there, and glared down at the tiles of the floor between his feet and Roy's. His arms were straight out, trembling now. He started gasping.

"I can't . . ."

Captain April stepped around Jimmy, got George by the shoulders, and pulled him away. Drake stepped back also, keeping Roy Moss at arm's length, and glaring warningly.

Keeping one eye on Roy too, Jimmy found the presence of mind to right a chair so his father could sit down again. As he arranged the chair, he looked at Roy.

Somehow Roy's expression hadn't changed, but *somehow*—there was a nasty victory in his face. Maybe it was the sudden relaxing of his eyebrows or a new set of his upper lip, but it was there, and it was nasty and Jimmy didn't like it. Roy hadn't won. He *hadn't*.

Why did he seem to think he had?

Jimmy could only hold on to the back of the chair and glare at him. *You didn't win, you snot. Don't stand there, blinking at me.*

Beside him, his father let himself be steered into the chair, then leaned against Captain April and shook his head over and over, gasping, "I can't . . . I can't hit a kid. . . ."

That was enough. Jimmy sidled away from them, took hold of Roy's elbow in an authoritative grip, as any good Security officer would—

"I can," he said.

In the textbook of street survival, it was called a roundhouse right. In Jimmy Kirk terms, it was short, low, quick, and a big surprise, and served a little pouched lip on top. A bit of the dirt.

In anybody's book, the blockbuster punch knocked the cockiness right out and left Roy Moss flat on the interrogation room floor.

Drake Reed scooted backward on all ten toes, hands in the air, and blurted, "Per-*cussion!*"

Near the toppled table, Robert April held George by the shoulders, looked down, and just chuckled irreverently.

George was still gasping, but now it was a happy gasp.

"Wow . . . how 'bout that. . . ."

## Part Five

# HARD ABOUT

# THIRTY-TWO

USS *Enterprise* 1701-A

"Captain, massive power drain!"

"All stop! Shut down."

Something in the way the captain responded made the bridge crew know that he had expected this. Or at least he had expected a change, had been thinking ahead, and was saving up those four words.

The bridge crew flew into response.

"Navigation, all stop, aye!"

"Helm, aye! Full drift, sir!"

"Engineering, aye, all remaining thrust shut down, sir."

"Long-distance communications just buckled, Captain," Uhura said loudly but calmly. "Unable to communicate with Starfleet."

"Don't try," Kirk snapped.

"Aye, sir, silent running."

"Mr. Chekov, calculate our ahead reach and make sure we're not going to hit anything."

"Ahead reach, aye," Chekov responded, already frowning over his navigational instruments. "Calculated, sir."

"Transfer it to the helm and stand by."

"Transferring . . . standing by, sir."

The ensign with the pretty eyes at the starboard submonitors—Devereaux—suddenly gulped a chunk of air and blurted, "Reading flushback again, sir! Magnitude nine!"

· "Confirmed." Spock's baritone supported her squawk. "But this time—*we* are the source."

The captain absorbed that statement and all its dozen implications, then moved only his eyes.

"Funny," he said. "I didn't feel us explode, did you?"

Still peering into his monitor, Spock said, "According to any recorded science, the only source of antiproton flushback is the explosion of warp engines. The only source of warp engines is hyperlight vessels." With unmistakable curiosity, he turned his head and somberly added, "And I can confirm that we did not explode."

Kirk didn't wait for reports from anyone else in the bridge crew.

He ignored glances from the two engineers behind him, went straight to his command chair's commlink and tied himself directly in to Commander Scott in main engineering.

"Scotty, Kirk here. Start talking."

*"Captain, this is Engineer's Mate Tupperman—Mr. Scott's unable to respond—he's hands-on up in the tube, sir!"*

"Throw a communicator up there."

*"Yes sir, he asked for one . . . but we had to call down to supply—"*

*"Scott here, Captain. It's a core-invasive dampening effect at the matter/antimatter mix level. It negated our warp field. Power slipped in one big drain down to twelve percent before we could grab it back, but I've got the twelve in abeyance. We've encountered this type of damper before, and I'd bet a bundle we can isolate the invasion and use our remaining twelve percent to push against it. On your orders."*

"No, Scotty, stand by on use of the power. Isolate the invasion formula and prepare to act against it, but for now I want you to maintain an illusion of total shutdown. Keep the twelve percent in abeyance and in the meantime let's pretend we had a total shutdown."

Scott paused, then said, *"You're implying it's not natural? There's someone you want to corner?"*

Jim Kirk got a clean mental image of Scott's squarish face

buckling into a combined snarl and furrow, one eye narrowing as the chief engineer anticipated going after somebody who would do this to their *Enterprise*. Scotty and the *Enterprise*. Duck and pond.

"That's right," Kirk said. "We may need that twelve percent later, and I want to keep it in my back pocket. For now, play dead."

*"Whoever's doing this, we may need to distract them while we're doing the necessary technological voodoo."*

"I know how that works," the captain said. "I'm usually the distraction."

*Uh . . . aye, you are, at that. I'll buzz as soon as we have the option, sir. Scott out."*

Without turning, Kirk tossed over his shoulder, "Uhura, get Dr. McCoy back up here. Spock, anything?"

Spock's elegant form straightened in the upper deck shadows, and he turned to speak quietly to the captain.

"Sir . . . I believe I have a fix on the *Bill of Rights*," he said. "Alive and intact."

A cloudburst of relief crashed over the bridge with such palpable force that every crewman physically wobbled and engaged the purely human tendency to look around to see if anybody else was wobbling.

James Kirk stepped up onto the quarterdeck to Spock's side and asked, "If *Bill of Rights* didn't explode, then what caused the flushback?"

"Evidently it is related to the dampening field that has stopped us."

Kirk got up out of his command seat and prowled the bridge, glaring at the forward screen, which showed him nothing more than the barren Faramond system and its little star. "What's the location of the *Bill of Rights?*"

"She is in stable orbit at the Faramond excavation planet, but otherwise appears immobile."

"Can we adjust our drift? Come within hail of her?"

"Possibly."

Spock didn't like to guess or bluff, or take half-informed stabs, but he had learned to do all of those after decades among humans, who would try anything rather than give up. He stepped closer to the captain and offered a theory that would have turned him inside out two decades ago.

"The dampening problem is more an envelope than a curtain, if you will forgive my metaphors. Your order to review the earlier encounter with Faramond has given me some pause regarding deflector shields, and I analyzed the changes in shield technology over the past fifty years. In keeping with the original design, this ship was mounted with older-style starship shields, of the type that can be focused to specific types of energy. The type meant for hard-core exploration rather than exploration, research, patrol, and transport."

"In other words," Kirk said, *"Enterprise* shielding was made for a savage, unsettled galaxy, meant to guard us when we didn't know what was past the next star."

One of Spock's brows lanced upward. "Bluntly accurate, sir. *Bill of Rights'* shields are stronger inch by inch, but are more general and less selective. *Enterprise* may have a chance that *Bill of Rights* did not have. We may also be able to actually extend our older style shields to include the *Bill of Rights."*

"And communicate with her?"

"Exactly. We may also be able to protect her long enough for her to rebuild her own power."

The captain's eyes grew slim and sparkled with angry anticipation. "Do it, Spock," he said.

Spock nodded toward the helm. "Gentlemen . . . dead slow."

"Dead slow, aye."

"Aye, sir."

"Captain?" Uhura interrupted. "I'm getting something from Captain Roth . . . I think."

"Why do you think?"

"It's an old code . . . very faint blips." She leaned toward her equipment, her wall-relief eyes taking on severity, and she tampered with her earpiece and the equipment that fed it. "Part Morse, part Lonteen's Light . . . I believe it's intended to be that way—a combination."

"Definitely Roth," Kirk said. "Definitely someone who served in my crew. She knows you're a specialist in old codes and not every starship has you. It's a bet I'd take. Can you read it?"

"Yes," she responded with a touch of hesitant humility now that he'd crowned her. "Attention . . . *Enterprise* . . . have possession . . . Faramond diggers . . . beamed whole colony . . ." She frowned, gritted her teeth at her equipment, then shook her head. "Blotted out, Captain. Interference from a third source. Direction is vague . . . a planetary source."

Kirk swung around to Spock, partly to leave Uhura alone with her aggravation, and partly to grab the sense of impending advantage he felt picking at him. "They beamed up the archaeologists!" he said. He looked hungrily at the main viewer, which showcased the dinky star system, its ornery little star, and the four unimpressive planets of which Faramond was one deep space chunk of dirt. "Better hostages aboard *Bill of Rights* than sitting in a cave on Faramond. Uhura, stop attempting to communicate with *Bill of Rights.* Try to break through to Faramond."

She turned toward him. "Will there be anyone there now, sir?"

"We'll know in a minute."

"Yes, sir."

She tapped and annoyed her instruments until they chirped at her.

"Sir, you're right," she said. "Making contact. I can give you audio."

When she gave him the nod, he stepped down to his command center, turned to that main viewer, and talked to open space.

"This is Captain James T. Kirk of the USS *Enterprise.* I want to speak to Roy Moss."

A dim, eerie pause held the breath of all who heard. Clearly, there was someone on the other end, listening.

Everyone on the bridge knew what that sounded like. It was different from the sound of no contact.

The pause was broken only by the meager interruption of the turbolift door emitting Dr. McCoy. He came down to the captain's level just in time to hear a new voice from the machines.

Kirk concentrated on the screen and repeated, "This is the USS

*Enterprise,* James T. Kirk commanding. Is Roy Moss on the planet?"

He almost felt foolish asking again, but the whole idea was foolish. Just a hunch. Just a guess—

*"This is Roy Moss. Who up there knows who I am?"*

"I'll be damned," the captain whispered.

He circled his own chair, one hand lingering upon it. He digested that voice. Tried to hear the sound again in his mind, then reach back forty-five years to see if it was the same. He couldn't tell. Forty-five was a lot of years for a voice to stay the same.

"This is James Kirk," he said again.

*"So?"*

Dr. McCoy stepped down and leaned toward him. "He doesn't remember you, Jim," he murmured. "It all fits."

Kirk wanted to commend the doctor for having done his homework, but the torch of anger that burned through him caught all his attention.

"He almost killed me, but he doesn't have the humanity to remember. I remember every crewman and even every enemy who died under my command, but he doesn't remember me."

McCoy leaned even closer and muttered, "People don't impress him."

Kirk's brows tightened downward and he raised his voice. "You've come a long way from the Blue Zone, Moss. But you're still a petty little tyrant, aren't you? Still just stealing."

*"Who* are *you!"*

Another pause like the first one—a pause of thought or realization.

*"Ohhhhh! . . . Jim Kirk! I know who you are! I haven't thought of you in years!"*

"Nor I you," Kirk shoved back without a beat.

*"How did you find me? Why did you come?"*

"You're holding a starship hostage. Did you think we wouldn't notice?"

*"How did you even know? They can't contact you, there's no long-distance blipping, they can't move or signal—"*

Squinting bitterly, Kirk taunted, "Maybe we're smarter than you are."

*"Yes, you're brilliant as ever, Kirk, caught in the same trap as the other ship. Sure, I remember you now. I ought to leave your ship dead in space for what you did to me. What the hell, I just might. I don't need two ships."*

Kirk started to speak again, but Ensign Devereaux squeaked, "Sir—uh-oh!"

"Specify, Ensign," Spock told her.

"There's a . . . some kind of a laser hitting our hull, sir. It's old and weak, but it's heating up on our unprotected hull."

*"Scott to Bridge. Captain, you might have to use that twelve percent you're holding back for the shields. That's a weak wee heater, but it's building up on us. Permission to power up?"*

"I agree. Maybe we can make a deal. First you tell me what this is all about. What is it you want this time, Roy?"

*"Why don't you just beam on down and I'll show you."*

"Why should I?"

*"Because you're itching to. For the same reason you couldn't just get away forty-five years ago and had to bust your way onto my ship. And I want to see the look on your face when I make your whole career meaningless."*

"I'd like to see you try," Kirk said. "We're not in transporter range."

*"Hah! That's beautiful. Not in range. That's poetry, it's really poetry. Yeah, a transporter's not much good from way out there, is it?"*

Nervous at Moss's odd sense of humor regarding the fine, dangerous science of transporting, Kirk moved along the back of his command chair. "Why don't you let us come into transporter range?"

Roy Moss just laughed and laughed. *"You'd love that, wouldn't you?"*

"What's so funny?" Kirk challenged. "Afraid I'll beat you again?"

The laughter stopped abruptly, and that hideous pause reprised.

*"You never beat me,"* Moss said. *"Come on down in a shuttle. Then you'll really appreciate what I've got. But you come down alone, got it? All alone."*

"I've got it."

*"If you try to screw me up, I'll drag that other ship right down into the atmosphere and burn her into little pink bits of metallic dust. You got that?"*

"I said I did. I'll be right down."

*"You be forewarned . . . I'm not a teenager anymore."*

The threat made everyone on the bridge look up. There was something very cryptic and not at all silly about the last words as the communication abruptly cut off and the bridge went silent.

The captain sensed what was happening, but ignored it.

"Neither am I," he uttered.

Kirk swung around to Uhura and made a slicing motion across his throat. When she signaled that communication was definitely cut off, he vaulted to the upper bridge. "All stop."

"All stop," the crewmen at the helm responded in chorus.

"Secure from battlestations. Go to yellow alert."

"Aye, sir, secure from battlestations . . . secure from red alert, aye . . ."

"Yellow alert, aye, sir."

Spock seemed uneasy with the level of cross-grained bluffing and restraint, but contented himself with technicals as he said, "This man obviously fails to understand his own science. He possesses a warp-dampening field. Each time the *Bill of Rights* attempted to go into warp, the field would be countered and drained, sending out waves of antiwarp, or flushback. The flushback reaction moves at hyperwarp, faster than a ship, and can be detected light-years away. He can lure a ship to the planet and hold it there, but does not understand that his trap launches its own warning signal."

"He's a genius," McCoy added, "but there are gaping holes in his knowledge. He accepts ninety percent knowledge as one hundred percent. He didn't realize this thing could be detected from so far away. He's always been this way, hasn't he, Jim?"

"Always, considering a forty-five-year hole in *my* knowledge about him," the captain droned. "Roth must have bluffed him somehow. Or outguessed him fast enough to beam up the Faramond archaeologists." He aimed toward the turbolift, fists knotted, and turned at the last moment.

"We may be able to use that somehow . . . before he can make good on that threat. I didn't come all this way to find the *Bill of Rights* intact just to lose her again. All hands, general quarters until further notice. Commander Chekov, you're in charge until Mr. Scott's engineering voodoo is ready. Communicate with Captain Roth if you find any way to do so. Mr. Spock, Dr. McCoy, both of you come with me. Mr. Chekov, notify the flight deck to prepare a shuttlecraft for launch. The three of us will be down on Faramond . . . being damn distractive."

He mounted the short steps toward the turbolift—and found himself blocked by Dr. McCoy and a very fierce glare that was part country doctor and part pioneer gunfighter.

"Jim, what's making you do this?"

Kirk glowered at him. "Do what? Go down and take care of the problem?"

"No. Go down and take care of this *particular* problem. Do you really know what motivates this man?"

"It's just revenge, Doctor. Stand aside."

But McCoy wouldn't get out of his way. "Revenge doesn't motivate Roy Moss," he said. "He doesn't care about those things. Doesn't understand intangibles like duty, self-worth, satisfaction, and betterment—only that he has a bigger pile of whatever than anybody else."

"Make your point," the captain demanded.

"I am making it. You're the one who ordered me to become an expert on this man, and I did. Roy Moss never grew up. He's still nineteen years old. He hasn't learned a damned thing in forty-five years."

"I'll tuck that away."

The captain started to step past him, but McCoy actually bumped into the frame of the lift door and grabbed the captain's upper arm in determination to stop him and get his say. By now the whole bridge was watching.

"Where would you be if not for Roy Moss?"

Kirk's shoulders squared self-consciously. "Where would *I* be?"

"Oh, yes. You thought I was paying attention just to facts on those archives you send down to me. A chief surgeon has to also be trained in crew psychology. I know you were out in space for only the second time, and I know what happened the first time. Those pirates would never have attacked your ship without Roy's shields. Without Roy Moss, would sixteen-year-old Jim Kirk ever have become the Jim Kirk of Starfleet? You probably wouldn't have gone into the Academy, and you certainly wouldn't have made it if you had. And all the things pioneered by you and your crews and the *Enterprise* might never have happened." The blue eyes flared suddenly. "You didn't think about any of that, did you?"

"He wanted to bring glory to himself, not to me. Get to your point."

"We never get over some things from our teenage years," McCoy pestered—truth in the form of needles. "I'm just asking, is this the best thing for you to do? If this wasn't Roy Moss . . . would you go down there at all?"

Suddenly on a roll, McCoy sucked a breath and kept hammering, heedless of the taupe fire in the captain's eyes and the tightening he saw in the captain's jaw. He took no warnings, but kept on.

"Despite all you've achieved," he drilled, "could it be that you still want to best Roy Moss in a one-on-one contest? Could it be that after all these years you still have to prove who's the better man? Could it be that *you're* the one who wants revenge?"

Kirk felt his face flush. His eyes started to feel like pincushions, prickled and burning.

"It was his psych file I had you analyze, Doctor," he warned, "not mine. Now, get yourself the hell out of my way."

# THIRTY-THREE

———————— ☆ ————————

The gritty, druidic landscape crunched under his feet as James Kirk stepped out of the shuttlecraft after piloting through the narrow tube that led them inside the atmospheric dome on an otherwise unlivable planet. The domes themselves were impressive—five of them, each ten miles long, three wide. Ah, technology.

He paused and gazed at the planet's purple-on-gray surface. It looked like elephant hide with crystals spilled on it.

"Well, Dad," he murmured, "forty-five years late, but I made it."

"You say something, Jim? Lord amighty, who'd want to set up a colony on this dry cracker?"

Kirk was deciding whether or not to respond to McCoy, when a bright, violent curtain of screaming light struck them and they huddled. Blinded, they stood their ground, but all arms came up to protect their eyes, and Spock shouted over the whine, "Sensors, Captain!"

With a nod Kirk said, "Stand your ground!"

The sensor screamed and crawled over them, then a voice bellowed as though through a bullhorn. "Drop the phasers and all three communicators. Smash the communicators. I want to have the only one."

"Golly, who can that be?" McCoy dryly grumbled as the light snapped off as suddenly as it had hit them.

"Do what he says," Kirk ordered.

A few seconds were lost as they blandly removed their weapons and dropped them on the dirt, then ground the communicators into the dust with their heels.

Kirk scouted the land, then walked the necessary twenty yards and confronted Roy John Moss as though they'd seen each other yesterday.

"All right," he demanded. "What's so funny?"

Roy Moss stood a few feet above them on a raised piece of ground, holding a phaser on them in one hand and a fairly basic non-Starfleet communicator in the other. There was something hooked to his belt that looked like a control box chirping for attention like a baby bird, but he ignored it.

He seemed more fascinated by the forty-five years' difference in their appearances, and scrutinized his old adversary for every line and every curl that was new, trying to see through the decades to the scrubbed, freckled, muscular blond boy who had given him such trouble at that key time in his life.

Moss himself had taken on a coarseness that hadn't been there in his youth, was grayer and somewhat thicker at the waist, but other than that he was recognizable by anyone who knew what he was looking for—and Kirk did.

Yes, this was Roy Moss. Even the ponytail was still there. Iron-gray, but still there. So was the distrust in the eyes. The startling intelligence right on top of the distrust. Yes. The same person.

There were ghostly lines and glimpses of Rex Moss in his face now that he was so much older, none of which had emerged yet at the age of nineteen. Back then, he and his father hadn't appeared related at all. His nose was meatier now, as Rex's had been, and there was more flesh at his throat. There was a beard now, a Galahad-type pointed beard, a few shades lighter gray than the ponytail, and small mustache that was almost white.

That's what the years had done—put the father into the son. The age around his lips, the yellowish-whiteness in his eyes, the thinness of hair in spite of the persistent ponytail, the color of his skin— those were from Rex. Sometimes resemblances took twenty years to show up. Or forty years . . .

*Do I look like my father now? Are there hints of him in my eyes that my mother would recognize? The way my cheeks crease when I'm angry, or the tuck of my chin?*

Ghosts from the past.

The eyes were the recognizable. Strange, Kirk noted, that the glare could look so familiar after so long. A chilling sensation . . .

Moss involved himself in his memories for a few seconds, seemed to relive the whole experience on the *Shark,* then leered with a weird fascination at Spock and McCoy as they came to Kirk's side.

"Said you'd come alone," he pointed out.

"I lied," Kirk said.

Moss tipped his head, and after a moment even nodded. "That's good. I like that. I'da lied."

He gestured them toward him, but he was holding a phaser on them from enough paces away that they couldn't jump him.

"It helps me," he went on almost as though he were talking to himself. He attached the control box to his belt next to his communicator, made a long grab for McCoy, and yanked the doctor toward him. "It keeps you under control. One move from you, or the Vulcan and I'll shoot this other guy. I know your type. You'd rather I shoot you than him, so I'll shoot him if you do anything."

Spock made an instinctive move to put himself between McCoy and Moss, but Kirk motioned him off with just a flick of his brows. Moss would indeed kill McCoy if he decided to. Moss would kill—there was no reason to doubt it forty-five years ago or now.

"They're each here for a reason," Kirk told him.

"What reasons?"

"You figure them out. You're the genius."

"All right, I will. Just give me some time. And if any of you try to knock me over, I'll just shoot wild. See that dome over us, pretending to be a sky? That's what I'll hit. Then we're all dead. I guess that's simple enough, even for you tough guys, right?"

Kirk didn't even glance up at the poor excuse for blue overhead. He knew this was a lie. Roy wouldn't hit their only protection.

But Roy's eyes still had the glint of assumption, as they had in his youth, and the Starfleet officers took this as the warning it was meant to be.

Kirk looked past Moss to McCoy—the one who was here to deduce Moss's psychological condition.

The doctor bit his lower lip and raised his brows in an expression Kirk had seen before. *Don't push.*

"So," Moss said, "you're here in the Constitution-style ship, aren't you? Sounds familiar now that I think about it. Kirk . . . captain . . . weren't you an admiral for a while? I remember the colonists babbling about this. Now you're back captaining the old version of starship?"

"The first version," Kirk corrected. He didn't care if arrogance came off in his tone.

"Thicker walls," Moss said, "trimmer decks, different thrust-to-mass ratio, touchy intermix formula," he rattled off, "and nothing inside but a few hundred crewmen. I wouldn't trust that many people. Of course, all the ship is, really, is big speed. Just big fast. That's all your old starship is. Basically a house for its own engines. Weapons and science labs can be mounted on a barge, after all. Starship isn't a starship unless it's fast . . . and I'm about to use one of them to make them all obsolete."

Kirk glanced at Spock.

The Vulcan offered an expression in only his eyes that the captain read as a shrug. Use the *Bill of Rights* in some kind of experiment?

Three Starfleet spines suddenly went rigid, and they stopped and glared at him.

"Keep moving!" Roy ordered, jamming his weapon into the soft place under McCoy's ribs. "I'll slaughter him first and your old ship second."

"It's not an old ship," Kirk snapped. "It's the second starship *Enterprise.* A remake of the first Constitution-class sh—"

"Who cares? It uses a classic deflector-shield method, doesn't it? *My* method . . . which *I* never got credit for?"

Moss phaser-pointed them across the bleak, rocky landscape pocked with a few archaeological tents and pathetic excuses for hiking paths, under an eerie, unnatural glow from the miles-long dome, but he kept his phaser at McCoy's back and eyed the others the whole time, and they eyed him back.

"Hmm?" he badgered. "The method which was stolen from me? Any of you going to admit it?"

"There were others working on it who would've broken through soon," Kirk said. "You never got credit because you didn't stick with the project. You didn't do the development."

"Because I was sitting in a rehab colony, thanks to you and your papa. I sat there till I was twenty-five. Thinking the whole time. Then, I came here."

Moss didn't sound angry, yet his tone was laced with a disturbing irony and a devious grin that bothered the Starfleeters. He obviously liked the bothering part.

Spock's voice buttered the crunchy purple landscape.

"We diagnosed your special deflector shield decades ago. You found a way to focus the deflection against isolated threats, and no more. It made your shields seem a hundred times more powerful than they actually were. Federation engineers dissected your theory, applied it, combined shields with sensors—"

"Stole my ideas."

"Expanded," Spock repeated firmly, "your theories and further developed them, because they know that every scientist stands upon the shoulders of those who come before. It is a building process."

"And you're a needle-eared regurgitator. Big deal. It's all talk."

Jim Kirk suddenly stopped walking and scraped around in front of Moss. "You think everyone else should start from scratch at the Stone Age, even though you didn't, right?"

Stock-still, Moss gripped the phaser tightly between them. "People who came before me were idiots."

"You don't give any of them credit for the foundation you're standing on. Take from all, give to none, share nothing, fear being robbed—your obscurity was your own choice. You could've continued work on those shields, but you fumbled the ball, Roy. You made your own purgatories. Don't blame anybody else."

"Purgatory?" Moss waved his free phaser in a big arch. "I don't need any security out here! Tourists come and go, delegations come and go, diggers come and go, boatloads of students . . . I've been working here undisturbed for thirty years. I wasn't going to take any chances that a little oinker like you would ruin my plans again. Now I'm ready. All this ancient equipment is lined up and cleaned—it's fairly simple. I figure it all happened about a hundred thousand years ago, and the problem was that the stars have shifted. So I had to recalibrate it."

Kirk felt his features crunch when the subject suddenly changed in such a bizarre way. He used what he knew about Roy Moss to try to deduce what was happening. His feet got cold, as though he'd just stepped into a pool of ice water.

"'It'?" he prodded.

Moss glared at him analytically, then all of a sudden looked at Spock. "Ohhhh . . . you brought the Vulcan here to figure out my science, didn't you? That means this other one . . . is a psychiatrist. He's supposed to figure out my motivations or my mental stability, right?"

McCoy gave him a dirty glare. "I'm Leonard McCoy, ship's chief surgeon. I'm here in case of injuries."

"And in case of insanity," Moss was sure. "The other side of the balancing act. I know how these command things work. And everybody sends the chief surgeon down in case of skinned knees and splinters. That's all right—you're still a hell of a good target, Doctor, and your captain over here knows I'll drill a juicy hole in you if they don't behave, so go ahead and analyze me up and down the cliffs for all I care."

He waggled his phaser directly at McCoy's head to make his point, and something about the way he did it erased any doubt that he would shoot.

"Get down there. Down that ladder."

He pointed to some kind of geological bowl, crater, or dried pond bed that opened before them and went down two choppy levels, where he had put a simple wooden ladder.

Moss grinned as they started down before him, and he stayed up on a small, glittering promontory, then pulled the ladder up behind them, and they were trapped.

"You should see the looks on your faces. You'd think you were midshipmen."

"Why don't you get to the point?" Kirk demanded. "What is it you want?"

"Respect."

"You won't get it from me. You've got to earn it."

The words were barely out and—*zing*—back forty-five years to the sound of his father's voice. The same words, the same feelings, new dangers.

"You'll give it to me," Moss said, "when you see what I got here. About four thousand miles from here, there's a machine. Its power core is a hundred and sixty miles straight down underground, so your ships can't find it. Here—watch this. You'll like this."

He fingered his control box without even taking it off his belt, and things started to change in the very rock.

Behind Moss, a picture of the *Bill of Rights* formed as though projected on the rock. There was no projector, but there was the picture, as tall as Moss.

"Jim, look out!"

McCoy shoved him from one side and Spock pulled him from the other just in time to keep him from dropping into an opening that appeared at the pond bed's center. Before they could react any more than that, a set of dull-colored pill-shaped orbs the size of melons rose in no particular order out of the ground. There was no noise, no metallic substance about the oblong things, and they were disturbingly unarranged.

"Control center, Captain," Spock said. "Probably a computer access. Obviously built to the social taste of the ancient culture."

"They must have thought Faramond was pretty, then," McCoy commented when the orbs stopped rising.

Only to the educated eye did this smooth collection of bowling balls appear to be a computer of any kind. To a child it might look like a gathering of balloons, each independent with a glowing interior and a pliant, almost gummy surface, all different colors, but all versions of the ivory-to-ash spectrum.

In the side of the pond bed, right out of the dry rock there, part of the rock separated and revealed what looked like a child's idea of a library—books or tapes, stacked side by side, in long, curved racks. Apparently, these and the balloons were meant to be used together.

At least, that was the symmetry of their movements.

Spock's eyes lit up when he saw the volumes, but he didn't say anything.

Kirk and McCoy pushed up behind Spock for a look at the

brilliant past culture. Certainly the collection seemed alien. Though neither captain nor physician dared touch the balls, Spock was on them like a bee on pollen.

His long fingers left marks on doughy surfaces, but the marks filled in almost immediately, as though he had pressed wet mud.

"Poke all you want," Moss said. "Unless you know the order of information feed, you're just poking at rubber. At first I thought they might be kids' toys."

"Where is your power center?" Spock asked him.

Roy looked at him in a disgusted manner. "It's built in."

"But *where* is it," Spock emphasized. "Physically?"

"Underground, I told you."

"How do you know?"

"Because I put it there. It's the only thing that was missing. It took me my whole adult life, but I added a matter/antimatter converter to the central core complex. It's almost as powerful as what you have on your pretty ship, Mr. Brock."

"Spock," McCoy corrected fiercely.

"Fine. Where did you idiots think I was getting the power for my dampening field? Magic? Anyway, the machine is ready to go and all I have to do is turn it on. All you have to do," he added, "is watch."

"What does this machine do?" Kirk asked. "Wait a minute! Don't start it up yet! Tell us what it *does!*"

Moss squared off before them, squared his shoulders, squared his brows, squared everything about his posture, as though to build himself into a castle before their very eyes.

"I'm going to move the fastest thing in the galaxy a hell of a lot faster than it can go. I'm going to show how you move things around if you're Roy Moss. I'm going to take your big fancy *Bill of Rights,* all its six hundred eighty crewmen, and all the Faramond archaeologists, and transport them all the way back to Starbase One in a single beam. And you're going to serve as my living witnesses. How's that for a destiny, hm?"

Roy Moss stood above them, looking from each to the next as though to taunt them. His eyes were wide, brows up, arms fanned outward.

"You haven't figured it out yet, have you?" he quizzed. "I've given you enough information—"

"You have discovered a long-distance transporter," Spock said. His interruption sliced Roy's insult in half. "Some form of frequency-focus method of travel."

Moss confirmed Spock's words by looking a bit disappointed.

"Wait a minute," Kirk said. "Is this thing operative? Do you understand *how* it works?"

"I don't have to," Moss said. "I've figured out how to operate the controls. You drive that ship up there, but could you build a warp engine? Of course not. You don't need to. That's for mechanics to do."

Jim Kirk moved dubiously from one side of the dry bed to the other, just as he had paced the sunken command deck of his bridge, never taking his eyes from Roy Moss.

"This thing has been shut down for a hundred thousand years," he said, "and you're going to plug power into it and go from there?"

"I've got it aimed. What can go wrong?"

"Have you tested it? Put any power to it before today?"

"No. Why would I?"

McCoy rolled his eyes. "Uh, boy . . ."

Moss looked at the doctor. "If I did that, Starfleet would have heard it and come in and taken it all away from me. After all, one little buzz and here you are, right?"

Above them on his ledge, he huffed a sigh, pushed his phaser into a pocket, and looked at the ground.

"I'm the only one who figured out how to make it work," he said. "Faramond's an old, cold system and I'm the one who made it warm again. When I was fourteen, we salvaged a ship on its way back from here—"

"You mean you pirated a ship," Kirk drilled.

"Shut up. The ship had all kinds of relics from here that made the Federation decide to dome and dig. But archaeologists are always looking backward. Even though I was fourteen, I was the only one who looked forward. I'm the one who figured out the normalized symbols, that the language over here under this rock was the same as the language over there under that outcropping . . . I found the commonality and discovered that it was a device for frequency-focus travel . . . instantly stop existing here, start existing there. What would *that* be worth to the settled galaxy? The Fabrini and a half-dozen others have found this stuff, and none of them knew what to do with it."

All three Starfleet men surged forward.

"The Fabrini were here?" McCoy gasped. "Have you had this checked?"

Even Spock let a trace of shock run through his question. "A race as advanced as the Fabrini passed this by?"

Kirk stepped as far forward as possible and pressed, "Doesn't that tell you something?"

Moss couldn't ignore their reaction. In fact, he seemed proud that an extinct but far superior race had come here and gone away without the prize.

"They just couldn't figure out how to work it," he said. "I've turned up a dozen artifacts from past digs of other visiting civilizations. None of them were as patient as I was. They came and went, and after a few years they got used to me and I just went about my work."

Kirk felt Spock step forward to ask a question, and caught his old friend by the wrist just in time to keep him silent. "How do you know you're doing all this correctly?"

"Because it was *simple!* You don't think for a hobby, do you? If I took your shuttlecraft back a couple hundred years, it would still be obvious which way it points and where the pilot sat, wouldn't it? Drop a World War Two biplane into King Arthur's age, and a clever person could figure out how it steered." Moss nodded at them with raw pomposity. "I told you—I had it figured out when I was a kid. Before I even met you, Jack."

"Jim," McCoy spat.

"Yeah, Jim, Jim, right. All I had to do was ask *why* any advanced race would put an instrument here. It's a cold system, right? Nothing growing, no heat, no life—a giant gravitational field and not much else. A big magnet. So that's what I went looking for. I let the Federation archaeologists set up the domes and the artificial atmosphere, then I started picking."

Moss pecked at the dirt and stone with his toe, as a child pecks at beach sand.

"Those Federation dopes ran around here, scooping up trinkets and brushing off fossils, while this incredible technology sat idle just a few miles away. They never figured out what happened to the Old Culture, and I had it figured out when I was fourteen." He looked at them as though to be sure they were paying attention to his win. "Somehow the gravity or mass of this planet, or maybe its effect on surrounding space, were necessary to their project. But why a cold planet? I asked myself that question—and I answered. They needed an inactive core, because that's exactly where the heart of their transporter is—at the gravitational dead center! That's where I found it when no one else was smart enough to look. Great, right?"

Pacing again, he started grumbling as though talking only to himself.

"I tolerated those piratical pigs in order to get my stake for the big score, then you came along and set me back years. I never depended on anybody else again. Just me. I knew what a long-distance transporter would be worth to the Federation. Or anybody. Klingons, Romulans, I don't much care. It'll make me one of the most powerful beings around to control the LDT. The LDT . . . good sound to it, doesn't it?"

"Yes, Roy"—Kirk glared up at him and pushed—"you cling to that 'it.' You don't have anything else. You've always expected 'it' to come in the future. Forty-five years and you still have nothing but a someday. Even after all these years, you still have no *today.*"

Silence fell suddenly and left only the buzz of the dome.

Roy Moss had counted on having to immobilize a starship to use as his example. He hadn't counted on having to immobilize Jim Kirk.

Deprived of respect, he went hunting for it. His eyes were boiling.

"What do *you* have?" he asked. "You're a captain. So what? You've risked your life a hundred times, I'll bet. What've *you* got to show for that? A couple of stars and bars? You're at the end of your career, you've run all over the galaxy, you've gotten a lot of people killed, and for what? You don't even own that ship out there! Everybody says 'Kirk's ship,' but it's not your ship. You've been in charge of a machine that could lay waste to anything! You could've flown into orbit around some planet and declared yourself god to any culture fifty years younger than yours, and there's nothing they could've done about it. They'd have to say, 'Yes, you're god, you sure are.' You never knew what you could've had! Which of us has wasted his life?"

Abruptly, cruelly, Jim Kirk's attention was dragged back to the most potent weapon anyone could strike him with, and he went bitterly silent, a prisoner to the words from up there.

"If you hadn't stopped me forty-five years ago," Moss badgered, "I would've developed this back then! All the deaths in four decades of exploration and accidents at high speeds—they're all your fault! Who are you now, Jim Kirk?"

To Spock and McCoy's unexpected dismay—a dismay he could feel on either side of him—the captain didn't say anything.

The control box on Roy's belt started yelping at him, and he grabbed it and read something on it.

"All right, what're your friends doing in that stupid ship?" he demanded.

"Okay, I'll just hit 'em with another damper. I'll just go pull the stopper out of the bathtub again. Something must be broken. Equipment failure or something. Stay down there, because you can't get out. I've got the area electrically sealed. Sure, Mr. Vulcan, I see your face—play with the machine all you want. You couldn't figure it out in twenty years, and you couldn't hurt it with a phaser. Even I don't know what it's made of. I'll be back as soon as I beat your friends off. I can't wait to see your faces when you see history happen."

"Spock," the captain said.

Immediately Spock turned to the ancient, alien controls and the snakelike shelving of ancient books, or cards, or whatever they were. He scanned the books first with his eyes, then with his tricorder, then picked up one and began leafing through its stiff, leatherlike pages.

"I am uneasy with this," Spock puzzled. "Others have been here, including races as advanced as the Fabrini, yet even they could not make the long-distance transporter operate. It is unlikely that Roy Moss is the most brilliant creature to come along in the galaxy . . . ever."

"Don't tell *him* that," McCoy drawled.

Spock turned to him and added, "There must be a reason these intelligent races have left this mechanism alone. His assumption that we could not locate this machine's core simply because it is underground—"

"Makes perfect sense, Spock," McCoy shoved in, "given his psych profile. He only sees weaknesses in others. He was never formally trained, learned everything on his own, and didn't even realize his flushback could be detected from far away. One of us said it before—gaps in his knowledge—"

"Spock said it," the captain supplied.

"Well, one of us said it," McCoy went on. "Moss is smart, but he's learned only enough in life as he's needed to know to achieve his goals or protect himself. He sees no value in knowledge itself, did you notice that? Only in knowledge as it leads to power."

"Or recognition," Spock added.

"Jim—Jim, what's bothering you?" The doctor stepped toward Kirk, ignoring their commander's attempt at solitude. "Jim, don't let him get to you. This man's psychological profile isn't any different from the one you handed me on board the ship. He hasn't changed in almost five decades. He's a textbook example of Huerta's Emperor Syndrome, and even that wasn't enough for him. He'd become an emperor, then spend all his riches trying to become a deity. I should write a dissertation on him! McCoy's Pharaoh Syndrome."

"If we survive, you can write a book." Kirk turned to Spock and said, "What do you think?"

"A long-distance transporter is a fabulous advancement, if he can indeed do it," the Vulcan said fluidly as he picked through the ancient library. "No more death, no danger, no risk of travel at warp speeds . . . there could be instant exploration, far less cost and loss of life in the name of a single look at a new place or a contact with a new race—"

"I don't trust him." McCoy pushed between them. "Jim, how thorough could he have been? As critical as you were to the turns in his life, he didn't even remember you!"

"The incident meant a lot more to me, Bones," Kirk said. "All he remembers is that he lost. He's completely wrapped up in himself.

That's the scary part. Roy Moss doesn't think about people. If this thing works, even a little bit, even if it costs the lives of everyone on board *Bill of Rights* to find out how to operate it, he thinks the Federation will forget about those lives eventually and honor him for the discovery. And he's much more dangerous at sixty-five than he was at nineteen."

"This man," Spock said, "does not seem to consider the reality of probability, Captain. He accepts a ninety-percent chance of success, but not the ten-percent chance of failure. There are no allowances for failures of machines, failures of others, failure of himself. Yet—"

"Yes, he bets everything on every spin of the wheel," McCoy finished. "The hole in his plan is that he never sees the hole in his plan."

Kirk pushed his way out from between them so he could pretend to be alone again. "The *Bill of Rights'* crew and all the Faramond archaeologists might fall through that hole. The entire ship may die."

Kirk's thoughts were now with the *Enterprise.* The original.

But now that first ship was gone, burned up, sacrificed, and there was a replica in her place. A model of her, a tribute, yes, but not the original ship that had taken them through voyage after voyage, danger upon danger, and somehow survived. An incredible feat, considering that even poor docking could rip a hull apart.

The same style of ship, the same kind of hull structure, the same interior structure, the same mass to thrust, and all those other same things that Roy Moss had so casually tossed off. But it wasn't the same ship. This one hadn't earned her stripes. She hadn't been given a chance.

That was the miracle of the old ship . . . that she had survived all those dangers, all those storms, all those attacks, all those hands at her helm, all the brand-new things that no other ship had encountered because no other ship had gone out so far, and all the little mistakes that might have been made by whoever was at the controls from moment to moment—a compilation of survival and skill and luck that only old ships could show off.

She'd been lucky, the old *Enterprise.* This new ship was a tribute, yes, but she hadn't paid her way yet.

And now she wouldn't get the chance.

Starfleet had apparently already made that decision.

Spock and McCoy could see the gravestone sitting on Jim Kirk's shoulders, tooled with an inscription dictated by Roy John Moss. An era about to pass. Even the tribute was being decommissioned.

McCoy maneuvered closer, just to Kirk's periphery. "Moss has managed to incapacitate the *Bill of Rights* and the *Enterprise,* but he didn't count on the wild card . . . he didn't count on Jim Kirk being here again."

"Just as well," the captain said. "I'm tired of people counting on me."

The captain's voice lacked its old burn. A lot was missing that could be painted in colors of fire. Was this why men chose to retire? When the fire washed away?

If the pond bed had had bars, Jim Kirk's hands would have been wrapped around them. He would have been staring between them, the cold metal pressed against his face and blood running to his cheeks. His eyes would have been fixed upon the landscape, if there were one.

There was nothing in his eyes that had been there four or five decades ago. Today he wasn't the bulldoggish James Kirk he'd been on the bridge of his command ship, who flourished during danger, gone on the hunt for it, who tasted adventure on the tip of his tongue and had to bite.

He wasn't even the Jimmy Kirk he'd been on the bridge of the *Shark,* secretly enjoying the sensation that rashness had provided to a goalless teenager. That was the time he'd first learned that spunk could be put to a valiant purpose.

His dad had taught him that. . . .

All the red-blooded overzeal was gone from him now. He kept waiting for the valor to arise as it had in every other situation, but nothing came this time.

He had lost more than years when the first *Enterprise* went down, for he'd failed to go down with her. He was tied to his ship by the captain's string—and when a ship dies unhelmed by its master, the string draws tight and kinks the captain's spine for the rest of his life. He may never again walk as tall, move as swiftly, glare as fiercely.

Such was the portrait here. The captain without his ship. The mind without its heart. James Kirk without his *Enterprise.*

"My ship is gone," he murmured. "My career is ending. Maybe this is my best destiny, Bones. My full circle . . . from Roy Moss to Roy Moss. This is where it began . . . maybe this is where it's meant to end."

Usually an ardent man whose short words were delivered sharply, McCoy barely moved behind his shoulder this time, and had the good sense not to touch him.

Seconds whispered past.

The captain's phrases roamed and settled without really having anywhere to go. No one in here wanted them. McCoy didn't even have to glance over his own shoulder to Spock to know their thoughts were consonant.

"Spit in the eye of 'meant to,' Jim," the doctor said gently. "You always have before . . . why not this time?"

# THIRTY-FOUR

──────────── ☆ ────────────

Like boys telling ghost stories in a tent deep in the alien night, they kept their voices low.

"Is he right, Bones?" Kirk didn't look at him. "Did I prevent something from happening that could've kept thousands of people alive over the years? Of all the decisions I've had to make in my career . . . how many have been wrong—and I'll never know? Have I done more harm than good in my life?"

He turned and watched Spock move from the control bubbles to pick through the ancient volumes, as he had for what seemed much longer than twenty or thirty minutes since Roy left them here alone. Spock was working, yes, but he was watching Kirk too. And he was hearing.

"Oh, Jim, for cryin' out loud," McCoy muttered, carrying it on a sigh. "How much do you have to see?"

"I *see*," the captain snapped. "If Moss hadn't been smart enough to pursue power, he would've been frustratingly torturing little animals to get an illusion of power. If he'd gained power, he'd have found out it wasn't enough and would've had to blame somebody and started killing millions of people. That's how it starts—how do I know I'm any different? What would I have become if his father's ship hadn't attacked my father's ship that day? I was a frustrated boy, enticing others to follow me on crazy chances, making

369

decisions they should've been making for their own lives, and that's what I kept doing for the rest of my life."

McCoy shook his head as though somebody had hit him. "Now, you know that's not what I was getting at—"

"Yes, you did." Kirk nailed him down.

"Jim," the somber Captain Spock interrupted as he looked up from his instant education about the alien machine. He stood still, one hand holding a volume, the other on a bubble. "The past cannot be redrawn," he said quietly, "nor can the future be drawn in advance. You learned from your experience with Roy Moss. He failed to learn. He continues to underestimate those who are his equals or his betters."

Supplanted by the hum of the dome above them, his voice was the bass chord of a cello—soothing and simple.

"It is a classic error of military history. Disaster after disaster," he said, "because generals underestimate. Overestimate and be timid, underestimate and be destroyed. All leaders march that line . . . all captains sail it."

Though he paused, from experience the other two knew he wasn't finished.

"I have been content these many years," he said, "to march that line at James Kirk's shoulder."

Spock wasn't prudent about sentimentality as he had been when they'd first struck out together in the dawn of Federation long-distance exploring. In fact, now he was proud of it. How many Vulcans could be sentimental and still be Vulcan?

Kirk gazed at him, and for a flash saw the younger Spock. Then the flash ended, and Spock gazed back at him without the veil of embarrassment they had over the years torn down.

Moderately Kirk grinned at him with one side of his mouth. "How do you always know the right thing to say?"

"I do not," Spock said. "I merely estimate very well."

"What should we do, Jim?" McCoy asked. "Jump him?"

Kirk shook his head. "If this machine is on some kind of buildup, jumping him won't stop it," he said. "Spock . . . is he demented? Or is there something to all this—stuff?"

Spock frowned, still pressing and feeling his way across the floatless gray balloons. They knew from his expression that in a few short minutes he had analyzed Moss's data as Moss had failed to do in fifty years.

"It definitely is a computer," he confirmed. "I can deduce from this information here that Roy Moss is right."

"Ouch," McCoy said.

Spock looked up, then stepped to the racks of books or pamphlets or whatever they were, pulled one out, and showed them what looked like hieroglyphics with ink and fish soup splattered on it. "Fabrini, intermingled with a language I do not recognize. However, I can tell that he is right. This is a long-distance transporter . . . on the order of light-millennia."

McCoy turned serious and stepped closer. "Good Lord."

"I estimate that beaming the *Bill of Rights* back to Starbase One," Spock went on, "would barely warm up the machine."

Though he was impressed, though his iron eyes flashed with a scientific fascination that didn't come along very often these days, Spock's voice carried something that Kirk pounced on.

"But it's not going to work, is it, Spock?" he asked intuitively— not really a question.

Seeming relieved, Spock put the book in its place, then paused with his back to them and his hand on the rack.

"These books are scientific logs, and I do not believe they were left by the Old Culture originally at all. They were left by following visitors, and are purposely made in a low-tech way, so others would not be saddled with incompatible communication technology."

"Brother," McCoy drawled, "would I like to get a gander at your idea of 'low-tech.'"

"Not now, Bones," Kirk admonished. "Spock, go on."

"Thank you. The logs seem to have been begun by the Fabrini, but were added to by other races. None is complete, and each subsequent race apparently abandoned the attempt to use this machine."

"Why would they abandon it?" the captain persisted. "If it was so valuable?"

"Because," Spock said, "it seems to be missing a central connection. This is the terminal . . . but there is no core."

Kirk stepped away, then circled the leathery collection of bubbles. "Are you telling me this is a hulk? A shell?"

Spock turned around. "Yes, Captain. It will accept commands," he said, "but it has no place to send them."

He drew a long breath, knowing he was speaking to intelligent men, but attempting to put across a concept meant only for scientists who had no other life or concern than science.

"Moss is correct that if an old airplane were dropped into the Middle Ages, a clever individual could deduce how it may have steered and flown, but he may not realize it has no engine. What lies before us, a hundred sixty miles under the ground, and all that extends to the planet's core, is essentially a computer without software. The shell of the machine remains here, but the Old Culture took the important parts with them in case they should want to move again, or to prevent others from following, I would surmise. In our lifetimes, it will never work as a long-distance transporter."

"They didn't want us to come walking in their back door!" McCoy said excitedly.

Taking the Vulcan's nod as encouragement, Kirk empathized with those he would never meet. "So Roy decided what it was, then never considered that the people who built it were smarter than he was. I find it damned impolite to look back on the past and be arrogant toward those who invented our advancement."

"Well said," Spock commented as though they were sitting in front of a fire.

Then—maybe they were.

The captain spun toward him. "Is it useless, Spock?"

"Not at all." Spock raised his voice, his scientist's passion shooting through the sobriety. He yanked control back, but he was still excited. "Not at all—the remnants themselves can give our science tremendous direction, sir—"

"Jim, think about it!" McCoy interrupted. "We can analyze the metallurgy, the control techniques, the directional power transfers, the molecular structure—"

Kirk blinked at him for a moment, and realized how easy it was to forget that McCoy was very much a scientist, if a scientist of nature more than mechanics.

"Moss's shields from forty-five years ago are an excellent example," Spock said. "The technology Starfleet developed from their principles has given us nearly a half-century of relatively safe space exploration and battle survival rates." His large, elegant hands swept the gray control center, then the racks of volumes, then all of Faramond. "This can be a leap in technology to rival the Theory of Relativity or the discovery of the space warp. Captain, think of it." He stepped forward, as close to excited as the Vulcan ever became. "The Old Culture used this single compact mechanism to beam their entire civilization countless billions of miles from here—what can we learn from what they left behind?"

"Yes . . ." the captain said. "Yes, but, Spock . . . if the Fabrini and others got to a certain point, then stopped . . . what will happen when he puts power to a mechanism that was meant never to be used again?"

There was a pause, then McCoy was the one to answer.

"Probably the same thing that happens to the medieval guy when he tries to fly that biplane off a mountainside."

# THIRTY-FIVE

☆

"My God, that's the scariest thing I've heard in—hell, must be a half-hour . . ."

McCoy echoed his own grumbles and paced, but there was real fear in his voice and no one attempted to scold him for making a joke.

In fact, Kirk wheeled toward him and spoke with zeal under his own dread. "The entire civilization just picked up and beamed out of here together?"

"Millions of people," Spock agreed, "billions of miles away, thousands of years ago. They are, as you say . . . long gone."

McCoy scowled at him. "Why? Why would a whole culture want to beam across the galaxy?"

At his side, the captain yanked attention back to himself, and to the glitter in his eyes. "Why would a man get in a reed boat and try to cross an ocean? Why sit on top of a Roman candle and try to break out of a planet's gravitational pull? Why are you and I here today? Why, Bones! Because the whole culture wanted to go *look* . . . go see what it's like in another place . . . think of it—an entire culture that said, 'Let's go!'"

He found himself staring upward and wishing the dome would go away so he could look at the stars and think about what was beyond them. His entire body pushed upward, his arms, his shoulders, his chin and thighs, and one foot even went up on a toe.

374

McCoy winced, then ambulated his brows and said, "I'd've liked to see *that* ballot."

But the captain had already moved away a few steps, though the ground shuddered and made a rumbling growl beneath his feet, still looking up. In his eyes a hunger began to reignite even as they watched. In a moment he began to speak, and there was something in his voice that neither of his closest companions had heard in a decade.

Maybe two.

"Bones . . . it's us. It's humanity. We said, 'Let's go!' And so did they!"

Paces away, McCoy was poking Spock in the shoulder with a long forefinger and holding very still, hoping Spock was looking too and would be a witness.

James Kirk gazed up at the atmospheric dome as it turned nauseating colors above him, yet saw not a bit of it.

"Think about that," he murmured. "Think how far there must still be to go . . . what must still be out there. . . . I haven't thought about it in years! He asked me what we get out of what we do, but he doesn't understand it's not like looking for gold. Exploration is an end in itself! *That* is what we get!"

As he was gazing upward, the poison came back into his periphery.

Roy Moss, back on the promontory in front of the projection of *Bill of Rights* on the rock wall, was annoyed and bitching.

He pointed at the projection.

"They're finding little ways around my damper! Why do people even try? What's this guy's name? What's he doing?"

"As if we'd tell you," McCoy high-browed.

Moss stalked around on his promontory, picking and twisting at his control box, shaking his head so that the ponytail swayed, and spitting insults.

"Moss," Kirk began, "are you paying attention to me?"

"I heard you," Moss said. "What else? You're only twenty feet down."

"Good. Now, pay attention. There's nothing here but the controls. The other civilization left a hulk. They took it all with them.

They didn't want to be followed! Putting power to it could create a disaster."

Stopping whatever he was doing, Moss looked down. "Oh, how nice. You figured this out in the thirty minutes I was gone, did you?"

"I'm serious."

"Oh, you're 'serious.' I'm glad you know so much more than I do. When the *Bill of Rights* suddenly appears in orbit at Earth, then everybody'll know a lot. And I'll have six hundred living witnesses."

McCoy pushed forward to the bottom of the promontory. "What if they're not living! Maybe this thing wasn't meant to transport humans! Have you considered that?"

"I don't care about that. It's so simple, what can go wrong? Besides, if they die, they die. Even if the transporter works enough to move the ship, it'll be justified in the long run. Nobody'll care who lived or died. How many of Columbus's sailors died of dysentery on the trip from Spain? Who cares, right?" He pointed at the projection of the trapped starship and said, "When that monster appears at Starbase One, what can anyone say but 'thank you'? The victors write the history books, Doctor. Now, back off before I make you history! Look at my hands," he said. "Look at them! Left! Right! I've got the only phaser! I've got the only communicator! I've immobilized your magnificent prizes! Your starship! I've frozen Starfleet's best ships! There they are, hanging there!"

He whisked his hand across the little viewscreen's image of *Bill of Rights.*

"This is my planet now! On it is the only thing the Federation doesn't have! You were here at the beginning, Kirk, and now you're here to see my reward! You . . . watch!"

He went after his control box like a squirrel going after a walnut.

Nothing happened.

Roy looked at them, and they looked at him.

Then Roy looked at the picture of *Bill of Rights* and held his breath.

Still nothing.

Roy looked at the ship, looked at his hand-held activator, gave it a little shake, put it to his ear, looked at it again.

From below, Kirk asked in a low voice, "Did you put any safeties on it?"

"What?"

But the captain's words weren't really a question at all. "You didn't put any safety backups on your equipment, did you?"

Moss just gaped down at him as though he were the crazy one.

Behind Spock, one of the balloons hissed, and broke open. Steam fizzed from it. Then the steam turned into a spray.

Then the spray turned into a geyser. . . .

## USS *Enterprise* 1701-A

"Mr. Scott, to the bridge!"

The bridge of the sparkling new "old-style" starship thumped with frantic movement.

Pavel Chekov bounded out of the command chair and took his more comfortable position at the science area. He'd always felt better here than in any facet of command.

"Chekov, take the conn," he muttered as he glared into the science monitors. "Chekov has better things to do—"

"Pardon, sir?" a fresh-faced lieutenant called from the science station down the starboard control board from him.

"Nothing," he clipped, his Russian accent adding a certain scissor to his word. "What takes Mr. Scott so long to get up here?"

"No idea, sir," the science lieutenant said noncommittally, but he and Devereaux exchanged a glance.

They knew what it was. Mr. Scott didn't want command either. He wanted to be down there with those engines.

Want or not, responsibility had them all by the throat, and Montgomery Scott thundered out of the turbolift, barking orders.

"Red alert. Battlestations. Stabilize all external systems. Police all local frequencies. All weapons on line. And see what you can do about that bloody communications problem."

Warning alarms erupted—somehow comforting those who had been on edge waiting for them—the ship darkened to alert-status maroon lights, the graphics came into crisp, bright focus, and the bridge rippled into a series of "ayes."

And Uhura's voice throbbing through the entire vessel—

*"Battlestations . . . all hands to battlestations . . ."*

"Reading matter/antimatter power feeding through the core of the planet Faramond, Mr. Scott!"

"Ah, that's just a duck flapping in your ear," Scott growled as he pressed himself into the command chair. "It's a dead planet."

The lieutenant pushed a flop of thin blond hair out of his eyes and insisted, "Sir, there's a massive runaway matter/antimatter reaction generating power through the interior of the planet!"

"Slow down, lad. Just man your post."

The lieutenant sucked a breath, held it, then said, "The core is starting to become molten again, sir."

Scott looked at him a moment, divided the panic from the young man's ability to read the science equipment, then decided to believe him.

"Can the planet take it?" he asked.

"After being cold for millions of years? Doubt it, sir. All the energy is being taken up by the body of the planet itself and it's all going to become molten."

"It's reverting," Scott said. "It's all going to go up. The whole planet's going to explode!"

"Yes, sir—and, sir? *Bill of Rights* is in orbit. She's going to be swallowed by the blast!"

Scott hit the young officer with a look of the obvious, then arranged himself in the command chair, leaning hard on one side. "Not to mention our personnel sitting down there on that bomb. Pull up that twelve-percent power, lad. Divide it half to thrust, half to shields."

"Aye, sir. Power coming up . . ."

"Shield engineering acknowledges, Mr. Scott," Devereaux called from the port side.

"Impulse engineering signals ready, sir," Chekov told him.

"Ahead one quarter impulse. Let's show 'em what this ship can do."

"One quarter impulse, aye!"

"What's happening, Spock!"

Kirk stumbled toward the control balloons as Spock and McCoy joined him there. The balloons were beginning to dissolve, one at a time.

"He activated it," Spock said simply. "The power—"

A fissure opened in the pond bed not ten yards from them. For a terrible instant they had to work to keep each other on their feet.

Was there any feeling worse than the planet itself coming apart under those who must live upon it?

"Mr. Moss!" Spock called over the volcanic noise. "You were right. The entire planet is a giant transporter conductor! That explains why the Old Culture chose a cold rock for their project! But the control mechanism was beamed away too! The power you have put into it now has nowhere to go!"

"A huge short circuit," Kirk muttered.

"I beg your pardon?" Spock shouted over the sound of a planet tearing itself apart from within. "I failed to hear you, Captain!"

"Moss!" Kirk staggered toward the rock wall. "Moss, if you don't want to listen to me, at least listen to him!"

He waved at the smoke pouring from the cracking shells of the ancient computer controls and found his way toward Roy, but McCoy grabbed for him and hollered, "Jim, we've got to get away from here!"

Kirk ignored the flaming obvious, shoved past him, and choked out, "Moss! We've got to get off this planet!"

"No, no," Moss said. Insanely calm, he shook his head and smiled. "You just want me to leave. I'm not leaving my prize."

"You idiot, the entire planet's melting under us!"

Spock twisted toward them without taking his hands off the cracking balloons. "Captain, planetary surface is collapsing."

"The surface is collapsing!" Kirk repeated to Moss. "The planet's melting! Give me the communicator!"

"It's not melting," Moss insisted. "You must have done something. What did you touch down there?"

Looking up from the grotto at the hunched shoulders and brittle outline of his oldest enemy, Kirk felt his fists ball up and his arms go hard.

"It wasn't *us,* you spoiled maniac," he snapped. "Wake up and get over it!"

Moss actually cocked a hip despite of what was happening around them. "Get over what?"

Kirk pushed forward, his hands on the rocks now.

"So you had a bad father! So what! Parents don't last forever, good or bad! Get over it! Comes a time when there's no excuse. 'Poor me, I had a bad life, so I get to go out and be bad to others.' Like hell you do. You've been dragging that fat corpse around for forty-five years waiting for it to sit up and say, 'Son, you did a good job.' It's not going to happen! You're never going to get his recognition! You're going to have to grow the hell up!"

From the vantage of his promontory, Roy huddled his shoulders and they could see, in spite of the banging, clanging, heat, sweat, and burning, a big shiver go through him. "Don't . . . don't speak to me like that. . . ."

"That's your problem right there," Kirk growled up at him.

"Captain!" Spock called.

McCoy cranked partly around at Spock's shoulder and shouted, "Jim, you better look at this!"

"Captain, continents are collapsing!" Spock continued. "Dry oceans are beginning to break open!"

"I'm about to break open myself." Kirk climbed toward Moss. "You're going to give me that communicator, you whining baby. Don't you understand? There's nothing here! The Old Culture didn't go out in a radius from a central hub! They *moved the hub!*"

Moss was thrown to one knee, and had trouble rising, but the shake-up made him really feel what was happening to the planet.

"No . . . no, that's not right. You see, I've—"

Kirk waved a hand dismissively. "You can't do this because they didn't want to be followed! They took the secret with them! No excuses anymore! You've had gold fever for a half-century, fixated on gold that's not here! Your own dream blinded you! You're a spoiled, angry kid, still looking for the same things you were looking for when we met! And you still haven't found them!"

The captain felt the swirling tempest of conflicting atmosphere tearing at his hair as the dome above them shuddered and began to lose integrity—the only thing still keeping them alive. Once the dome went, there would be nothing but a scalded ball in space.

He didn't care. He saw only his anger. He started climbing the crystal rocks, using the anger as his staircase. The crystals cut into his fingers as he climbed, an inch at a time.

"And I'm not going to let you have it. You can kill me, but I'm going to take it all with me. You're still getting nothing!"

"You stop talking like that to me!" Moss bellowed, his diaphragm crushing inward. He shot a hand toward the artificial sky, finger pointed. "I'll drag that ship of yours down! I can do it! I'll drag it down!"

Suddenly, Kirk stopped climbing. He straightened and pressed his lips tight, his glare the kind that cuts.

Then he said, "Go ahead."

Behind him McCoy kept poking at Spock, until Spock had to shrug him off, but they were both staring, neither moving at all, certainly not daring to interrupt.

Above, Moss tilted his head. "What?"

"You heard me," Kirk said. "Go ahead and try it. Those people up there are better than you are."

Roy's mouth twisted and flinched. "Are not. Now . . . you think —you think about it. They are not. I have the only communicator. I can tap into my power stations and haul that ship down. Then what'll you have, *Captain?*"

The man he tried to taunt merely straightened a little more on the rocks under him and had no problem staring upward in spite of crashing and howling planetary collapse.

"I said go ahead."

"Oh, you're bluffing, come on," Moss said. "I mean, I know the tactics, right? We're both too smart for that."

"Try me."

The words, the eyes, the man himself, suddenly statuesque— there was no dare about him. No game. Nothing.

He meant what he said.

Moss glowered down at him, huffed reflexively a few times,

grinned without thinking about it, then brought his communicator around tightly to his chest and started pecking at it.

Past his hands and the small black mechanism, though, were the eyes of James Kirk.

Antique-gold eyes and low brows. Wind ripping at the soft taupe hair and the undone chest flap of the burgundy Starfleet uniform he'd earned the hard way. Shoulders that had never been square but had remained unbending under a weight few could carry for so long, and not a flinch now. Less than ever, in fact.

Below, Spock lost the last of his interest in the gurgling computer controls. At McCoy's side he turned to watch what would happen. Life was ultimately more captivating than any machine, even though that life stood on a precipice and threatened to jump or be pushed.

Moss was clearly irritated. "I'm going to do it," he said.

Kirk didn't move. "I know you are."

Moss pointed upward again, but in a smaller way. "Your ship. Your big identity."

"I know what it is. Our only way off the planet. Yours too."

Shifting from one foot to the other as the promontory started quivering, Moss added, "Your whole crew, y'know."

"They swore the same oath I did. They're ready."

"Wait a minute . . . am I missing something?"

"As usual. And we don't have a minute. Go ahead."

Curious as much as afraid he was missing something, Roy asked, "Why doesn't this bother you?"

"Why?" Kirk's mouth took on a bitterly satisfied grin. "Because I've gotten more out of this in five minutes than you've gotten out of it in fifty years."

"How d'you figure?"

"Because, you brat, I know those people went somewhere. They left the machine, but they took their dreams with them. And somewhere far away from here they built on those dreams. There are ways to meet them, but my ways, not yours. There are more places to explore—more people to meet—I've got your dream, Moss. And you can't have it."

"What," Moss asked, his voice getting high, "what are you . . . talking about?"

"I'm talking about your dream!" Kirk said. His words shot out like staples. "I'm gonna take it. If I leave here, I'm gonna take it. And if you kill me, I'm still gonna take it."

Moss stood over him, fundamentally baffled. Never mind the frantic environment and the planet falling down around them, Jim Kirk stood below him with his arms casually at his sides and a damning chalk drawing of satisfaction instead of anger on his face, one foot up a little higher than the other on the uneven terrain and a hand resting dynamically upon it. He looked like a painting, he really did—he was *enjoying* this!

"I was ready to give up," Kirk told him, "but if I live through this, I've got you to thank for the rest of my life. And if I don't live, I've accomplished things I never dreamed would have my name on them when you and I first met. All because you helped turn me around forty-five years ago."

Rocks cracked off points and fell around them. Pieces of the interior shell of the dome chipped away and spun like giant needles into the ground inches from them, shattering and spraying them. Each jolt of the planetary core reinvigorated the knowledge that James Kirk was not his ship, or even his rank.

Kirk barely moved. He never took his eyes from Moss, and he never even raised an arm to protect himself from the fallout.

"You think those ships up there are Starfleet?" he said, rolling a hand upward as though this conversation were happening in a lounge instead of in the midst of a planet pulling itself apart. "I've been through that," he went on. "I've scuttled my ship. I took her out and watched her die in space. *I* made that decision. And I'm still here! Those are ships, but that's all they are—vessels for ideals. The ideals . . . you can't kill." He nodded at Moss, and at the communicator. "You have the ship. Go ahead—crush it. You can't kill the dream."

Strange how softly he was speaking. Strange that Moss heard him, or read his lips, or got it telepathically—no one could tell. Strange that Spock and McCoy watched from below and saw what was happening, and somehow also heard in spite of the great collapse. Strange that Jim Kirk, a boy on a bridge, saw so well that there was no one thing that could be an answer to a dream.

"It doesn't matter if you're captain or admiral or emperor or god," he finished. "Reach the position at which you can be of most value. But you didn't do that, Roy. You wanted shortcuts. All this time you've been wrong. Forty-five years, dead wrong. All you have is a big short circuit. And my ship?" He tucked his lip and shook his head. "Still wrong. The man isn't his ship. The ship is the man. So go ahead. The only one here with anything to lose . . . is you."

No matter how McCoy had analyzed Roy John Moss, no matter how over decades Spock had learned to be more interested in life than in machines—no matter anything that had happened to them in the past ten hours or ten years, James Kirk still knew Roy Moss and men like him better than anyone else including Roy Moss.

The captain who knew everything he needed to know now began to climb again. Crystals chipped under his fingers and his boots, but he kept going until he was all the way up, standing beside Roy Moss and in front of the weapon leveled on him that Kirk had dared and dared and dared to go ahead and put a hole through him.

Because no hole was going through what he sculpted out of the raw rock of Jimmy Kirk over the years. No holes.

Shuddering, Roy Moss grew smaller and smaller, staring at Kirk.

Kirk jabbed out a confident hand, caught Moss by the wrist, and pressured the bigger man down toward the cracking rock.

As Moss crumpled, he let the communicator fall out of his hand and into Jim Kirk's expectant grip.

The dirt was still in him, and he was taking Robert April's advice. He brought out the gangster to understand the gangster, and he knew Roy Moss didn't have a Starfleet oath in his soul—the oath to sacrifice himself for anything, or anyone, or any dream.

With Moss hunched at his ankles, Jim Kirk flipped the communicator upward.

"Kirk to *Bill of Rights*. Four to beam up, priority one!"

# THIRTY-SIX

☆

The three from the *Enterprise* burst onto the bridge of the class of starship that was going to make everything they had known obsolete—the Excelsior-class starship *Bill of Rights*.

Behind them, two beefy, armed, and mean Security men in helmets hauled the shackled man who had insisted he was going to make even this ship obsolete.

Going hand over hand along the starboard side of the rocking vessel, Spock invited himself to the science station to peer over the shoulder of *Bill of Rights'* science officer, but kept his hands to himself. McCoy stayed to one side also on the upper deck, but was chewing on some crack about who was going to make what obsolete.

Captain Alma Roth swung around in her command chair, her dry brown hair flying in three directions, and she looked like she'd just gotten up after a bad night's sleep. Instantly she found the face of the man she wanted to talk to.

"The ship is completely drained, sir! Transporting you took the last of our batteries," she said as Jim Kirk stepped down to her side. "We're being pummeled by power surges and massive waves of radiation! There are indications of imminent antimatter detonation inside that planet in roughly eight minutes! It'll tear us apart and—"

She stepped very close to him and grasped his sleeve.

"I really don't know what to do," she whispered. "I really don't."

He gazed into her pale face, noted that she suddenly looked a lot older than thirty-seven, and evenly told her, "It takes guts to admit that. Give yourself credit."

"They promoted me too fast, sir," she said. "Do you want me to admit that too, in front of my crew? I should have, and long before something like this."

Kirk scowled and grinned at the same time. "Alma, I'm surprised at you. What do you take us old fogies for? Think we'd give a ship to someone just because we're tired of making decisions ourselves? Look me in the eye and say, 'No, Jim.'"

She sucked in a shuddering breath and through her teeth she actually laughed and said, "I can't call you Jim!"

"Have you got a fix on the *Enterprise?* They're not drained yet."

From behind, Roy Moss said, "Like hell it isn't drained."

"Shut up," one Security guard snapped, and tightened the shackles on Moss's arms just to prove who was in charge.

Kirk glanced back, but resolutely stayed with his conversation with Roth. He'd already been informed they only had eight minutes, and he needed one of those to explain.

"Is the dampening field gone?" he asked, raising his voice but trying to keep from shouting in spite of the alarms whooping and the ship shaking. He crossed in front of Roth to squint at the diagnostics on the starboard side.

"Yes!" Roth said, following him. "But the ship's power is down and we can't regenerate under this bombardment of radiation! According to my engineers, it's compromising our own intermix stability ratios!"

"All right." He turned to her, one hand on the bridge rail. "Use your impulse reserves just enough to turn the ship toward *Enterprise* as she moves in." He looked up at the science officer and asked, "Is *Enterprise* any closer than she was an hour ago?"

"Aye, sir!" the officer said. "She's within two hundred fifty thousand solar miles!"

"Puffed in on that twelve percent," Kirk thought aloud. "Close enough for shield extension in less than thirty thousand miles—"

"Sir," Roth began. She dug her fingernails into his sleeve, and this wasn't the grip of a person who wanted to give up. "I don't understand."

The statement was perfectly clear. No argument, no panic, no demands.

Kirk whirled around. "Spock! Explain to the captain."

Spock was already dropping to the central deck behind Roth's command chair. *"Enterprise* can make her shields specific to the electromagnetic resonance of the planetary radiation waves and extend the shield to protect *Bill of Rights—"*

"And keep us stable enough to regenerate?" Roth interrupted.

"Yes," Spock said simply.

Kirk confronted Roth again. *"Enterprise* needs thirty minutes to regenerate. What've you got?"

Roth panted a few times, desperate and excited, and her eyes got wide in what could almost have been conspiracy. *"Bill of Rights* only needs five minutes! *Enterprise* can shield us from the radiation, then we can pull *Enterprise* away before the planet explodes! Captain Kirk! You have the conn!"

She gestured him with both hands to her command chair, and actually stepped out of his way.

But he shook his head and spoke quietly in spite of the Klaxons and the flashing and the running.

"I don't need the conn, Captain. Mr. Scott on *Enterprise* knows what we need. Just wheel *Bill of Rights* around into that shield envelope and take it one step at a time. After all, you've got almost five minutes."

Reinvigorated as a plebe, Roth drew her shoulders tight and spun to her left. "Lieutenant DesRosiers! Digest and calculate!"

"Aye, Captain! Minimal impulse on line! Turning toward *Enterprise!"*

A hum of effort rose through the ship, and with it a lance of hope went through everyone there, piercing what Kirk recognized as that crew sensation that the ship might be sinking and their next moves might be their last and most desperate, nervously expecting the abandon-ship to be the next order.

Suddenly all that changed. Alma Roth grabbed tight hold on the idea that the time-hardened *Enterprise* and her technical eccentricities and the new-age *Bill of Rights* could combine their skills and gamesmanship and yank both out of a maelstrom even as it bit at them from beneath.

Within fifty seconds the ship jolted.

"Mr. Scott on *Enterprise* advises we are in their shielding envelope!" DesRosiers shouted over the red alert whooping in their ears.

"Shields are around us, Captain Roth!" the science officer shouted. "We're stabilizing!"

"Intermix!" Roth ordered, smashing back a handful of flying brown hair. She even found an instant in her gasping and ordering to throw Kirk a wild-eyed grin. Then she flung herself to the port side, grabbed the bridge rail, and shouted at DesRosiers, "Prepare tractor beams for immediate lock-on as soon as we're hot!"

"Aye, aye, intermix formula calculating. Traction on line!"

Kirk backed off a few feet to let the process happen. Somehow he managed not to blow everybody's flush by crossing his fingers.

As Roth barked orders to her crew and relayed cooperations back and forth from engineering and from communications with the *Enterprise,* Kirk stepped to the upper deck, jabbed a thumb at the two Security men to stand aside, and moved in on Roy Moss. He grabbed Moss with both fists and forced him to look at the forward screen, at the planet that was burning up from inside out.

He felt his own eyes like scorched nuggets in his head.

"Look at it!" he said through his teeth. He took Roy's collar and choked him until he looked. "A hundred thousand years of culture and technology, and we're losing it! All because of you. For generations after we're all dead, Roy Moss will be equated with stupidity. The one who lost Faramond for us and everything it could have taught us. You got what you wanted, Roy. You're going to be famous. Humiliated before the known galaxy. Your name will go down in history as the biggest buffoon of all time."

At first he thought his words weren't getting anywhere, just as no one's words had gotten anywhere with Roy Moss—

Until he felt the quiver at the ends of his hands. The shudder.

He looked from the screen to Moss, and found himself holding a red-faced, weeping old man.

Dampened and brought to bay this time not by a fist but by facts, Moss slipped back against the consoles, and Kirk let him go. Moss could swallow anything but humiliation, and Kirk had given him a mouthful.

The Security guards closed in again as Kirk moved away, but there was no protest from the quivering, gurgling, whimpering mess that once had threatened them all.

Kirk found himself near the turbolift, beside McCoy.

He blinked at the doctor. "You were right. It was revenge," he said.

McCoy nodded, not quite as flippantly as usual.

"I liked it," Kirk added.

Any smug responses were cast aside as a force grabbed the ship and threw everybody grasping for handholds.

When the warp engines came back on line, they all felt it. The ship whined and hummed beneath them, and the bridge flashed like firecrackers, and howled with warning whistles and alarms as if she were some great locomotive ready to haul a record line of cars, and Roth's crew scrambled at their emergency stations.

"Compensators!" Roth was calling, on line to her chief engineer. "Implement traction on the *Enterprise,* and let's get both ships away from that planet!"

Kirk grabbed for McCoy as the doctor stumbled when the countertractors activated, then the three of them retreated even farther into the turbolift vestibule to stay out of the way.

All this time the captain's string had been pulling on him like a long, quiet noose. Now it would be the other way. The string would reach from the past, from *Enterprise* to *Enterprise,* to keep all ships and all who sailed them alive.

"Look at them, Spock . . . Bones," Kirk said. "I've been talking about retirement as though it's all over. As though I've done it all. And I haven't done anything close to all. We're all young—so's the human race," he added. "I don't know about you, but I'm going to keep on going."

At his side, Spock was gazing at him but remaining appropriately silent, and Kirk knew what that meant.

At his other side, Leonard McCoy clung insectishly to a handhold and grumbled, "I knew you were gonna say that, I just knew it. Now Scotty's got to sell his boat and I've gotta send back the firewood I just had delivered to my cabin, and Spock'll have to starch his backup uniform—you know what a problem you are? Lewis and Clark and Kirk—"

# THIRTY-SEVEN

☆

*Forty-five years earlier . . .*
Officers' Lounge, Starbase One

Fingers were funny things. Open 'em, close 'em, imitate 'em with prosthetics . . . lose 'em altogether . . .

Boot heels caught in the struts, Jimmy lazily sat on a turning stool in front of the big viewport at Starbase One. Beside him, the beauty of Earth was settled like quartz in the soil of space. From their orbit he could look up from appreciating his fingers and appreciate the Northern Hemisphere, the wide United States, and even thought he could see the Skunk River, and the rope bridge if he squinted. Yep, there she was, hanging like wet laundry.

He rubbed his sore knuckles with which he had cashiered Roy, and almost let in a flicker of self-pity, but then thought about Veronica and flushed the self-anything.

The door panel brushed open behind him, and he cranked the stool around enough to see the carrot-red hair, the ruddy cheeks, and the other reds and blacks of his father and the Security uniform that so ideally blended with George Kirk's personality.

Neither of them said anything.

George was petrified. He inhaled nervously several times before he could even remember to exhale. The officers' lounge wasn't very

391

big, and it was completely empty except for them, because this was the weekend and everybody was planetside.

George took the long, long way around to getting anywhere near his son.

His boy was looking at him, at least. Well, that was something.

He steeled himself for the inaccessibility that had been lurking under the freckles just days before, and the wall behind which his son had withdrawn, the sun of sociability, and the mean falcon's glare from that apricot face.

There was still a touch of unripe, inharmonic youth, a stroke of skepticism groping for something to disbelieve—

Or was it the shadows in here?

Jimmy just sat there on the stool, his muscular shoulders hunched and his hands folded, legs kinked up on the supports of the stool, and waited.

"Don't know what to say," his father mumbled. "I was hoping I could give you a perfect . . . y'know . . . perfect voyage."

Jimmy nodded. His dad was very nervous. Funny, but he'd never noticed that his dad could be nervous before. Just hadn't ever seen it. Maybe he just hadn't ever looked. He'd seen a lot of things in the past few hours that he'd never looked at before.

For an instant he was back in the airlock, about to be launched on a desperate journey, the last breath of the living. In his head rang the things he was going to say, the awkward apologies, the painful confessions, all the things that had pushed at his lips while he sat on the needles of loss only hours ago.

Would his dad be embarrassed if those words were spoken now?

There must be a better way to say those things than blurting them out like a bad commercial. Some better way than words. There would be time, Jimmy thought, and a better way.

Maybe he'd look around for that too. A way to talk without talking too much.

After a few seconds of fidgeting from his father, Jimmy offered a shrug, then pursed his lips. He gazed at his father, and made his own eyes shine with the ancient Rosetta trinary, the human confidence of Starbase One, and the snow-white sorcery of a starship.

And as he gazed, his eyes told about the bloody cry for help scrawled on a piece of metal, and about a boy's last good-bye, this time to himself as a boy.

Jimmy wanted all those to be in his eyes for his father to see. He refused to look away, or down, or at anything other than his dad's eyes, because this time the message knew where it was meant to go.

"Don't worry about it," he said soothingly. "Perfection stinks."

George gaped, blinked, shook his head, then tried to talk again and failed.

After a few bad seconds he managed to say, "I know I've let the years slip away . . . guess there's no way now to convince you space is worth seeing. Sure don't blame you . . . and I, uh, I want you to know I'm done."

Jimmy looked sidelong at him. "Done?"

"Y'know—done . . . sticking my nose in and trying to change your mind. I'm done with that."

George anticipated a typhoon by squinting into what he thought might be the first wind, but nothing came. Jimmy just sat there, swinging idly back and forth a few inches, hands clasped.

His son nodded. "Thanks."

A message was just getting through George's hard hide that he'd underreckoned his boy again. Maybe Robert was right . . . Robert had been impressed all along by the fire and underlying survival instinct of Jimmy Kirk.

Time for me to be impressed too, George thought. Late with everything.

He cleared his throat and paced sheepishly around the clean deep-plum carpet, thankful that he had something freshly vacuumed to stare down at instead of his own feet.

"Your mom and I always accused you of running away from everything," he said sullenly. "We didn't understand."

He cranked on his throat muscles until he managed to look up at Jimmy. A man should have the guts to look up at a moment like this.

"You were running *to* something," he finished.

Moved by his father's confession, Jimmy thought back on the quiet gallantry of sacrifice from his father, Captain April, Veronica

Hall, and Carlos Florida, who were willing to save him while giving up their own lives to a purpose. He'd found out how critical it was to do a job and just *do* a job. On board a ship, no matter how menial a job was, if it didn't get done by the person assigned to it, then somebody else would have to do it. Nothing could just go undone. Nothing could go judged by the doer.

His dad was still looking up. "I'm sorry for not understanding," he said.

Jimmy raised his shoulders, then let them drop. "No problem. But there's something I'm going to tell you."

"Anything. Go ahead."

"I'm not going into the pre-Academy program at high school."

His dad licked his lips, shrugged sadly, looked down again, and groped, "Can't . . . say I blame you."

"I'm going directly into the Academy itself."

The astonishment in those ruddy cheeks and dark eyes was like getting a medal all by itself.

Jimmy liked the feeling of causing surprise to pepper that face. Wanted it again.

"Wha—what?" his dad gasped.

"I want to go right into the Academy. Captain April said he could arrange it, so I'm going to let him. I promised I could get my grades up and stay out of trouble. That's the deal. I'm going to do it."

"But—but—but I thought—I thought—"

"Well," Jimmy popped off, "we can't let criminals like the Mosses think they can just have their way out there, can we?"

"No, no, no . . . we . . . uh . . . no, sure can't . . . but, uh, Jim, not everybody gets in, you know . . . I never did . . ."

"Dad," Jimmy said, and slipped off the stool to stand before his father with the big viewport as his backdrop and all of Earth as his mantle. "I'm *going* to the Academy."

George tried to take a step, but his legs locked. He might prick something. Break the bubble. What was he seeing in front of him? Who was he seeing?

Terrified he might blunder what was happening, he stammered, "You, uh . . . you'll have to give up your . . . your . . ."

"My gang?" Jimmy slid off the stool and moved forward, coming toward his father with a confidence that didn't include the flippant disgust that had always been there before. He was almost George's height and much steadier.

He took his father's arm and turned him toward the door. "I don't think I need them anymore, do you? If they need me," he added, "they can join Starfleet."

Through blurring eyes, George Kirk was taking that real first look at this son of his.

At this man.

They walked together toward the doors of the Starbase One officers' lounge.

"I'll be darned," he murmured. "I guess they can . . ."

As the wide doors opened before them, they caught at the same moment a glimpse of the brass placard on the beautiful polished walnut panels. Neither mentioned the placard, but father and son felt it go by, and felt it breathe on their shoulders its blessing for the valiant of Starfleet.

> *Sail forth—steer for the deep waters only,*
> *Reckless O soul, exploring, I with thee, and thou with me,*
> *For we are bound where mariner has not yet dared to go,*
> *And we will risk the ship, ourselves, and all.*
>
> *—Walt Whitman*

# EPILOGUE

## USS *Enterprise* 1701-A

*"This is the president. My greetings, Captain."*

"Mr. President, hello."

*"I must add once again our profound thanks. How many times can we thank you for your superhuman feats?"*

"Only human, Mr. President. I do have a special notice, however."

*"Go right ahead."*

"We're not decommissioning this vessel, or retiring the Constitution-class of starships."

*"We're not? But the Admiralty—"*

"Will have to consider new facts. I have evidence that the older style of starship construction and power ratios may prove indispensable. The galaxy is only partly explored, and we can't prudently shelve valuable capital. We will make a new decision."

*"I see . . . very revealing, Captain. Certainly we cannot ignore your conclusions. And obviously when we needed the* Enterprise *this time, she was there for us—again. I risk being presumptuous, but I agree a growing Federation should not cast away our early strengths. I have authorized your command crew's reprieves from retirement while I call a special congress of the Admiralty for you to address. I look forward to the result . . . there are those of us who cling to the*

*Constitution-class for more than tangible reasons. We may be glad you can provide tangible reasons, sir. Visit me upon your arrival."*

"I will, sir. I'd like you to be my guest in the officers' lounge. There's a plaque there I'd like to polish with my elbow."

*"My pleasure to witness it, Captain."*

"Thank you. Kirk out."

*"This is Starbase One, out."*

James Kirk drew in a deep cleansing breath, then took a moment to flick a hangnail off his thumb. All of a sudden a little piece of him was embedded in the plush carpet of the new ship's bridge. All of a sudden it was a little more part of him than it had been a day ago.

Ships were like that. Something had changed in the ship's heart. Suddenly she wanted to be part of him instead of the other way around. They had saved each other's lives, and the lives of others.

Strange, how things could change.

He glanced around him, at the upper deck, where McCoy stood beside Uhura, where Chekov stood beside Spock, and over to port, where Scotty was leaning on the glossy new engineering section, and all at once the ship wanted them, and wanted desperately to prove she was worthy of them.

That light was in all their eyes, and it was in his. The let's-fly light.

Jim Kirk patted the arm of his command chair, and told her in his mind that the captain's string was still in his pocket.

"Mr. Chekov," he said, "reverse the ship."

"Reverse the ship, aye. All decks responding."

"Mr. Spock?"

"Captain?"

"Bring her about . . . steady as she goes."